PRAISE FOR *TURNING HOME*

"Johnson has a gift for portraying emotional depth and vulnerability in just a few subtle glances and fleeting touches. . . . This is sure to win readers' hearts." —*Publishers Weekly*

"Well-written with complex, realistic characters. . . . A touching story." —The Avid Reader

"A wonderful story of healing hearts and new beginnings." —Pink Granny's Journey

MORE PRAISE FOR THE NOVELS OF JANICE KAY JOHNSON

"Janice Kay Johnson wins our hearts with appealing characters in this poignant tale of sacrifice, healing, and family relationships." —*Romantic Times*

"Well-written characters living through complex situations that are neither glossed over nor magically solved. . . . A lovely romance with strong, likable characters." —Her Hands, My Hands

"Johnson writes in a way that conveys real life very well and, at the same time, makes romance seem possible for normal people in everyday places." —All About Romance

"Believable characters that demonstrate admirable growth and sensitivity. Remarkable in scope, beautifully realized with plot and characterizations. . . . Very highly recommended." —Word Weaving

Finding Hope

❧

Janice Kay Johnson

JOVE
New York

A JOVE BOOK
Published by Berkley
An imprint of Penguin Random House LLC
penguinrandomhouse.com

Copyright © 2021 by Janice Kay Johnson
Scripture taken from the New King James Version®. Copyright © 1982 by Thomas Nelson.
Used by permission. All rights reserved.

ISBN: 9780593198001

First Edition: June 2021

Printed in the United States of America
1 3 5 7 9 10 8 6 4 2

Book design by Gaelyn Galbreath

Chapter One

❧ ◆ ❧

HANNAH PRESCOTT STIRRED the fresh rosemary she'd chopped into the mix of melted cheeses and cream. Inhaling, she smiled. This was one of her favorite dinners—who didn't love mac and cheese?—and she thought her take on it, after much experimentation, was divine.

Too bad her boss refused to even consider adding it to the menu.

"Don't care how good it is," he'd told her. "It's macaroni and cheese. People expect it to come out of a box. That's not what they want when they pay good money to go out to the hottest restaurant in Lexington."

End of subject.

Well, to heck with him.

She added salt and pepper, tasted, and stirred in the penne rigate pasta before pouring it all into a ceramic baking dish. After popping it in the oven, she set the timer and took out asparagus from the refrigerator.

Her phone rang from somewhere in the living room. She hesitated, hoping it wasn't Greg desperately needing her to fill in because someone hadn't shown up to work and the restaurant would be jam-packed tonight.

He didn't do that often, so if he needed her, she'd go in. But when she picked her phone up from where she'd left it on the coffee table, she saw the number was her mother's. Since Hannah hadn't talked to her in . . . oh, it had to be close to a month, certainly longer than they usually went between calls, she answered with cautious pleasure.

"Mom."

"Sweetheart." Jodi Prescott had a dreamy voice men tended to like. "It's been forever since we talked! I always worry about you, and you haven't kept me up to date. Are you still seeing that other chef?"

Hannah had to cast her mind back. The last time she'd dated . . . "Grant Summerlin? No, we didn't go out for long. Chefs work long and inconvenient hours. You know that. Since he's the executive chef at a trendy new restaurant, his hours are even worse than mine. Coordinating our rare evenings off was a nightmare. And . . . it just wasn't worth it."

Sad to say, that's what she concluded every time she became briefly interested in a man. There'd been a couple of really nice guys from her church who at least shared her values, but neither had enough patience to accommodate her work schedule. And really, there hadn't been any zing.

"What about you, Mom?" she asked. Her mother almost always had a man thinking he was privileged to take care of her.

Well, except for the losers expecting *her* to take care of them. Hannah's mother had never had good instincts where men were concerned.

Which might be why her daughter had surrounded herself with a force field that refused to let anyone in. Once you lost the ability to trust, regaining it became a task that resembled climbing Mount Everest without oxygen or a guide. Especially without a guide.

"Oh, Dale and I broke up," her mother said, something a little off in her tone. "Listen, I have a favor to ask of you."

Hannah braced herself. Her mother trailed unpaid bills the way a pickup truck did plumes of dust on a dirt road.

"This will sound really silly," her mother said, "but I don't want you to answer any calls from unfamiliar numbers. I'm sure they'll try to reach you, but they've made *awful* accusations, *none* of which are true, and I don't want you involved."

Not what she'd expected. "What kind of accusations?"

"What *difference* does it make?" Jodi sounded suddenly petulant. "There's no reason for you to be involved, that's all. You have to trust me and . . . and not talk to anyone! Can you do that? Just promise me?"

"Is this someone I know?"

"No! It doesn't have anything to do with you!"

Blinking in bewilderment, Hannah asked, "Then why would these people want to talk to me?"

Her mother began to cry. Whether Mom did it consciously or not, she had a way of turning on the hysterical tears to get her way whenever an argument took a turn for the worse—from her point of view, of course. The tears worked splendidly on the men in Jodi's life, until the enchantment wore off—or said men didn't turn out to be as useful as she thought they would be.

Hannah winced at her cynicism. She was being uncharitable, and she did love her mother despite everything. How could she not? Mom was all she had. Still, Hannah had become hardened to the weeping ploy many years ago.

Trying for a soothing voice, she said, "You know I'll help if you tell me what you need."

"I need you not to talk to any strangers who call!" her mother screamed.

Hannah held the phone away from her ear. What on earth—?

"Promise me?"

"Mom . . ."

"Oh!" her mother exclaimed, and ended the call.

Shocked, Hannah discovered that she'd retreated to the kitchen while they talked. Always her refuge. Now, she backed up until she could sink down on a stool. Still clutching the phone, she stared into space, not really seeing the tiny table with a place set for one, or the bunch of daffodils she'd impulsively bought to bring spring indoors.

Jodi had never been the cookies-and-milk-after-school kind of mother—any cookies came in packages from the grocery store or, once Hannah was ten or eleven, were baked by her—but the call had definitely been weird, even by her standards.

What kinds of accusations could anybody make now? When Hannah was a child, school authorities or social service workers had definitely circled, suspecting Hannah's mother wasn't providing a secure home life for her, one reason for the frequent moves that meant constantly starting over. But Hannah hadn't been a minor in a long time—she was twenty-seven now, and hadn't lived with her mother since she graduated from high school.

Nearly a decade ago.

Had someone Mom lived with died, and she was considered a suspect in an investigation? Or did this have to do with drugs? Hannah didn't think her mother had ever used illegal drugs, but some of the men who came and went in their lives had. Now, who knew? But that wouldn't have anything to do with her daughter, who hadn't seen her since Christmas, which they'd celebrated here.

A thought crept into her head. Her mother had never been willing to talk about Hannah's father. Not a word beyond an insistence that he couldn't be bothered with them.

What if these accusations had something to do with *him*? As an adult, Hannah had speculated about why her mother had never remarried. If she was widowed or divorced, wouldn't you think . . . ?

A buzzer went off, and she jerked.

Oh, my. Her macaroni and cheese was done, and smelled amazing. To heck with the asparagus, she decided. Right now, comfort food was exactly what she needed.

Hands enveloped in two quilted potholders, she carefully removed the casserole dish from the oven and set it on the stove. Even as she reached for a serving spoon, she asked herself the big question.

What if her phone did ring, and that unfamiliar number came up? Should she answer? Or do as her mother asked?

But it wasn't really even a question, was it? Hannah knew herself too well.

MIDAFTERNOON THE NEXT day, she'd just stowed her purse and thin jacket in a locker in the small break room at work when her phone rang. The number and area code were both unfamiliar. Oh, boy—this was lousy timing. She hesitated, then looked toward her boss, who both owned the restaurant and was executive chef.

"This is important. I really need to take it."

Greg's bushy eyebrows rose, but he nodded. In the three years since he'd hired her as his sous chef, she'd never once taken a phone call during working hours. Since she seldom dated and had few friends outside her co-workers, the phone didn't actually ring very often.

The next minute, he slapped a firm hand on the back of a young kitchen helper, knocking him forward a step, and began a lecture.

Hannah turned her back and answered. "Hello?"

"Is this Hannah?" a woman asked her tremulously.

"Yes. I'm Hannah Prescott." Closing her locker with a clang, she went out the back door and sat on a wrought-iron chair that was part of a set placed out here for employees but seldom used, because they rarely had a moment to sit down. Given that this was an alley with a few parking spots, the view wasn't sublime, but traffic noise was less distracting than people talking.

"Jodi's daughter?" the woman pressed.

"Yes."

"Oh, my goodness. I was so afraid I'd never have a chance to hear your voice again."

"I don't understand," Hannah said. "Who are you?"

There was a small sniff. "I'm your grandmother."

Her mouth fell open. "I . . . why haven't I ever met you?"

"You have," the woman said sadly. "Your grandfather and I saw you at least once a week until your mother took you away when you were five. You don't remember?"

Hannah's memories from that early were next to nonexistent: a jumble of faces, images, and sounds. The clop of horse hooves. The glow of hot metal, a deep rumble of laughter, the texture of a man's wiry beard. An older man and woman were in there somewhere, but—

"Mom said you were dead."

"No, and you still have another grandmother, too. We just couldn't find you. We hired a private detective twice, and he'd find traces of where you'd been, but Jodi had always taken you and moved again. And then—"

When the woman—her grandmother?—spoke again, she sounded broken. "And then we were told you'd both been killed in a car accident."

"What?"

"Oh, yes. That's when you would have been eleven or twelve. The man who called identified himself as a police officer. He sent us a copy of the death certificates."

Winded, Hannah tried to understand. For all her mother's flaws, she wouldn't have done something that awful, would she? Feeling sick, she said, "We lived with a police officer for about a year. In Illinois, I think, although that might not be right. We moved a lot."

"The death certificates were from Jackson County, Illinois." There was a pause. "Your mother admitted to us that a sheriff's deputy she had . . . dated made the phone call and was responsible for creating the false death certificates. She was just so afraid we'd find you, Jodi said. She wanted us off her back."

That was grief Hannah was hearing, pure and simple. An echo of it seemed to be awakening inside her. "I don't understand any of this," she admitted.

"I don't, either," her grandmother said with aching slowness.

My grandmother. And grandfather. She had one of those, too.

"Where do you live?" Hannah asked, as if that were the most important thing she needed to know.

"Tompkin's Mill. It's a small town in northern Missouri. That's where you grew up until Jodi left your father."

Hannah's heart hammered. Her father. She swallowed. "Is *he* alive?"

"Yes, and he's never been able to put you out of his mind. I haven't let him know yet, because I thought I'd call you first. Is . . . is there any chance you can come for a visit?"

"Missouri." Oddly, she visualized a map. "I don't think we ever lived there. We moved all around it—Illinois, Iowa, I think Indiana once, Kentucky, Tennessee, Arkansas, Oklahoma, Kansas. I'm not sure about Nebraska."

Her grandmother understood. "You circled around Missouri. Around home."

Like a dance, Hannah thought, except nothing about their late-night departures and the shabby apartments or houses they'd left behind had been graceful.

"Until we were told both of you were dead, we kept

thinking Jodi would call, if only to ask for money, but she didn't until now."

"That's why you've talked to her." Hannah felt dumb, not having even wondered. Although, her mind swarmed with so many questions it was hard to pin any one down.

"Yes." There was the weariness, the sadness, again. "It sounds like she just . . . ran out of resources. Didn't she call you?"

"She's borrowed money a couple of times in the last six months, but she knows I don't have much to spare." Hannah frowned. "She gave you my phone number?"

"In exchange for a check."

So Mom was desperate.

Jobs and men both might be harder to come by for a fifty-year-old woman than they had been when she was twenty or thirty, Hannah realized. Jodi had kept her figure, mostly, but she was developing arthritis in her hands, and when her expression changed, the lines in her face didn't smooth out as quickly as they used to. Of course, Jodi would never let herself turn gray, but the roots of her hair must sometimes betray her when she couldn't afford a touch-up at a salon.

Mom had given her parents Hannah's number, then panicked. *These* were the accusations she'd feared. The lies. Hannah's grandparents weren't dead. They had grieved for their lost daughter and granddaughter all these years.

And my father. To let *him* think his child was dead . . .

How could Mom have done that to all of them? Hannah asked herself on a painful stab of anger. *To me?*

"I didn't think to ask your name," she said. "Except, I guess it has to be Prescott?"

"No, and unless Jodi married a man who adopted you along the way, it isn't your name, either. Or hers. I'm Helen Hinsch. Your grandfather is Robert."

She couldn't breathe. Whispered, "Then . . . what is my name? What's my father's name?"

"He's Samuel Mast. Like I said, unless you were adopted, you're Hannah Mast."

That seemed like an odd last name, but . . . familiar? Now *she* panicked. No, it couldn't be. She hardly remembered a thing about those years, certainly not a last name.

The back door to the restaurant opened behind Hannah. She turned her head to see Greg, wearing his white toque and crisp white double-breasted chef coat.

"You're still on the phone?" Then he seemed to look more closely at her, and his expression altered.

Hannah lifted her hand to discover her face was wet with tears. She hadn't even noticed.

Appearing alarmed, he backed up. "Don't worry. We'll be fine. Take your time." The door swung shut behind him.

"Hannah?" asked the quiet voice from her phone.

"Sorry. I'm at work. Actually, in our break area. That was my boss. He said no hurry."

"Your mother said you're a cook?"

Wiping at her tears, Hannah almost laughed. Her emotions were swinging that far. "I'm a chef. A sous chef, in my current job, which basically means I'm second in command. I approve menus, I cook, I oversee staff, including waitstaff. I went to culinary school in New York."

"I see," her grandmother said doubtfully.

"Mom hated cooking. You probably know that."

"I do."

"I . . . took over shopping and meal preparation when I was ten or eleven. I always loved it."

"Ten years old, and your mother expected you to put meals on the table."

It wasn't a question. It was . . . more grief, although Hannah wasn't sure she understood it this time. *She'd* made the decision to take over housekeeping and cooking, not Mom. Mom . . . just didn't care. She'd have been fine with fast food or nothing at all some of the time. She ate like a bird—a wren, not a duck or goose that could be aggressive about food. Hannah knew, after visiting farms while she was studying culinary arts. Ducks thought toes looked edible. A big white goose had bitten Hannah's finger. She had a scar from it.

She corralled her wandering thoughts.

"I'm okay," she said. "I love my work. Mom didn't abuse me."

"Let's not argue about this." The tremulous voice hardened. "I love my daughter, despite the inexcusable choices she made, but she kidnapped you. She tore you away from your family. From what she said, the two of you moved frequently. Did you even go to school?"

"Yes." She hesitated. "Mostly."

"How many schools?"

"I . . . don't know." Hannah closed her eyes. "I lost count."

Her grandmother made a raw sound of pain.

"I did graduate from high school." Probably a miracle, considering that none of the schools she'd attended had taught the same things at the same pace. She'd be ahead, or behind—mostly behind—and scrambling to catch up. Confused, humiliated, spending her school days with her head ducked, trying to avoid any eye contact with students who might make fun of her. She'd quit trying to make friends— why bother, when four months later, she and Mom would be on the move again?

She occasionally watched a TV show or movie that portrayed what was apparently a typical family, and realized she couldn't relate at all.

And yet, she'd told the truth; her mother was affectionate and fun. Creative, delighting in fantasy—and always sure the next man would truly love them both and give them the stability, the steady income, the chance to stay in one place that Hannah had craved but never believed she could have.

She'd managed it herself, having come to realize that was the best way to achieve any dream.

"Your grandfather's health isn't good," her grandmother told her. "He has congestive heart failure. We're in our early seventies, but heart disease runs in Robert's family. His own father dropped dead of a heart attack in his fifties. I'm hoping . . ." She hesitated.

"I'll ask for a few weeks off," Hannah said instantly. "I'll come to Tompkin's Mill. As soon as I know when, I'll call."

"You have no idea what this means to us."

"It means a whole lot to me, too. I wanted family. I could never understand—" Her throat closed. And yes, she was crying again, her nose running. She tried for steady breathing—in through the nose, out through the mouth—except her nose was hopelessly stuffed up. "Can you give me my father's phone number?"

There was a moment of silence that made her wonder if she'd been cut off. She pulled the phone away to look at it, then heard a tiny voice and hastily put the phone back to her ear.

". . . message only."

"What?"

"Some Amish use phones in their businesses, and several households will share a phone in a shanty by the road, mostly for messages and emergencies."

Hannah was stuck on the beginning. "Amish?"

"Yes, your father is Amish. We aren't, but you were raised Amish until your mother took you away."

She'd seen horses and buggies in some of the areas where she and Mom had lived. Women wearing those white caps with trailing ribbons or black bonnets, men with suspenders and hats and long beards but shaven upper lips. They were an odd religious sect she'd hardly given a thought to.

And now she was supposed to believe *she* was Amish, on some level?

The clop of horse hooves, the sight of a horse's rump swaying back and forth right in front of her.

She opened her mouth, about to say, *I don't understand*, then closed it. Why bother with the words? Her entire life had just been upended.

Chapter Two

❧◆❧

GIDEON LANTZ TRUDGED across the farmyard, trying to hide his limp from his son, who bounced around him bragging about how much help he'd been throwing out hay for their horses and cows.

Resting a hand on Zeb's head and ruffling his hair in an effort to calm him down, Gideon said, "*Ja*, big help you were," even though that kind of help had doubled the time it took to feed the animals. Just as his six-year-old daughter's help doubled, or even tripled, the time it took to get a meal on the table. "Where is your hat?" he asked.

His boy looked up at him. "My hat? I don't remember. I had it when I got home from school."

Well, that was something. If he'd lost it on the walk home from school, they might never see it again.

Tonight, Gideon wouldn't have to prepare dinner with the help of his *kinder*, but even tired and hurting from having one of the draft horses step on his foot, his fault, he almost wished that wasn't so. Without a wife to take care of Rebekah and Zeb, Gideon had no choice but to hire a young woman to watch over them when he was working, and to do some of the household chores. Since moving to Tompkin's Mill a year and a half ago, he'd hired and lost three different women. This latest one, the fourth, gave him an uneasy feeling. He suspected she saw herself becoming a permanent part of his household.

If he were to remarry, he would not choose a nineteen-year-old girl.

If? Ach, he knew better than that. Eventually, he'd have to marry for the *kinder*, if not for himself.

When he and Zeb stepped in the house, he could smell chicken frying, and his mouth watered. Despite his caution where Rebecca King was concerned, tonight it would be good to wash up, sit down, and be able to eat immediately. He hoped this was one of the days that she would go home to eat with her own family, but he'd noticed that, increasingly, she lingered to sit down with him and his *kinder*. How could he say, *You should go home*, when she'd cooked the meal?

"Daadi!" His daughter rushed to him for a hug. She hurried everywhere. He wished he could borrow some of that energy. Like her *mamm*, he sometimes thought, but did his best not to make that comparison. Thinking about Leah always left him hurting and angry both. Complete forgiveness and acceptance might have let him heal, but he feared neither would come while he kept painful secrets to himself. Telling himself he hid nothing from God didn't seem to help.

He swung Rebekah up into his arms and smiled at her. "Did you have a good day?"

He thought her smile dimmed a little, but she said hastily, *"Ja,* I helped. We did laundry today, and hung it all on the line. Well, Rebecca did, because I'm not tall enough, but *I* shook out the wrinkles first."

"Good for you." He kissed her cheek. Almost done with her first year of school, pleasing her teacher and making friends. She had come a long way from the dark year or two after her *mamm*'s death.

"I wish I'd grow faster," she said wistfully, then squirmed to be let down.

Rebecca King—that was another thing he didn't like about having her here, the confusion of having two Rebeccas—turned from the stove to smile at him. "Dinner will be on the table in just a minute. We made rhubarb crumble for dessert. Rebekah says that's your favorite."

He feared his answering smile was more of a grimace. With only a polite nod, he hung his hat on a peg on the wall and went to the downstairs bathroom to wash up.

Once they were seated around the table and he'd signaled the start of the prayer before meals, Gideon bowed his head and thought, *Forgive me, God. Rebecca King is here when she promises to be here. She keeps my kinder safe. We're blessed to sit down to such a fine meal. I have nothing to complain about.*

Except that when she popped up to refill his coffee cup as any Amishwoman would do, she laid a hand on his shoulder when she poured, and leaned so close he felt her body brush his upper arm.

At twenty, he'd have been flattered. She was a pretty girl. Now, he felt like a buck startled in the woods by the sight of two strange creatures freezing to point long sticks at him. Not *knowing* he would be prey; how could he? But fearing.

Was there a way that wouldn't humiliate her for him to let her know that he wasn't looking for a wife?

All he said was, "*Denke*," and asked Zeb a question about school.

Only a few miles outside Tompkin's Mill, Hannah got stuck behind a black buggy pulled by a single horse. The narrow shoulder of the highway prevented the buggy from moving over, and traffic was just heavy enough going the other direction, she hesitated to pass for the moment.

She could be patient. In fact, the slow pace gave her the chance to really look around, take in the bright green, leafy splendor of the wooded hills rising from each side of the highway, which followed a small river tumbling over rocks. Pretty now, this country would be spectacular in the fall. The town ahead sat in a bowl surrounded by hills.

An opening in the other lane encouraged her to put on her turn signal and accelerate past the buggy and horse, giving it a wide berth as she passed. She caught only a glimpse of the driver, clearly a man, but a black-clad shoulder and the straw hat that shielded his face weren't revealing.

She had just veered back into her lane, the horse and buggy receding in her rearview mirror, when a thought struck her.

That could have been her father.

If not him, it might have been an uncle, or cousin, or—

She was panting as if she'd run on her own two feet past the buggy instead of speeding past in her aging sedan. Moaning, she told herself to rein it in . . . and then whimpered at the bad pun.

Yes, her father lived in the area, but from what she'd learned online, there were at least three church "districts" clustered around this typically rural Missouri town. What were the odds she'd happen to pass him?

Once she did meet him, she might recognize the horse, it occurred to her, except she'd only been aware it was a high-stepper with an arched neck and mane flying. Brown. She enjoyed watching the Triple Crown races on TV, and it seemed to her that the Thoroughbred racehorses were all some shade of brown. Probably the buggy horses were, too.

So much for that plan.

The dense deciduous woods gave way to farms that looked well kept. Rows of green shoots emerged from rich brown earth. She had no idea what crop—or crops—she was seeing. Corn? Tobacco? Fences were mostly solidly constructed from boards, not wire, many painted white, as were a lot of the houses and even barns.

Electrical wires. That's what distinguished an Amish home from an *Englisch* one. She'd learned that term, too, from her online searches. Now she paid attention, seeing the wires strung from the main line along the highway up to the next house—but the farmhouse across the road had no electrical wires leading up to it. Which meant . . .

That could be where I grew up.

Wow. She had to quit thinking like that.

She passed a large building set back from the road with a sign that read "Produce Auction House." Although it didn't seem very busy right now, there were two cars in the parking lot as well as two buggies with horses presumably used to waiting.

The town sprawled to each side of the river, Hannah discovered, two concrete bridges connecting it. Tompkin's Mill was bigger than she'd expected, although she didn't see any buildings taller than three stories. The speed limit dropped to thirty-five, then twenty-five miles per hour. The outskirts had some of the same businesses you saw anywhere: a convenience store, several brand-name gas stations, a McDonald's, and a Subway. What looked like a tacky gift shop that advertised "AMISH" in big letters.

But a few blocks farther, downtown was classic small-town America: a clothing emporium, a bank, a pharmacy, a corner business with a classy-looking sign reading "Bowman & Son's Handcrafted Furniture," a jeweler, and down the block, what appeared to be a fabric and quilt store. A hat store, a—

Wait. She needed to be paying attention to cross streets. She was supposed to turn left on Dogwood. Had she passed it . . . ? No, it was the next street.

Left took her over one of the bridges and through another part of town, past a hardware store, a plumbing supplies business and a business labeled only: Buggies. Her head turned as she tried to take everything in. Modest older homes partly showed their age by the size of the trees shading them: oaks, maples, and sycamores, and others she didn't recognize.

And there was the senior housing complex right where it was supposed to be. Much newer than the surroundings, it consisted of an attractive building that had several wings. Separate, smaller buildings included an adult day care and a child day care as well as what were probably maintenance buildings.

Hannah's grandparents had sold their home and moved here when Robert's health declined, a year after his heart condition was diagnosed. From what her grandmother had said, this was the kind of facility with several stages. When he needed more help, they could move to a smaller apartment where round-the-clock nursing care was available. Right now, they had the option of cooking meals in their own apartment or eating in a common dining room.

Hannah parked, surprising herself with her bout of nerves. Her grandmother had sounded nice. She'd even spoken briefly with her grandfather on the phone. He'd been breathless but deeply emotional about meeting her.

Her problem was that she'd never had family, and didn't have the slightest idea how to be part of one. She was actually a little bit glad that her grandparents didn't have a guest room to offer her, so she'd been able to make a reservation at a hotel that was apparently on the way out of town without hurting anyone's feelings. She could retreat to a room that was hers alone.

She hadn't succeeded in talking to her father, although she'd left him a message and he'd left her one in return, telling her in strongly accented and oddly constructed English how much it meant to him that she was coming home. She was to go to his house for dinner tomorrow, where she would also meet her other grandmother, her stepmother, and four half siblings.

"We will start small, *ja*?" he'd said with apparent humor. "The rest of the family can wait."

How many others? There must be some aunts and uncles and cousins, as she'd imagined. It sounded like Amish families tended to be large, so her father might have had five or six sisters and brothers, maybe more, and if *they* each had four to ten children . . . Hannah's mind boggled.

The one person she hadn't talked to was her mother. Hannah's decision. She was too mad, and afraid of what she'd say if she did answer one of Mom's calls. She'd have to eventually, of course, but by then she'd know more about what her mother had hidden from her all these years.

One thing that did make Hannah uneasy was wondering where Mom was. Surely she hadn't lingered here in Tompkin's Mill now that she had money in hand.

Hannah so hoped her mother wasn't anywhere close by. She hadn't even begun to grasp the magnitude of her mother's lies, or to meet the other people who might have been hurt as much by those lies as Hannah was. She wasn't ready for a phone call, never mind a face-to-face confrontation.

She got out of her car, locked it, and started for the main entrance, telling herself she was mostly excited and only a little nervous.

A receptionist inside sent her to the right elevator, and a minute later she knocked on the door marked 219. It opened to reveal a white-haired woman who looked astonishingly like Hannah's mother, from brown eyes to the slightly pointed shape of her chin and the height Hannah had inherited.

"Oh, my," her grandmother said, surveying her. "Oh, my." Already, her eyes were damp. "I can see Jodi in you, but also your father."

Hannah's own eyes stung. "You look so much like Mom."

When her grandmother's arms opened, Hannah unhesitatingly stepped into them. Locked together, both women wept.

HELEN SAID, "I'M afraid Jodi is still in town. She has friends from high school, and she's probably staying with one of them. The last time I talked to her, she insisted she had to warn you, that she wasn't going to let us all brainwash you. She's upset that you aren't answering her calls."

Robert made an incoherent sound. He sat by his wife's side on the sofa, a tube connecting him to an oxygen tank. Talking had him breathless so quickly, he mostly listened. When she'd hugged him earlier, his eyes shared the wonder she felt, though.

"What did she mean by that?" Sitting in an easy chair, Hannah held a glass of iced tea.

"When she left Samuel—your father—she claimed he was abusive, that Amishmen all were. Behind closed doors, Amishwomen were the next best thing to slaves, that she wouldn't leave you alone with Samuel."

Disturbed, Hannah said, "You didn't believe her? Domestic abuse is pretty common." She'd hidden her head under a pillow some nights when her mother and the man du jour screamed at each other, when she heard slapping sounds and crashes. Although . . . if Samuel Mast had been abusive, wouldn't you think Mom would be more careful where men were concerned?

Helen frowned. "It was so . . . out of the blue, you see. There'd never been any hint before. Samuel and Jodi had us out to their house often. Jodi was all smiles, and from the minute you could toddle, you'd run right to your daddy, completely trusting him to swing you into the air, or push you on a rope swing, or put you on one of the horses' backs." She hesitated. "Also, Jodi has been a worry to us since she reached adolescence. Either she could never stick to anything, or she was never satisfied. I guess that's why I doubted a sudden story like that. A job or class in school was always fine one minute, and the next she'd claim an instructor was sexually harassing her, or that the employer's practices were unethical and she refused to go along with it. She'd also refuse to report them, though. I don't think she ever lasted on a job for more than a few months."

"She still doesn't," Hannah said quietly, feeling as if she was betraying her mother, but also grateful that for the first time in her life, here was someone she *could* be honest with about Mom.

Her grandmother's smile was sad. "I'm sorry to say, I'm not surprised. She started college twice and dropped out both times without even completing a semester. When she first told us she was converting to be Amish, we were alarmed. But, well"—she glanced at Robert, who reached over and clasped her hand—"Samuel was kind and several years older than her. He seemed so steady. We hoped their deep faith and the routines and boundaries of the Amish were just what Jodi needed, so in the end we supported her decision. And, at first, it seemed we'd been right to do so."

"At first?"

"She got pregnant, oh, six or eight months into the marriage. She was so excited! And I'd swear she adored you, but you weren't very old when I saw signs of restlessness. I'd spot her in town with friends who must have picked her up with their cars. If I asked her about it, she'd lie and say I was mistaken, or insist she was entitled to have friends who actually wanted to have fun. At first, she seemed to be earnestly trying to fit in, but it wasn't long before I realized that Samuel's female relatives seemed to be doing most of the cooking and plenty of housework besides. Jodi would reheat dishes, or Samuel would, even though he looked exhausted after a hard day of work. He's a farrier," she added.

Hannah nodded. Helen had told her that in an earlier phone conversation.

"When we were there, Jodi would dart around as if entertaining us was her only obligation. We worried about you, but your other grandmother or one of Samuel's sisters or nieces always seemed to be there, warm and loving."

Robert wordlessly handed Helen a big, white handkerchief, which she used to wipe her cheeks and blow her nose.

"I started to wonder why she hadn't gotten pregnant again. The Amish mostly have big families. Was she secretly using birth control?" Her mouth compressed. "Whatever we expected, it wasn't what happened. Samuel came to see us, distraught. She'd taken all of the cash they had on hand—and, I gather it was several thousand dollars, at least. He hadn't seen any necessity to bank more than every few weeks. He thought she might have been taking some over the past months, too, a hundred dollars here and there. She left a note on the kitchen table, and was gone. Their second horse and buggy was there. A friend had to have picked her up. She called us two days later to tell us how horrible her marriage had been and how afraid she was for you, pleading for some money and our support. When I told her running away was wrong, well, that was the last we heard from her. Until this week."

Twenty-two—almost twenty-three—years later.

"I'm so sorry," Hannah whispered. "I wish . . ."

Robert said, "Not . . . your . . . fault. Scared . . . for you."

"I'm ashamed that I don't even remember you. Except . . . since you called, I keep feeling as if more memories are lurking than I knew." She bit her lip. "This one time I asked Mom if I could ride a horse, and she told me it wouldn't be safe at all, since I'd never been on one before. And . . . I was maybe seven or eight, and we passed several Amish buggies on a road. I got excited, but she rolled her eyes and said, oh, of course I'd seen them around, because Amish did have communities in . . . I don't remember. Indiana or Iowa or wherever we were. If she did that enough times—"

"You'd doubt your own memories. And . . . start suppressing them yourself."

"Yes." Hannah sat quiet for a minute. "I'm going to my father's house for dinner tomorrow night."

Her grandmother nodded. "He let us know."

"Did he divorce Mom? Or . . . ?"

"No. If she'd sent divorce papers, he might have signed them for her sake, but with his faith, he would have still considered himself married. He didn't remarry until, oh, ten years ago, long after we were told you and Jodi had died."

"You stayed in touch?"

"Oh, yes." Helen's smile warmed. "Samuel invited us to occasional gatherings, and now that Robert can't easily attend, Samuel still drops by every so often with a basket of fresh produce, a delicious pie or cobbler, or honey from one of his neighbors. He told me that when we need help, to let him know, that we were still family." More huskily, she added, "Always family."

"You believe he's a good man?"

"I truly do. And saying that, I'm ashamed of my own daughter."

Hannah saw that Helen and Robert's handclasp had tightened. Comfort offered and received. They had to have been married fifty years, and yet, unless she was imagining things, the love they felt for each other was still palpable.

Hannah wanted that, with all her heart, but didn't know whether she'd be able to stand so much closeness, or was capable of sustaining love and trust. The only relationship of any meaning she'd had was with her mother, who was affectionate, lighthearted, and imaginative, but also inconstant and useless where the practicalities of life were concerned. As it turned out, those were trivial flaws compared to what she'd done to her parents, her husband . . . and her daughter. Thanks to her mother, Hannah had never known a sense of security. What foundation did that give her?

Unless, a voice seemed to whisper in her ear, her first five years of life, her grandparents, her father, and her extended Amish family had provided the bedrock she could trust. Just because she'd blocked it out didn't mean it wasn't still there.

A loner now, she was almost afraid to find out.

Chapter Three

❖◆❖

ANNOYED BECAUSE A delivery of fertilizer hadn't arrived when promised, Gideon decided to check for a telephone message. He considered leaving the *kinder* playing, since they seemed happily occupied kicking a ball back and forth on the lawn, but decided he didn't dare. Most of the time they were responsible, but Zeb was at an age to be reckless, and Rebekah never slowed down long enough to *think* before she tore off to her next discovery.

When he said, "We must walk to the phone shanty," they both brightened. The ball rolled away.

"Do I have to hold hands, *Daadi*?" his daughter asked. "If we do, I want to hold yours, not *his*."

Zeb curled his lip. "Who'd want to hold *your* hand?"

Best friends one second, squabbling the next.

"You and I will hold hands once we reach the road," he said.

"Race you!" Zeb cried, and tore down the driveway. His sister ran after him.

"Stop before you get to the road!" Gideon called, increasing the length of his stride, but not worried. The most important rules, they knew to obey. He trusted them not to run out onto the road.

It was a quiet, rural road, not like the highway, and most of his neighbors on this stretch were Amish, but *Englisch-ers* used it, too, and they often drove too fast. Especially the tourists, out hunting for any glimpse of the Amish. Tourism was good for Tompkin's Mill, keeping the restaurants busy, including the Amish-owned Country Days Café, and plenty of other businesses in town, too, many of which were also Amish-owned. Bowman & Son's Handcrafted Furniture sold almost entirely to the *Englisch*, for example.

Well, let the tourists go into the stores and stare all they liked, he thought, but stay away from his farm. He hated to look up when he was plowing a field to see a car parked by the side of the road so a row of strangers could snap pictures of him at work as if he were part of an exhibit. It wasn't as bad here as it had been back home, in upstate New York, but Missouri had plenty of those people curious about the Amish for no reason Gideon could fathom.

A faint smile twisted his lips when he remembered Miriam Bowman, now Miriam Miller, a member of his church district, telling him that the tourists were excited because the Amish drove and farmed with horses. "If we used tractors and cars, they wouldn't care what we wore," she'd told him.

That might be so.

And he knew that growing up as one of eight *kinder* crammed into a three-bedroom house had left him with a craving for solitude that partly explained his choice of work. None of the *Leit*—the people—liked the curiosity of *auslanders*, but he more than most felt their intrusion.

His own *kinder* had skidded to a stop short of the pavement and now ran back toward him.

"Are you going to call someone?" Zeb asked him.

"Probably not, just listen to messages." He explained about the fertilizer, and his son nodded solemnly.

Rebekah, not at all to Gideon's surprise, looked messy—her formerly crisp white *kapp* was hanging by a pin or two, and her hair, also dripping pins, had fallen down around her shoulders. Part of that, he would concede, was his fault; even after a couple of years, his fingers still felt thick and clumsy when he tried to fix her hair.

How could Leah have done this to her family? he asked, as he still did too often. He didn't want to think he was begging for an answer from God. He tried to have faith his Lord had His reasons for taking her, but even his family and members of his church district back home had questioned his decisions and Leah's behavior to the point where he had to believe that he bore some responsibility for her death, that it was not all God's decision. Left confused and hurting, he had made the decision to move away, where people didn't know what had happened.

It was better here in Missouri than it had been in New York, where the endless whispers sometimes felt like a horde of whining mosquitoes intent on sucking all the blood out of him and the *kinder*. But living without his wife, the *kinder* without their *mamm*, had become no easier. Nor had his own questions about the accident.

A *kind* on each side of him, he was walking the short distance on the shoulder of the road to the phone shanty he shared with three other households—Esther Schwartz, a widow; Isaac and Judith Miller as well as their son and his family; and Bart and Ada Kauffman—when he heard a car approaching. It was crawling along, by the standards of the *Englisch*. He turned to see why, not liking how exposed he and the *kinder* were to cameras and rude questions.

The driver was a lone woman, however, no one he'd seen before, but at least she didn't appear to have a camera. She did brake beside them and roll down her window. "Do you speak English?" she asked.

Beside him, his *kinder* gaped at her. Both had probably learned enough English now to understand her, Zeb more than Rebekah.

"*Ja*—yes," Gideon said. "Are you lost?"

He had the surprised thought that she was pretty, but not in a showy way. Which meant she wasn't wearing the makeup most *Englisch* women did, he realized. Her dark blond hair was confined in a knot at her nape, and her eyes were green and gold with maybe a hint of brown. He guessed she might be tall, for a woman, and thin. And why he was bothering to wonder, Gideon didn't know.

"Not lost, I don't think," she answered. "Just . . . I'm a little confused by the house numbers."

He nodded his understanding. "That's because when the road took that sharp bend half a mile back, the numbering changed."

"But I'm still on the same road. Aren't I?"

"No. This is Two Hundred Seventy-Fourth now."

"Shoot. I must have passed the house I'm looking for." She smiled. "Thank you. *Denke*."

"Who are you looking for?" he asked, not sure why he didn't just nod and keep on his way, which was what he would normally do.

"Samuel Mast."

Was this the long-lost daughter everyone was talking about? He had no excuse for asking.

"Then go back to the bend, and his farm is the second driveway on the left."

She offered another smile, aimed at Zeb and Rebekah as well as him, thanked him again, and drove the short distance forward to the Millers' driveway to turn around.

With another smile and a wave, she passed them again and went on her way. As Zeb, incurably curious, asked who she was and why she, an *Englisch* woman, would go to Samuel's house, Gideon thought she probably was Samuel's daughter—because her long, slender fingers had been gripping the steering wheel too tightly, and her eyes and even those smiles showed tension.

Scared to meet her *daad*, who was probably just as nervous. Someone had said she'd been snatched away when she was just past her fifth birthday, and had only now discovered who her father was.

Gideon looked down at his own six-year-old daughter, feeling as if the hollow left inside him where Leah had been had suddenly expanded. Even with his trust in God, if he lost Rebekah or Zeb, that would be hard to survive.

He imagined Samuel pacing the floor or perhaps out front in the yard, waiting for a first glimpse of that little girl, now grown up.

"Here we are," he said, stepping into the three-sided wooden structure where a telephone and answering machine sat side by side. A red light blinked on the answering machine. A lower shelf held a couple of tattered spiral-bound notebooks and a cup with pens and pencils. Anyone who checked the answering machine would make note of messages for the neighbors.

Picking up a pen, he smiled at Rebekah. "Would you push the button to start the messages?"

She beamed and reached out.

Zeb complained, "Why can't *I* . . . ?"

A man started talking. The message was for Gideon, saying just what he'd expected. The fertilizer was to be delivered tomorrow. "Without fail," the man concluded.

Gideon snorted and erased the message.

For no good reason, even as he listened to his *kinder* chattering and answered endless questions on the return walk, his thoughts strayed to the *Englisch* woman and to Samuel Mast. Would anything come of this meeting? It seemed unlikely, after she'd been out in the world so long.

But just knowing she was alive and doing well, that would be a blessing for Samuel they would all celebrate.

HALFWAY UP THE driveway, Hannah's foot jerked to the brake when she saw children chasing each other around the lawn in front of the large white farmhouse. Her sisters and brothers? As she made herself start forward again, they all stopped where they were and turned to stare at her car. The oldest girl suddenly lifted her skirt and raced for the front porch.

By the time Hannah parked in what seemed a reasonable spot where the hard-packed lane turned toward a barn, a man had come out on the porch.

Even more nervous than when she'd met her grandparents, she grabbed her handbag, climbed out of the car, and walked toward him as he descended the steps and came to meet her.

He wore the same kind of suspenders over the same color shirt as the man with the two children down the road had. Heavy work boots, too, and a straw hat. He was blond, with a beard that was a shade darker, almost a match to her hair, she couldn't help thinking. The beard with a shaved upper lip looked odd to her.

"Hannah?" he said. "My Hannah?"

"Yes." Oh, heavens, she was going to cry again. "Yes. If . . . You must be Samuel Mast."

Astonishingly, he had to swipe at his cheeks, too. "*Ja*. Yes. I thank God for bringing you home."

She bit her lip and nodded.

He lifted his arms, then let them fall. Hannah took an equally hesitant step forward and then thought, *This is my father.* Feeling her lips tremble as she tried to smile, she took that last step, and felt his strong arms come around her.

His beard was wiry against her cheek. He wasn't a tall man, no more than a couple of inches taller than her, but solidly built. She had the bewildering thought that he smelled familiar.

"*Daadi*," she whispered.

He lifted his head and let his arms fall. "You remember?"

"No." She sniffled. "But . . . sometimes I think I do."

"You were very young." Bright blue eyes met hers. "I never forgot you. When your grandmother let me know you and your *mamm* had died—" He took a couple of deep breaths. "My heart broke."

"I'm so sorry—"

"No." He stopped her with a hand on her arm. "You knew nothing about that. You were only eleven when your mother asked that man to make it look like you were both dead. Still a girl."

She barely remembered the sheriff's deputy Mom had stayed with for something like a year. Mom must have done it just because she finally had someone she could coerce who might—as it turned out, *did*—know how to fake a death certificate.

But why, *why*, had Mom been so determined for Hannah never to meet the rest of her family?

Looking at the kind face of this man who had mourned her all these years, Hannah came closer to hating her mother than she had ever imagined she could. She had moments of bitterness about going hungry because Jodi had quit another job, staying in homeless shelters because they'd been evicted, fleeing whatever they'd called home in the middle of the night because creditors or social service workers were about to close in—or because a man had become too demanding, or too rough. She'd fought that bitterness, almost convincing herself that Mom had done the best she could.

But all of that was nothing compared to the cruelty of stealing her daughter from so many people who had loved her, leaving them not knowing what happened to her—until they were told, falsely, that she was dead.

Eventually, she'd ask Mom why she'd done such a thing . . . but how likely was it that her mother's answer would even approach the truth?

"Come. My wife and your sisters and brothers are eager to meet you." Samuel held out a hand to her and smiled.

Hannah's stomach seemed to flip. She *knew* that smile. Not from memory, but because it looked so much like her own when she saw herself in the mirror or a reflection on window glass.

Fighting to resist new tears, she started forward again.

HANNAH HAD CONFINED herself to small servings of everything, because she'd seen the array of desserts on the counter. Since she especially loved to bake, she could hardly wait to sample the pies and cakes for which the Amish were well known.

She felt so odd, looking around the table, almost dizzy with the wonder of being here. She'd long since given up on ever finding out who her father was—as an adult, she'd decided he was one of her mother's transient "boyfriends" and that maybe Mom herself didn't remember which one. But now she not only knew, she was sitting at his table, stealing astonished peeks at the bearded face that really didn't look like her, but had already slotted into a place in her mind where she'd kept a blank labeled "Father."

I must remember him. What else could explain how right he feels?

And then there was the rest of the family, starting with her other grandmother, Samuel's mother. A tiny woman, Ruth Mast had the most wrinkled face Hannah had ever seen, yet she was still lovely. Her skin looked soft, as if delicate fabric had crumpled. The shape of those lines described her character to anyone looking at her. Smiles had to come most naturally to her. She was almost eighty, Samuel had told Hannah quietly. She'd had eight children, Samuel the youngest. She moved between the homes of all her children, but several were out of state, one south in the Ozarks, and she didn't travel well anymore. She currently lived in what he called a *grossdawdi haus*, a wing built onto the farmhouse that was apparently a self-contained mother-in-law apartment—with his sister and her family. There'd been a time she traveled between her many sons and daughters, but no longer.

"I went to get her tonight. Lucky it is that she's here right now, when you came back to us."

When Ruth could reach Hannah, she'd pat her arm or cheek ever so gently, but her English was broken and her accent strong enough that Hannah had trouble understanding her. Still, her delight at Hannah's presence was palpable, her smile a blessing. This woman had cared for Hannah when she was young, cooked and cleaned for the family. Loved this granddaughter.

Hannah's stepmother, Lilian, was likely ten or even fifteen or twenty years younger than her father, but had been a widow when she married him, already having a child. *Daad* had beamed as he laid a hand on the shoulder of a lanky boy who was fourteen years old, claiming him, saying he was their oldest. The boy's name was Mose. Hannah's half sisters and brothers stairstepped down from there: a shy girl named Emma, ten years old; Adah, eight; Zachariah, five; and Isaiah, three. Hannah had the impression that Lilian was pregnant again. And if *Daad* was . . . heavens, he was a few years older than Jodi, according to Helen, which meant he was at least fifty-three or fifty-four, possibly even older. Lilian was certainly in her mid- to late thirties, at least.

The two little boys didn't understand a word she said. Her father explained that Amish children didn't begin to learn English until they started school at age six.

"Although you were different, of course," he added.

With the little Emma had said—whispered—she had a

strong accent, as did her mother. Adah, too, but she was a chatterbox. Mose just seemed alarmed by this much older sister. His cheeks flushed whenever she spoke to him.

Samuel or Lilian translated much of what Hannah said for the benefit of the younger children—*kinder*, they called them. Hannah found herself silently shaping the sounds and the words: *mammi*, *daadi*, *grossmammi*, *stoppe*, *schnell*, *sehr gut*, *komm*, *wilkom*. Zachariah called his brother *doppick* and was scolded by his mother. Hannah had to hide a smile.

She understood more words than she would have expected, partly because plenty were self-explanatory, possibly because she'd taken German in high school, even though she didn't get very far because most of the schools offered only Spanish or French.

The desserts were every bit as delicious as she'd expected, although she could eat only a bite or two of each, to the apparent astonishment of everyone present except her *grossmammi*, who had also eaten lightly.

"I've always picked at my food," she tried to explain. "I guess you can tell I'm not a big eater." She wrinkled her nose. "Plus, I'm a chef, and we tend to taste often but not really sit down to a meal."

"A *chef*?" her daad asked, obviously not knowing the word.

"Well, a cook."

They all beamed.

"I went to school to learn how to cook, and now I work at a fancy restaurant. We create dishes instead of using ones from recipes."

"Ach, we do that sometimes, too," Lilian agreed.

"I've loved to cook since I was a girl. My mother mostly opened cans or bought frozen food to be heated in the microwave." Maybe it had been tactless for her to mention her mother at all, but she forged ahead anyway, although she wasn't about to tell them how often there just hadn't been any food at all. "So, well, I took over."

Lilian turned her smile on her oldest daughter. "Emma is already a fine cook, and Adah is learning, too. Mose just eats everything set in front of him and then asks for more!"

Mose turned beet red.

"Boys do that," Samuel said tolerantly. "Hard worker, he is."

When Lilian and the girls rose to clear the table, Hannah jumped up and tried to help, but Lilian wouldn't let her. She gave her a quick hug and murmured, "Your *daad* has waited so long to be able to get to know you."

Hannah hesitated, but sat down at the table again. Her grandmother—her *grossmammi*—smiled gently at her. The two little boys had disappeared toward the living room, Mose out the back door.

Samuel lifted his coffee cup to his mouth, but watched her over the brim with keen blue eyes. "How long will you stay?" he asked, before taking a sip.

"I . . . don't know." Already, she was in turmoil about this. "I asked for a two-week break from my job, but . . . I think I'd feel guilty leaving that soon. You know my grandfather is in poor health?"

"*Ja*, Helen told me, but I could see for myself." His voice was kind. "It's a blessing he was able to see you."

"Yes." Her smile wobbled. "I don't want to say, 'Hi, nice to meet you,' and just leave. You know? I think Grandma Helen could use help, and . . . I've missed so much. I didn't think I had any family except for Mom, and now—" She shook her head. "I always wondered especially who my father was."

He took her hand in his work-roughened one. "Losing you was terrible. You were so bright, so happy, everything a father could want."

"Grandma said, oh, that I'd run to you to be swung into the air, always trusting you to keep me safe."

A spasm crossed his face, and she felt guilty because they both knew that he *hadn't* been able to keep her safe.

But all he said was, "*Ja*, we were close. Your *mamm* . . ." He paused.

Hannah saved him from having to criticize her mother. "I know what she's like. She was always loving, and really good at playing—she made up wonderful stories—but . . . I still love her, but . . . she wasn't responsible."

Still isn't responsible, she silently corrected herself. Had her mother ever really grown up?

Then an awful thought struck her. "You married again because you thought she was dead."

Samuel grimaced. "*Ja*, I have talked with the bishop about this. To make things right, I've asked your *gross-mammi* Helen to speak to Jodi about filing papers to get a divorce in the *Englisch* court. Not what I would have chosen, but—" His eyes rested on his wife, washing dishes as his oldest daughter dried them while sneaking peeks at her *daad* and this strange new sister.

Not his oldest daughter, Hannah corrected herself. The thought was somehow startling. *I am.*

"Mom could remarry, then. I always wondered why she didn't. Although . . . I never had the feeling she especially wanted to."

"I think," he said a little gruffly, "she got tired of being married quickly. Or maybe it was our way of life she didn't like. She was fun loving, as you say, but not so happy about digging into work."

"I know," Hannah whispered.

"I can see her in your face, but are you like her in other ways? I don't see that."

"No, I don't think I am." In wondering about herself, she reflected often on Proverbs 22:6. *Train up a child in the way he should go, and when he is old he will not depart from it.* Jodi hadn't really trained her daughter in any meaningful way. Could it be true that her father and grandparents and the aunts Helen told her were often there, cooking and watching over her, might really have given her that foundation? Trained her in the way she should go? She'd have to think about that later. Although . . . that especially made sense since she'd so instinctively taken to cooking and felt such unexpected joy the first time she went to church.

What had she been? Eight or nine? Jodi had assured the man she'd begun to date that naturally she and her daughter attended church every Sunday. Hannah didn't say a word. The relationship fizzled without really going anywhere, but they'd gone to several services, Jodi restless and bored, Hannah enraptured.

Shaking off the memory, Hannah continued with what she'd meant to say. "And right now, I'm mad at her for what she did to you and to my grandparents. And to me, making me believe I had no family. It was so lonely."

Her father's hand covered hers. "*Ja*, I understand, but you must forgive her. Our Lord tells us that if you forgive the trespasses of others, your heavenly Father will also forgive you. But if you do not forgive the trespasses of others, neither will your Father forgive yours."

She smiled shakily. "Matthew is my favorite book in the Bible."

"You're a churchgoer?"

"Yes. Once I was old enough that Mom didn't pay much attention to what I was doing, I'd find a church wherever we went. The services opened a door for me. My faith gave me solace."

Samuel nodded, sadness deepening some of the lines on his face.

Why, Mom? Why?

Chapter Four

❖◆❖

"THE CUCUMBERS ARE coming along well," Hannah commented as she swiftly pulled weeds and dropped them in her bucket. The first time she offered to help in the garden, Lilian had been careful to show her what was a weed and what was a plant to be encouraged.

"*Ja*, May will be the start of our busy time." Two rows away, Lilian, too, was weeding. Her girls were currently in school, while the boys were with Samuel in the barn. Lilian continued, "Peas, potatoes, rhubarb, and strawberries. But later, so much ripens it's hard to keep up."

"I can only imagine." Hannah had never had the chance to garden, and the extent of her experience preserving fruits or vegetables had been making freezer jam.

This garden was vast, at first sight looking like a commercial enterprise, but Hannah was slowly learning what it took to feed a family of seven, soon to be eight—well, already often eight, as much time as she was spending here. This family raised enough vegetables and fruit to keep them year-round. Lilian and her girls must can daily for several months on end. They purchased only what couldn't be raised here in northern Missouri, or not without devoting entire fields to it, like wheat and sugar. They kept chickens and pigs, traded eggs with a neighbor for milk. They raised a couple of beef cows each spring, too.

An enterprise like this first surprised, then impressed and intrigued Hannah. To cook with ingredients you'd raised from seed or egg was something she'd never pictured doing, probably because it wasn't common in this country anymore, certainly not on this scale. This wasn't a backyard garden that provided treasured, if limited, sweet corn or peas for a few nights' worth of dinners.

The sun felt wonderful, although Hannah had plastered herself with lotion to keep herself from burning. She didn't tan well at best, and working lunch through dinner and into the night until the restaurant kitchen was clean didn't allow her many daytime hours to hang out at the park or the public swimming pool. Since she lived in an apartment with a tiny balcony, the only gardening she did was plop some geraniums and the like in pots.

Thank goodness she hadn't started any annuals, she thought, because they'd be brown and brittle by now with her away so long.

She reached the end of a row and straightened up, stretching her back.

"I'm thinking of looking for a rental in town," she announced. "And probably a short-term job, too. I'm not ready to go so soon. I've loved getting to know all of you, and then there's my grandfather."

Even though Lilian had already started down another row, she, too, straightened. "*Ja*, Samuel doesn't think he has long."

"No." She hesitated. "I've been meaning to ask about *Grossmammi*. Is she well?" They'd gone to *Aenti* Gloria's house for dinner one night, and Mose had gone to get *Grossmammi* another evening.

"Stronger than she looks," Lilian said, "but . . . fading a little. In her mind, you understand?"

"*Ja*. It's hard for me to tell because I can't totally understand what she says anyway." She frowned. "Although I'm getting better."

Lilian smiled warmly. "Mose says he has been giving you lessons in speaking our language."

"*Ja*, he's patient. I sit and watch him measure and saw and nail while he grills me." As young as he was, Mose had an apparently thriving business building doghouses, most sold at the local lumberyard and farm store. To his *daad*'s disappointment, he had no interest in becoming a farrier like his father, or metalworking in general. Samuel had told her with open pride that Mose was determined to build houses someday.

"Grills?" Lilian's forehead crinkled.

"Tells me words, makes me repeat them, then waits a little while and demands I come up with the right word again." She grinned. "He can be sneaky. He makes me *work*."

Lilian laughed. "*Ja*, his sisters, he helps them with their homework. Harder on them than their teacher, Emma says."

Hannah laughed. "I believe it. He's a smart boy."

Mose's mother looked justifiably pleased.

The two women worked in harmony for another two hours, until Hannah's back ached and she began to fear she should have reapplied the suntan lotion. Finally, on completing a row, she said, "I promised Grandma Helen I'd have dinner with them, and I'd better go by my hotel room to shower and change clothes first."

Lilian took a swipe at her forehead, beaded with sweat, and studied Hannah. The knees of her jeans were stained with green and brown, and she had wet circles under her arms and probably between her shoulder blades. Feeling like a weakling, Hannah couldn't imagine working this hard in the garden in July or August when the temperatures climbed into the nineties and hotter.

Lilian went with her to dump their buckets in a compost bin—a whole row of them, some full and only being turned, others empty or partially filled, containing every-thing from grass clippings to kitchen waste. Saying she thought she'd had enough, too, and must get supper cook-ing, she walked Hannah to her car.

There, she startled her with a hug. "Will we see you to-morrow?"

"You must be getting tired of me."

"Never," Lilian insisted. "God brought you to us. Sam-uel has never been happier, and the *kinder* all love you, a new big sister."

Swallowing a lump in her throat, Hannah said, "Thank you for saying that. Yes, I'll come help you in the garden again tomorrow, if you'll let me make any desserts for dinner."

Lilian's plain but sweet face lit with happiness. "Certain sure!"

Hannah surprised herself by hugging Lilian in turn be-fore jumping into her car and starting it.

Paradise was supposed to be a beach in the Caribbean, the sand white and the water turquoise, wasn't it? So why was she increasingly feeling like this farm was the most wonderful place on earth?

REBECCA KING'S ENTHUSIASM for the job of caring for Gideon's *kinder* as well as doing basic housekeeping and cooking had noticeably dimmed in the past two weeks. To his relief, she hardly ever stayed to eat with them, but the quality of the meals slipped along with her attendance.

Today, rain threatened, so Gideon forced himself to col-lect the clean laundry Rebecca had left on the clothesline.

A wind had picked up enough to snap the sheets out of his grip. One billowed and flew away. Zeb and Rebekah chased it, but when they handed it over, he could see that it would need washing again.

"Rebecca must have forgotten to take down and fold the laundry," he said in an attempt at good humor. He was hungry, and had a bad feeling that they'd finished the fried chicken from last night at *middaagesse* today.

"She said she didn't have time," his daughter told him. "Some boy is taking her to town for a hamburger and fries."

"Her *mamm* and *daad* said she could do that?" he said in surprise.

"The boy is *Englisch*." Zeb looked envious. "She says he has a red pickup truck."

"They're going to the Sonic Drive-In," Rebekah added.

Gideon's gathering frown momentarily silenced his *kinder*. He made himself smile at them. "Ach, she's having her *rumspringa*. Let's hope the boy doesn't drive too fast."

Gideon didn't like the expression that flitted across Zeb's face. Many Amish boys were drawn to the idea of driving a fast car or flying an airplane until they became settled in their faith and understood why so many modern ways had to be resisted. But he wouldn't have expected it of his own son, not after what happened to Leah. That wasn't a subject he wanted to raise with his *kinder*, however, not when he'd been glad to see them start to step out from under the shadow cast by their mother's death.

"Well, when you see her tomorrow, you can ask her about eating at the Sonic Drive-In," he said.

"Oh!" His daughter looked guilty. "I almost forgot, she said to tell you she won't be here tomorrow."

She'd left a message with a six-year-old girl, but hadn't been able to tell him in person when he harnessed her horse and wished her *gut'n owed*? Although he might not have said good evening, if he'd known her plans.

Gideon silently went back to taking down the clean

clothes, dumping more than folding them into the basket. He could feel dampness in the air. If he and his *kinder—and* the clothes and linens—ended up sopping wet, he was going to be annoyed.

He'd hoped Rebecca King would be a good employee. She'd seemed cheerful and willing when she first came, but he was wishing he'd never hired her. Firing her would be awkward when her family was part of the same church district as his. If she'd done something like leave the *kinder* alone because this *Englisch* boyfriend came by to take her for a ride, he'd have fired her anyway. As it was . . . she might have a good excuse for tomorrow. And who could he find to take her place? Some help was better than none.

He let out a heavy sigh. It was times like this when he missed having family nearby, the men who would expect to help him plow and harvest, the women who wouldn't hesitate to step in when he needed them. And, *ja*, he knew perfectly well that most of the women in the church district wouldn't hesitate, either, but he didn't like to ask.

Pride. He grimaced, dropping clothespins into the basket.

"Hurry!" Zeb exclaimed.

Gideon looked up to see a wall of slanted gray rain engulfing the barn and heading for them. "Run," he told the *kinder,* snatched up the overflowing basket, and jogged for the back door right behind them, abandoning some of the clothes still on the line. They could dry the next time the sun came out.

SHOWERED AND PRESENTABLE, Hannah was on her way out to her car when her phone rang. Immediately tense, she groped for it in the side pocket of her handbag. *Please don't let Granddad be having a crisis*, she prayed. Or worse.

But the caller was Mom.

She had to talk to her eventually. Why not now?

The day was gray and drizzly, so she unlocked her car as she was answering. "Mom." She slid in behind the wheel and shut the door.

"You've been ignoring me," her mother said piteously. "And after I asked you to trust me."

Her heart hardened. "Trust you? When you kept me from the rest of my family? Do you know what it means to me to meet my grandparents and my father? Not to mention my half sisters and brothers?"

"Illegitimate, since your dear father is a bigamist."

Hearing the spite, Hannah thought her head might explode. "How can you say that? You had—what was his name? Kevin?—call to say we were dead. You had him *fake* death certificates for us. *Daad* remarried in full faith that he was a widower."

"Why do you believe *them* instead of me? I didn't do that. Why would I?"

"Because you were trying very hard to be sure we weren't found."

"For a good reason." Was that an admission that she had been responsible for those death certificates? "Can't you understand? I ran away because I was scared for both of us, and my parents wouldn't help. They said I was married and had to go home, that I had to live with my decisions." Mom was crying. "I was hoping you never had to find out how awful it was."

"Tell me." Hannah didn't sound like herself, and didn't care. "What did *Daad* do that was so terrible? What did Grandma and Granddad do but bail you out of trouble over and over, pay for college classes you never completed?"

There was a gasp in her ear. "You believe everything they told you without ever asking me about what *really* happened? I raised you, protected you, loved you."

Hannah closed her eyes. "I know you loved me. I'm not sure moving from a battered women's shelter to a sleazy apartment to living with an abusive man was exactly _protecting_ me."

"I had to keep running, or _he_ would have found us!"

"_He?_" Hannah said inexorably. "The kind, steady man I'm getting to know, the man whose children love and respect him? The man who would never go to the police, or hire a private investigator, or even search records on a computer?"

"It's pretend!" her mother screamed. "They're vile people! They were hateful to me!"

"Including my sweet _grossmammi_?"

"Don't use that horrible, crude language with me! I'm your mother!"

Voice shaking, Hannah blurted, "Do you have any memory of how often we went hungry? Do you remember the creep you moved in with who whipped me with his belt? The ones who beat _you_ black and blue? Do you have any idea how hard school was for me, when I could never even complete a semester at any one school?"

"You're being hateful." Her mother's breath hitched. "I've never given you an excuse for that." And she was gone.

Hannah closed her eyes. Feeling both sick and remorseful, she had to ask herself: Who would she be, if she couldn't forgive?

"I DID IT," she told her grandparents a few days later. She'd come over to join them for lunch in the communal dining room, but arrived a little early. "I quit my job."

"Oh, honey, I'm sorry," Helen said with regret. "I hoped your boss would give you longer."

"He really was generous. And you know, he did pay me for a week on top of the two weeks of vacation time I was owed. He offered another two weeks, paid, but he can't do any longer without a sous chef. It sounds like there have been lots of problems. He needs to find someone who isn't just filling in, who's good."

Letting her ideal job go hadn't been easy, but she wasn't ready to tell her father and grandparents what a pleasure it had been, and then leave Tompkin's Mill, either. Leave with no idea when she could take the time to come back for more than a weekend. One comfort was that Greg had promised her he'd give her a good reference when she was ready to focus again on her career.

Right now, that was low on her list of priorities. No matter what her mother said, Hannah had to discover what really having family meant. She was a little scared that she'd find dark secrets among the Amish, or just that Samuel would quit hiding a brutal streak once they were past this . . . well, *honeymoon period* wasn't quite right, but close enough.

And what if her grandparents *were* lying to her, excusing their own failings with a daughter who'd had no one else to depend on?

Hannah didn't believe any of that—but she'd have told anyone that she knew her mother's weaknesses, through and through. Mom didn't hesitate to use what she called little white lies, but to fake her own and Hannah's deaths? And, really, to take off the way she had in the first place, instead of contacting social services, filing for divorce, insisting on supervised visitation for Hannah with her father? There was a right way to do things, and a wrong way.

"It's okay," she said. "I know I told you I was going to look for a rental, even if it was just a room, but *Daad* and Lilian have asked me to stay with them. I was a little bit horrified because they already have such a crowd, but it turns out *Daad* has an office downstairs. He plans to move the desk and file cabinet out to the living room so I can have a bedroom to myself. I couldn't say no when they looked so hopeful."

"Of course you shouldn't say no!" Helen insisted. "You need to get to know your father and the rest of your family. This will be perfect."

Hannah thought so, too, except that the differences between her, raised *Englisch*, and her father's family weren't so important when she was there just for a meal or to help out in the garden. Living there, though, would be different.

They wouldn't have wireless, so she might as well leave her laptop locked in the trunk of the car, but she couldn't exactly whip out her mobile phone and check the national news in front of them, could she? If nothing else, she'd be setting what they'd see as a bad example for the children, especially Mose, at an impressionable age. Then there was her wearing pants or skirts that only came to midthigh, and the fact that a car would be semipermanently parked in their driveway, and the kids would see her driving into town to do errands and visit her other grandparents. What if they asked to ride in the car with her?

Maybe this wasn't such a good idea, she thought, deflated.

A few minutes later, after having pushed her grandfather in his wheelchair into the elevator and downstairs so that he could join her and her grandmother at a small table in the dining room, she said, "*Daad* thinks he might have found a job for me, too."

Robert watched her with surprising alert eyes.

"Do you need to work?" Helen asked in surprise. "If you're living with them, I mean?"

"I should contribute—"

"We'll be glad to help you out financially."

Hannah shook her head firmly. "Thank you for offering, but I'd rather work at least part-time. If nothing else, I need to let *Daad* and Lilian and their children be a family without me some of the time."

Helen smiled her understanding. "What kind of job is it?"

"Childcare and, I guess, some housekeeping and cooking for a widower with two kids. I've never spent time with children, so I'm nervous about that, but you know how much I love to cook."

Her grandmother laughed. "Just so there's not a baby! That would have you diving in at the deep end."

"I'll find out more tomorrow." She smiled her thanks at the waitress who set her entrée in front of her. The food here wasn't up to her standards, but she guessed the elderly residents preferred bland to subtle or spicy. "I have an interview."

"Is the widower Amish?"

"Yes. He may decide not to hire me once he realizes I don't speak the language."

"It wouldn't be bad for you to learn some of your father's language."

"I . . . already am. I've actually surprised myself. It's coming fast enough, I have to wonder whether . . ." Would it sound silly if she said—

"You already speak it?" Her grandmother had either read her mind or thought the possibility to be logical. "There are concepts a four- or five-year-old wouldn't know, but otherwise you were fluent when Jodi took you away. Maybe this will be more like opening the gates to release water from a dam than learning the language afresh."

"Maybe." What an odd thought—but her earliest vivid memory was of her first weeks of kindergarten at a big elementary school in . . . She didn't remember. She'd been paralyzed. Mom told her she had to quit being so shy. On a new spurt of anger, she realized that she'd been confused by the chatter of so many surrounding children all speaking English. She must have been bilingual to some extent, speaking English with her mother, but now, she thought she'd spent more time with her father and all those female relatives than she had with her mother. "Do you know how fluent Mom got in *Deitsh*?"

"I heard her say things, but . . ." Helen looked at her husband, who only shook his head. "Mostly she spoke English when we were around. And knowing Jodi . . ."

Hannah didn't blame her for not wanting to finish. Her mother had disappointed her a thousand times, but it would be even worse when it was your own child. Your only child.

So she said, "If this interview doesn't work out, I could probably get a job cooking here in town."

That idea held little appeal. Slapping hamburgers or pouring premixed pancake batter onto a grill wasn't her idea of cooking. And . . . she wanted to immerse herself in the Amish culture. Learn to feel at home among the people and with the faith she'd lost when her mother decided Hannah was better off forgetting her early years.

Under the table, she crossed her fingers—and pictured the tall, stern man with the two children who had given her directions to her father's house.

She tried to justify her hope that he was the man needing to hire someone by thinking about how likable the children seemed . . . but she knew that wasn't all of it.

Thinking it through, Hannah realized she'd been touched by the way the man had rested his hand on his young daughter's shoulder in automatic reassurance. Hannah had wanted that, so much. This little girl would feel safe with her father standing solidly behind her.

While that was perfectly true, she tried to be honest with herself.

She'd reacted to the man himself. His height, his strong body, his handsome face, and his strikingly dark eyes and hair. He was so . . . physical, nothing like the guys she'd known who had muscles only because they worked out at a gym.

She'd felt heat in her cheeks and a quiver low in her belly at her first sight of the Amishman. That happened to her rarely to never.

All of which meant it would be very bad if the prospective employer was him and he hired her. Right? What she should do was cross her fingers that Gideon Lantz was someone else altogether.

Chapter Five

❧✦❧

GIDEON PACED FROM his front door to the back before retracing his steps, then doing it again. The woman wasn't late yet, but he was already regretting having told Samuel that he'd talk to her. How could he hire an *Englischer* to watch over his *kinder*? Especially given their *mamm*'s history, her clinging to her *Englisch* friend even when it wasn't wise? And, aside from his fear of how this Hannah could influence them, he had to wonder whether Bishop Amos might question his judgment as Bishop Paul had back in New York. Though the fact that Hannah was Samuel Mast's daughter would weigh with Amos, too.

Gideon wouldn't have considered this if she'd worn makeup when she stopped to ask directions. She'd looked . . . plain in some ways, except for the lack of a *kapp*. What he'd seen was an honest, open face with big eyes and a sweet smile.

Gideon groaned, not liking the turn his thoughts had taken. It was not good that he'd been drawn immediately by her appearance. Even born Amish, she *wasn't* a plain woman. She was an *Englischer*, through and through, with her car and the blue jeans he'd heard she wore to work in the garden and the phone she carried everywhere.

This was foolish. If *he* had a phone closer to hand than the shanty, he'd call her to cancel.

That was when he heard the sound of a car coming toward the house. He grimaced. He couldn't forget that he was considering her because no other good possibility had emerged to replace Rebecca King, and he was already falling behind on his work after only a few days of trying to do that work and also take care of his *kinder*, feed them all and do a poor job of keeping the kitchen clean, never mind the rest of the house. They would have nothing clean to wear if Judith Miller hadn't insisted on doing their laundry last week. He wouldn't be surprised if she was organizing a group of women to sweep in and scour his house from top to bottom, as they'd done when Judith's son, David, had moved into the house he inherited from his *onkel*. He should welcome such generosity, but instead shrank from it. Kindly meant, that kind of work frolic also said, *You can't take care of your* kinder *without the help of your neighbors.*

The women in his own family back home had often said such things, sure to notice and speak out when laundry didn't get done or Rebekah's *kapp* had gone missing or either *kind* was *strubly* on worship Sunday. His mother and two of his sisters had tried to talk him into letting Rebekah and Zeb stay with them. His father chastised him for resisting.

Ja, that was another reason he had decided to start over far from that family. He had told himself they spoke up out of love without ever thinking how inadequate they made him feel or noticing how Rebekah and Zeb shrank from criticism. He was glad to move before he had become resentful.

For the sake of his *kinder*, he could never let these new neighbors know he felt anything but grateful.

Gideon sighed and went to the front window.

If he hired Hannah Mast, he wouldn't need the members of his church district to take pity on him, at least not if she did an adequate job.

And, *ja*, he knew better than to be too proud to accept help when he and his *kinder* needed it. Hadn't God said, *Therefore, whatever you want men to do to you, do also to them, for this is the Law and the Prophets*?

Had he not joined with the members of his church district to help others, such as Esther Schwartz, the widow who lived next door? He should rejoice that they would joyfully help him in return.

He watched the woman drive up his lane so slowly, he could have walked as fast. Certainly, his buggy horse would leave her behind. At least she wouldn't make Zeb envious when she sped away.

Once she parked, he decided to be polite and go out to meet her. She might be *Englisch*, but she was also a church member's daughter, living with him and his family.

She saw him as she got out of the car, and walked across the lawn toward him. He was pleased that she wore a skirt with a short-sleeve blouse that didn't reveal much more than an Amishwoman would when she rolled up her sleeves—except for the slender calves and ankles showing beneath the knee-length hem of the skirt. She was tall, although still well below his height of about six feet. Slim, too. And, *ja*, as pretty as he remembered.

She'd brushed her hair, a shiny light brown streaked with blond, smoothly back from her face and secured it in a bundle at the nape of her neck. She offered a tentative smile, her beautiful eyes hopeful.

"We meet again."

"Ja." He hesitated. "Why don't we sit on the porch?"

"That sounds good. The breeze feels wonderful. I guess you can tell I've been getting too much sun helping Lilian in her garden." She touched her nose, which would be peeling any day. "I'm not used to being outside so much."

"Do you come from someplace that's cooler?"

"No, I've been living in Lexington, Kentucky, the past two—almost three—years. But I work indoors."

He leaned against the porch railing. At his gesture, she sat on the porch swing, her knees together, her hands folded on her lap, composed so carefully she must be nervous. She'd apparently left her handbag and keys in the car, but a pocket in the khaki skirt showed the outline of her phone.

She saw the direction of his gaze and said, "I wouldn't keep this with me, but . . . I don't know if Samuel has told you that my grandfather has congestive heart failure. He had enough of an incident this morning, the paramedics came out, but decided he didn't have to be hospitalized. I don't want to be out of touch if my grandmother needs me."

Gideon nodded his understanding, reassured by her concern for these grandparents she hadn't even known that long.

"You saw my *kinder.* Zeb is eight years old, Rebekah six. Both are in school right now. Their mother died three years ago. Zeb remembers her, but I doubt Rebekah has many memories of her *mamm.*"

"And you don't have photos of her."

It wasn't a question, so she must know they refused to be photographed. He couldn't decide if her soft voice was making a judgment, or simply expressing sympathy.

"No."

"I understand how your daughter must feel. I didn't remember my father."

He cocked his head. "You were five, weren't you?"

"Days past my birthday, I'm told. But . . . my mother discouraged me from remembering." She looked away from him, as if hoping to hide what she felt. "I ended up confused, not knowing what was a real memory and what I'd made up."

He should ask the questions he'd planned, not talk about her past, but he couldn't help himself. "Why would she do such a thing?"

"I . . . don't know. She has stories about why she had to escape, but I find it hard to believe her now that I'm getting to know my *daad*."

Interested in how naturally she'd said that, even as she was otherwise speaking English, Gideon said, "My daughter speaks only a little English. Our *kinder* don't learn until they start school, and this was her first year."

"So I understand. But Zeb speaks more?"

"*Ja*, some." He wasn't sure, because they didn't use it at home. How would she communicate with his *kinder*? This suddenly seemed like an even worse idea than he'd thought.

"I'm trying to learn to speak *Deitsh*," she said hastily, as if she'd been able to tell what he was thinking. "Mose especially has been helping me." A smile played with her mouth. "I think he was scared of me at first, so now he enjoys being the teacher. He can scold me when I don't remember part of the lesson."

Gideon chuckled. "Mose seems like a fine boy."

"*Ja*." Continuing in *Deitsh*, this Hannah Mast said, very slowly, groping her way, "My sisters and brothers have all been good to me."

His eyebrows rose. "*Sehr gut.*"

She gave him a saucy grin. "Do I get a gold star?"

Gideon had to laugh. "If I had one."

Sobering, she said, "Will you tell me more about the job?"

"I need someone to watch over Rebekah and Zeb after school from Tuesday through Friday and all day on Saturday. I'm also asking for at least some housework and laundry if you have time. Cooking is the other big job. I'm fine with breakfast, but when I have to prepare other meals, either we eat really late or I cut my work short."

"What do you do?"

"I'm a farmer. That means I'm usually nearby, but often out in the fields with my horses, plowing, fertilizing, harvesting, maintaining fences and buildings, feeding animals, pruning trees or vines, mending equipment, or sharpening blades. I work long days. In the past two years, I've had four different young women work here to take care of the house and my *kinder*, but none have lasted long."

Hannah studied him, her high, smooth brow crinkled. "Is there a problem causing them to leave?"

"I don't think so." Her asking seemed reasonable. "Sarah—she was first, was already planning for her wedding, so I knew we wouldn't have her for long. Eva left when her *mamm* became ill and needed more help at home. Naomi also left to marry. Two weeks ago, Rebecca took a job at a café in town for more money." If he were Rebecca's *daad*, he'd be worried about her increasing interest in *auslanders*, and he thanked God that he wasn't responsible for her.

"Oh. Well, I assume *Daad* told you that I might not stay for more than two or three months."

"He said that you're staying because of your grandparents."

"Yes, and . . . well, I want to get to know my *daad* and Lilian and my sisters and brothers. My Amish *grossmammi*, too." Emotions welled in her richly colored eyes. "Before, I didn't have any family. Sometimes I don't know what I'm supposed to do or say, but . . . I want to learn. I don't want to give any of it up. I've waited my whole life to find them."

A tug in his chest, Gideon felt sad for everything she'd missed. He understood, since with this move to Missouri, he and the *kinder* had said goodbye to the rest of their family, from an *aenti* who'd cared for Rebekah and Zeb after

Leah died to the brother Gideon had been closest with. His *mamm* and Leah's, too. He still thought he'd made the right choice, but it was hard. Letters were not the same, and visits would be rare, especially since many members of his family had opposed the move. He had yet to find time to take the *kinder* back to New York, and only one of his sisters had come here for a two-week stay.

He wouldn't tell anyone else how relieved he was that the distance made much contact difficult.

"Even a month or two would be a help," he said to Hannah. "That would give me time to find someone for the summer." At her nod, he continued, "What did you do for work before you came to Tompkin's Mill?"

"I'm a chef." She told him about her training and her recent job at a restaurant in a city in Kentucky.

He didn't want to insult her, but had to be sure she understood what he needed. "We don't expect our meals to be fancy. I work hard, and eat heartily."

"I've seen that with my *daad*. Lilian and I have been trading recipes. I love to cook. I enjoy playing with recipes until they're as good as they can be, but I'm happy to cook the kind of food you're used to. And I love to bake." She raised her eyebrows. "I assume Rebekah is learning to help?"

"Some, but not the way she would be if her *mamm* was here." He'd been disappointed when he would come in for a cup of coffee and see her sitting at the table coloring or just kicking her heels while Naomi and then Rebecca worked on dinner. "The young women taking care of the household wanted to get each job done, not make it slower by teaching a girl as young as my daughter."

Hannah frowned. "That's wrong. Helping her discover what she can contribute should be a joy, not a trial."

Surprised and pleased, Gideon knew right then that he would at least give her a chance. He wondered if her cooking would be better than Rebecca King's. It couldn't fail to be better than his.

Her face brightened. "Do you have a garden? I've spent a lot of time with Lilian in hers."

"A small one. I don't have time for more than what I already do. We keep plenty of the crops I grow to sell. Corn, raspberries, sweet potatoes, and watermelon. We do have fruit trees, too."

"I see." She looked past him, her lips curving. "Your *kinder* are coming."

Gideon turned. "*Ja*, a neighbor and I take turns walking our *kinder* to school and home at the end of the day. The road isn't that busy, but the *Englisch* drive too fast sometimes." He was immediately embarrassed because he'd forgotten *she* was *Englisch*.

Except she laughed and said, "Not me."

He suppressed a grin. "I have noticed."

Her eyes shied from his as if he'd startled her, but he didn't know why that would be so. He thought she might be blushing.

"I'm bold about some things—trying different spices in a recipe—but timid in other ways," she said hastily. "My mother didn't have a car, and I didn't learn to drive until I was almost twenty. And then I was in a city, and it was scary. Everyone rushing around. I still don't enjoy it." She shook herself.

Zeb and Rebekah spotted the two of them on the porch and broke into a run. Winning the race, as he always did, Zeb thudded up the porch steps and came to an abrupt stop, gaping at the *Englisch* woman. Rebekah followed, but went straight to Gideon, clutching his hand.

Hannah smiled and rose to her feet. *"Was bist du heit?"* How are you?

Zeb responded with a burst of speech.

Hannah almost immediately had to shake her head and

say apologetically, "I only speak a little *Deitsh*. I'm just learning."

"I can teach you," he said eagerly.

This smile was more polite. "We'll have to see if your *daadi* decides to hire me first."

Zeb looked at Gideon with eyes as dark as his *daad*'s. "Will you?"

"We'll see." He bent to kiss the top of his daughter's head and then ruffled his son's hair. "Now you go on in, and let us talk."

"But I can—!"

Gideon raised his eyebrows. Zeb sighed and trudged into the house. At least he held the door until his sister slipped in with him instead of letting it close in her face.

Amusement danced in Hannah's eyes. "Well, he's not timid, is he?"

He laughed and shook his head. "Not anymore. After their *mamm* died, he quit talking much. Rebekah, too. Before, she had so much to say, for her age, but after, I'd see her watching me, her eyes so worried . . ." Gideon shook his head. "Now she, too, is a *blabbermaul*." Seeing Hannah's expression, he said, "You don't know that word yet?"

"No, but I can guess. A chatterbox, like my sister Adah?"

"I don't know that word, but I think we're saying the same thing." They looked at each other for a minute.

"I would like to hire you, at least for both of us to try it out. I need you to work full-time." He needed more than that, of course; he needed a wife. "I can feed the *kinder* breakfast, but I start the day early. I hope you can come early enough to make lunch for Zeb and Rebekah to take to school—or prepare lunches the day before—and walk with them on the days that are my turn, then do some laundry or housework, make dinner. Once you've caught up on the housework, you could cut your hours if you don't want to work full-time. For dinner, you can stay to eat with us, or leave to eat with your *daad*'s family, whichever you'd like." He told her what he could afford to pay.

"You come in for lunch, surely," she said in apparent surprise.

"*Ja*, but . . ." He hadn't thought about that, the two of them alone. Because of his unease with Rebecca King, he'd gladly had her not start work until after lunchtime except for Saturdays, even though the house had suffered.

"Once you let me know what you'd like, I can make lunches, too."

He saw that it hadn't occurred to her to be uncomfortable because the two of them might sometimes be alone. Because she was *Englisch*, of course.

He could discuss this with the bishop.

She gave a decisive nod. "That schedule sounds fine, as long as I can change it if necessary. And that you understand I might have to rush to town if my grandfather suffers a crisis. I'd need to know where to find you, or who I could leave the *kinder* with if that happens and they're home but you're not."

"We can plan for that," he agreed. "Almost any of my neighbors would take them, or Lilian would. Her girls go to school with Zeb and Rebecca."

She grinned suddenly. "But he's a boy."

"I think he objects to them being girls." They exchanged smiles that felt more than friendly. As if, for that moment, they'd been of one mind.

Gruffly, he asked, "When could you start?"

"Tomorrow?"

Gideon felt as if she'd lifted a weight from his shoulders. "That would be good. *Denke*."

They agreed on a time. She said, "Please tell me if I do something you don't like," nodded, and went down the porch steps.

A minute later, she'd managed to turn around in front of the barn and drove slowly down the lane.

HANNAH HAD A bad case of nerves the next morning when she parked in a spot she hoped would be out of the way and started for the house. Had this been a terrible idea? She could have easily found a part-time job in town, instead of committing herself to trying to take the place of these two children's mother, and her not speaking their language well at all. She'd lain awake worrying last night. For heaven's sake, she wasn't even sure how they did laundry when they didn't have electricity—that was a job Lilian must have done on a day when Hannah wasn't there. What if she couldn't find ingredients or implements she needed to cook?

Those were problems she could take to Lilian, she reassured herself. But what if she and that poor little girl were completely unable to communicate?

Worse, what if she blushed every time Gideon looked at her with the darkest eyes she'd ever seen? She knew perfectly well she had at least once during the interview, when a contagious grin crinkled the skin beside his eyes and transformed a sometimes stern face into a heart-stoppingly handsome one. She could only be grateful he didn't notice how she'd been affected, or surely he wouldn't have hired her.

There he was already, coming out the back door to meet her. He was about six feet tall, not huge, but muscular with broad shoulders, and imposing. He was a rarity among the Amish she'd seen so far, with his hair and beard a very dark brown, almost black, and then those eyes. She liked his lightning smiles, but he was otherwise hard to read. Deeply reserved, she'd thought first, but believed she'd seen bleakness in his eyes and the set of his mouth.

And, ach—she consciously borrowed from Lilian—why was she fussing about how he looked? She worked for him, that's all.

"*Gute mariye*," she called, pleased to have the right *Deitsh* words at hand. Very appropriate, since this was a beautiful, sunny morning.

"*Gute mariye* to you, too," he returned, some of the lines on his forehead easing. "Glad I am to see you so early."

She couldn't lie and say she was an early riser; given her career, she was more often up late and then slept late. But she could adjust. "I hoped you could show me where to find things. Unless Zeb and Rebekah can do that?"

"No, I'll start, at least."

He led her to the garden patch, which was indeed disappointingly modest, although neatly tended. Some rows were made up of green shoots, but the peas were coming along, and she spotted a head of cabbage ready to be used. Greens, too; Lilian usually served a salad of some kind along with meals. Plus a nice patch of strawberries and substantial clumps of rhubarb.

Hannah opened her mouth to ask if he'd mind if she enlarged the garden, but then shut it. She'd better find out first how busy she was with the children—the *kinder*, she corrected herself—and the cooking and housework. Both would certainly be more labor intensive than running a vacuum around her apartment or tossing dirty clothes in the washer—or using a blender. Also . . . what if she created a larger garden, then left? Would Gideon feel constrained to keep it up?

He gestured toward a grassy bank with a metal door inset. "The storm shelter."

"Have you had to use it?" she asked apprehensively.

"Not yet. I pray we don't need to, but am glad it's there."

She was on board with that sentiment.

At the chicken coop, he grabbed a basket and collected eggs, showing her how to do it without getting pecked.

"Zeb usually does this, but just in case you have to. He also cleans the coop. He likes to forget, so you should remind him after school."

She nodded, eyeing the chickens, red with speckled feathers. Having an awful thought, she asked, "Do you . . . *eat* your own chickens?"

Chapter Six

❧ ◆ ❧

HANNAH FELT DUMB. *Doppick*. This was a farm. Of course they raised chickens not only for the eggs, but to eat.

"*Ja*, certain sure," Gideon said matter-of-factly. "Not the good layers, but I can show you which—"

Feeling foolish or not, she shook her head vigorously and took a step back, even if she risked irritating her new employer. "I've never killed anything but bugs. I don't want to."

He studied her. Blinked a few times. "I will do it for you when you want to cook chicken."

Here she'd been wallowing in the idealistic vision of farm-to-table without letting herself think through the reality. He probably raised pigs and steers to eat, too—just as her *daad* and his family did. Hannah ate meat, which made her squeamishness hypocritical . . . but she still didn't know if she could wring a neck.

After a moment, she squared her shoulders and nodded. "But not until I learn how to, well, pluck the feathers and get it ready to cut up and cook."

He seemed mainly bemused, but might be *a*mused, too. "We have plenty of beef and pork in the freezer."

Hannah relaxed. At least he hadn't fired her on the spot. She took in the orchard of well-cared-for fruit trees, many in bloom, others shedding pale pink or white petals that carpeted the grass. Beyond, tied to taut wire strung between posts, were a few short rows of berries that he said were marionberries.

"At the back of the property, near the pond, I've put in some blueberry bushes, too, not big yet, but I think we'll get a good crop this year. We catch some fish in the pond, too. Zeb enjoys fishing. The raspberries are that way"—he waved vaguely—"but they don't come ripe until July at the soonest."

A huge old walnut tree shaded the yard just behind the house.

Hannah turned in place. A woodlot screened the property from its neighbor. A silo topped with a conical aluminum roof gleamed white. She caught a whiff of what might be a pigsty, but not so close as to be offensive. A few cows grazed in a field along with four massive draft horses and a smaller horse with a coat that was more red than brown, accented with black mane and tail.

The grass was recently mowed; the paint on the side of the barn and the house behind her as well as the board fences was a crisp, clean white, the sky an arch of blue. Gideon Lantz must work hard to keep up his house and farm so well. Something of a perfectionist herself, she admired that.

They entered the house through a combined mudroom and utility room, where she saw what had to be a hand-cranked wringer washing machine. She recognized it only from old photographs. Hannah hoped Gideon didn't see her wince. Beside the washer sat a basket filled with clothespins. She had only vaguely noticed the lines outside, but had seen laundry on the line at her *daad*'s house.

Inside, she greeted the *kinder* still at the kitchen table. Zeb gave her a big grin, while his sister looked shy and ducked her head. Ignoring her, Zeb started telling her what he liked taking for his school lunch, mixing English and *Deitsh* words in a way that made her laugh.

Gideon stopped to lay a gentle hand on his daughter's shoulder and spoke in his own language. Hannah made out her name and the word *gut*. As in, Rebekah was supposed to be good for this strange woman, Hannah guessed. That gentleness with his daughter made her heart squeeze again. The juxtaposition with his big, work-roughened hand . . .

Hannah closed her eyes. She had to get over this acute awareness of Gideon, or she wouldn't last in this job for two days.

She made herself glance around the kitchen. As at her *daad*'s house, the stove and refrigerator would be fueled by propane. No dishwasher. Cupboard and counter space was generous, and a long, sturdy farm table in the middle of the large room would give her another prep surface.

Gideon led her down steep steps into a cellar, cool and earthy smelling. The kerosene lantern he lit and carried illuminated walls lined with shelving that held some canning jars but nowhere near what Lilian still had laid by from last year. Several chest freezers were also hooked up to propane, Gideon told her. One was reserved for meat. Wooden bins held potatoes, onions, and dried-up apples.

Those apples would make fine pies, she thought. Turning, she felt her upper arm bump Gideon's.

She glanced up to find him watching her with unexpected intensity, seeming . . . perturbed. Was it their proximity? Hannah became acutely aware of how close they stood to each other, how small this space was.

That might be why he said so abruptly, "Use anything you can find. Now I have to get to work."

She felt an unfamiliar tremor inside, a reaction to the look in his eyes.

Not a minute later, after leading her up to the kitchen, he strode out the back door, leaving her staring at his *kinder*, who stared back.

THE WARMTH AND rich aromas of the barn welcomed Gideon once he'd fled the house. Or was that *fled from the* Englisch *woman*?

This morning, he'd seen clearly all the problems with having her here. He was afraid she wouldn't last any time. Frowning, he thought, maybe until the weekend. That would at least give him a respite.

He shouldn't have hired anyone whose primary skill was fancy cooking. Who wouldn't kill a chicken and didn't even know how to pluck the feathers. What clsc would they find that she couldn't or wouldn't be able to do?

Guilt stewed in his stomach, too, at the memory of his daughter shrinking into herself because this woman he'd hired could neither talk to her nor understand her.

For that reason, he wouldn't plow today, although he was already behind. He should have every field seeded by now, but still had one large one to go. He intended to plant sunflowers this year, reducing the acreage he'd have in corn since there had been a glut of it last year, with prices sagging.

He started the morning mucking out the stalls, adding to his compost pile behind the barn before spreading clean bedding. In no time, he had rolled up his sleeves and hung his hat on a nail, but still began to sweat.

Then he milked their three nanny goats before turning them out as well. Carrying the milk into the house gave him a chance to find out how the new woman was coping.

He was met by silence. No one in the kitchen. Before he could panic, he realized that she would be walking Zeb and Rebekah to school right now. Possibly already on her way home after leaving them. Tomorrow, he should join them so that Hannah could meet Susan Miller, his closest neighbor with a school-age *kind*. If she'd trust Hannah to escort her son, they could continue sharing the task.

Putting the two cans of milk in the refrigerator, he returned to the barn. This would be a good day to clean harnesses and sharpen tools, the kind of small jobs that too often went undone when so much else demanded his attention.

His buggy horse, Fergus, would soon be in need of shoeing. It occurred to Gideon he could ask Hannah to speak to her father. Samuel was the farrier who took care of all Gideon's horses, and she could arrange a day for him to come.

And here he was, loitering in the kitchen as if he had nothing better to do. Even an *Englisch* woman couldn't get lost following the road back from the schoolhouse.

The cherry tomatoes were planted close enough to the house he'd hear Hannah calling for him if she needed assistance. Gideon picked up a hoe from the barn and strode around it. Weeds not only drew nutrients from the soil, if they grew too tall, they would make picking the tomatoes difficult. Having to weed by hoe and hand was a nuisance, but vine-ripe, flavorful cherry tomatoes brought in high prices at auction and would be worth the more intensive labor. Or so he hoped.

His goal was to get certified to sell his crops as organic, but that took proof of not having used pesticides for three years. In the meantime, he intended to try a variety of crops rather than only the corn, soybeans, and wheat common to local Amish farms. The produce auction house in town, so close, gave him options he hadn't had as readily where he'd farmed before in New York.

Gideon did still have two large fields planted with soybeans; once those were harvested, he'd plow under the stubble and replace the soybeans with corn. And, of course, he had a sizable field with early hay. Otherwise, he had planted pumpkins, squash, and the tomatoes. If he'd had a larger family to help pick, he could do more with tomatoes and the raspberries, but he'd decided that this year it wouldn't hurt to try small amounts of a number of different crops. That was a good way of protecting himself from too much loss if one crop failed because of drought or pests. After a rainy spring in New York and an attack of rust, he'd had to tear out his raspberry plants. It hadn't quite been a disaster, but closer than he liked, teaching him a valuable lesson.

He saw Hannah striding up the driveway a short while later, her head turning, but as far as he could tell, she didn't see him. He wondered which chores inside would seem most urgent in her view. Lunchtime would come soon enough. He'd let her figure out how to get by on her own until then.

He just wished he had more confidence in a woman who knew almost nothing about their ways.

The morning passed far more slowly than usual, with him worrying. Finally, his stomach growling and the sun high in the sky, he started back toward the house, stopping for a moment at the sight of clean sheets, towels, aprons and white undergarments hanging on the clothesline.

He relaxed slightly. It would be good to sleep with clean sheets tonight.

When he walked in the back door, he was greeted by aromas that had his mouth watering. He took off his hat and hung it on a peg on the wall, his eyes on Hannah, removing something from the oven.

She must have heard his footfalls, because she turned with a smile. She'd covered her shirt and khaki skirt with an apron that fell well below the hem of her skirt. Her cheeks were pink from the heat of the stove.

"Rebekah was good about helping me find things this morning," she said.

How had she asked for what she wanted in a way his daughter understood? he wondered. But he only nodded. "She likes to help."

He washed up in the downstairs bathroom, and returned to find a spread on the table more than ample for only two adults.

Surveying it, Hannah wrinkled her nose. "I may have overdone."

Schnitz un knepp—ham and dried apples—was the centerpiece, accompanied by creamy scalloped potatoes, cornbread with flecks of bacon, and a salad with fresh greens. She'd set out applesauce as well, and he saw apple pies cooling on the counter. The coffee she'd made was dark and strong, just the way he liked it.

"I think this may feed us tonight, too," he agreed. "But it looks good, and I'm hungry."

The words were inadequate, but the right words didn't always come to him, particularly when he was speaking English.

With a shy glance at him, Hannah took a seat across the table. When he bent his head in prayer, she did the same. Was she only being polite, or did she pray? She'd moved in with her *daad* after the last worship service. Would she attend the next service with her family? Gideon wondered. *Ach*, why would she? It would be a misery, when she couldn't understand hymns or sermons.

Suddenly realizing he had yet to pray, Gideon did so hastily, hoping she wasn't wondering what had taken him so long. When he lifted his head, she did as well. He reached for the plate with the cornbread.

She dished up a small helping of the *schnitz un knepp*. "I met Susan Miller this morning. She was just coming out with her boy, and was glad to let him go with us. I told her I'll be happy to pick them up, too, because otherwise she has to get Judith—her *mamm*? Jacob's *mamm*?—to watch the rest of her *kinder*."

"If you don't mind the walk."

"Not at all. And it must be harder for her to get everything done with young *kinder* at home. Two not yet school age, and a baby, I think she said."

"*Ja*, their family is growing fast. Judith and Isaac are Jacob's parents. They have one other son who inherited a farm a mile or so down the road from an *onkel*."

"Oh." He watched her ponder that. "So Jacob will take over his *daad*'s farm?"

"*Ja*, I think so." She'd obviously realized that Jacob and his family lived in a small house on the same property as his parents. Gideon had heard talk that Jacob's family and his parents were planning to switch houses, since Isaac and Judith no longer needed so much space.

Everything Gideon put in his mouth was delicious. The cornbread and the dressing on the salad were subtly different from any he'd had before—the cornbread spicier than he was used to—but both were so good, he was afraid he had stuffed himself too full to appreciate the pie the way he should.

Except, once Hannah served him a large slab, he realized he'd been wrong. The crust was flaky and the apples just sweet enough without being too sweet. He ate his plate clean, then sighed.

Expression anxious, she said, "Was it all right?"

"*Ja*." He smiled crookedly. "Almost too good. Now I don't want to go back to work."

Looking around, he saw that the kitchen was cleaner than it had been in a while, too. Hannah had worked hard this morning.

"Was there anything you needed you couldn't find?" he asked. "Either for cleaning or cooking? I can shop if you give me a list."

"Why don't you let me? If you don't mind, I'd like to buy more spices and bags of beans. Oh, and split peas. I didn't see any. The flour is getting low, too."

Since he wasn't growing wheat this year, that was something they'd have to keep buying. He told her about Troyer Bulk Foods, owned and run by Bishop Amos Troyer, where he did much, although not all, of his shopping. "The prices are good on what is carried at that store."

"I hadn't noticed it." She listened to his directions. "We're not out of anything, so I'll probably wait and run to town tomorrow or Thursday."

He agreed, gulped the last of his coffee, and fled for a second time that day. Sitting at the table talking to Hannah felt both natural and deeply uncomfortable. Gideon didn't like noticing the sheen of her hair, or the delicacy of her collarbones and length of her slender neck. He must guard himself when he was near her, especially when they were alone.

At the same time, he hoped Amos would not ask him to let Hannah go because she was *Englisch*. Despite his doubts, she'd already showed herself to be as hard a worker as any Amishwoman. As a man who enjoyed his food, he looked forward to the next meal she prepared . . . and all of the meals she would cook for him and the *kinder* in the days to come.

GLAD FOR HIS obvious pleasure at the meal, Hannah reluctantly tackled another load of laundry. Her arms ached by the time she had rinsed the clothes and was done running everything through the ringer for the second time and carried it out to hang on the line.

This load of laundry had gone better than the first, which she'd started to hang on the line out back before realizing the fabric was weirdly stiff because she'd forgotten the rinse stage entirely. And then when she'd carried it all back in—grateful Gideon was nowhere in sight, or she might have had to explain what she was doing—she'd come way too close to getting a finger, or her entire hand, crushed in the wringer when she reached out to adjust a sheet that had clumped up. It took half an hour before the spike of adrenaline from her close call subsided.

Given the sunny day and slight breeze, her first batch was already dry, so she was able to carry it in and fold everything, although the shirts and dresses needed to be ironed. She'd have to ask Lilian how to do that, when she obviously couldn't plug an iron into an electrical outlet on the wall.

Upstairs, she made all three beds, resolved to sweep and dust up here tomorrow and take all the rugs in the house out to the lawn to beat them. She added weeding the garden to her mental list. There was so much to do.

She'd washed all the windows on the inside and the downstairs ones on the outside by the time she had to pick up the *kinder*. If she got there a little early, she'd be able to see Adah and Emma, too, and maybe get a peek in the schoolhouse.

According to Samuel, she would have attended school in the same location, but not in the same building. That one had been severely damaged by a tree falling during a storm. A new, larger schoolhouse had been built in its place.

Everything she learned was creating an echo, or maybe a shadow she could now almost see. *This* was the life she would have had if her mother hadn't stolen her away. At moments, she almost felt as if she had never left, that this was where she should be—but then she'd be jarred to remember she wasn't Amish. She wasn't home. She was an *auslander*. She felt as if her cheeks had been stung by a slap when her ignorance about something essential to their lives or faith was exposed, or her hands fumbled when they should be steady. Worst of all was when Gideon or even a member of her own family looked warily at her.

Hannah suspected that friends her age would be horrified by the idea of spending their days in such hard labor when modern technology would have allowed the work to be done so easily. So far, she wasn't bothered; she had always worked hard at whatever job she held.

The paternal structure of Amish society would offend most modern women of her generation, too. Probably her mother's as well, which might have contributed to Mom's disillusionment. But again, none of the jobs Mom had held out in the world—the way Samuel put it—had been anything but menial and low paying. Hannah was willing to bet that most of those bosses her mother had resented were men, too. She had yet to see any sign that Samuel and Lilian had anything less than a partnership.

The *kinder* were pouring out the open schoolhouse door when she reached the clearing, joining half a dozen other adults already waiting. Several had driven buggies, including Lilian, who called, "Hannah!"

The two women hugged, and Hannah hugged Adah and Emma, too, when they ran up. Zeb and Rebekah followed them, Zeb saying, "Hannah works for my *daad* now," in an important voice to the Mast girls.

Emma rolled her eyes. "We *know*. She's my sister."

His frown expressed as much puzzlement as annoyance. It seemed he hadn't entirely worked through Hannah's place in the community. No wonder, when her place was so fragile and temporary.

"I wish I could drive you, but—" Lilian made a gesture of helplessness when three other *kinder* piled into the buggy, too. Hannah already knew these were Sol and Lydia Graber's *kinder*, Noah, Neriah, and the youngest, Rebekah's age, Beth.

Hannah smilingly greeted all of them, too, before shaking her head at Lilian. "I enjoy the walk. Especially after doing laundry."

Her stepmother gave a merry chuckle. "*Ja*, hard work that is. Will you be home for supper?"

"No, I think I'll eat with Rebekah and Zeb and their *daad* for now, until I'm sure they're happy with what I cook."

"I wish I'd had a cookie for lunch," Zeb grumbled.

Hannah only laughed at him. "I only started the job this morning. Where was I supposed to get a cookie?"

She felt sure he didn't understand everything she said, but enough to get the gist. He wrinkled his nose at her before running over to walk with a couple of boys starting toward the road on their own, all three jostling and laughing.

When Hannah held out her hand to Rebekah, Gideon's daughter bent her head shyly again, but took her hand. Once they caught up with Zeb, Hannah asked, "Doesn't their *mamm* or *daad* come for them?"

"No, they don't walk on the road. See?" He pointed as the two boys turned onto a narrow trail that cut through the woods.

"*Ja*," she agreed.

As they walked, she practiced her limited *Deitsh* on them, making faces when they laughed at her and trying again. She corrected Zeb's English, too; Rebekah wasn't ready to try hers out with this strange woman.

Once home, Zeb ran off to find his dad, calling, "I'll come back if he doesn't need help."

Hannah smiled at the six-year-old. "Let's bake cookies."

She'd already located most of what she'd need, but she made a silly game out of having Rebekah teach her the names for foods and utensils.

The bottle of dark molasses was *melassich*, for example. Whether that was German or original to the dialect called *Deitsh* or Pennsylvania Dutch, or simply a slight alteration of the English word, Hannah had no idea.

As they assembled ingredients, Hannah repeated the words, trying to absorb them. Wheat flour was *weezemehl*, sugar *siesse*, butter *budder*.

It was unsettling how easily they came off her tongue, along with others she didn't remember anyone saying. All she could think was that she'd heard Lilian ask someone to hand her an *abbutzlumpe*, a dish towel. Or that *reseet* was "recipe," *teeleffel* a teaspoon.

Soon Rebekah, enveloped in the smallest apron Hannah could find, stood on a stepstool stirring their cookie dough while Hannah checked the heat in the oven—*offe*—and greased the cookie sheets. Once the first batch was baking, they cleaned up enough to start on dinner preparations.

Hannah felt sure they did have enough *schnitz un knepp* left for dinner, but decided to save the leftovers for lunch tomorrow instead. She was having fun cooking with Rebekah. Fortunately, she'd already defrosted more meat.

Rebekah got chattier by the minute, and Hannah understood more and more of what she said, as if—no, it didn't matter why. Either she was soaking up the language fast, or it was bubbling forth from her subconscious. Did it matter? It helped that the Amish all seemed to sprinkle in a fair number of English words, too.

The cookies smelled fabulous baking and cooling on the counter. It had to be the aroma that magically drew Zeb from wherever he'd gone. He snatched several even though he'd grabbed ones that had just come out of the oven and he had to juggle them from hand to hand. He said, "*Daad* will want some, too," and raced back out the kitchen door.

Hannah smiled, anticipating the expression on Gideon's face when he ate this meal.

Mattsait. Supper.

Chapter Seven

❖❖❖

GIDEON AND AMOS Troyer walked as they talked. Gideon had noticed before that Amos liked to keep moving. Personally, he wouldn't have minded sitting and sipping a cup of coffee, after working hard all day, but he'd had to bring Zeb and Rebekah with him to Bishop Troyer's house. Amos's wife, Nancy, had happily taken charge of them while her husband and Gideon went outside to stroll toward the garden and orchard behind the house.

Dusk deepened the sky purple. A bat flitted by.

Gideon knew he'd deliberately downplayed his concerns about Hannah. He'd simply said, "I'd like to know I have your blessing, since she isn't one of us."

Now, Amos asked, "Do you know what Hannah and the *kinder* talk about? If she questions our faith or our ways, that would trouble me. You know we are counseled to be cautious about linking our lives with those of unbelievers."

Gideon knew the passage well. Too well, thanks to his wife's close friendship with an *Englisch* woman. Were it not for the outcome of that, he'd be less concerned about Hannah and his instinct to trust her.

"Samuel says she is a churchgoer," he remarked. "He hopes she'll attend one of the next services with the family. Maybe not this one, with her not speaking enough of our language."

Amos dipped his head.

"Your *kinder* both speak some English."

"*Ja*, but she seems intent on learning to speak *Deitsh*. She has only worked for me for three days, but already she surprises me, learns new words every day."

"She does live with Samuel and Lilian."

"Their two youngest speak no English," Gideon agreed. "She seems to like *kinder*." He surveyed the large vegetable garden Nancy tended, and wished he'd been able to do as much. "Hannah is working hard to be able to talk with Zeb and Rebekah, but she's nowhere near fluent. I don't think she could criticize even if she wanted to."

"But if she keeps learning so fast . . ."

It hadn't occurred to Gideon that she might try to undermine his faith or his authority with his own *kinder*. He clasped his hands behind his back as he mulled over the possibility, finally shaking his head. "I think she wants to live the way we do. Become one of us as much as she can in a short time."

"You believe she'll leave soon?"

"She told me intends to stay for a month or two, at least."

"Do the *kinder* like her?"

A low branch on an apple tree brushed Gideon's shoulder as they circled through the orchard.

He smiled at the question. "*Ja*, she's become a favorite fast. She's the best cook I've ever known."

Amos's bushy eyebrows rose at that.

"A boy Zeb's age is hungry all the time," Gideon continued, "and he likes his sweets." As did Gideon. "Also, she's encouraging Rebekah to help her cook in a way none of the other girls I hired did. Rebekah is excited to feel like an important part of the family." He remembered how Hannah had described it: the joy of contributing.

"You're satisfied with her work, then."

"Very. She took over weeding the garden right away, we have clean clothes and sheets again, good food always prepared, and she makes work fun for Zeb and Rebekah. I'll only have to walk them to school and pick them up on Mondays."

"Samuel was pleased when you hired her," Amos said thoughtfully. "He shod our horses yesterday, that's why we talked. He says she is full of new questions for Lilian every night, studies her recipes, looks less sad and more happy." He paused. "He worries because her *mamm* is in town, staying with friends, he thinks. Keeps calling her."

Gideon frowned. "Does she answer those calls?"

"Not when he's seen. She told him she keeps the telephone close only because of her grandfather's failing health."

"She told me the same."

"When Hannah did talk to her mother after coming to Tompkin's Mill, that woman spewed poison about Samuel and about all of us. Samuel doesn't think Hannah believes her *mamm*, but if she hears it over and over . . ." Amos didn't need to finish.

Newly disturbed, Gideon said, "She hasn't said much about her mother. More about her grandparents." There'd been passing references to her *daad* and Amish family, which had reassured him. Perhaps he'd been too willing to be reassured. Perhaps he should quit fleeing her, and spend time talking to her instead. She wasn't Rebecca King; he didn't think Hannah would be so bold as to pursue him.

Still, he had to abide by Bishop Amos's judgment.

Amos looked down at his feet and walked in silence until they were almost to the house. Finally, he said, "Samuel says she's a good, kind, hardworking woman. I think it's fine for her to work for you, so long as her mother doesn't come around, or you don't overhear her say anything you don't like." He cast an unexpectedly mischievous grin at Gideon as they started up the porch steps. "Nancy misses having *kinder* in the house. She baked all afternoon."

Gideon sighed. "They already had a fine dessert, and plenty of it."

"I think now they've had plenty more."

HANNAH HEARD THE back door open and close. Even with that warning, she felt jumpy whenever she turned to see Gideon walking into the kitchen. More than that, it was suddenly harder to breathe. He dominated any space in a way that unnerved her.

But if he ever noticed how she reacted to him, he'd be uncomfortable and she wouldn't be able to keep working here. So she smiled and said, "Your timing is good. The stuffed bell peppers are almost ready to come out of the oven."

Gideon greeted her gravely, in his usual way, and went straight to the half bathroom under the stairs to wash up.

She hoped he didn't mind that more of today's meal was cold than usual; they'd had meat loaf for supper last night, and with plenty left over, she'd cut thick slices and put them out with two types of cheese to make sandwiches. She'd already sliced the bread she'd baked yesterday. Leftover potato salad and sauerbraten completed the meal. She was always astounded at the quantity he could put away while remaining lean and muscular. She'd probably have one of the stuffed peppers, some sauerbraten and a taste of the strawberry-rhubarb fry pies she made from one of Lilian's recipes, and that mostly to determine whether she could improve them.

Gideon waited until she put the last serving bowl on the table and sat before taking his own seat. He immediately bowed his head.

She'd learned the Amish prayer before meals now, and thought it fitting.

O Lord God, heavenly Father, bless us and these Thy gifts, which we accept from Thy tender goodness. Give us food and drink also for our souls until life eternal, that we may share at Thy heavenly table, through Jesus Christ.

When Gideon murmured, "Amen," and lifted his head, she did the same.

As he ladled generous helpings on his plate of the salads and stuffed pepper, he said, "You're spoiling me. You're a fine cook."

She grinned at him. "So you keep saying. If you're not careful, I'll start getting full of myself."

"We would say you are getting a *gross feelich*. A big feeling. That means pride."

"Well, too many compliments will definitely give me a *gross feelich*."

His chuckle lightened his often stern face. "Don't people who eat in your restaurant tell you how good your food is?"

She looked down at her plate, bothered to realize that the answer was more complicated than it seemed. It was a moment before she responded.

"The waiters will pass it on when a diner says something like, 'Compliments to the chef.' But I might have made only a side dish they ate, like—" she scanned the table "—the stuffed peppers. If the executive chef had made the meat loaf, and a pastry chef baked the fry pies, then we all tell ourselves we did a good job, but we can't get too swelled a head." Her smile flashed again. *"Gross feelich."*

"So it's like our fellowship meal, where many women bring food."

She nodded. "We'd call that a potluck."

Gideon assembled a sandwich, slathering on horseradish. "Did your *mamm* teach you to cook?"

Hannah went still, then forced a smile. "No, she never liked to cook. Until I got old enough to take over, we mostly ate frozen meals that we heated in the microwave, or fast food. You know, french fries, cheeseburgers, chili dogs. She'd buy those packets of oatmeal you just pour boiling water on. Things like that. Nothing very healthy."

He watched her instead of eating until she went on. "When I was ten or eleven, I asked to buy some pans at garage sales. And utensils like a pancake turner and a whisk. I found a few cookbooks that way, too. I just . . . took money from her wallet and bought groceries. If I was careful, I didn't spend any more money than we already were, often less, and we had better meals." She wasn't eating at all, only staring past him, lost in her memories. "Then, I didn't even ask myself why I wanted to cook, or thought I could. Now . . . I think I must have learned enough before *Mamm* took me away."

The sympathy in his espresso dark eyes made her eyes burn, but she blinked away any incipient tears. "So I've thanked *Grossmammi* and my *aenti* Sarah, who *Daad* says was most around, for what they taught me." She imagined the women she didn't even remember standing just out of sight, yet guiding her hands, praising her efforts, gently correcting her. As a little girl, she might have helped Helen bake cookies or make dinner, too, it occurred to her.

But never her mother.

"Did it make you angry, having to be responsible for there being meals on the table?" Gideon asked.

"No." She met those very dark eyes. "No, never. I loved cooking and feeding us, even whatever man we were living with. *They* liked me, because I was a good cook."

Gideon's expression darkened. "Whatever man . . . ?"

Wishing she hadn't said that, hoping he wouldn't think less of her now that he knew a more sordid part of her past, Hannah said, "Mom always liked having a man around. A . . . boyfriend." She couldn't tell if Gideon understood that word. "Mostly, I tried to avoid her boyfriends when we were living with one of them. Either they'd get tired of her, or she'd get mad at them, and we'd move again."

Twice, she'd left her clothes behind because packing her kitchenware had come first. Mom had been mad when she had to take Hannah to a thrift shop to outfit her before she could start school.

"It was, um, a strange childhood." She shrugged awkwardly. "Stranger than I knew then."

He still hadn't taken another bite, and Gideon was a man who ate heartily, as he'd put it. Muscles bunched in his jaw. She couldn't decide if he was angry on her behalf, or stunned, but whatever he felt was powerful. Hannah only hoped it wasn't pity.

"If your *daad* had known . . . ," he said roughly, shaking his head.

"He says he imagined everything. And then when he was informed I was dead—" She shivered.

Gideon opened his mouth, then closed it. Had he stopped himself from expressing an opinion about her mother?

"I don't know why I'm telling you all this," she said suddenly.

"I asked. I wanted to know." His forehead creased, although it wasn't quite a frown. Maybe he'd rather not be curious about her? Still, he asked another question. "Do you still see your mother?"

"I did until Grandma Helen called me, and I found out I had a father, grandparents, half sisters and brothers. Since then, I've only talked to Mom once on the phone. I'm so angry—"

A warm, calloused hand covered hers. Astonished, Hannah looked down to see that she'd balled both of her hands into fists on the table. That he'd wanted to comfort her gave her a sweet yet painful sensation beneath her breastbone.

After a suspended moment, Gideon erased any emotion from his face as he took back his hand and resumed eating.

"Our Lord asks that you forgive her."

"*Daad* said that, too. How *he* could forgive her, I don't know. I'm . . . trying."

Gideon nodded and cleared his plate. She rose to refill his coffee cup and set a platter of the fry pies in the middle of the table.

"I found a few strawberries ripe in the garden, and discovered you have a patch of rhubarb. Actually, Rebekah showed me. I'm leaving most of it for another few weeks, but I liked the idea of using fruit from the garden to bake."

"*Denke* for taking over the weeding," he said. "You didn't have to."

"I actually enjoy working outside. But if you'd rather I didn't—"

"No. I have too much to do, and never enough time. A big help you've been this week."

There was more of the cadence of a *Deitsh* speaker in that than she'd become accustomed to from Gideon, but she liked it.

"Would you mind if I expanded the garden a little to put in some peppers and more beans?" She heard how fast she was talking, but couldn't seem to stop herself. "And, well, maybe some herbs? Most of them grow fast."

He studied her, finally nodding. "*Ja*, that would be fine."

Neither of them said anything while he ate several fry pies and she nibbled at the corner of one, evaluating whether she should have used a little more—

"I ask you not to bring your mother here."

Stung by the words and his forbidding tone both, Hannah jumped to her feet. "I wouldn't."

Without looking at what she was doing, she gathered up serving dishes and took them to the counter by the sink. Probably what he'd felt earlier was shock, because he'd been foolish enough to trust his children to the daughter of *that* woman. He hadn't been thinking of *her* at all. Except, her hand still tingled from his touch.

Her back to him, Hannah said, "She's not dangerous, but . . . do you think I'd take any chance at all with Rebekah and Zeb?"

He doesn't know me, she reminded herself. *This is only my fourth day working for him.*

She shouldn't feel . . . hurt.

Behind her, the chair legs scraped on the floor. She waited to hear his receding footsteps and the sound of the back door closing. Instead, there was silence, until he said heavily, "I don't think you would, but I'm their father. I thought I should say it anyway."

"Fine." She scraped the remnants of the sauerbraten, left from last night, into a compost bucket, then turned on the water in the sink to rinse out the bowl.

By the time she turned around, he was gone.

"HANNAH SAID SHE'D make pancakes if we waited until she got here," Zeb announced. With typical energy, he was bouncing around the kitchen like a rubber ball. "I bet she cooks really *good* pancakes."

Gideon bet she did, too. He'd intended to fry some hash browns, probably plain because he didn't have time to fancy them up, but if he dawdled a little . . .

Rebekah dashed into the kitchen from the front of the house. "Hannah's here! I saw her car coming."

He hadn't hired her to cook his breakfasts as well as the other two meals, but if she'd already promised the *kinder* . . . He poured himself some coffee, and leaned back against the countertop, crossing his booted feet.

"Can I help you today?" Zeb was begging, when Hannah let herself in the back door carrying a couple of bags filled with groceries.

Gideon straightened. He'd forgotten she had promised to do the shopping. "Do you have more?"

She didn't want to look at him. "*Ja*, but I can—"

He went out the back door, well aware that he'd damaged the new trust between them by questioning her judgment. He didn't like feeling in the wrong, or wondering whether she'd ever smile so openly at him again.

By the time he returned with five more bags, all but one from Troyer Bulk Foods, Hannah had a griddle heating on the stove and was mixing batter in a big ceramic bowl with his daughter's assistance. Rebekah squeezed out orange juice as Hannah grated the zest.

He heard her say in *Deitsh,* "Now we need—" and then smile when Rebekah handed her a small box of baking soda. *"Denke."*

She fried bacon as Rebekah, frowning in concentration, spooned the first circles of batter onto the griddle.

Savoring the delicious combined aroma, Gideon settled at the table with his coffee and just watched as Hannah effortlessly juggled tasks while interacting with both his *kinder.*

Minutes later, Zeb triumphantly carried a platter heaped with crispy bacon to the table, as pleased as if he were responsible for it. "I got it out of the freezer for Hannah," he told Gideon.

"It's good that you do what Hannah asks of you."

Because of the juice, the pancakes were tinted orange and sprinkled with bits of cranberry. Instead of syrup, Hannah supplied a spread that was cream cheese with more orange zest in it along with . . . maybe cinnamon? Gideon wasn't sure, but they were so good, he ate until his eagerness to get to work waned.

Ach, there was plenty of time for another cup of coffee, he decided.

As usual, Hannah ate so little, she was long since on her feet cleaning up by the time he finished. When Rebekah tried to jump up before she'd cleared her plate, Hannah leaned over and whispered in her ear, her smile . . . beautiful. Rebekah forked up another bite.

At the same time as Zeb declared himself ready to go to work, Gideon drained his coffee. After pushing back from the table, he hesitated. *Thanks* and *goodbye* were taken for granted among the *Leit*, but today it felt wrong to walk out without saying something, especially considering how Hannah had changed toward him since he'd said that about her mother. She was as warm as ever toward the *kinder*, but she held herself back from him, guarded. A little stiff. That might be for the best, but he missed their former comfort, the feeling he could talk to her, that she was happy in his home.

So he said, "*Denke*. That was the best breakfast I've had in a long time."

With a dishrag in her hand, Hannah lifted her eyebrows. "What do you usually have for breakfast?"

"Oatmeal," he admitted, "but not from little packets. Hash browns, toasted bread, eggs."

"Well, I'm glad this was a treat." She gave *him* one of those smiles, the kind that both warmed him, and worried him.

This was an *auslander*, he reminded himself, when he shouldn't have to. She'd driven here in a car. She'd worn trousers today that outlined her hips and legs. He must not forget who she was. And yet that smile—

"What are we going to do first, *Daad*?" Zeb asked.

"Actually," Hannah said tentatively, "I was hoping you could help me for a little while." She must have seen Gideon's surprise. "Today's a perfect day for gardening. I'll bet you'd be good at digging, ain't so?"

Ain't so? She must have picked that up from Samuel or Lilian.

"I can do that," Zeb said. "Can't I, *Daad*?"

"*Ja*, I think you'll be a big help." He rested a hand on his son's thin shoulder. "When Hannah doesn't need you anymore, come and find me. Today, I'll spray manure on the back field."

Zeb wrinkled his nose.

Gideon laughed and looked at Hannah. "It's a stinky job. You'll smell it, too. I waited until a day when there's no breeze to carry the stench to neighbors, but it has to be done."

She chuckled. "A neighbor of *Daad*'s did it the other day. It was pretty awful, but that's country life, I guess. Maybe Rebekah and Zeb and I will hurry to get our work on the garden done, and then hide in the house without opening any windows."

"That will work," he agreed, and grinned at her. "Until I come in for lunch."

"Maybe we should make *Daadi* eat in the barn," Hannah suggested, a smile quivering on her lips. For his daughter, not him, but he liked it anyway. "What do you think, Rebekah?" she asked.

His daughter had understood enough of Hannah's mix of *Deitsh* and English words to be shocked. Her mouth fell open. "That would be mean."

Hannah's laugh sounded young and carefree. "I was teasing. We'll just hose your *daadi* down before we let him in. Zeb, too, if we have to."

Rebekah looked aghast.

Gideon was still laughing when he reached the barn. Ach, there'd been too little laughter in this house before Hannah came.

His step checked when he remembered how soon she'd be leaving them. She had worked for him such a short time, and yet felt important to them all. Because of her cooking and kindness and ability to make them all laugh, he told himself, not because she filled the empty place in their small family in a way the other young women he'd hired hadn't.

No, he wasn't foolish enough to believe an *Englisch* woman could ever do that.

Chapter Eight

❖◆❖

As MUCH AS Hannah had enjoyed the week working with Gideon's *kinder*, she'd also looked forward to Sunday. She needed a reality check. However natural her relationship with Zeb and Rebekah felt, how . . . comfortable she was managing the Lantz home, her job was to be a substitute.

Unfortunately, her attraction to Gideon hadn't waned. If anything, it had gotten worse since he'd let her see his dry sense of humor, his gentleness with his *kinder*, what a hard worker he was. She'd just have to keep hiding what she felt. Honestly, the idea of their having any kind of relationship beyond employer and employee was ridiculous. She was in Tompkin's Mill for the sake of her grandparents, and to get to know her father. Period.

She would have nodded in satisfaction, except she hadn't entirely convinced herself.

A health aide was to stay with Robert while Helen and Hannah attended church. She'd promised to bring the makings for a midafternoon meal she could put together in the small kitchen.

Thank goodness Robert had bounced back after Monday's scary episode. Hannah had called her grandmother twice this week to make sure all was going well.

She parked in a visitor space outside the complex, collected the grocery bags from the back seat, and straightened, almost bumping into someone.

She knew before she even turned around.

"Sweetheart," her mother said, holding out her hands. "Can I carry one of those?"

Hannah's hands tightened. Anger felt like a spike thrust between her ribs. It frightened her to feel like that.

"Did Grandma Helen invite you?" she asked.

Her mother looked woeful. "Do I need an invitation? Mom mentioned that you'd be going to church with her this morning . . ."

In other words, no. It had never occurred to Hannah that her mother might appear at church, but apparently she'd go to any lengths. It wasn't as if Jodi had ever been a churchgoer, except now and again when she'd been trying to impress some man. Probably thanks to her parents, she knew how to go through the motions, but that's all it had ever been.

Hannah knew her resentment was unchristian and uncharitable, but church was her refuge. Of all times for her mother to show up.

"I'm not ready to talk to you," she said, still not moving.

Of course, tears shimmered in Jodi's eyes. "Can't you believe that I love you, and did what I believed with all my heart was best for us?"

"I know you love me." Hannah was ashamed of her stony voice, but that's how she felt. Hard. Unforgiving. "I think you did what you thought was best for *you*, not me."

Those brown eyes widened. Teardrops trembled on her mother's dark lashes. "You don't know everything. If you'd just let me explain . . ."

"You've had more than twenty years to explain. Instead,

you lied." Hannah shook her head. "If your parents welcome you in their apartment, I won't argue. But I'm not willing to listen to your excuses."

Jodi backed up a few steps to let Hannah close the car door and lock.

"What did Helen say when you asked if you could join us this morning?" Hannah asked, still stonily.

"They're my parents! I . . . didn't think it was necessary to ask," her mother said with fragile dignity.

"That's between you and her. Just don't upset Granddad."

"I would never do that! How can you think—"

Hannah gritted her teeth and marched toward the big building. Did her mother think those counterfeit death certificates hadn't upset anyone? They were just a little excuse for not staying in touch?

The slap of Jodi's footsteps came behind her. "You're being cruel," she cried.

That might have penetrated Hannah's armor if she hadn't known her mother so well. Jodi Hinsch aka Prescott used helplessness like the police did tear gas to bring people—especially men—to their knees. The better Hannah got to know her *Englisch* grandparents, Samuel, Lilian, *Grossmammi*, and the rest of the family, the less well her mother's tactic worked on her.

Cruel. Of all accusations, Jodi couldn't have picked a more ironic one.

At the glass doors, she hesitated, then stopped. "I do love you," she said to Hannah's back, her voice soft.

Her own eyes burning, Hannah kept going.

She could only feel grateful when her mother didn't follow her into the building.

"WE'VE ASKED THAT she not be allowed in," Helen explained. "It's not foolproof, but there's almost always someone stationed by the doors."

They had just gotten into Hannah's car to drive the dozen blocks to the Congregational church where her grandparents had gotten married, and worshipped in for all the years since. The first Sunday Hannah had joined them, she tried to decide if anything about the handsome old church felt familiar, but she couldn't decide. Her grandmother said that Jodi had sometimes brought her small daughter to worship with them on the "off" Sundays, when the Amish visited rather than holding a service.

Hannah started the car and put it in reverse. She wished she knew what her mother was driving. "Has Mom tried to get in?"

"Twice, according to the front desk." Helen's face crumpled with distress. "I have no idea what she wants, unless it's more money. Or why she's staying in the area."

Hannah gusted out a breath. "She may be genuine in fearing that she's lost my love."

"That doesn't explain why she's battening on us."

"Unless she truly has regrets."

They stopped at a red light two blocks from the senior complex.

"Has she expressed any to you?" Helen asked.

Hannah ached. *I must forgive her, but . . . I pray God understands why I'm not ready.*

"No," she said. "She begs me to understand why she did what she did. She hasn't once said she's sorry, or that she could have handled any part of leaving Dad differently."

"She hasn't to me, either," her grandmother said, voice low and sorrowful. "I begged her to tell me how she could have done that to us, and she just claimed it seemed like the best thing to do at the time. I feel as if I'm trying to reason with a temperamental toddler."

Her mother always had been childlike in many ways, Hannah reflected, except for the need to have a man adoring her, not to mention her ability to organize their regular escapes whenever anyone dared question her, or when her latest swain became disenchanted.

"She just doesn't get how angry I am, or why." Hannah bit her lip. "I'm hurting her, but I need for her to see this from my point of view."

"I don't know if she's capable of that," her grandmother said raggedly. "I wish I knew what we did wrong."

Hannah took a hand from the steering wheel to squeeze Helen's. "She may be mentally ill, you know."

"Then why didn't we see it sooner?"

"People mature at different speeds." Some, out of necessity, did very young, Hannah couldn't help thinking. "You know how silly a lot of people still are in their twenties."

Had these well-meaning people spoiled their daughter by never insisting she suffer the consequences of her own actions? As kind as they seemed to be, that was a possibility—but not one Hannah would ever say to either of them. She and *Daad* hadn't really talked about her mother yet, either, but Hannah knew they'd have to eventually.

"When Jodi married Samuel, I thought she finally knew what she wanted." Helen tried to smile. Tears made her eyes look even more like her daughter's. "And then when you were born."

Her mother hadn't been ready to have a baby, Hannah knew. When she took an incomplete in a class or quit a job without giving notice, the only one she was hurting was herself.

"Did she really *believe* she was ready to make that kind of commitment?"

"She said she was." Helen stared straight ahead. "And if she needed someone to lean on, Samuel wasn't anything like her previous boyfriends. He seemed so strong, so steady."

"I think he is." Hannah hated that he'd had to grieve for so many years. She couldn't help thinking about how different her life would have been, too, if Mom had left her with her *daad*. She wouldn't be the same person, that was for sure.

She'd be Amish, looking askance at those *Englischers* with their fast cars and reliance on the phones they couldn't be parted from. Maybe in a rural part of Missouri like this, most of those *Englischers* did attend church regularly, unlike moderns in much of the country. But Hannah somehow doubted they lived their faith in the way she saw the Amish doing every day.

And that was making her examine her own relationship with God. Reading her Bible last night, she'd pondered another passage from Matthew.

Enter by the narrow gate; for wide is the gate and broad is the way that leads to destruction, and there are many who go in by it.

Because narrow is the gate and difficult is the way which leads to life, and there are few who find it.

Much of her life had been a struggle, but not because she'd chosen to pursue the narrow path to life eternal. Did her Lord ask for His faithful to make every decision in life with an eye to whether it kept them close to Him or led them away?

Nobody in her life had ever suggested that to her, including the many pastors she'd heard speak in all those different churches she'd attended. The Amish were surely not the only people who sought to live their faith, down to the smallest choices, but in so few weeks, she was coming to see that they were remarkable. She admired them—and felt an ache for what she'd lost.

And yet . . . she wasn't the woman she would have been. How could she be her?

She still found a smile for her newfound grandmother, and said, "I think the church service is just what we need right now, don't you?"

Helen's answering smile trembled. "Bless you, Hannah. You're what Robert and I needed most."

As HE SET the oven to preheat Sunday morning, Gideon felt both gratitude and remorse. By ordering Hannah not to allow her mother on his property, he'd both insulted her and, he feared, hurt her feelings. And then what did she do, along with caring for his *kinder*, teasing him, digging up sod and enriching the soil in the new part of the garden, whacking clean every rug in the house, and making both lunch and dinner, but also prepare a breakfast bake for him to warm this morning. Not just that; after she'd left, he'd found several fresh-baked loaves of friendship bread on the counter.

She was an astonishingly generous person. Unfailingly cheerful with Zeb and Rebekah, too, even as he sometimes caught sight of sadder emotions beneath.

Her loneliness, he recognized. He knew better, and yet it was all he could do sometimes not to reach out to her in comfort and perhaps because *he* would then feel less alone. Remembering how fragile her hand had felt when he did touch her unsettled him.

His . . . regret at hurting a woman who had been hurt too many times stuck with him through breakfast, while harnessing his bay gelding, Fergus, hitching him to the buggy, lifting Rebekah up onto the seat and waiting while Zeb scrambled up to join her. Had he really believed for a minute that Hannah would allow the mother who'd stolen her from the rest of her family to come near his *kinder*?

"Is Esther riding with us today?" Zeb asked, nose wrinkled.

"*Ja*, and I don't like that face you're making," Gideon said mildly. Esther Schwartz, his next-door neighbor, was not the most likable member of their church district. There'd been a time when she repelled Gideon's every offer of help, but she seemed to have softened since last summer, when two work frolics were organized to paint her house and barn, and reroof her house. A widow, Esther had lost not only her husband, but her only *kind*. That could sour anyone.

Although Gideon doubted that Samuel Mast had been anything but good-hearted and stoic after his wife ran away with his daughter.

As it happened, after they'd picked up Esther and reached the road, Samuel's buggy passed. He had—and needed—a large one, a family sedan, to seat his growing family. Gideon couldn't get a good look inside at the back seats, but didn't see Hannah.

Samuel nodded at him, and the two girls waved at his *kinder*. Rebekah, of course, waved back, while Zeb pretended not to see them. Gideon hid a grin.

The bishop and his wife were hosting today's service for the first time since Gideon and his *kinder* had moved to Missouri. He'd initially joined a different church district, but the farm he'd chosen to buy was in the middle of Bishop Troyer's district. Unless Gideon had wanted to drive the *kinder* a distance and then have to pick them up, too, five days a week, it had made sense for them to attend the school right down the road. Inevitably, they'd made friends among neighboring *kinder*. He was glad now to have made the change to worship with these neighbors who had quickly become his friends, too.

Once he reined Fergus in line alongside the fence paralleling the long farm lane at Amos's home, only one buggy separating his from Samuel's, he let Zeb and Rebekah run ahead to find their friends. Esther accepted his help to descend, then set off with a covered dish.

As Gideon spoke to the boy who was one of several who would watch over the horses, another large buggy drawn by a handsome, high-stepping black gelding came to a stop beside his.

Because of Hannah, he'd been thinking about Luke Bowman and his formerly *Englisch* wife, Julia, this week, so he greeted them and waited while Luke, a tall man about Gideon's age, lifted his small, blond daughter down and steadied Julia as she descended, holding their baby son.

Not quite six months old, Nathan Bowman was as large for his age as Zeb had been, and had his *daad*'s blue eyes and his *mamm*'s dark auburn hair.

It was impossible not to grin back at him. Gideon said hello to Abby, too. Five now, she would be starting school with his *kinder* come fall.

When he asked her about it, she said, "I wish I could start *now*! 'Cept Leah is my best friend, and *she* has to wait to start school for a whole *year*!"

Amused at her vehemence, he said, "You'll make many more friends."

"I already have lots," she assured him.

This girl had been so shy she'd barely speak when Gideon first got to know the Bowman family, but that had changed.

Laughing, Julia set off toward the house with the *kinder* while Luke replaced his horse's bridle with a halter so that he could graze.

When he was satisfied, the two men fell into step together.

"I hear Samuel's daughter works for you now."

Luke must have guessed why Gideon had waited for him.

"*Ja*, although she may not stay more than a month or two. I don't think she knows." He sighed. "She is a very fine cook. We'll miss her when she goes back to her job."

Luke's keen blue eyes met his. "You don't think there's any chance she'll stay?"

"You know how few *Englischers* convert."

Luke's gaze lifted to his wife and *kinder* ahead. His mouth curved. "*Ja*, but sometimes they do."

"Hannah might like to talk to Julia." This, Gideon admitted if only to himself, was why he'd hoped to have a chance to talk casually with Luke. "Right now, she goes back and forth between her *Englisch* family and her Amish family. It must be confusing."

"Pulled both ways." Luke sounded thoughtful. He would have felt that pull, having left the faith and gone out among the *auslanders* for over a decade, from what Gideon had heard, before returning to his faith. "I'll suggest it to Julia," Luke said. "Is Hannah here today? We just passed Samuel's buggy."

Pulled both ways. The words reminded Gideon of things he'd rather forget, but couldn't. Had Leah felt that pull to the *Englisch* world, or was she only loyal to an *Englisch* friend? Her death had stolen any chance of an answer from her. Either way, she had died in a head-on collision of two cars *because* of her determination to hold tight to a bond that fell outside of her family and faith in God, to which she owed her first loyalty.

Struck anew by his profound sense of loss and the anger he had still not overcome, Gideon took a moment to say, "I don't think Hannah is here. She's learning our language really fast, but she doesn't speak it well enough yet to understand the sermons."

"Julia didn't, either, the first time she visited."

Gideon had been aware that several families streamed up the lane behind them, calling greetings and instructions to their *kinder*. Most women, including Julia, went to the house first to leave their contributions of food. Clumps of men and women visited with friends, and *kinder* ran around playing impromptu games, their parents hoping they'd wear themselves out enough to be patient during the three-hour service. Luke stopped walking, but didn't join any groups of friends or family.

He asked, "Would you mind if Julia came to your place someday?"

"No, she would be welcome," Gideon said with a nod, even as he wondered why he was making any effort to help Hannah understand the Amish. That was for her father to do. She was a modern, with her car and her phone, an *auslander*, and hadn't given any indication she would consider choosing her Amish roots over the rest of her life.

Yet she rarely used her phone, and drove the car as timidly as a woman would the first time she held the reins to drive a horse and buggy.

He decided this was not a good time to think about whether he was trying to help because Hannah was such a good worker and her conversion would please her *daad* or whether he was being foolish enough to think there might be any chance . . . *No.* Gideon steeled himself. He liked Hannah Mast—might have more than liked her if she were Amish—but he would never let himself care for a woman tied to the *Englisch* world.

"Daadi!" Rebekah raced up and flung herself at him for a hug. "Can I sit with Beth?"

"Did her *mamm* say that was okay?"

"Uh-huh. Can I?"

"Ja." Rebekah was getting old enough to start sitting among the women and girls instead of with her *daad* on the men's side. She still wasn't doing that for every service, but for most. When she spun to race away, he called after her, "Wait. Did you take the bread to the house?"

"Of course, *Daadi!*"

"Denke. Go. Be good."

She giggled and took off at a run, just as she'd arrived.

Beside Gideon, Luke laughed. "You need a lead rope for that one."

"Or a bridle and reins," Gideon agreed ruefully.

Luke's eyebrows rose. "Have you taken up baking?"

"Baking?" He felt some heat on his cheeks as he realized what Luke was asking about. "No. Hannah and Rebekah baked several loaves of friendship bread yesterday.

Different kinds. We brought one that Rebekah says is lemon poppy seed."

"And kept the rest to yourself." Luke shook his head as if reproaching him.

"We almost finished a whole loaf this morning." Mostly him. He restrained himself from patting his belly. Most Sundays, he would be eager for the fellowship meal. Today, he could only hope his appetite recovered in time.

Once other men joined him and Luke, conversation became general.

Chapter Nine

❖✦❖

TUESDAY MORNING, HANNAH lay awake listening for Lilian to come downstairs. The minute she heard the soft foot-steps on the stairs, she leaped out of bed and hurriedly dressed.

What Hannah wanted to do was dash out to her car and drive straight to her new job, but they wouldn't expect her so early. Gideon hadn't hired her to cook breakfast along with the other meals. The pancakes last week had been a special treat. She'd look pathetic if she started showing up the minute they climbed out of bed. Apparently, she'd spent the week fantasizing that Gideon, Zeb, and Rebekah were her family, their house her home.

Well, that was natural, as much time as she was spend-ing with them, and doing it while she was actively trying to see herself in the life she could have had. The one she could almost see if she looked over her shoulder quickly enough.

Because by now I would have had *a family much like theirs, if I'd grown up here.*

And Gideon was exactly the kind of man she would

have chosen: a hard worker, a perfectionist who still didn't demand too much from his children. A man with a sense of humor. Trustworthy, and able to weaken her knees with the way his gaze sometimes lingered on her.

She made a face.

Uh-huh. One week, remember? Partly, she was here, staying with her father and his family, working for another Amish family, to learn for herself whether there was any basis for her mother's accusations.

More likely, she loved her job so far because of the children. The *kinder.* She'd never had a chance to spend time with children, not since she was one, and even then the frequent moves meant she gave up trying to make friends by the time she was seven or eight. But she was finding she enjoyed both her sisters and brothers—especially shy Emma, *blabbermaul* Adah, and Mose, a confident, kind teenage boy showing every sign of growing into a man as fine as Samuel—and her new charges, Zeb and Rebekah.

Yesterday morning, Hannah had wished that she was supposed to work. In only a week, she'd begun to think of the garden behind Gideon's house as hers, too, and hoped somebody had thought to water the newly planted seeds yesterday or today. Even though this was just a job, she was eager to explore the kitchen cupboards and cellar more thoroughly to find out whether there were enough canning jars for her to start in on the rhubarb in the next couple of weeks, now that she'd canned her first batch with Lilian and knew what to do. The strawberry bed would barely provide enough berries for them to eat fresh at a few meals and bake with the rest. While prices were low, though, she might pick up some flats at the store and freeze them to use later.

The thought jolted her. *For Gideon to use later,* she corrected herself. Gideon, and whatever woman he hired to replace her. Or whatever woman he married, as she expected he would do sooner or later.

She greeted Lilian cheerfully, then smiled at the two girls who appeared right behind her. Both were sleepy eyed and barefoot. Adah had forgotten her *kapp*, and her blond hair was straggly. But the two girls began helping their mother cook breakfast, neither needing instruction or reminders. Truthfully, Hannah felt as if she was in the way, even as Lilian found small tasks for her to do.

Maybe *this* was why she'd rather be in Gideon Lantz's kitchen. There, she was in charge. The executive chef instead of the new hire lucky to be allowed to chop scallions.

Once the family had eaten, Lilian flapped her apron at Hannah and said, "Go to work. There'll be plenty of dirty dishes waiting for you there, uh-huh. No need to do more here."

Laughing, Hannah fetched her handbag so she had her driver's license, car keys, and phone, and went out the door. Indeed, by the time she waved goodbye, the girls and Lilian already had a good start on cleaning the kitchen.

No, they hadn't needed her.

It was silly to feel a little sad at that realization. Of course they didn't! The whole family welcomed her and were coming to love her, Hannah believed, but still, she was the odd puzzle piece that didn't belong in this box. If Samuel had raised her, all these years later she wouldn't be underfoot in her *daad*'s already crowded house.

When she parked in her usual spot at the Lantz home, the back door of the house flew open and both *kinder* ran to meet her.

"Hannah! I skinned my knee Sunday and put a hole in my pants," Zeb blurted in English even before he reached her.

"People said the friendship bread was the best they'd ever had!" Rebekah exclaimed in *Deitsh*, dodging her brother's elbow. "They said I'm getting to be a good cook."

Hannah was startled to realize she understood almost every word. Any loneliness she'd felt evaporated like steam from a teakettle. She bent to hug Rebekah and said, "I'm glad you thought to take some of the bread with you." And, to Zeb: "Will I be able to mend your pants?"

"For working around here, maybe," he said doubtfully. "It's a big rip. And *Daad* says they were getting too short already."

She had noticed that Zeb was outgrowing not just his pants but his shirts, too. What about his shoes? Had Gideon thought to poke his toes to find out?

Was sewing new clothing another task expected of her? She'd never done anything but mend her own garments, stitching up small tears, sewing on buttons, and, occasionally, shortening a hem on a dress or skirt. Lilian would help, she felt sure . . . but what if she asked Judith Miller instead? She helped with her grandchildren, but without *kinder* at home might have more time to spare than Lilian or Susan Miller did. Hannah remembered seeing a fabric store in town.

In the kitchen, Gideon was swallowing the dregs of his coffee and pushing back in his chair when she entered with his *kinder*.

"*Gute mariye*," she said.

He nodded, surveying her with his dark eyes. "And to you." He turned to his children. "Better get ready for school."

Both scuttled upstairs.

"I hear Zeb skinned his knee," Hannah offered, to fill the silence.

The boy's *daad* shook his head. "Not for the first time, or the last."

"No, I don't suppose so." She hesitated. "Do you have a mending basket somewhere?"

Faint hope showed on his face. "*Ja*. It's near the washer. If you have time . . ."

She had a vague picture of an old hamper full of what she had assumed were rags. "I'll try."

"*Denke*." He shoved fingers through his hair, as if ill at ease with her.

She hated knowing how often he *was* uneasy in her presence. Because he barely knew her, and because she was an *Englischer.* An outsider.

Some of her confidence shriveled.

"*Denke* for breakfast Sunday, too," he added. "And the bread. It was very good."

"Is it all gone?"

Now he looked embarrassed. "*Ja*, we took a loaf for the fellowship meal Sunday, but we've eaten most of the rest."

She smiled at him, even if she wondered whether he thought she was demented. *He* didn't smile often.

"That's what it was for," she assured him. "Did you have a favorite?"

"All but the chocolate."

She crinkled her nose. "Well, it does tend to be women who like chocolate."

Gideon tipped his head, looking interested. "Is that so?"

"That's been my experience. Did Zeb like it?"

"*Ja*, but he likes anything sweet."

She chuckled. "Speaking of . . . I'd better make school lunches."

Gideon reached for his straw hat. "And I should get to work instead of standing here talking like a *dumkupp*."

"Oh—did you water the garden?"

"I sent Zeb to do it yesterday."

"*Denke*."

She had the distinct feeling he was relieved to escape out the back door. Feeling hurt . . . that was absurd. He wasn't a chatty man, and . . . some things were impossible. She needed to be glad for his approval and her weekly pay—and to quit having the weird experience of having something like double vision. The real here, and the might-have-been here.

Anyway, it wasn't as if she didn't have plenty to do. And why that made her feel energized, she couldn't have said.

Only now that he was gone did it occur to her she'd need a sewing basket with needles and thread, at the very least.

If such a thing existed in this house, Rebekah might know where it was.

But right now, she had to make those lunches.

GIDEON CAME IN for lunch even filthier than usual. A bath sounded good, but would have to wait for late afternoon or evening.

Hannah looked startled at the sight of him.

"I'm plowing today," he explained. "And not finished."

"Oh, while we were walking to school, Zeb said something. I saw you were harnessing all four horses."

He nodded and went to wash up, as best he could. Gideon recognized that his sense of anticipation wasn't only for the fine meal Hannah would have waiting on the table for him, but for her conversation. Used to eating his midday meal in solitude, he now found himself eager for the tentative steps taken to get to know another person.

Over the weekend, he'd convinced himself he had just been alone too much since the move, that it was good to escape his own thoughts.

She'd prepared potato soup and fried tomatoes and had sliced roast beef and cheese to make sandwiches with whole-grain bread he could tell had just come out of the oven.

"Oh, and there's rhubarb cake," she told him. "I hope you don't hate rhubarb, since you have a big patch of it."

Once she'd sat down across from him and they were dishing up, Hannah asked if there were any foods he didn't like.

Gideon pondered that. As a *kind*, he hadn't been given any choice in what foods were put in front of him, so there wasn't much of anything he wouldn't eat. Even since then, nobody had ever asked him that question. Not even his wife. In such a short time, Hannah had surprised him often.

"Peanut butter," he said finally. "My mother used to

make a peanut butter sheet cake. Even that I didn't especially like." He had a moment of amusement. "And cooked
spinach. I don't like that."

He could see her absorbing what he said. "I'll keep it in
mind."

He'd no sooner finished his bowl of soup than she
jumped up to refill it.

"Did you have a good weekend?" he asked, feeling obli-
gated to fill the silence and curious, too. The members of
the church district all had routines similar to his. When
Hannah was here, she fit so well, and yet once she left in
that car, how she spent her time was a mystery.

"Oh." This smile was one of those meant to cover feelings she didn't want to share. "Yes. My grandfather isn't
well enough to go out, but Grandma Helen and I went to
church, of course, and then we cooked a meal together. It
felt . . . good. As if we'd always done that on Sundays."

"Was your mother with you?"

Hannah looked sharply at him. "Does it matter?"

He didn't allow himself to take offense. "For you, it
does." This time, he wasn't thinking of his *kinder*, but
rather Hannah and the sorrow he saw beneath her cheerful
surface.

She sighed. "I'm sorry. I shouldn't have jumped on you.
She's . . . sort of a sensitive subject right now. You know?"

He did know. How could she help but be mixed up about
the woman who'd raised her, who'd been her only family
until a few weeks ago?

Head bowed over her plate so he couldn't see her expression well, Hannah said in a low voice, "She was waiting for
me in the parking lot Sunday morning when I went to get
my grandmother. She thought we'd ask her to join us."

Gideon did his own waiting.

There was torment in her eyes when she looked up. "I
wasn't very nice. I told her I'm still too mad to listen to her
side of the story. She said I'm being cruel."

Gideon's jaw tightened.

"She left when I made it plain that she wasn't welcome." Her face twisted. "So there it was, Sunday, and Grandma and I went to church. All I could think was that God would be disappointed in me."

"Because you didn't invite her to go with you?"

"Isn't that enough?"

"I think our Lord expects you to forgive your mother, with your heart and mind. That's not the same thing as asking her to be part of your life, as if she never did anything bad. Or feeling the same trust in her."

Her lips curved into the most sorrowful smile he'd ever seen. "I'm not sure I've ever really trusted her. My own mother." Then she shook her head, as if dismissing the gloomy subject, and asked about their Sunday. "*Daad* said he talked to you."

"*Ja*, we arranged for him to shoe my horses." Something he hadn't managed last week. "Have you thought of attending one of our services?"

Her face brightened. "I think I might two weeks from now. Do I have to ask permission from anyone?"

He shook his head. "Samuel or I will mention to the bishop or one of the ministers that you might come, if we happen to see any of them. I'm sure you'll be welcome."

"The women and the men sit separately?"

"*Ja*," he agreed.

"Does Rebekah have to sit by herself on the women's side?"

"No, young *kinder* sit with parents. Now that she's school age, Rebekah sometimes sits with a friend whose *mamm* doesn't mind watching over her."

"Oh. Do you think she'd be willing to sit with me? Lilian has her two girls already."

"She will be excited," he said gently, having heard her underlying anxiety.

"You have wonderful children, you know."

"*Denke.*"

She rose and began clearing the table. The conversation was over. Gideon wasn't sure whether his reluctance to push back his chair was a disappointment because he liked talking to this woman, or an overfull belly.

Disturbed that he even had to ask himself such a question, given the gulf that lay between them, he decided he shouldn't indulge himself so much in the future. This was a good time to remind himself that the Lord cautioned his faithful not to allow themselves to be unequally yoked together with unbelievers. Hiring her to work for him was one thing; enjoying the time he spent alone with her too much was another. All he had to do was remember that she was *Englisch*, a word the pain of Leah's death had turned into the lash of a whip.

Feeling all too well-fed as he strode to the back of his property where he'd left his team tied in the shade did not stop him from speculating about what Hannah would serve for supper tonight.

Just as Hannah got out of her car at her *daad*'s house late at six thirty or so, she was surprised to see another car coming up the driveway. She groped for her phone, but there'd been no missed calls, and that wasn't her grandparents' car, anyway.

Samuel had *Englisch* customers, she reminded herself, and maybe even friends. But she hadn't gotten halfway to the front porch before the driver parked . . . and her mother stepped out of the passenger side. Hannah came to a dead stop.

A man behind the wheel of the car made no move to get out.

"Mom, what are you doing here?"

Her mother's nostrils flared. "Maybe I just wanted to see my old home."

Behind Hannah, the front door opened and closed, and

booted footsteps on the porch boards told her who had come out. She had a suspicion everyone else in the family, except maybe for the two young boys, was lined up at windows to see the *Englisch* woman who had once been married to Samuel.

Grateful when he stopped beside her, she gave his big, calloused hand a squeeze that he returned.

He dipped his head politely, not taking his eyes from Hannah's mother. "Jodi," he said, his accent especially noticeable. "I didn't expect you."

"I suppose not, but how else could I talk to you?"

He would have asked almost any other visitor into the house, insisted Lilian had made plenty of food, that of course they were *wilkom* to stay for dinner.

His expression placid, he asked pleasantly, "What is it you wanted to say?"

"To let you know I've filed for divorce. Hannah—" her gaze darted to her daughter "—reminded me I should do that to make things right with you."

That wasn't quite what Hannah had said, not the way she remembered it, but she wasn't about to step in between them.

Samuel said only, "I will sign the papers when they are ready."

"I'll bet your *wife* will be glad once they're filed."

"Lilian and I are married in God's eyes," he said, sounding unconcerned. "Glad I am to have Hannah back in my home."

Jodi looked directly at her. "How do you like the Amish lifestyle? Not that different from convict labor for the women, is it?"

The muscles in Samuel's jaw might have knotted, but otherwise his expression didn't change. The back of his hand brushed Hannah's.

"You chose to leave. Maybe that's why. I don't know."

For her *daad*'s sake, she struggled to moderate her tone. "But it's rude to come to a family's home to insult them."

Jodi tossed her head. "You didn't answer my question."

"I'm having a wonderful time getting to know everyone. I love cooking and gardening. And I have yet to work any harder than I've been doing for years in restaurant kitchens."

Her mother stared at her. "At least at the end of the shift, you can go home!"

"I work very long shifts." *And have no particular reason to be glad to be home.*

Jodi gave an incredulous laugh. "You're delusional, but you're not going to listen to me, are you?"

"Not until I have a chance to make up my own mind."

For what had to be thirty seconds, they all stood there without a word. It began to feel awkward, more than anything.

"I miss you." Her mother's voice cracked. "No matter what you think, I love you." She whirled and started for the car.

To her back, Hannah said, "I love you, too, Mom, but what you did was wrong."

Her mother went still between one step and another, but only for a moment. Then she hurried around the car and jumped in.

Samuel and Hannah didn't move. She caught one glimpse of the male driver as he turned the car around. He looked to be in his fifties, dark hair mixed with gray, handsome. Probably ready to hold Jodi when she cried. It would never occur to her to cry in the shower where no one could hear.

She's my mom.

The car receded, and turned onto the paved country road.

Samuel said calmly, "The others are probably waiting for us." This time in the evening, he read aloud from the Bible to his family.

"I suspect they're all dying to hear what my mother said," Hannah suggested.

The skin beside his eyes crinkled when her *daad* smiled at her. "*Ja*, they will have questions, certain sure."

Hannah was actually able to laugh as they walked toward the house.

Only then she had a thought. "I wonder if she came at this time of day so I'd be home."

The creases on Samuel's forehead deepened. "Does she know you have a job?"

"I don't see how she could. But she could have come by earlier and seen that my car wasn't here."

He patted her on the back as they mounted the steps. "You worry too much, daughter. You know that our Lord reminds us that being anxious gains us nothing."

Hannah laughed. "Yes, but how can we help it?"

Her *daad* smiled at her.

Chapter Ten

➤◆←

GIDEON KNEW THE minute he saw Hannah get out of her car Wednesday morning that someone or something had upset her. He had been waiting only until she arrived to go out and hitch up his four-horse team again to pull the disc harrow that would help break up and turn the soil in the back field he'd just plowed. Come afternoon, he hoped to change to the spring-tooth harrow that further broke down clods of soil and would also level the surface to prepare it for planting. Neither job was as grueling as plowing, but he and the horses would work hard today, for sure.

Now he walked toward her. He'd just sent the *kinder* upstairs to brush their hair and teeth and put on shoes and socks, so, unlike many mornings, they didn't immediately burst out the kitchen door.

She produced a smile and said her usual "*Gute mariye*, Gideon."

"Is it your grandfather?" he asked, his eyes lingering on her fine-boned features.

"What?"

Maybe not. He hesitated. "You look—" He couldn't decide, now that he studied her closely. Grieving, he'd thought, but that might not be it. Her mood was certainly shadowed.

Not a man who often searched for undercurrents, he felt uneasy to discover that he had gotten so good at reading hers.

"Not my perkiest, huh?" she asked.

"Perky?"

"Cheerful. Bouncy."

"Ah. No, you don't look cheerful or bouncy." He knew bouncy; if Zeb could jump instead of walk or even run, he did.

"I'm okay. Really." Hannah gripped that handbag of hers tightly. "I didn't sleep very well last night, that's all. My mother came out to *Daad*'s house. It was . . . strange."

He wanted to touch her, if only to lay a hand on her shoulder, but didn't dare. "Why would she go to Samuel's house, after leaving so many years ago?"

"Supposedly, to let him know she's filing for divorce in court. But she also made a few jabs at me, and . . ." Hannah shrugged, not finishing.

Jabs. Which particular ones had the woman chosen? *Auslanders* liked to see and even talk to Amishmen and women as if they were animals to be petted at the county fair. Others, including some local *Englischers*, didn't like the Amish. They had excuses for that dislike, complaining about the ruts worn by steel-rimmed buggy tires in paved roads, the manure dropped on streets in town, or what they labeled "unfriendliness." But he'd also heard them call the Amish "weirdos" and worse. Some people seemed to think that, because the Amish held themselves apart, they must have frightening secrets. They sacrificed children at their church services, maybe. He also knew many moderns thought Amishmen repressed their women. That was the word he'd read. Wouldn't let the women hold jobs and make money, kept them doing hard labor at home and raising *kinder*. Was that what Hannah's *mamm* thought?

Those same people never seemed to notice that several businesses in town were owned and managed by Amishwomen, or that other Amishwomen ran successful businesses out of their homes or worked beside their husbands.

He settled for saying, "I'm sorry."

She bobbed her head. "*Denke.* Oh." Her smile spread. "Zeb! Rebekah. *Gute marijye!*"

Ja, here came his *kinder*, excited as they'd been every morning since Hannah first came to take care of them.

She hugged Rebekah and exclaimed, "Here you are, all ready for school, and I haven't made your lunches yet."

He'd noticed that she had taken to starting before she left the evening before, setting out cookies and whatever fruit she could find on a shelf in the pantry, but making sandwiches in the morning. Did she ever fumble around in the kitchen, forgetting what she was doing or skipping a step or creating a big mess? Gideon didn't think so.

Zeb made a face. "Today's Susan's turn. I wish *you* were walking us to school."

"But I'll meet you at the foot of the driveway after school," she reminded him.

"*Ja*, but—" Silenced by one look from his father, Zeb turned sulkily back to the house.

Quietly, Gideon said, "Lately, he doesn't always think about what he says about other people, or having to do something he doesn't want to do."

"You mean, he's being a brat?"

"*Ja*. Not so bad, but I don't like it."

"You want to make sure I put a stop to it, too."

Maybe he shouldn't have said anything. "I can't expect you to discipline my *kinder*."

"That's not discipline. It's expecting them to be kind. I have no problem asking that from them."

For all that she was *Englisch*, Hannah was nothing like the other women who'd worked for him. Back home, the women in his own family were plenty willing to correct his *kinder*, although his son and daughter were both so young and sad then, they'd seldom needed even a chiding word. But Hannah . . . though she'd been here such a short time, she acted almost as if she were their mother. Never impatient, that he'd seen. Never acting as if they were getting in her way. Instead, she seemed to *like* listening to them, encouraging them, teaching them.

Just as she listened to him, as if she wanted to understand him.

As he wanted to understand her.

He knew his nod was abrupt, but he had to cut off this conversation as well as what he'd been thinking. He left her standing there when he walked away.

She wasn't Amish, and would never be. Why did he have such a hard time accepting that?

"Is the job still going well?" Helen asked that Sunday as she sliced the turkey breast they'd roasted and Hannah put a cookie sheet with sourdough biscuits in the small oven.

"I love it," she assured her grandmother, even though this week hadn't gone as well as the first one. Rebekah and Zeb hadn't changed, but their father had. Hannah had no idea what she'd said or done, but there had to be something.

She'd have asked Gideon, except he hadn't seemed annoyed at her, only distant, less willing to talk the latter part of the week. He was polite, the way she'd seen him be to a man from the sawmill delivering a load of wood chips for bedding. And, *ja*, that fellow was Amish, but from a different church district. Hannah had the impression they had never met before.

There was no reason whatsoever why Gideon's subtle change in attitude toward her should sting, but it did. She told herself it was just as well Gideon had used a scythe to slice off any unrealistic dream that she belonged in his home, mothering his children.

What humiliated her was wondering whether he'd guessed that she was attracted to him, drawn by his tall, strong body and the intensity in his dark eyes as well as the way he softened for his children. No, more than that—there was the way he listened to her, noticed when she was distressed even when she thought she'd hidden her feelings.

Had she flirted, or touched him when she shouldn't? If so . . . well, she wouldn't apologize. Better take her cue from him and stay cool, pleasant, and distant.

So she told her grandparents all about Zeb and Rebekah, and talked about her sisters and brothers, too. She bragged about her garden, with tiny new shoots already appearing from the seeds she and the *kinder* had planted so recently.

Several times Robert chuckled, which made her happy even if laughing also made him choke and gasp.

"Once I've canned the rhubarb, I'll bring you a few jars," she said. "Gideon won't mind."

"That would be lovely." Helen hugged her.

When it was time for her to leave, her grandfather stopped her with a knobby hand on her arm. It trembled, but his gaze was steady. "We . . . love . . . you . . . Hannah." He fought for air between each word.

Eyes awash in tears, she bent to kiss his cheek and whispered, "I love you, too."

As she waited for the elevator at the end of the hall, she railed against having found him when he had so little time left. Why not a year ago? Better yet, a decade ago?

All right, she conceded in anguish, why not even a *month* sooner?

This is the day the Lord has made; We will rejoice and be glad in it. The verse came to her, as if in the softest of whispers. Hannah drew a deep, cleansing breath.

Even though her eyes still sparkled with tears while she

crossed the parking lot, she felt both chided and grateful. She had found her grandfather in time to get to know him. He'd learned that his daughter and granddaughter weren't dead, as he had believed; he had seen them both again. When his time came, she had to believe he would have less to regret than he'd had before she came to Tompkin's Mill.

How foolish to wish for more than that.

AFTER LUNCH ON Tuesday, Hannah went straight out to weed the garden and decide what she could pick for dinner. A few cucumbers were ready, and she thought a first batch of peas, plus enough greens for a good salad. She was especially excited about the peas.

She'd straightened to stretch her back and ease her shoulders when she heard a horse and buggy coming up the driveway.

Gideon was cutting wood in the treed corner of his land, and splitting it for winter, he'd told her during lunch. He made a point every morning and afternoon of making sure she knew where to find him, should there be an emergency. She'd nodded pleasant understanding, sticking to her new determination to be professional.

If her heart ached sometimes . . . well, confusion was probably inevitable given the nature of this job.

She stood, swiped at the dirt on the knees of her jeans, dropped her leather gloves on her bucket, and went to meet the visitor.

A woman was driving the small, open-fronted buggy. She reined her horse to a stop at the hitching post near the house and got out, seeing Hannah.

"Hello!" she called before tethering the horse, which had already cocked one hip and appeared ready to sink into somnolence. The air was still and warm enough to encourage thoughts of a nap.

The hello had been spoken in English, which meant the visitor already knew who she was.

Hannah got close enough to greet her, seeing a woman she thought was a little older than her—early thirties, at a guess—with deep auburn hair and a complexion that should be creamy but had a hint of tan. Her nose was pink—as, Hannah feared, was her own.

She introduced herself, saying, "I guess you know Gideon hired an *Englisch* woman to take care of his *kinder* and home. And garden," she added, to explain the dirt stains.

The woman chuckled, continuing to speak in English with no trace of an accent. "I do know. I'm Julia Bowman. I was born and raised *Englisch*, too. I converted only a couple of years ago, and married an Amishman."

Hannah was afraid her mouth had fallen open. From what she'd been able to learn, that was incredibly rare. "If you don't mind me asking, how did that happen?"

Julia smiled. "Do you have time to visit?"

"Of course I do. Please, come in. I made lemonade earlier."

"Let me just get the baby."

To Hannah's surprise, a baby seat rested on the floor of the buggy. Seeing his *mammi* bending over him, the little boy in it let out a squawk, then began babbling to her as she released the buckle and lifted him out.

"Oh, he's darling." Hannah stepped closer, entranced by the bright blue eyes and a smile that conveyed wonder and delight.

"We think so." Julia kissed him on the cheek. "I suspect he won't keep the blue eyes, since mine are brown, but you never know. Meet Nathan Bowman."

"Hi, Nathan." She glanced up at Julia. "How old is he?"

"Six months."

They went into the house, where Julia took a seat at the kitchen table, Nathan on her lap. Hannah produced a set of measuring spoons for him to shake and bang on the table-top. Then she poured lemonade for the two adults.

"Does he drink out of a cup yet?"

"Not quite. I'm still nursing him—and may I say, these dresses aren't very well designed for that—but the last month or six weeks, we've started supplementing my milk with oatmeal and applesauce." She shook her head. "I swear, he's *always* hungry."

"A foretaste of his teenage years, from what I hear."

Julia rolled her eyes. "My mother-in-law tells me Luke and his brother outgrew clothes faster than she could sew them."

"Oh! Can I ask you some questions about that? After you tell me about yourself."

Julia laughed and began talking. Her brother was the Tompkin's Mill police chief, and she'd come to visit, decided she liked the town, and gotten a job. "With Bowman and Son's Handcrafted Furniture," she said mischievously.

Hannah laughed. "I gather the 'son' is your husband?"

"Yes. He and his *daad*, Eli, make spectacular furniture. When I first started working there, I'd sneak around stroking dresser tops and whisking drawers in and out just for the sensual pleasure of it. I'd never in a million years have been able to afford to buy any of it. But guess what?"

"You own some now."

"Bowman and Son's doesn't make cradles—there's another Amish furniture maker in town who does—but Luke made an exception for Nathan's. He chose cherrywood, and the finish is so silky, the lines graceful." She sighed. "I'll hate having to put it away for a crib, but Nathan is thinking about pulling himself to his feet."

She went on to tell Hannah more about her life once she'd moved here; she'd found herself increasingly drawn to the Amish for the sincerity of their faith and their unshakable belief in forgiveness. "And, of course, I toppled into love with Luke, practically from the day I started to work for him and Eli. He felt the same, but tried to keep his distance from me because I wasn't Amish."

That sounded painfully familiar to Hannah, at least from her side. Was there any chance Gideon was distancing himself from her because he was tempted even though she was an *Englischer*?

Fat chance.

There was more to Julia's story; Luke had spent over a decade out in the *Englisch* world himself, getting a college degree, working in the software field, before choosing to give up everything he'd achieved, come home to be baptized, and return to woodworking with his father.

"He had a daughter, too. Mine now, of course. Speaking of darlings. Abby is five, not yet in school, so I left her at a friend's house. She went from barely speaking to becoming a motormouth."

"A *blabbermaul*," Hannah said with a grin.

"*Ja.*" Julia smiled back at her.

Nathan was getting restless, so Hannah found a few more kitchen implements and a stuffed animal from Rebekah's room that he could play with. A piece of dry bread, part of a few slices she'd intended to crumble atop scalloped potatoes, for him to gnaw on, too. Julia bounced him on her knee, too, and answered every time he sounded chatty.

"So," she said, "I've heard about you, born and raised Amish but taken away by your *Englisch* mother."

Hannah readily told some of her story, and her struggle to forgive her mother for letting her think she had no other family. "Her father, my grandfather, has congestive heart failure. I doubt he has more than a few months left, if that. Just Sunday, I had an attack of fury because Mom had stolen the chance from both of us to know each other while he was still healthy." She sighed. "I had to remind myself that we're both blessed to have this time, however short it turns out to be."

"That's definitely a blessing," Julia agreed. "I do hope

we can become friends. Samuel is a lovely man, and Lilian has been really good to me. You may be here only for a visit, but I assume you'll keep visiting in the future."

"Of course I will. My father and stepmother and my half sisters and brothers have welcomed me so generously, I feel at home. In fact—" She hesitated, then went ahead and told Julia about the unnerving speed with which she was learning the language. "I think it's like taking a lid off a boiling pot. The vocabulary, even the sentence structure, is rising like steam, as if I've always known *Deitsh*."

"Which you did."

She nodded.

Within half an hour, Hannah felt as if, for the first time in her life, she had a best friend. Their reasons for being split between an essentially *Englisch* self and an Amish self were different, but they understood each other. Julia talked about the decision to give up her former life despite opposition from her parents and brother, about the hard transition softened by her husband's understanding and love, the generosity of his family, and her own increasing belief her choice had been right for her.

"I'm here anytime you want to talk. I'd encourage you to attend a church service, to help you understand the Amish."

"I plan to come to the next one." She looked down at herself and wrinkled her nose. "Not wearing jeans."

Julia chuckled. "Probably best not to. You know, I might still have the dress I made for my first time. Unless you have something suitable—"

"The best I can do right now is a few casual skirts."

"I'll look for it, then. Or have you considered dressing plain while you're staying with your Amish family?"

Hannah opened her mouth, closed it, opened it again. "I . . . sometimes I've thought, but . . ." She tried to untangle her thoughts. "It's true I'm always conscious of sticking out like a sore thumb. But . . . wouldn't that be, I don't know, presumptuous? I mean, everyone knows I'm *not* Amish."

"I didn't wear Amish dress until I made the decision to convert," Julia said thoughtfully, "but you're different. You're Samuel's daughter, born Amish. I have the impression you've been trying hard to fit in, so why not dress as we do, too?"

Was fitting in what she'd been trying to do? Or had she been striving to . . . oh, be invisible, so no one would mind her being here? She'd done a lot of that in her life, hoping to please the various men along the way with her cooking and go unnoticed the rest of the time.

Or were her goals since she came to Tompkin's Mill, the sense of longing she couldn't shake, more complicated than wanting to be liked and, yes, to belong in her *daad*'s household?

"I'm the only *Englisch* woman delivering *kinder* to school or picking them up," she heard herself say.

"You don't drive them, I assume?"

"In my car? Heavens, no! I never even suggested it. I feel sure Gideon—do you know him?"

"Not well, but he's in our church district, so I see him around. He tends to look stern until he's talking to one of his kids. Then he's tender, and has a wonderful smile."

Hannah hoped she didn't sound as rueful as she felt when she admitted she'd noticed. "He's been easy to work for. I was a chef, and I think he's really happy with my cooking."

"Then he's luckier than Luke." Julia made a face. "I was a quilter. I sew well, although the restrictions on what the Amish in any particular district wear doesn't leave much— actually, *any*—room for innovation. I guess I'm an adequate cook, but nothing I make ever comes close to being as good as my mother-in-law's food."

Hannah raised her eyebrows. "If you have time, maybe we should trade some lessons. I can thread a needle and sew a button back on, but that's about it. Unfortunately, Zeb, Gideon's boy, desperately needs new clothes. His wrists and ankles are sticking out, and he's put holes in the knees of every pair of pants he owns."

"And they don't have female relatives here, do they?"

"No. I'm not sure why they moved away from family. Gideon hasn't been quite that communicative."

"I haven't heard, either," Julia assured her. "I gather it's something he doesn't like to talk about. I think everyone assumed he'd remarry once he was settled here, but he hasn't showed interest in any of the *maidals* or single women who throw themselves at him."

"He may still be mourning."

"Maybe." Julia sounded doubtful. "From a practical standpoint, though, it's not easy for an Amishman to be a single parent, particularly one who doesn't have family nearby to step in."

"No." Hannah thought of all the tasks she'd picked up that weren't in the original job description. "I hate the idea of leaving Zeb and Rebekah. I know the last woman who worked here didn't give them even close to the attention they need. I'm seeing them blossoming. It's really hard not to let myself get more attached to them than I should."

Hannah thought to bring out the gingerbread cookies she'd frozen Saturday and defrosted this morning so she had something to send with the school lunches. She planned to bake a streusel cake this afternoon, but Gideon had seemed happy with the cookies at lunch, even though she was able to tell from the diminished quantity that he and the kids had eaten some on Sunday and Monday as well as for Saturday supper.

Julia swallowed her first bite, her expression blissful. "I think these are at least as good as Luke's sister Miriam makes, and she's famous for her cookies. Not that she lets herself get prideful, you understand."

"Of course not." They grinned at each other again.

"I should let you get back to work." Julia sounded regretful. "*I* need to start thinking about dinner. But what if I come, oh, tomorrow or Thursday again? I'll see if I can find fabric and buttons so we can get started making shirts and pants for Zeb. And I'll bring that dress, if I still have it."

Hannah asked tentatively, "How would I go about getting an Amish dress and apron and *kapp*, if I decide I should wear them when I'm here?"

"Scissors, fabric, thread. But I'll tell you what. You and I are close to the same height. And build, too, although I still haven't gotten rid of the baby pudge. Anyway, I'll bring one of my outfits for you to try, if you don't mind clothing someone else has worn."

"Of course not." They smiled at each other again. "Either day. Any day. And I'll plan something for us to cook together that you can take home and reheat."

The hug they exchanged saying goodbye was heartfelt on both sides, Hannah believed.

Chapter Eleven

❖◆❖

THE NEXT AFTERNOON, shortly after Gideon disappeared to the barn to harness his team of massive horses, Julia Bowman arrived again, this time with another woman.

Pretty, blond and pregnant, Miriam Miller was Luke's sister, Hannah learned, just married last fall. She, too, was a quilter, and still worked at the fabric and quilt shop in town.

Hearing that surprised Hannah. She hadn't known any married Amishwomen held jobs. When she said something, Julia told her she, too, had worked well into her pregnancy.

"And, while it's not common for married women raising a family to hold outside jobs, many do bring in income by selling quilts, honey from their beekeeping, garden plants they've raised from seed . . . I know several women who sell baked goods to the bakery or one of the cafés in town. Essentially, they hold part-time jobs. And many widows take over their husbands' businesses, or start their own."

"I've held a job for eight years now," Miriam put in. "Although I have given my notice." She wrinkled her nose.

"I'm almost six months along, and it's getting harder to be on my feet all day. I'd like more time to sew baby clothes, too." She grinned. "Today, we'll practice on older-boy clothes."

They started by slicing the seams on one of Zeb's more worn pairs of pants, using the pieces as a pattern—after adding Hannah's estimate of how much extra room, and especially extra length, he needed—to cut out the several yards of sturdy fabric that Miriam had brought along. There was plenty here for three or more pairs of pants.

She spoke English almost as fluent as Julia's, but with a slight accent and the occasional difference in sentence structure Hannah had noticed from Gideon's speech as well as Samuel's.

When Hannah was nosy enough to ask about her fluency, Miriam explained, "Just because I've worked at businesses in town for so long, dealing mostly with *Englisch* customers. My *mamm* hasn't worked out of the home, and her English isn't so good." She gave a sidelong, teasing look at Julia. "Although *Mamm*'s English has improved now that Sheriff Durant comes around so often."

Julia's brother, Hannah reminded herself. She learned that Nick Durant was particularly fond of Deborah Bowman's cooking.

As the afternoon went on, the three women took turns entertaining Nathan—Hannah thoroughly enjoyed cuddling him—and made great progress on the pants.

Julia had also, as promised, loaned her a loose-fitting, calf-length dress Hannah could wear to the church service. In addition, she'd brought an Amish dress, in a shade of green that Hannah knew would be a perfect color for her, as well as an apron and filmy white *kapp*.

Hannah hadn't decided how she felt about actually *wearing* this dress, but decided there was no harm in her trying it on. She hadn't expected to need a lesson in how to get dressed, but discovered she was wrong.

First, there was the fact that Amishwomen didn't wear bras.

Then, she learned the dress was fastened with straight pins rather than buttons or Velcro or any other sensible innovation from the last few decades. Or the last centuries. As she struggled with a pin, she said, "But *why*?"

The other two giggled. Julia grimaced at her sister-in-law. "Miriam says it is part of the Amish determination to avoid modern improvements that make life too easy—unless, of course, they're something really helpful, like diesel generators or modern appliances. 'Enter by the narrow gate,'" she quoted, "'for wide is the gate and broad is the way that leads to destruction, and there are many who go in by it.'"

Hannah laughed and finished the verse. "'Because narrow is the gate and difficult is the way which leads to life, and there are few who find it.' I was just thinking about that the other day." She looked ruefully down at the puckered seam she'd just pinned. "This is not what I was thinking."

"It was a while before I quit stabbing myself," Julia warned.

"At least we don't have to constantly sew buttons back on our dresses," Miriam contributed. She blew a raspberry against the baby's plump belly. "Isn't that right, Nathan?"

He chortled happily.

Miriam continued to stitch seams with enviable speed while Julia and Hannah cooked an enormous batch of beef stew that would also have dumplings, adding her own special touches. Hannah worried a little that one of the main ingredients for the stew was stout beer, but Julia didn't comment, and cooking took care of the alcoholic content, right? Julia followed along with utmost seriousness, tasting before and after the addition of spices, nodding her understanding.

Starting with a buttermilk base, they did taste tests so that Julia could decide whether she liked rosemary or thyme better in the dumplings. Hannah explained why she recommended freshly cracked black pepper rather than the kind of pepper that came in a can, and why serious cooks looked askance at salted butter.

"Salt is a preservative, you know. It can disguise butter that's going bad. Plus, if you're using a recipe that calls for unsalted—"

Julia wrinkled her nose. "Do you ever use recipes?"

"Well . . . not often." Hannah grinned. "But if you do, be aware that you can end up with too much salt in whatever you're baking."

"I use unsalted butter when I bake cookies," Miriam said from behind them.

"Which might be one reason yours are better than anyone else's," Julia remarked.

When the two women eventually departed, each carried casserole dishes with ample servings for their families that evening, and the kitchen smelled fantastic. Hannah decided to take the pants home tonight and keep working on them— although she definitely needed to acquire some new calluses, she decided. Thank goodness Miriam had thought to bring along a thimble. Now that she knew how to deconstruct and construct, she felt confident she could make shirts, too.

Miriam had told her that her mother owned an old treadle Singer sewing machine, which evidently worked splendidly and would make a huge difference to a woman who had to keep a large family clothed. Hannah hadn't seen Lilian sewing yet.

To Hannah's satisfaction, Gideon and both kids ate the stew with great enthusiasm.

The next morning, she arrived early enough to make Zeb try on the new pants so that she could hem them to the right length. Surprisingly, Gideon lingered, watching with amusement in those very dark eyes.

Hannah pinned them up, frowning to see how much fabric was left. "I won't cut off all this extra. If I make the hem generous, I can let the pants down when he grows some more." Or whoever took her place could.

That deep voice above her commented, "My *mamm* used to do that, but usually by the time I needed extra length, the pants had been mended so many times, she said they were good only for the ragbag."

"You, too, *Daad*?" Zeb exclaimed.

Hannah swiveled on her heels and looked up at the big man towering above them.

"*Ja*. Boys will be boys." Gideon turned a smile on his daughter. "But girls can be just as hard on their clothes."

Hannah had noticed that Rebekah's dresses and aprons always had grass stains and often rips, as well. She was an active girl, which Hannah liked to see.

"Run, run, run," her father said, his hand gentle on her head. "Never slows down. Now, put your *kapp* on and get ready for school."

The two raced each other upstairs, bodies bumping against the wall, Rebekah indignantly calling out her brother for cheating.

Gideon sighed, and Hannah laughed.

Eyes smiling, he said, "*Denke* for making those. He's in sore need."

"I'll sew a couple more pairs, then try a shirt. Rebekah would probably like a new dress, too, but her need is less obvious."

"*Ja*." His smile was long gone. "There is so much I can't do for them."

"All parents need help," she said gently. "I'm having fun learning new things, and getting to know other women."

"Julia Bowman, you said."

"Miriam Miller came yesterday, too. I think she picked up the fabric at the store in town, because she works there. Both of them are quilters."

"*Ja*, so I'm told."

"Although Miriam said she just gave her notice because of her pregnancy. She's something like six months along."

"Among us, the men pretend they don't notice until the *boppli* is born," he said gravely, but with that fleeting smile reappearing in his eyes.

"Oh. I'm sorry. I didn't know that. *Daad* talks about Lilian's——" Hannah flushed.

"That is because she is his wife. None of the rest of us who are men have seen that she's expecting another *boppli*."

"Some things are just obvious," she mumbled.

To her surprise, Gideon laughed out loud. He hadn't done that much around her this past week.

Warmth blossomed in Hannah's chest and probably on her cheeks.

Apparently, he realized he'd lowered his guard, because his expression regained its usual reserved aspect. "Ach, I must get to work. I'll be planting that back field today."

The glow died a quick death at his immediate retreat, but she kept her voice steady. "Isn't *Daad* coming today?"

"No, it will be tomorrow. Some fellow I don't know had a horse throw a shoe and has a split in the hoof wall that needs tending."

"Oh. Well. When he does come, do you mind if I watch him work for a few minutes? I haven't had a chance yet."

Gideon's face softened. "Watch for as long as you'd like. Hard worker, you are. You can take time to slow down."

"Denke." She smiled.

His eyes narrowed, and a flicker of some emotion shifted his expression and eased the set line of his mouth. Was he looking at *her* lips?

The thud of footsteps on the stairs erased whatever he'd betrayed. The next moment, he nodded and went out the back.

For some reason, Hannah felt a little shaky.

And—oh no!—she hadn't even started putting together school lunches.

* * *

AFTER DINNER THAT evening, Hannah followed her father out to the front porch, where he liked to sit as dusk softened the outlines of the barn, fences, and trees. The air felt pleasantly cool. She thought of this as his quiet time, so she said a little timidly, "Do you mind if I talk to you about something?"

"You can talk to me anytime," he said. "Sit."

She perched on the top step instead of joining him on the porch swing. "I'd like to attend the next church service with you."

"Glad everyone will be to welcome you." There was no doubting he meant that. "The hymns, you won't understand, but I think your *Deitsh* is good enough, you will be able to follow the sermons."

"I think so, too." She knew the hymns came from a very old book called the Ausbund and were in an archaic form of German. Taking a deep breath, she tackled another subject. "I've already been here for weeks."

He straightened abruptly. "You're not thinking we don't want you?"

"No." She shook her head. "No. Lilian and the *kinder* have been really good to me. They let me feel I belong." That wasn't a hundred percent true; their routines were so set, she was often more of a stumbling block than a seamless part of whatever task the females of the family were trying to accomplish. But they were trying to include her, she was learning from them, and she had faith they truly wanted her here. Still, she took a deep breath before she said, "Julia Bowman and I have gotten to be friends. And . . . I keep thinking about what my life would have been like if Mom hadn't taken me away. So . . . maybe this is silly, but . . . what if I tried living plain while I'm with you? At least . . . well, I have to keep my phone, because of Grandma and Granddad, and maybe the car for when I see them." She came to a stop. "I guess if the only change I make is what I'm wearing, I'd just be pretending, wouldn't I?"

"You would do that?" He looked both stunned and pleased. "Dress like our women do?"

She nodded. "I even have a dress to start with. Julia Bowman lent it to me, so I'd fit in for the service."

"I can teach you to drive a buggy," he offered. "For going to your job. I can take you to Gideon's place until you feel confident enough to drive yourself."

That was part of what she'd been suggesting, wasn't it? Because it was true, the clothing was a small piece of the commitment the Amish made. Giving up cars was a bigger one. And computers, for personal use. Makeup. Jewelry. She touched the small gold post earring in her right ear.

Did she really *mean* to go down this road?

Yes.

She bit her lip. "*Denke, Daad.* I'd like that."

"Lilian is too busy to do much sewing, but either she or her *mamm* would help you make dresses, I'm sure."

Julia and Miriam would, too.

A peaceful silence fell. Hannah wrapped her arms around her knees and pondered the changes she would need to make.

She hadn't touched her laptop since she came to stay with her *daad* and his family, so she wouldn't miss that much. She could read newspapers instead of following news online, and catch up on e-mails later. It wasn't as if she got that many.

Makeup—well, she rarely bothered anyway. In fact, she wasn't much for fancying herself up, as the Amish put it. Certainly, the holes in her ears wouldn't grow closed during the couple of months she was likely to be here.

If I leave.

Hannah ignored that thought.

Julia Bowman had chosen to stay. To make a life-altering commitment, to be baptized, to marry an Amishman.

Hannah's mother had made that commitment, too, then broken it. If her faith in God had ever been real, she'd rejected it.

Anyway, just because it *could* be done didn't mean Hannah had anything like that in mind. All she hoped to do was experience this way of life more authentically.

The life that could have been hers.

That could be hers, however unlikely that seemed, a renegade voice whispered.

Despite the peace of the moment, worries crept into her mind. She couldn't forget that her mother had run away for a reason, depriving them both of family. Mom was inconstant, selfish, Hannah already knew that. Helen had confirmed she'd always been that way. But wasn't it possible that something else lay behind her determination, given that Jodi had gone to such extraordinary lengths to keep them from being found?

One of these days, Hannah knew, she'd have to move past her anger enough to listen to what Mom had to say.

But especially now that she knew her mother had lied to her all her life, she wanted to find her own answers.

The longer she stayed in Tompkin's Mill, the likelier she was to learn any ugly secrets that might be hidden behind the forgiving, peaceful, faith-oriented facade that the Amish, the *Leit*, showed the world.

Even thinking that, though, had her picturing the small scene that morning, so typical of the family interactions she saw every day. The amusement on Gideon's face, his big hand resting so gently on Zeb's head, his smile for his daughter to be sure she didn't feel less important after his "boys will be boys" comment. The trust they so openly felt for their *daad*.

Would that be the case if such dreadful secrets existed?

Hannah's sisters and brothers, too, were invariably cheerful and eager to follow in their parents' footsteps.

However bewildered she was by her mother's choices, Hannah knew that learning to drive a horse and buggy was unlikely to pull back the curtain and expose whatever ugliness Jodi claimed she'd fled.

But Hannah had to admit she was just a little bit excited about that part. She'd gone through a horse-crazy phase when she was seven or eight. Since she never once came in touching distance of a pony or horse, she'd moved on in her interests—probably, come to think of it, to cooking. But now, she'd petted several horses, even fed them carrots—and, finally, she'd be the one holding the reins.

HANNAH HAD LONG since gone back in the house after watching her *daad* shoe Fergus, Gideon's buggy horse. Samuel waited while Gideon led the gelding to the nearby gate and turned him loose in the pasture, then went to get one of his draft horses.

The draft horses weren't shod unless it became necessary to correct a problem. Gideon had no reason to take them out on a paved road. Usually, he cleaned and trimmed their hooves himself, but when Samuel was here, Gideon liked to have him check to be sure he hadn't missed anything.

Greta was last. Like the rest of the team, she was a Belgian, enormous and powerful, with a red-brown coat and pale mane and tail. He had been thinking lately that he might like to have her bred. The *kinder* would enjoy seeing a foal grow up, and she was a fine horse.

He didn't say anything about that, though.

"Looks good," Samuel said, after lifting each hoof in turn and slapping her on her powerful rump.

Gideon took a carrot from a bucket and fed it to her in

chunks. She chewed with such enthusiasm, orange flecks and spittle went flying. He chuckled and wiped his hands on a rag.

"Is Hannah working well for you?" Samuel asked unexpectedly.

Gideon raised his eyebrows, but said, "*Ja*, certain sure. I've never seen a harder worker, and Zeb and Rebekah like her."

Like. That was an inadequate word for their enthusiasm. *Love* might come closer, but he hoped it wasn't quite that, since inevitably Hannah would leave them. Gideon hadn't entirely decided if he wished he hadn't hired her, setting his *kinder* up to be hurt, or whether he should be glad this *Englisch* woman was setting such a good example and giving them the priceless gift of her affection.

His thoughts kept churning as he turned Greta out to join her small herd.

For his own sake, hiring Hannah had been stupid. He shouldn't have ignored his first instinct.

Spending time with her was unavoidable. Like his *kinder*, he admired her willingness to extend herself far beyond what he could reasonably expect of an employee, the good humor she maintained however dirty or exhausting a particular task was, her kindness, generosity, thoughtfulness . . . *Ach*, he could go on and on. What was most troublesome for him was the awareness of her as a woman that he couldn't shake, the warmth he felt at her slightest touch, or her smile. All her smiles from the sad and delighted to those that conveyed how proud she was of Zeb or Rebekah. The sweet smiles, the shy ones, the teasing ones.

He needed to remarry; Gideon knew that. Hoping he would find the right woman in a different settlement had been one reason for his relocating with his *kinder*. But until now, he hadn't met anyone with whom he could imagine spending a lifetime.

How could he be feeling such things for a woman who, despite her birth, wasn't Amish?

What he ought to do was let her go . . . but how could he make his *kinder* understand why he would do that? What would that do to his relationship with Samuel Mast, obviously proud of the daughter God had brought back to him?

And then there was the sorrow he often saw in Hannah's eyes, an unguardedness. That made him feel . . . protective, which weakened his ability to hold himself separate. He didn't want to hurt her.

He was a little surprised when he came back around the barn to find that, while Samuel had loaded his tools in his buggy and removed the heavy leather apron he wore when working, he seemed to be waiting for Gideon.

"Has Hannah told you she plans to attend our next worship service?"

"*Ja*, she did say so."

Samuel tapped his fingers on his thigh. "She has decided to live plain while she's with us. I'll be driving her to work until she becomes comfortable enough to drive herself. You or Zeb might help her unhitch our mare and then harness her at the end of the day."

Stunned, Gideon had to corral thoughts that wanted to burst in a dozen directions like a startled covey of quail. "She plans to dress plain?"

"*Ja*. She will keep the phone, because of her grandfather. And maybe drive her car into town when she goes to visit her grandparents. We didn't talk about that."

Heart racing, Gideon didn't dare ask the important question.

Was Hannah giving thought to converting to the Amish faith and staying in Tompkin's Mill?

Chapter Twelve

❖❖❖

SMILING AT HANNAH, her father slapped the brown mare's shoulder and stepped back from the buggy. Just as he did so, the horse shook her head vigorously. The frail fiberglass buggy shifted. Hannah's hands clenched the reins.

"Ach, you'll be fine," her *daad* said amiably. "Such a short distance, you probably won't even see a car. And at the end of the day, Clover knows her way home."

She *didn't* know her way to Gideon's farm. She'd require steering. But not only did Hannah not say that, she forced a smile. "It's a good thing one of us knows what we're doing."

Samuel laughed heartily. "*Ja, ja.* Clover is a calm one. She'll take care of you."

Hannah bobbed her head, loosened the reins, and clicked her tongue. Clover started forward. The buggy swayed and creaked as the wheels began to roll.

This felt like a replay of the day after she'd received her driver's license and could set out alone. It wasn't as if she hadn't been behind the wheel before, but until then she'd always had an instructor ready to shout, "Brake!" if it was necessary. Same with this new skill; Samuel had been a good teacher, but heading out on her own was different.

The mare walked all the way to the paved country road, where Hannah signaled her to turn left.

Okay, that's part of what was different. The car wasn't *her* or *him*; it couldn't think for itself, freak out without any input from the driver.

Hannah reminded herself that she wasn't going very far. The temptation was to keep Clover at a walk the entire way. The only thing was, a slow pace would increase the likelihood of a car happening to come along and pass them. She'd found that terrifying when she was only a passenger, Samuel confidently driving his larger work buggy. On her own, Hannah was afraid she'd have a meltdown.

I wanted to do this, she reminded herself grimly, although she hadn't dreamed she'd be setting out on her own so soon. Samuel seemed confident she didn't need much practice.

Point the direction you want to go, sit back, and relax.

Apparently, *Daad* had plenty of faith in Clover.

Was a prayer excessive? she asked herself. Undoubtedly, but she whispered a verse from Psalms anyway.

"'Do not leave me nor forsake me, O God of my salvation.'"

Feeling remarkably silly but no less nervous, she made herself gently flap the reins and click her tongue again. Without hesitation, Clover broke into a relaxed, ground-eating trot. The untied ribbons attached to Hannah's *kapp* rippled. She'd have worried she hadn't secured the *kapp* well enough, except she wore a black bonnet atop the *kapp*. It seemed Amishwomen almost always did when they were traveling or in town.

"It helps to hide our face when the *Englischers* take pictures, too," Lilian had told her. Presumably, the brims on the hats worn by the men accomplished the same purpose.

Hannah realized she would be offended if some passing tourists took her picture.

Clover had reached the sharp right-hand bend that had confused Hannah the day she was trying to find her father's address, and followed it without any signal from her driver. From here, it wasn't half a mile down the road to Gideon's driveway.

She could do this.

Of course, that's when she heard a car engine. It was coming up behind her, so she wouldn't see the vehicle until it, too, came around the bend—and the driver wouldn't know a buggy was just ahead, either.

Hannah was so stiff she thought she might break. Clover never hesitated in her stride, seeming entirely unperturbed at the approach of what Hannah saw was a big pickup truck when it moved to the oncoming lane to pass her.

Her terror didn't subside even when she realized the truck was moving slowly and the driver had gone out of the way not to crowd her. An older man, he waved as he passed, and gradually picked up speed. Hannah would swear Clover's ears didn't so much as swivel. The mare was completely unconcerned.

Hannah had a bad feeling she'd find big circles of sweat under her arms when she got to Gideon's, but she blew out a long breath and tried to make herself relax. The sharp striking of Clover's hooves on the pavement and the whir of the steel-rimmed wheels were rhythmic enough to be lulling, had she been any less tense.

Her gaze latched onto the mailbox, today with the red flag raised, and she eased Clover to a walk and a turn into the driveway, then let her resume her trot.

She passed the house in favor of a hitching post beside the barn doors.

Reining in Clover—although she hardly needed to—Hannah bowed her head forward. She'd made it.

Thank you, Lord.

* * *

SATURDAY MORNING, GIDEON had just stepped out his back door to stretch, evaluate the weather, and take a deep breath of fresh air, when he heard the approaching horse and buggy. Samuel, to drop off Hannah, Gideon assumed. He was glad Hannah worked on Saturdays. Mondays were difficult enough, with his getting the *kinder* ready for school, walking them to the foot of the driveway, then remembering to knock off whatever he was doing at the time of day when they got home. At least he had a good part of the day to work in peace, although he had to prepare dinner.

That was less challenging than it had been, thanks to Hannah; Rebekah had truly become useful in the kitchen.

Still, Gideon and his *kinder* all dreaded Mondays and looked forward to Hannah's appearance Tuesday morning, him the most, although he made sure neither Zeb nor Rebekah guessed that was so.

Still hatless, he walked across the grass, his eyebrows climbing at the sight of the two-person buggy, and the horse he didn't recognize. And, ach, an Amishwoman driving. This was early for Julia or Miriam to come calling—

The brown mare stopped neatly in front of the hitching rail . . . and the woman slumped in her seat. Shocked although he shouldn't be, Gideon realized this was Hannah. She'd not only driven herself today but wore Amish garb. He would have recognized her sooner were it not for the bonnet. Why had she decided to dress plain for the first time at his house the same day she drove herself?

"Hannah?" he said.

She lifted her head and untied her bonnet ribbons with hands that he thought were shaking, then removed the bonnet to expose a white prayer *kapp* and the hair that made him think of corn silk after it had darkened.

"That was scary!"

A smile crept over his face. "Did something happen?"

She turned her big eyes on him. "A pickup truck passed me. A giant one!"

His smile died. "Speeding?"

"No." She sighed, making no move to get out of the buggy. "The driver was polite. He *waved*." She sounded as if she'd been insulted. "Clover didn't even twitch an ear. But I panicked. Wow. I don't know about this."

Gideon reached her side of the buggy and stopped, no more than a foot or two from her. "You've driven with your *daad*."

"That's not the same."

The Amish young spent years as passengers in buggies before they eventually learned to drive their own.

For Hannah, this small buggy, not even fully enclosed, must feel flimsy compared to the solid metal cars she was used to.

"You don't remember riding in a buggy when you were a *kind*?"

She accepted his hand as she climbed out. *"Denke."*

With the contact of their bare hands, Gideon felt all the small hairs on his arm lift. It was a shock of a different kind.

Hannah looked flustered, but he couldn't tell if she was reacting to his touch, or was only recovering from her new experience.

Gideon was careful to back up several feet, trying not to stare but unable to help himself. This wasn't the same Hannah.

"I remember talking about horses," she said, evidently in answer to his question, "and when we passed Amish buggies, I asked if *Daadi* was driving that one, but my mother always told me not to be silly, my father would never have driven a buggy. It got so I believed her." She offered him the smile that was twisted enough to show that it hid old hurts.

His least favorite of her smiles.

"I'm sorry."

Her head turned. "Where are the *kinder*?"

"Upstairs getting ready. Or squabbling or playing, I'm not sure."

Her chuckle lifted his spirits. Still . . . he struggled to align his knowledge that this was Hannah, his *Englisch* employee, with what his eyes told him. A tall, slim Amishwoman stood in front of him, the forest green of her dress bringing out the green in her eyes, the white gauze of the *kapp* framing her fine-boned face. If she were a visitor attending their worship service, he wouldn't have been able to look away any more than he could now.

"Your *daad* said you planned to dress plain, but . . ." He shook his head. "You took me by surprise."

"Since this is the only dress I have"—she plucked at the skirt—"I decided to save it for the big day when I could drive myself. And I'll have to try to keep it clean so I can wear it again tomorrow for the service."

So she would be worshipping with them.

The back door of the house opened and the *kinder* burst out, running halfway before seeing the buggy and an apparent Amishwoman.

"Daadi?" That was Rebekah, who could still be timid.

"It's Hannah," he said, outward calm hiding an inner turmoil that confused him.

Hannah turned to the *kinder*, held out her arms, and twirled around once. "So, what do you think?"

Zeb gaped at her. "You look different."

Rebekah got over her surprise and ran to her, throwing her arms around Hannah's waist. "You're dressed like me! I like it."

"Good." Hannah touched her head gently. "We have lots of baking to do today. Except, um . . ." She turned back to Gideon. "I don't know what to do with Clover. *Daad* started to teach me how to harness her and take it off, too, but I kept making mistakes."

Gideon prayed his chuckle hid these strange feelings inside him. "Samuel already asked me to take care of your horse once you made it here. I'll harness her for you at the end of the day, too."

"Then, *denke* again." She steered the *kinder* toward the house as Gideon spoke quietly to the mare and unhitched her from the buggy.

Hannah's car and her *Englisch* clothing had been a good reminder that she was an *auslander*. With her speaking *Deitsh* so well, too, anyone meeting her would think she was Amish.

He must take even more care where she was concerned.

THE FAMILY WAS too large to squeeze into even Samuel's family buggy, or sedan, as he called it. So on Sunday, Mose and Hannah drove themselves separately, in the same small buggy she took to go to work. It was actually Lilian's. Having loaned it out, Lilian now either did errands or made visits on Mondays, when Hannah was home, or took Mose's wagon, good for carrying lumber. Because of Mose's age and determination to build a business, the family already owned three harness horses. Her usual good-natured, placid self, Clover pulled the buggy this morning. Mose had offered to let her drive, but Hannah had politely declined.

"I'll watch you."

He smiled in his reserved way. "Doing it yourself is better."

"Maybe two weeks from now. Right now, I'm feeling good because I made it back and forth to work yesterday without getting knocked into a ditch, or doing something to make poor Clover bolt."

"Bolt?"

Able to tell he didn't get her meaning, she said, "Run so I can't stop her."

"One of those big trailer trucks could go by, filling the road, the driver blasting his horn, and Clover wouldn't even think of running."

"Really?"

"Really. We drive on the busy highways, too, you know."

Remembering the buggy she'd passed on the highway when she was arriving in Tompkin's Mill, she couldn't help her shudder. "You do. I'll stick to back roads."

"*Mamm* stays on back roads, too."

"I hear some of the young men race their buggies during their *rumspringa*," she said, shifting her gaze from Samuel's much larger buggy preceding them to Mose's strong, already calloused hands, so confident on the reins. "It sounds crazy."

"*Ja*, that's true. And it is crazy. I will not be doing it." He nodded ahead. "We're almost there."

"Oh. That wasn't so far."

Today's service was to be held at the home of Melvin and Rosaria Esch. Lilian had explained that, like Julia Bowman, albeit thirty years earlier, Rosaria had become a convert to the Amish faith, her family Italian immigrants to this country who had taken up farming.

"She speaks three languages," Lilian had marveled.

Personally, Hannah thought the fact that nearly all Amish spoke *two* languages with reasonable fluency was impressive enough. Teaching foreign languages in school didn't work very well in this country. It was too easy to forget the French or Japanese—or German—you never had reason to use outside of class.

Following the rest of the family, they turned up a typically long driveway, more like a pair of ruts separated by a grassy hillock, that led between cultivated fields. Even Hannah recognized the corn growing on one side. At least ten buggies were already "parked" facing the fence on the left side. Samuel pulled into place, Mose following suit.

Nerves fluttered in Hannah's stomach. With lots of people chattering, her limited fluency was likely to break down. And what would the Amish who hadn't already met her think of her? Would they be pleased she'd dressed plain, or disdain her for pretending to be something she wasn't?

She took out the cheese pie with a potato crust she'd made this morning, and joined Lilian, who was carrying her own offering. Emma solemnly carried yet another dish, and Adah a loaf of fresh bread. Hannah worried whether she should have been so generous with the chili pepper in the filling of her pie. Maybe nobody would like it. They certainly wouldn't expect it to be so spicy. And . . . did her determination to distinguish her offering from others mean she was too prideful?

Mose and Samuel paused to speak to a boy who seemed to have been assigned to watch over the horses, and the women went ahead, Zachariah and Isaiah scampering along with them. They hadn't yet reached the large lawn in front of the typical two-story, white-painted farmhouse when a girl broke away from one of the groups and raced to meet them.

"Hannah!" Rebekah cried.

"I really am here." She smiled at the girl. Lilian and the girls greeted her, too.

"I'm going to sit with Hannah," Gideon's daughter told them proudly. "She asked if I would."

"That's good of you," Lilian assured her. "I hope you two will sit with us."

"Can we, Hannah?"

"Of course we can. Samuel is my *daad*, you know, Adah and Emma are my sisters, and Zachariah and Isaiah my brothers."

Rebekah knew that, on one level, but still showed puzzlement. How could this *Englisch* woman nobody knew really be her friend Adah's sister?

She pointed ahead. "There's *Daadi*."

Her pulse quickening, Hannah had already seen him,

even in a cluster of other men, all clad in dark coats and broad-brimmed dark felt hats. He was taller than most, of course, but that didn't explain her easy recognition. It was just something about the way he carried himself, the tilt of his head as he listened to another man speaking.

Hannah was afraid she'd know him in the pitch dark, which was a very bad sign.

Gideon Lantz would never see her the same way, and for good reason.

Suddenly, she felt like a fraud, dressed to blend in with all the other women. She wasn't one of them. They knew it, and so did she.

Her cheeks hot, she felt a cowardly desire to slink around the barn and hide until it was time to go home.

No, not home. She was a visitor. She certainly wasn't Zeb and Rebekah's mother, the way she sometimes wished she were.

But hiding wasn't an option. Her *daad* was so happy that she had come today. She had to hold her head up and make him proud.

ONCE GIDEON SAW Hannah emerge from the house and start across the lawn toward the barn where the service would be held, he left the group of other men who were still discussing an offer from a frozen food packing company made to two of them. The representative who had visited the men, both of whom grew primarily corn, said he could guarantee a price now, in the spring, protecting them from the possibility that they'd lose their crops through drought or other disaster—and from the chance of a glut of corn again come early fall.

Of course, the offered price was extremely low.

Glad he had decided to diversify, Gideon walked to meet Hannah. Lilian and her *kinder* trailed behind, Rebekah chattering with Adah.

"It's good to see you here," he said gravely. "You may have a backache by the time the service ends."

She wrinkled her nose. "So people keep warning me. I think I'm sturdier than that."

"*Ja.*" He had to clear his throat. "I've seen how strong you are."

For a fleeting moment, their gazes held. She wasn't as lighthearted as she'd seemed, he saw, and he had no idea what she read on his face.

Then Rebekah dashed over and hugged her *daadi*'s legs, as if they hadn't parted barely ten or fifteen minutes ago. People started moving toward the open doors of the barn.

"Oh, I pray my *Deitsh* doesn't fail me," Hannah whispered.

He resisted the urge to squeeze her hand in reassurance. Others would see . . . and talk.

"It won't," he murmured, before they had to part, him to join the men while looking around for Zeb, still too young to sit with his friends. *Kinder* were usually nine or ten before they could be trusted not to make trouble.

At least Hannah would not be alone, he saw at a glance. She and Rebekah had been neatly inserted in the usual order between Lilian and her daughters and Julia Bowman, who held her small daughter's hand and cuddled her *boppli* against her shoulder. Miriam Miller appeared, too, her hand pressed to her back as if it ached before she even sat down on the hard wooden bench.

Zeb wriggled through the gathered men to sit beside Gideon, ready to lean close to read the words of the hymns in the Ausbund that Gideon spread open on his lap. As had become habit, Miriam's husband, David, sat on his other side, followed by his brother Jacob, who had two young sons with him. Luke Bowman joined them on the same bench with his younger brother, Elam, who had married their hosts' daughter just last fall. Gideon liked feeling that he was sitting among friends. When he moved here, everyone had been welcoming, but that wasn't the same.

Light came between cracks in the barn walls and from a loft above as well as through the broad opening. Doors were usually left open, as nursing mothers or a parent with a toddler disturbing the service sometimes had to slip out, returning when they could.

Gideon tried not to be obvious when he kept an eye out for Hannah, but hoped others would assume he was watching for his daughter. Ach, and there they were, Rebekah clutching Hannah's hand. He made sure to turn his head away before they saw him.

"Nathan won't last three hours," Luke muttered. "Maybe I should have kept Abby with me."

Since his young daughter also sat with her *aenti* Miriam and was surrounded by other caring mothers, Gideon felt no need to comment. He did catch Elam rolling his eyes.

Silence fell.

Chapter Thirteen

❖

GIDEON TURNED HIS head when he heard a flurry of whispers in the back. Older boys, for sure. He was glad he had kept Zeb close.

The *Volsinger*, John Mast, announced the first hymn, and lifted his voice in the traditional, solo beginning. The purity of it always moved Gideon. Then the rest of the congregation joined in, young voices, old, women and men. Even caught in the beauty of the slow, measured cadence, sorrow blended with hope and faith, Gideon wondered what Hannah would think of what was closer to chanting than the songs he heard on the radio in stores or in bursts from passing cars with open windows. He wanted to watch her face, but couldn't let himself.

As an adult, he didn't waste much time thinking about what other people meant by saying or doing this or that, and even less time examining his own feelings. He had focused always on what had to be done next, rarely permitting himself to try to look through the eyes of other people.

He had been different as a boy, always questioning, worrying about matters that weren't his concern, or so his father told him. Punished severely when he spoke up or rebelled even in small ways, he had learned that rebellion achieved nothing. Everyone had eventually been convinced that he was a dutiful son, following the path his father laid for him.

Not until he married did he deliberately veer from his father's rigid path. He determined to be a good and loving husband and father, not so rigid he would expect his word to be law without listening first to suggestions or arguments from Leah and his *kinder*. Had he been wrong to deviate from the way he was raised? He still asked himself whether he should have exercised more authority as a husband and father. How could he help but wonder whether he'd been careless in allowing Leah to make choices he hadn't liked—and whether she had secretly longed for a life he couldn't give her?

Even after her shocking death in a speeding car driven by her *Englisch* friend, and the chiding—most loudly from his *daad*—and murmurs that followed it, he'd held tight to his faith in God. It had helped him stifle his resentment for what the bishop said to him.

The move had been mostly for his *kinder*, he still believed, but maybe more for himself, too, than he'd known. Once he'd bought the farm here and they were settled, he hadn't let himself dwell on his motives. What did they matter? What was done was done.

He'd certainly never let himself wonder throughout a service how an *auslander* would see it. The separation of men and women, the use of backless benches that surely were intended to keep anyone from slumping into inattention. The sermons, sometimes powerful and speaking directly to his heart, other times wandering or repetitive. Did preachers in *Englisch* churches often apologize for their clumsiness in trying to share God's word before they began their remarks?

He did glance to see that Hannah joined the others kneeling to pray when they were called to do so. Did she understand that they chose to worship God in the simple surroundings of homes and barns rather than in fancy churches to express their humility? That they blended their voices into one as part of their belief in community, in *Gelassenheit*, the giving over of individual will to a higher authority?

Gideon didn't understand himself, asking these questions. Questioning tradition wasn't the way of the *Leit*. That he was letting himself be swayed even this much by a modern woman disturbed him.

And yet, she was here, dressing plain, keeping her promise to her *daad* and to Rebekah.

Dismayed to realize Amos was giving the benediction and that it was time for the closing prayer, Gideon feared he had missed much of the preaching. He couldn't even remember the topic of Josiah Gingerich's sermon, and Josiah was forthright and hard to ignore.

Grateful that there was no members' meeting today, he joined other men in carrying the benches out onto the lawn, where some would be converted into makeshift tables for the fellowship meal. Zeb ran off with other boys his age. A volleyball net had been set up, and Melvin Esch maintained a baseball field, probably because of his large family of primarily boys.

Hannah, of course, appeared among the other women carrying dishes out from the kitchen, Rebekah at her side clutching silverware. If his family were intact, she'd have eaten with her *mamm*, as young as she was, but usually he called her to his side. Today, he felt sure she'd prefer to stay with Hannah. Zeb had recently taken to eating with the other *kinder* after both the men and women had finished rather than with his *daad*.

Gideon didn't like the spear of loneliness that slid between his ribs. His *kinder* were growing up, looking to other people rather than just their father. That was as it should be, except that Rebekah's attachment to Hannah laid bare how much she needed a mother to guide and love her. That was something he could provide for her. *Should* have provided for her . . . but right now, the only woman he might have been able to see making his wife was not of their faith.

And he was being foolish to let himself think such a thing.

Yet his gaze followed her, this graceful, good-hearted *Englisch* woman who was dressing plain and had given up her car on an everyday basis in favor of driving a horse and buggy—however much that scared her.

NOT UNTIL AFTER everyone had eaten did Hannah come face-to-face with Gideon again.

She'd been foolishly aware of him all along, noticing that he was readily accepted by the other Amishmen his age, yet often seemed to stand on the outskirts of any group. Perhaps it was because he was a relative newcomer to this settlement, but that might just be his nature. He had a way of listening to others talk, watching each speaker in silence, before he contributed himself. When he did, she saw other men nodding, as if he'd clarified their thinking.

An older woman caught her watching Gideon—or at least the group he stood with—and smiled. "You work for Gideon Lantz, *ja*?"

Chagrined to have been caught gawking at him, Hannah returned her smile. "*Ja*, I'm Hannah Mast." It was getting easier to say that, instead of Prescott.

"A quiet one, Gideon is. Keeps his thoughts to himself."

"He's been good to me. And I love his *kinder*."

The woman chuckled. "Hard not to. I'm Martha Beiler."

"It's nice to meet you. *Denke* for letting me join you today."

"Ach, Samuel's daughter. You belong with us."

Hannah opened her mouth to thank her again, but a squeal from a *boppli* had her turning to find Julia at her side. Nathan was grinning and verbalizing while bouncing in his *mammi*'s arms.

Martha chucked him under the chin. "Busy boy. And so good during the service!"

After she hurried off in response to a signal from someone else, Julia made a face. "If it hadn't been for the rest of you taking turns with him, I wouldn't have heard a single word of either sermon."

"No one would think less of you if you hadn't. And you know perfectly well we all wanted to steal him from you."

Julia's smile lit her face to beauty. "I'm so glad we've become friends. I pray you decide to join us. Having someone who understands my challenges is such a blessing."

This new friend was the first person to say out loud what Hannah hadn't even allowed herself to consider as a possibility: that she would choose this faith, this life, so different than what she knew. The life her mother had run from like a wild animal ripping its paw from a trap. Even Samuel hadn't said anything like that to Hannah, although she didn't doubt he was thinking it and hoping.

"I . . . don't know about staying," she said haltingly, determined to be honest. "I'm pretty mixed up right now, after finding out so much about my life I didn't know. And with my grandfather ill, and—" She didn't say that she wondered if the depth of her faith equaled theirs. How could she be sure?

Julia touched her hand, her expression soft. "I understand. I shouldn't have said that. My parents weren't happy about me converting, but I never had any doubt that they loved me or would support me whatever I chose to do. You must be especially mixed up about your mother."

Hannah tried to smile. "*Denke* for understanding. And helping me *look* as if I belong today."

"I'm glad you wore that dress. The color is good on you." She lowered her voice. "Not that we are meant to be vain."

They exchanged grins.

"What did you think of the service?" Julia asked.

"I meant to ask the same question."

Hannah jumped at the deep voice coming from just beside her. Or maybe it was only her heart that jumped.

"Do you have a backache?" Gideon asked, a possible twinkle in his eyes.

"A tiny bit," she admitted. "I'm more used to standing than sitting."

"I tell myself I need a rest," Gideon said. "God is good enough to give me one every two weeks."

Julia laughed. "That's one way of thinking about it."

"As for the service . . ." Hannah sifted through her impressions. "I almost cried during the hymns. We sing in other churches I've attended, but I've never felt as if everyone truly *joined* in prayer that way."

Julia nodded. "That's how I felt, the first time I came. As if I was hearing one voice, raised to God. As if everyone felt the power of that joining. No whispers, or congregants getting a verse wrong, or phone ringing in someone's purse."

"Yes!"

When her son batted her cheek, Julia smiled ruefully. "Of course, then I didn't have a little one trying to contribute, too."

Nobody within several rows could have missed hearing Nathan's excited babbling.

"What singing could be more beautiful than that of a *kind*?" asked Hannah.

Gideon's gaze, resting on her, seemed to hold a weight, but she knew perfectly well that she was likely imagining something that wasn't there. She really needed to curb feelings she had no reason to think were reciprocated. Even if they were . . . the gulf between them was surely too deep.

She decided to return to the original question. "I mostly understood the sermons. Josiah—that was Josiah, right?" At Julia's nod, Hannah continued. "I felt as if he was talking to me. That was sort of unnerving." The younger of the two ministers had started with a verse from Matthew.

Therefore do not worry about tomorrow, for tomorrow will worry about its own things. Sufficient for the day is its own trouble.

"Worrying about tomorrow is my specialty. He made me realize how much I've missed by not rejoicing in the present."

Gideon nodded. "I think he was talking to the farmers among us, too. Every day we labor while knowing that the rain may not come when the crops need it, or it comes in buckets two days before we bring in the hay. We try to accept God's will." One corner of his mouth lifted. "'Sufficient for the day is its own trouble.' That I can mostly accept."

The two women laughed, even knowing that on one level he was serious.

"I suspect Hannah had the right idea," Julia said, after a seemingly thoughtful moment. "'We will rejoice and be glad in it.'"

Gideon bent his head in assent. "That's a good reminder. I'm happy with the day the Lord has made." He looked past Hannah. "Esther seems tired. I should gather the *kinder* and go."

"Oh, I forgot you usually bring her," Julia said. "That's good of you."

"It makes no trouble. She's my neighbor," he said simply, and walked away, heading toward the baseball diamond. Hannah was still disconcerted by the Amish habit of skipping niceties like hello and goodbye.

Beside her, Julia sighed. "I should collect my dishes, too."

"I'll come with you. I have no idea if Mose will want to

linger or go home as soon as possible. I don't think he's very interested in girls yet. Baseball, I'm not sure about."

"You'd better hope not, or you might be stuck here for hours." Julia grinned at her. "Have you seen David and Miriam?"

"Pretty sure they left. She told me her ankles are swelling."

"Ugh. Mine did that, too."

Such a prosaic conversation to give Hannah a severe attack of envy. Until she came to stay with her father—and work for Gideon—she hadn't realized how much she wanted children. A real family. Here, she was surrounded by extended families. Within the church district, only Esther Schwartz, Gideon's neighbor, seemed to have no one—but from what Hannah could tell, her needs were still met, church members visited her, invited her to quilting frolics, treated her as if she were their own widowed *mamm* or *grossmammi*.

And then there was Gideon, a widower who had moved away from his extended family—and presumably his dead wife's family, too. Hannah would give a great deal to know why he'd done that.

And no, it wasn't any of her business, except that she'd come to care entirely too much for Rebekah and Zeb.

Not to mention Gideon, she could admit only to herself.

CONSIDERING WHAT A short time she'd been dressing plain, Hannah didn't know why it felt so odd to change back into her everyday clothes. Her *Englisch* clothes. When she came out of her small bedroom, everyone in the kitchen turned as one to stare. Even three-year-old Isaiah, who sat on the floor building a tall structure with wooden blocks, stopped to gape at her. Adah and Emma looked astonished, as if they'd forgotten she wasn't really one of them.

"I'm going to visit my grandparents," Hannah said unnecessarily. She might go back tomorrow, too, but somehow it seemed wrong not to see them on Sunday. She'd planned in advance to take them dinner and stay for a couple of hours this evening.

She'd considered not changing, but if other drivers in town saw an Amishwoman driving a car, she might be enough of a distraction to cause an accident.

Lilian produced her usual, warm smile. "*Ja.* Don't forget the casserole and cookies. And the peas! They'll enjoy peas fresh from the garden, for certain sure."

Hannah smiled. "Ach, I remember fine."

Her teasing passed unnoticed.

"And be careful driving home in the dark," Lilian added.

Adah carried the lidded container filled with cookies while Hannah managed her rarely used handbag, the covered casserole, and the peas, picked just before she went in to change.

The drive should have given her time to decompress— *think of it like Superman's telephone booth*, she told herself wryly—but it didn't really work. The less often she got behind the wheel of the car, the less she enjoyed driving. It was silly, given that the whole route was on country roads, but her timidity came out when she got stuck for a stretch behind a wagon pulled by two draft horses. The bed of the wagon was piled high with lumber and a couple of doors and some wrapped objects that might be windows. She started to edge out once to pass, but an oncoming car was so close, it scared her back into her lane.

On her way home this evening, she'd probably drive ten miles under the speed limit. She never liked driving in the dark.

Finally in town, she parked at the senior complex, looked nervously around in case her mother was lying in wait, and then piled the cookies atop the bag of peas and the casserole and went up to her grandparents' apartment.

When the door opened, she was smiling . . . until she

realized it was her mother there in front of her. Inside her grandparents' apartment.

For a too-long moment, she didn't move.

Jodi didn't even acknowledge the shock on Hannah's face, only exclaimed, "Oh, you're here at last! I'm so excited. It's been ages since I've eaten your cooking. And, of course, I'm excited to spend time with you."

Hannah flicked a glance beyond her mother's shoulder, but couldn't see Helen. "You set a trap," she said flatly, keeping her voice low. "You know I can't turn around and walk away."

Mom did sad eyes so well. "Oh, but . . . I've missed you so much."

Hannah opened her mouth, but shut it when Helen appeared behind her daughter, smile bright but worry in her eyes.

"Hannah, I'm so glad you could come. I was talking to Jodi earlier, and, well—"

"She inveigled you into inviting her." She managed to keep her tone light, and was glad when she saw the relief on her grandmother's face.

"What an armload!" Helen said. "Let me take—"

"Oh, I'm closer," Jodi said sweetly, taking the top few items from the pile Hannah carried. "Oh, my! What did you bring?"

"Nothing that fancy. A casserole, and fresh peas straight from the garden. And cookies."

Jodi headed toward the kitchen, saying blithely over her shoulder, "Have you had Hannah's cookies, Mom? She's the world's best cook."

Helen gripped Hannah's arm to stop her. "I'm so sorry," she whispered. "I should have warned you."

Giving her grandmother a one-armed hug, Hannah said, "It'll be fine. As long as she doesn't demand a heart-to-heart with me."

"I'll make sure she doesn't have a chance," Helen said firmly.

Hannah said hi to her grandfather and kissed his cheek before going to the kitchen, where she popped the casserole in the oven for a quick reheat. Knowing where everything in the small kitchen was kept, she took out a pan from beneath the stove for the peas and began shelling them.

"Why don't you let me help you?" Jodi suggested. Her voice had a lilt, because she was sure they were all so happy. She still sounded girlish.

And yes, Hannah thought fiercely, it felt more natural to think of her by her name than as Mom. Since Hannah had reached adulthood, her mother had liked being called Jodi. She would giggle and say, "Because I can't possibly be old enough to have a child in her twenties!"

I don't feel *the same about her.*

She said, "Thanks, but I'm quick. Fresh peas don't take long to cook, you know."

Helen asked for help setting the table. Her back to them, Hannah closed her eyes for a moment. She remembered praying that first time she drove a horse and buggy, but now . . . no. She could be nice for her grandparents' sake. This would be another important memory for Robert: his entire family, sitting around the table, everyone smiling.

Helen helped her husband move to the small dining area, his oxygen tank with him. Hannah placed the hot casserole dish on a pad in the middle of the table, the bowl of peas beside it.

Once they'd all taken their seats, Helen prayed. Hannah had already begun a silent one of her own. Not the Amish Prayer before Meals, but rather the Lord's Prayer.

Our Father who art in heaven,
hallowed be Thy name.
Thy kingdom come.
Thy will be done
on earth as it is in heaven.
Give us this day our daily bread,

and forgive us our trespasses,
as we forgive those who trespass against us,
and lead us not into temptation,
but deliver us from evil.

Oh, yes, she needed the reminder. She greatly feared she'd never feel the same about her mother again, but she had to find forgiveness in her heart.

Chapter Fourteen

❖◆❖

GIDEON FORKED A bite of scrambled eggs into his mouth, Zeb and Rebekah doing the same. He swallowed before, without a word, reaching for the saltshaker. Pepper, too, he decided. His scrambled eggs did not taste like Hannah's. She'd spoiled him. Not only him, he saw, watching his *kinder* push their eggs around on their plates with an obvious lack of enthusiasm.

Mondays had become his least favorite day of the week, he thought, and not for the first time.

Fortunately, Hannah had baked enough bread Saturday afternoon to keep them until tomorrow. He reached for a buttered slice of toast, certain to be good.

"Daadi?"

He smiled at his daughter. *"Ja?"*

"I liked seeing Hannah Sunday. Is she Amish now?"

"No, she was only visiting. She has been dressing plain out of respect for Samuel and the rest of her family."

"And us." Zeb lifted his chin pugnaciously.

"Ja. And us." Although he had no idea whether that was

true. "You know she only plans to stay for a couple of months. I should start looking for someone to replace her."

"No!" Tears filled Rebekah's eyes, and she scrambled off her chair. "I don't want anyone else! I want Hannah!" She ran for the stairs, her breakfast barely touched.

Gideon shoved back his chair. "Rebekah!"

Upstairs, a door slammed.

He bent a warning stare on Zeb, who resumed eating.

It was a mistake not to go after Rebekah—but her distress was real. She never caused him trouble. Being hungry this morning at school would be consequence enough.

His interest in his own breakfast had waned, but he made himself continue eating. Unlike the *kinder*, he could slip back to the house for a sandwich after he walked them to school, but he didn't like to dump food in the compost bin, and there was nothing wrong with what was in front of him.

"Hannah is really going to leave?" Zeb asked in a small voice.

"So she said. She warned me when I hired her that she could only stay for a month or two. You knew that. It's been a month already."

"Maybe she changed her mind."

Gideon wished he felt as hopeful as Zeb sounded.

Maybe *he* should ask her.

And maybe it would be better if she left soon. He'd never anticipated his *kinder* getting so attached to her. The feelings she stirred up in him put him in danger of forgetting who and what he was. He couldn't let those feelings lead him into temptation, even if her generosity, her warmth, her vulnerability, and, *ja*, her slim, strong body with a woman's curves had captivated him from the beginning.

"She's a kind woman and a good cook," he told his son, "but she's not one of us. We can't forget that."

Zeb nodded, but he didn't meet his father's eyes. Instead, he picked up his plate and took it to the sink.

Gideon ended up scraping food from three plates into the kitchen waste container.

ZACHARIAH FRETFUL, HIS cheeks flushed, Lilian picked him up and cuddled him close. "Poor little one," she crooned, and laid her hand on his forehead. "Ach, he's getting sick."

"Just a cold, maybe," Hannah suggested.

"He has asthma. Usually he's fine, but whenever he's sick . . ."

"Is there anything I can do?"

From her seat beside the five-year-old, Lilian looked up. "Will you find Mose? He'll have to drive the girls to school."

"Mose's gone, remember? He's delivering one of his doghouses."

Lilian squeezed her eyes shut. "*Ja*, of course he is, and to Jacob Stutzman, all the way the other side of town."

Hannah had no idea who that was, but did know that "all the way the other side of town" encompassed another church district, the farthest geographically from her *daad*'s.

"I can drive them. *Daad* already harnessed Clover, didn't he?" The school wasn't much over a quarter mile past Gideon's farm. Okay, maybe a half mile.

"*Ja*, he said he would. Are you sure?"

She couldn't blame Lilian for the doubt in her eyes. It was the equivalent of an *Englisch* mother sending her young children off with a sixteen-year-old driver who had only had a learner's permit for a few weeks.

"I'm sure," she said steadily. "It's not that far past Gideon's. But, oh, you pick up the Graber *kinder*, too, don't you? Maybe it would be better if I take care of Zachariah while you go."

There was a distinct pause before her stepmother said, "No, no, if you'll drive the girls, I'll be glad. No need to pick up any other *kinder* today. I have the girls' lunches almost ready . . ."

Hannah touched her on the shoulder. "I'll finish them. Zachariah needs you."

Samuel hadn't, as it turned out, backed the mare between the shafts; however, Hannah had been watching him five mornings a week. Clover obligingly did her part, and Hannah was confident she'd fastened everything that needed to be attached.

"*Mamm* usually takes the other buggy," Emma commented as they set off.

"*Ja*, because she has to have room for the boys, too. Mose needed it this morning to haul a big doghouse."

"Clover knows the way," Adah assured her.

Hannah laughed and hugged her, knowing she was right. Probably, she didn't have to do a single thing. The mare would deliver them to the school doorstep, and take Hannah home after.

She was pleasantly surprised not to have a single panic attack during the drive, though two cars went by going the opposite direction and another one passed them.

Clover made the turn onto the hard-packed lane leading to the school. A tall man stepped to one side to let them pass, guiding his *kinder* to the verge, too. Feeling a quiver of surprise, Hannah waved as Adah and Emma shouted greetings.

The mare came to a neat stop next to another buggy, currently disgorging three *kinder*. By the time the girls jumped down, Rebekah and Zeb had run the rest of the way.

"Hannah! Why are you here today?" That was Zeb.

"I didn't eat *any* breakfast." Rebekah looked beseechingly at her. "I missed you."

"I saw you yesterday," Hannah reminded her. "We sat together for worship *and* for the fellowship meal."

The young girl's lower lip pushed out. "But—"

Having approached unseen, Gideon laid a hand on her *kapp*, firmly enough to compress the pleats.

Silenced, Rebekah ducked her head.

Suddenly noticing the bagged lunch forgotten on the floor of the buggy, Hannah called, "Adah!"

Of course, chatty Adah was already in the middle of a group, and Emma didn't hear Hannah call out, either. She smiled at Rebekah. "Would you take Adah's lunch to her?"

Rebekah gave the tiniest sniff. "*Ja*, she's my friend."

"I know she is."

"You're coming tomorrow, right?"

Very conscious of Gideon's presence, Hannah said, "I am."

"*Daadi* said—"

This time that big hand came to rest on her shoulder. "Not now, Rebekah. See, Tabitha is about to ring the bell."

The young schoolteacher had indeed appeared on the porch. Several late-arriving *kinder* trotted past Gideon. The other buggy—Hannah recognized the woman in it, but couldn't remember her name—circled around in front of Clover and, after a cheerful wave, set off down the lane.

"Would you like a ride?" Hannah asked, feeling a little foolish.

His eyes seemed darker than ever when he looked at her, and creases in his forehead deepened, but then he nodded. "*Ja*, just down the road. *Denke*."

The buggy rocked when he climbed in, taking up more space than the two girls combined. Gideon's muscular arm brushed her shoulder.

Painfully self-conscious, Hannah twitched the reins, and Clover pulled them in the tight semicircle to reverse direction.

"Rebekah seemed sad," she said, unable to withstand the silence.

"She wasn't happy this morning." He paused. "She didn't like my scrambled eggs."

He was speaking English, she realized. Because he didn't know some of the words?

"Really? There's not much you can do to ruin them."

His shoulders tightened, then loosened with a long breath. "They were runny. I should have used more salt."

"Oh. A little grated cheese can do wonders." Feta was even better, but she suspected that wasn't a usual part of the Amish diet.

"I'll remember that."

"If you had bread left, you could use it to make French toast. If you add cinnamon—" Hannah throttled the rest of her happy homemaker advice. It occurred to her that he might be using the switch to English, rather than their usual mishmash, to set her at a distance. Or was he just being considerate?

Clover slowed, and Hannah checked both ways to be sure there was no oncoming traffic before they turned onto the paved road. They'd be at Gideon's driveway in minutes. She knew he'd refuse any offer to take him all the way up to the house.

"She was unhappy for other reasons," he said suddenly. "We can talk about it tomorrow."

"Okay." Hannah had become accustomed to Rebekah's sunny, willing nature that had increasingly blossomed now that she felt less vulnerable.

"I was surprised to see you this morning."

"Zachariah looked like he has a fever. Lilian says when he comes down with a cold, he has trouble with asthma." She had a sudden thought. "He doesn't go out that often. I hope it wasn't going around yesterday. A bunch of the *kinder* might get sick."

"*Ja*," Gideon agreed, with no apparent concern. "It happens."

Of course it did. Colds and the flu and even measles had roared through the students at schools she'd attended. Those had been among the loneliest times in her life, when she'd been left home alone and sick because her mother couldn't take time off from her job. The only time she'd been really scared to be alone was when she had the measles. She'd been seriously ill. Mostly, she understood. Mom had to work to get paid so they could buy groceries and pay rent.

That time, though, Mom had had to take her to a walk-in clinic. The doctor had been really annoyed with her mother, who hadn't kept up with Hannah's vaccines.

Predictably, Gideon said, "You can let me out here. I need to check phone messages."

"Oh. Sure." She reined the mare to a stop.

He didn't move immediately. "You saw your mother yesterday, didn't you?"

She let herself meet his eyes. "How can you tell?"

"You're like Rebekah today." His answer seemed to disturb him. "Sad, or worried, I don't know."

"I took supper to my grandparents last night. She was there."

"You didn't know?"

Hannah shook her head. "Grandma and Granddad are mad at her, but she's their daughter. I understood, even though . . ." She stopped. "For them, seeing her after all these years may be bitter, but also sweet."

He frowned, but also nodded. "*Ja*. Have they forgiven her?"

Hannah hadn't thought of it that way, but seeing the way Robert watched his daughter had almost made her cry.

"I think so. I'm glad they did, for Granddad's sake."

"You're still angry."

She heaved a sigh. "I am."

There was the lightest touch on her arm, and then he got out. She turned her head to see a gentle expression on a face more often impassive.

"Forgiveness is necessary, but there are times we all

struggle with it," he said unexpectedly, then turned his back and stepped into the three-sided phone shanty.

Deciding to follow his example, she skipped the whole "goodbye, I'll see you in the morning" thing, instead clicking at Clover. A few strides later, the mare achieved her usual smooth trot.

GIDEON DISLIKED FEELING indecisive, a state that had come and gone ever since he'd pushed aside his doubts and hired Hannah. Now that he knew her so much better, he was even more confused.

Until yesterday morning, he had let himself almost forget that Hannah was here temporarily. The reminder was best; he and the *kinder* had grown too comfortable with her, letting themselves need her in a way that could leave them bereft when she left.

He should press her for an end date so that they could prepare themselves, yet he didn't want to. He hadn't asked around about any young woman—or older one, a widow—who might step in when Hannah was gone. He dreaded the many irritations he'd felt with his previous employees, and worried especially about Rebekah.

Walking from the barn to the house for lunch on Tuesday, anticipating a good meal, he did battle with his reluctance to find out how little time they had left . . . even as he suspected it would be just as well, for many reasons, if her remaining time *were* cut short.

Hearing him come in, Hannah looked over her shoulder. He wasn't sure her bright smile reached her eyes.

"We're mostly having cold foods. I've never paid that much attention to temperatures before, but, wow, it's really starting to get hot out there."

Gideon hung his hat on the wall. "*Ja*, for May. Nothing compared to July and August."

She wrinkled her nose. "I'm used to air-conditioning in my apartment, my car, and the restaurant, not to mention all the stores."

He didn't know what to say. He did shop in stores in town that were air-conditioned, but for him stepping from the hot sun into an icy temperature was a shock, not that pleasant.

By the time he returned from splashing water on his face and neck, and scrubbing his hands and forearms, Hannah had set two places at the table and put out the usual array of serving dishes.

She'd made a cold potato salad today as well as a cucumber salad, also serving applesauce and sliced ham and cheese for sandwiches. The only hot dish was one he didn't recognize. He'd never seen a sauce that was green.

This wasn't the first time she'd tried new dishes with them. On a Saturday, they'd had tacos, refried beans, and spiced rice. That one hadn't been so strange, as there was often a taco stand at street fairs and mud sales. He, Zeb, and Rebekah had all loved her spaghetti with meatballs, and even an eggplant Parmesan she'd served with what she called tortellini soup.

They bent their heads in prayer. When that was over, he dished up the potato salad and a spoonful of the unfamiliar dish.

"That's, um, a Thai green curry. I just thought I'd keep experimenting."

She watched somewhat anxiously as he took a bite of the vegetables coated in the sauce. Gideon tried to hide his reaction, but could tell from her face that he'd failed.

"So much for that!" she said, too brightly. "Don't worry, I won't make it again."

"I'm sorry—"

She jumped to her feet to grab the coffeepot and whisked the bowl holding the green curry to the counter. "I don't know what got into me. You notice I didn't try it on the kids.

I'm sure you'll be happier to hear that I also made my first ever shoofly pie," she told him as she poured his coffee. "I hope it's good."

"I haven't eaten anything you've ever made that wasn't good."

"Until now," she said ruefully.

"I might be able to get used to this Thai curry."

"Why do that?"

Gideon couldn't think of an answer. After a while, she asked whether he was pleased with Tabitha as a teacher.

"This is only her second year, but from what I've seen and the *kinder* tell me, *ja*. She's strict, but good with praise, and seems to know when the students are getting restless. She takes them for walks to collect leaves or seed pods to learn what grows around us, and borrowed a telescope from an *Englisch* neighbor so that one night the *kinder* could look more closely at the stars. When a student has a special interest, she brings books from the library." Which had gotten her into trouble a few times; the school board chairman, an unimaginative, strict man, had been unhappy that she'd fostered Paul Fisher's interest in medicine or Katie Wagler's in art. Gideon had heard talk that the Fisher boy wanted to be a paramedic or even a doctor, either of which would take him away from the *Leit*, but Gideon didn't think encouraging reading was necessarily a bad thing. Paul could use some of the skills of a paramedic as a volunteer firefighter, which many of the Amish were. Anyway, interests changed.

Although his former bishop had believed Gideon needed to be less accepting of anyone and anything outside their faith and their small community.

He was probably frowning by the time Hannah said, "She looks so young."

She? It took Gideon a moment to realize Hannah was talking about Tabitha.

"Only eighteen, I think. Our teachers are usually young women. Once they marry, they're replaced."

"Do you think eight years is enough education for anyone?"

"*Ja*, to live as our Lord asks of us. So much that is modern pulls a person away from a life based on faith." He hesitated. "Many also learn by becoming apprentices, and we allow our youth to take some additional classes." He studied her. "It's hard for *kinder* drawn by a need to serve as a nurse or doctor, or fascinated by computers. Not everyone chooses to keep the faith. But some leave, and come back when they understand what they've lost."

"Like Luke Bowman."

"*Ja*, he's one. I always knew I wanted to farm. I didn't need more school. And you. What use was what you learned in your high school classes once you were in the kitchen?"

"Probably not much, but I did go to culinary school." She told him some of what she'd learned, but admitted that much of that was hands-on.

"Is fancier cooking really better than what you make here?" he asked, genuinely curious.

"Honestly? I'm not so sure. I like to experiment, but sometimes restaurant critics rave about entrées that are innovative but not necessarily anything I'd want to eat."

As he hadn't wanted to eat that green curry.

"A lot of chefs are competitive—they live for getting the best reviews, opening their own restaurants where they can make the final decisions—but I've come to realize I'll never make it to the top. I'm glad when diners let the server know that they loved something I made, but . . ." She stopped, appearing bothered, but shaking her head. "It doesn't matter."

He wanted to pursue the subject, but her decisions once she left Tompkin's Mill didn't concern him. Even if she returned to visit her *grossmammi* and *daad* and his family, Gideon wasn't likely to see her.

And *that* was what they needed to talk about.

Setting down his fork, he said, "Yesterday morning, I had to remind the *kinder* that you don't intend to stay for very long." He hadn't meant to sound so brusque, but didn't apologize.

Dismay on her face, Hannah said, "That's why Rebekah was upset."

"*Ja.*"

"Sometimes I forget . . ."

When she stayed silent after letting her words trail off, Gideon asked, "What do you forget?"

"Oh, that I don't belong." One shoulder jerked. She wasn't looking at him. "That I'll be leaving."

He didn't like knowing that he'd stripped away any joy she'd had in the day. It confused him, too, that she looked sad about leaving.

"Why do you think you don't belong?" he asked. "Your family is here."

"Because I'm not Amish! They may be, but I'm not." Her eyes flared with anger, although he wasn't so sure that's what he was seeing. She yanked at a ribbon dangling from her *kapp.* "I'm pretending, and everyone knows it!"

For the first time, he wondered *why* she had started to dress plain and given up the technology that had to have been a big part of her life. Was it respect, as he'd assumed? Just an experiment? Fun, maybe, to get a good feel for what her life might have been like if her mother hadn't taken her away? If she were another woman, he'd have thought she would turn it into a big story she could tell her *Englisch* friends, except Hannah wouldn't do that. But now he became aware of an odd drumbeat of hope, an echo of one he'd felt Sunday.

Was it possible she had been testing the Amish life to find out if it was for her?

So he said, "You could become Amish, like Julia Bowman did."

Hannah's eyes widened, dilated pupils surrounded by

that swirl of green and gold. At last she stuttered, "But . . . but I'd be giving up so much."

"What would you be giving up, Hannah?"

She only blinked at him, seemingly dazed that he'd suggested something so wildly unlikely.

His appetite vanished. Gideon pushed back his chair. "I need to get back to work."

"But . . . there's pie."

"It will be good for dinner." He clapped his hat on his head and walked out, dodging the clean clothes and sheets hanging on the line outside. He was almost to the barn before he realized he had forgotten to ask his real question: *when* she expected to leave.

Chapter Fifteen

❖

HANNAH ADMIRED THE decision Julia Bowman had made. She did. But there were reasons most American women wouldn't make the same one. Especially women of their generation.

Obviously, it had been a mistake to try to blend in with her Amish family and the members of their church district. How many of them were assuming she'd convert? Thinking to themselves, ach, Samuel's daughter, of course she would.

As Hannah made the beds with clean sheets, replaced towels on racks and in the cupboards, and folded or hung clean clothes, she was conscious of strange, electric zings beneath her skin.

Panic. It had to be panic.

Instead of trying to find the source of the panic, she stayed busy. As she should. This was her job.

She swept, mopped the kitchen and downstairs bathroom floors, waxed the hardwood floors. Windows—no, it was time for her to leave to fetch Zeb and Rebekah. Windows tomorrow.

Usually, she'd be walking Jacob and Susan Miller's boy home, too, but when the schoolhouse door opened, the numbers that spilled out were much diminished.

Surprised, Hannah joined a couple of mothers to talk to Tabitha.

"All getting sick," she told them, resignedly, "only a cold, I think, but it's spreading fast."

"What happens if you get sick?" Hannah asked.

She looked surprised. "I have an assistant. You haven't met her? We will hope only one of us catches this cold."

"If that's all it is," a mother—Mara Eicher—muttered.

The others chimed in their agreement.

Hannah expected to have to cull Rebekah and Zeb from their friends, but today the two of them stood apart, as if no other *kinder* were present. Her instincts sharpened at seeing expressions that were so reserved. That was not natural for either of them.

She smiled, hugged Rebekah, and briefly touched Zeb on the back, and then looked around for Enoch Miller. When she called to him, he joined her.

His English, she'd discovered, was inadequate for conversation, so she switched to her less-than-perfect *Deitsh*. "Did you have a good day?"

"Ja!" Clearly in a good mood, he said, "We sang my favorite hymn, and Tabitha hung my drawing on the wall. We played baseball, and *Mamm* sent a *big* molasses cookie for my lunch."

"That does sound like a good day." She gave him a sidelong hug as they started walking.

This was Enoch's first year of school, as it was Rebekah's. Susan had said that he'd be turning seven in June.

She turned her attention to Zeb and Rebekah. "How about you two?"

Zeb shrugged. Rebekah mumbled something Hannah didn't make out, but she decided not to press the issue until they were alone.

When they reached the road, Zeb found a rock to kick, and kept kicking with a viciousness that startled her. She'd say something if he left it on the road, since she wasn't sure what would happen if the narrow wheels of a buggy ran into it, but he obviously needed to vent anger somehow.

They walked Enoch halfway up his driveway, at which point they could see Susan on the porch of his house waving. Yelling, *"Mammi!"* Enoch broke into a run, and Hannah waved back. Then she and Gideon's *kinder* turned around.

Expecting one or the other of them to start complaining right away, she was surprised by the continuing silence. Zeb all but had a dark storm cloud hanging over his head, while Rebekah's shoulders were hunched as if in preparation for blows. They might dread going home if they'd done something to stir their father's temper— But she knew right away that wasn't it. They'd been cheerful this morning during breakfast and the walk to school. No, whatever had happened was during the day.

Zeb found his rock again and gave it a huge kick, almost falling down before he regained his balance.

"Can we talk about why you're mad?" Hannah ventured.

"No!" he shouted, and ran up the driveway.

Rebekah trudged along beside Hannah, never looking up.

This time, Hannah asked, *"Was is letz?"* What is wrong?

After a minute, the little girl said, "They were talking about our *mamm* today, and they never even *knew* her! When Zeb told them to shut their traps, he got in trouble with Teacher Tabitha."

"I'm sorry. Was it all your classmates?"

"Mostly some of the girls." She named several, the names familiar to Hannah but not matching up to faces. Older *kinder*, then.

"We should have told them they're *doppicks*!"

"You know what the Lord would say about that," Hannah said gently.

Rebekah stole a look at her. "You mean, to turn the other cheek?"

Zeb had disappeared, Hannah hoped into the house and not off to hide in the woods or the huge, shadowy interior of the barn. "I was thinking of Proverbs," she said. "'A soft answer turns away wrath, But a harsh word stirs up anger.'"

"Oh. But it's not fair if we can't argue!"

Hannah smiled, even though she didn't feel like it. "I didn't say you can't, but there is a smart way to do it instead of an angry way that only makes the other person mad."

Rebekah's face crumpled. She cried, "I don't want to go to school tomorrow," and ran for the house.

Hannah hesitated only briefly. Longing to find Gideon—he was the one who should be having this talk with his *kinder*—she wasn't willing to leave them alone. He'd be in for dinner in only another two hours. Keeping them busy might be a better idea than trying to find out what the older girls had actually *said*.

BOTH *KINDER* SAT at the table, backs to him, when Gideon came in through the mudroom. There was no sign of Hannah. The kitchen smelled enticing, but it puzzled him that neither of the *kinder* so much as turned a head. Had they gone deaf?

Zeb appeared to be doing schoolwork. Hunched over it, he kept bouncing the heels of his boots on the legs and rungs of the chair as if he wanted to break them. Intent on her task, Rebekah used the open mouth of a canning jar to cut out dough before dropping the circles onto a cookie sheet. She was only concentrating, he hoped, but had a bad feeling.

"It wonders me that nobody wants to say hello to their *daadi*," he said.

Zeb gave him a sullen look. "I have to finish this."

"I'm helping Hannah," his daughter said.

After hanging up his hat, he went to her and kissed the top of her head. "Where is she?"

"The cellar."

Fortunately, Hannah appeared just then, two jars in her hands. Was that relief flooding her face? What could be so wrong?

"Gideon. We're a little behind on dinner."

"So I see."

"I'm sor—"

"I can wait."

He thought she might be trying to send him a message with her eyes, but he didn't understand it.

She set the jars on the counter and faced the rest of them. "This might be a good time to talk to your *daad*," she said quietly.

Alarm brought Zeb's head up. "It was just dumb girls! *Daad* doesn't have to hear about it!"

Rebekah kept her head down.

"Do you think the girls made up what they whispered about?" Hannah waited. Neither of the *kind* responded. "Or were they repeating something they heard at home?"

Now both Zeb and Rebekah gaped at her.

"If adults are gossiping, too, your father *does* need to know."

"But . . . *Daadi* won't like it," Rebekah said.

"It's his job to protect you, not yours to protect him." She knotted her fingers together in front of her.

Thinking about her mother, Gideon guessed. The mother who hadn't always protected her.

But he had to concentrate on his *kinder*, who had heard whispers today they thought might hurt him. Already suspecting the topic, he circled the table and pulled out a chair so that he could look into their faces.

"If people are saying bad things, we can't hide from it," he said. "It's better to set them right."

"I wanted to tell them they're *doppicks!*" Rebekah burst out.

Zeb's expression grew rebellious.

Behind him, Hannah asked, "Would you rather I leave early so you can talk alone?"

He should say yes. She was an *auslander*. But his *kinder* showed renewed alarm . . . and she spent so much time with them these days, keeping disturbing rumors making their way around at school from her wasn't practical.

"*Denke* for offering, but it would be good of you to stay." He turned in his seat. "Unless you'd rather—?"

"No. I'll keep working on supper. Are you done there?" she asked Rebekah.

"Except there's more dough."

She spoke as kindly as always. "Let me ball it up and flatten it out."

"I hope you didn't call anyone a *doppick*," Gideon said to his small daughter.

"Uh-uh. But Zeb said—"

Her brother knocked into her with his shoulder. "You're a big fat *blabbermaul!*"

"I am not! *Daadi*, tell him!"

"You don't talk to your sister like that," Gideon said sternly. "You know better than that."

"She's just trying to get me into trouble."

"You already *got* in trouble," Rebekah retorted, glaring at Zeb.

"You don't have to tell everything!"

"Quiet," Gideon snapped. "Both of you."

Expressions sullen, they both shut their mouths.

His gaze went first to Zeb. "How did you get into trouble?"

He shot an evil look at his sister. "I told those girls they didn't know what they were talking about, and they should shut up! Only, *they* went running to Teacher. She made me sit by myself facing the wall."

Gideon shook his head. He had been in more trouble than that as a schoolboy. He wouldn't make an issue of this, since Tabitha had already dealt with Zeb's behavior in the way that seemed best to her at the time. This was one of those times when Gideon refused to follow his own father's example of wielding a leather strap on his son's bared back.

Tears springing into her eyes, Rebekah said, "Hannah told me . . ." She looked an appeal at the *Englisch* woman. "What was it you said?"

"It was a quote from Proverbs." In a gentle voice, she said, "'A soft answer turns away wrath, But a harsh word stirs up anger.' I've always found that to be true."

Surprised that she'd turned to the Bible, although he didn't know why as it wasn't the first time she'd done so, Gideon only nodded. "*Ja*, I, too, have found it so." He was ashamed to have erupted in anger a couple of times after Leah's death, his grief eroding his self-control. That anger, as much as grief and bewilderment, played a part in setting him and his *kinder* apart from their brethren. Now, he was able to continue calmly, "And nobody likes to be called names. Did these girls tell you what they'd heard to your face? Or were they gossiping and didn't mean you to overhear?"

"Half the students were out sick today," Hannah put it. "The group was small."

"They saw us," Rebekah said. "And they were talking *loud*."

Gideon nodded meaninglessly. Dread filled his chest until he felt as if he might be sick, too. But avoiding a problem never did any good.

"What was it that these girls said?" he asked.

Zeb and Rebekah exchanged a glance, the squabbling between them set aside.

Rebekah answered. "I heard Bernice telling her friends that our *mamm* was running away from us when she was killed. That she was going and wouldn't come back, and she was always at the bottle." Her tone suggested she didn't know what that meant, but it was obvious from Zeb's fierce scowl that he did.

"And Zillah told Yonnie that *mammi* was in the car with a *man*." Zeb threw his pencil across the room. "And he was *Englisch*!"

Gideon closed his eyes. He didn't bother asking himself how such stories had reached their settlement in Missouri from so far away. The Amish were noted correspondents. All it would have taken was for one of the local women, writing to a cousin or friend, to mention that a Gideon Lantz and his two *kinder* had moved from New York to join their church district not that long ago. The surprise was that this hadn't happened sooner.

He liked his neighbors and sisters and brothers in the church. He called several men friends. But if two of the girls at school were talking, that made it likely these hateful stories had already spread locally. Why had no one come to him? Although, with the exception of Jake Miller, whose boy was in his first year, none of Gideon's closest friends had *kinder* of school age and might well not have heard this talk.

Had somebody in his old settlement actually written such vicious untruths? Or did the recipient enjoy adding nasty detail to an already hurtful truth?

And what was he to say to Zeb and Rebekah? They had been so young when their mother was killed in a car accident, he hadn't told them everything. They didn't need to know more than the basics. He'd believed *he* didn't need to find out whether his own wife had been drinking alcohol. He wouldn't permit himself to doubt her. Now, he thought maybe he should have agreed to allow the authorities to check her blood-alcohol level, too. If nothing else, that might have silenced some of the most poisonous talk.

Swallowing, he opened his eyes to take in the scared faces of the two people he loved most in the world.

"First," he said, praying they wouldn't notice the roughness in his voice, "your *mamm* was not in the car with any man. Do you remember her *Englisch* friend? Brooke Stephenson?"

"I think so," Rebekah said uncertainly.

Zeb frowned. "I always thought that was a funny name."

"Not funny, only *Englisch*."

Behind him, Hannah remained utterly silent but for the occasional clatter of a spoon on a bowl or the hiss of oil heating on the stove. He wished he knew what she was thinking.

"But she was nice," Zeb said. "*Mammi* wouldn't let us get in her car, but Brooke brought us cheeseburgers and french fries sometimes. Or pizzas."

In allowing the friendship, one of the restrictions that Gideon had set in place was that their *kinder* never get in the car, even when it was parked. How often had he wished since then that he'd also insisted his wife never go with her friend in the car? Brooke could have visited Leah at their house or met her in town. But rationally, he knew that being on the road in a car was no more dangerous than being in a buggy. Less so, maybe.

Being in a car with a drunk driver, that was something else.

"Brooke was driving when the accident happened. And your *mamm* was *not* leaving us. She would never have done that. She loved you so much."

Him, too, he thought, but he had, from time to time, wondered whether her close friendship with Brooke suggested Leah had regrets. She'd committed herself; he had never doubted she would keep that commitment. But she had been so excited when she drove away in that car with her single friend for a visit, or for an adventure. She wasn't as excited about visits with her Amish friends, or to worship with her sisters and brothers in the church.

Although perhaps the way of her death had altered his memories of his wife.

Whatever those private thoughts, he would never cast any shade on his *kinder*'s memories of their mother.

Zeb and Rebekah stared at him, maybe sensing there was more he didn't want to say. But wasn't that the important part? Leah was with a female friend; she was certainly not running away from home. They had both died in a car accident.

"Now you can tell anyone who speaks about her that the stories they heard are false. Brooke had been your *mamm*'s very good friend from the time they were three or four years old. Brooke's parents lived right next to your grandparents' land. Baptism and marriage don't mean an Amishman or woman has to cut off a good friend." He did believe that, but guilt still nudged him to fear that his failure to set boundaries on that friendship made him partially responsible for the tragedy. And keeping an *Englischer* as a friend was fine—as long as that person wasn't trying to undermine the Amish person's faiths and values. As Brooke may have been doing. He went on, "Most of us aren't quite so close to any *Englisch* friends as your *mamm* was, but many Amish have them. So long as they respect our beliefs," he tacked on, "it is always good to have friends."

"But . . ." Rebekah spoke barely above a whisper. "Why was *Mammi* in a *car*? We're never s'posed to drive in cars."

"That isn't true. The three of us came all the way to Missouri on a bus. You remember that." It had been a nightmarish trip, his *kinder* sunk in gloom yet also having trouble sitting in one seat for so many hours. He had been plagued the entire way with fear that he'd made a mistake leaving family and a prosperous farm behind, tearing his young *kinder* from everything loved and familiar.

But not from everything safe, Gideon reminded himself. They had shrunk from whispers, as he had, and become increasingly fearful. Rebekah and Zeb had clung together, even sharing a bedroom for comfort. He'd had to sit with them at night until they fell asleep. Many nights, one or the other woke crying out from a nightmare. They were afraid riding in a buggy, afraid anytime he was out of sight.

He had increasingly believed he had made the right decision. Until now.

"We are permitted to ride in a car when we have good reason—to visit someone who lives too far away for us to go in a buggy, or if an emergency arises. When Hannah's *grossdaadi*, James, had a stroke, Samuel and Lilian called George for a ride to the hospital so they could get there as fast as possible."

"I saw Toby Esch riding in a car with an *Englisch girl*," Zeb said.

Gideon hoped he hid his wince. "During your *rumspringa*, you will be allowed to do things like ride in cars, have a cell phone and even an iPod to listen to music. I hope, when you reach that age, you won't be foolish, but it's important to look outside our Amish way of life to be certain that you can be baptized with a whole heart. Once Toby is ready to be baptized, he won't ride in a car again just for fun."

Looking thoughtful, Zeb nodded. "So *Mammi* wasn't doing anything wrong when she was in the accident."

"That's what you should say," he agreed. "I'll need to talk to the parents of some of the *kinder* who were telling tales, and probably Bishop Amos, too."

They sat quiet for a minute. Finally, Zeb said, "*Daadi?* Can we have dinner now?"

"*Ja*, certain sure. We'll all like that. And then we can have pie."

"I bet Hannah makes the best shoofly pie."

Gideon assumed the same, but would have to talk to Zeb someday about using a word like *bet*. Laying bets was not something a good Amishman would do, nor did they believe in luck. They trusted in God's will.

Only moments later, Hannah and Rebekah, who scrambled off her chair to help, had filled serving bowls and placed them on the table. When Hannah poured coffee for him, her eyes met his, and he had the very bad feeling she knew he hadn't told his *kinder* everything. When they were alone, would she challenge him, or keep her opinion to herself?

Strangely, Gideon didn't like either option.

Chapter Sixteen

❖

THEY ALL FELL back on routine with relief.

Rebekah helped put leftovers—and there were far more than usual—into containers to go into the refrigerator, then dried dishes as Hannah washed.

Zeb went out to spread seed for the chickens and close them into their coop for the night, after which he joined Gideon feeding animals, putting some in stalls, making sure gates were closed as they ought to be. Hannah knew one of Zeb's jobs was to fill the food and water bowls for the barn cats, too, before closing the big doors.

Once Hannah dried her hands and took a last look to make sure the kitchen was spotlessly clean, she walked out with Rebekah. Giving her a hug, she said, "I'll see you in the morning."

Small, thin arms squeezed her waist. "I wish you lived here," Rebekah whispered.

"Oh, honey . . ."

"I know you can't, but—" Rebekah released her and backed away. "Zeb and I are going to play baseball."

Really, she'd try to throw a plastic ball near enough to her brother for him to hit it. The first time Hannah saw them doing it, Rebekah had also been required to run and fetch the ball wherever it landed. Gideon spoke to his son, and now they took turns with the fetching. Zeb even reluctantly let her bat sometimes.

"Have fun," she said.

Zeb raced past her toward his sister, calling, "Bye," over his shoulder.

Gideon had already harnessed Clover and was backing her between the shafts. Hannah thought she could do it all now, but would hate to find out she hadn't connected something important when horse and buggy separated halfway home.

Not home.

The reminder came by rote, but she had to keep renewing it. She didn't understand why, since she and her mother had never lived anywhere long enough for her really to feel as if she were home. Samuel's house was at least her original home, yet while her *Deitsh* had come back, not many memories had. The warm welcome to her *daad*'s house, even the knowledge that it once had been home, didn't make her feel any less like a guest. Someone temporary, as she'd always been.

She'd lived longer in her apartment in Lexington than she had anywhere else since her mother stole her away, but she suspected apartments never quite felt like home. Right now, she couldn't think of anything she'd left behind that she missed.

Remembering what Gideon had said was inescapable. *What would you be giving up, Hannah?* His question had nibbled at her when she was on the edge of sleep at night.

The panic intensified. Throw over the life she had? At least it was familiar, safe.

Lonely.

She hadn't been in Tompkin's Mill very long, certainly not long enough to think about taking such a drastic step as Gideon had suggested. Was she capable of trusting in God that much?

Be practical, she told herself. Small steps. She wasn't making enough money working for Gideon to be able to keep paying for an apartment she didn't live in. What she should do was hire someone to pack up her stuff and store all of it until she knew where she was going next.

Hannah hated the not knowing. It brought back too many bad memories.

She reached the buggy and, as always, said, "*Denke*, Gideon. I guess I'm not quite ready to harness Clover myself."

"It makes no trouble. I would prefer to keep doing it for you," he said with a finality that didn't surprise her.

She nodded and got in, repeating, "I'll see you in the morning."

"*Ja.*" But he didn't step back. "You were a help with the *kinder*, when they were upset."

Surprising herself, she said, "I know what it feels like to hear other people whispering about you at school. Or even saying awful things to your face."

A frown creased Gideon's forehead. "Why did that happen to you?"

She shrugged, as if to tell him it hadn't been a big deal then, and certainly wasn't now. When that, of course, was a lie.

"We were always poor. I had to wear dirty clothes sometimes, and there were stretches when I got the free school lunch because Mom couldn't afford to give me money for hot lunches, and there was nothing in the house for me to take. Usually it was something like a peanut butter sandwich. Everyone who saw me eating knew I was one of those kids. A few times, one of Mom's men hit me, and I had to hide bruises."

He looked stunned at that, or perhaps at her entire speech. Kindness and charity, qualities that mattered to the Amish, had been notably missing in much of her childhood.

"She ran away from Samuel for men who would hit a *kind*?" he asked incredulously.

"That's one thing she didn't put up with, not violence aimed at her or me. But when she left them, we'd have to move again and start all over." In her recent impassioned speeches, Jodi claimed Samuel *had* hurt her. The fact that running away from him fit her pattern introduced some doubt in Hannah's mind. Doubt she hated to entertain.

She had no idea why she'd just told Gideon all this. Because she'd sensed his humiliation at the stories being passed around at school?

"I guess I grew a thick skin, eventually. Ah . . ."

"I know what that means." He rolled his shoulders in an unusual betrayal of his discomfort before saying abruptly, "I think tomorrow I should walk Rebekah and Zeb to school so I can talk to Tabitha."

Telling herself she was just as glad he hadn't felt an obligation to express sympathy, Hannah pulled herself back from hurtful memories to the current situation.

"That might be a good idea, although it will embarrass them if she says anything to the class in general."

He nodded. "I've decided I should speak to our bishop next. Better he should talk to the parents than me."

Was he asking for her opinion? From the way he watched her, she thought he might be. "Talking to the parents individually would be really awkward. They might feel like you're challenging them, on top of criticizing their *kinder*. Some people would get defensive."

Gideon nodded, turned away, and strode toward the house.

He planned to keep his secrets, then. Twitching the reins to start Clover in motion, she asked herself why she'd thought for a minute he would tell her what he hadn't wanted his own *kinder* to know.

She wished she didn't have an uneasy feeling that Zeb, at least, had noticed the gaps around the little his *daad* had been willing to tell them.

NOT LIKING TO waste half a workday, Gideon had driven his *kinder* to school a little early and spoken privately to Tabitha. Only now, on his way to town, did he realize how difficult that had been. *Ja*, she was the teacher, but he didn't like having to share painful events from his past with a woman . . . ach, not quite young enough to be his daughter, but closer than he liked. If she'd been ten years older, seasoned by life, he might have talked to her for more than five minutes. As it was, he told her no more than he had Zeb and Rebekah.

He could have waited until evening to meet with Amos Troyer, but then he would have had to ask Hannah to stay late or taken the *kinder* with him. He wouldn't want her to have to drive home in the dark. Anyway, it was a rare day that Amos couldn't step away from his business for a few minutes to speak with a member of the church.

The bishop was actually behind the counter of his thriving bulk-food store when Gideon came in through the front door. Just done ringing up the purchases of an *Englisch* couple on an old-fashioned cash register, he nodded at Gideon while chatting amiably with them. After they left, he came to Gideon.

"Are you here to shop?"

"No, Hannah has done all of our shopping since she started. You may have seen her."

"*Ja*, I have. Loading her purchases in the back of her car."

Gideon felt an instinctive need to defend her. "She drives

it each weekend when she comes into town to see her *Englisch* grandparents. I think she isn't yet confident enough to take a horse and buggy onto busier streets."

Amos chuckled. "I'm not surprised. I passed her one day, out with Samuel's buggy and mare. I waved, but she was concentrating so hard, she didn't see."

Gideon grinned. "The first day she came to work in the buggy by herself, she was shaking, so scared."

"Ach, we'd be frightened if we had to drive a car on the highway," Amos said tolerantly. He glanced toward the counter, where an Amishwoman had planted herself after placing her few selections to be tallied. "Come in back with me. I'll send Obie out to wait on any customers."

He did greet the woman on the way back, saying someone would help her in just a minute. Obie, a scrawny Amish boy with acne, abandoned a carton half-emptied and hurried to the front, leaving Gideon and Bishop Amos in a cavernous space with a huge door that currently stood open as if a shipment was expected or had just been received. Boxes towered along walls, smaller ones filling rows of metal shelving. No break room—three metal chairs had been set up in a corner by a whiteboard on the wall that displayed a hand-scrawled work schedule.

Amos waved Gideon to a chair and sat himself. "What troubles you, Gideon?"

Gideon was glad that, when he first moved to Missouri, he'd told Amos some of the reasons he'd chosen to leave his former church district. *Ja*, he had kept his guilt and doubts to himself, but he had even been frank about the tongue-lashing from his former bishop he'd been compelled to accept with bowed head. Perhaps he had earned it, but he'd needed something besides a heavy dose of blame when he was grieving for the wife he'd loved and for all his *kinder* had lost. Later, he could have listened to criticism of his own choices in the spirit of *Gelassenheit*, but just then, hurting, he'd needed support.

Now Gideon repeated what older students at school had been whispering yesterday. "Maybe not whispering," he amended. "Talking loud enough for Rebekah and Zeb both to hear."

Creases on Amos's well-worn face deepened. "I hadn't heard any of this."

"I assumed you hadn't, but these *kinder* must have heard these rumors from their parents. Why did nobody come to ask me about what they'd been told instead of spreading gossip? I know I'm a newcomer—"

"You're a member of our church district." Amos rarely interrupted, but he made an exception this time. "You've been generous with your time and money for those who needed help, kind to some of our more difficult members." Not some: Esther Schwartz. "I will certainly speak to the parents. If you find there are others, let me know."

"It's likely all the other students heard the same things Rebekah and Zeb did, and will go home to tell *their* parents. The one blessing is that the younger ones won't pay attention."

Sharp brown eyes examined him. "Is there any truth to these stories beyond what you've told me?"

Throat tight, Gideon squeezed out what he must say. "You know my wife's friend was speeding and caused the accident. She hit another car head-on. That driver died, too. He was a teenage boy, an *Englischer*. At first the police assumed he'd been speeding, a new driver and young, but they can map what happened by rubber the car tires leave on the road. It was Leah's friend who was driving too fast, who crossed the yellow line." Here was the part he hadn't said. "She was drunk."

Amos blinked and sat back. "Your Leah?" he asked, after a minute.

"They had no reason to test her blood, since she wasn't driving. She was a modest, loving woman, a good wife."

"She must have known her friend had been drinking."

"*Ja*, but what was she to do?" he asked. How many times had he tried to put himself into her head? "The walk home would have been many miles. We checked telephone messages every few days, maybe. If she'd called, she'd have had to wait for hours wherever she was, until I grew worried enough because she was late coming home to check messages at the phone shanty. Perhaps her friend had had a few drinks before when they had lunch, but driven safely. I don't know."

"Not knowing what she thought and felt is the kind of thing that can torment a man."

"It is," Gideon conceded. "I pleaded many times for God not to forsake me, and I have faith that He didn't. It's said He is near to those who have a broken heart, and I felt that. For the *kinder*, understanding that He called Leah home because He needed her is harder, but they try."

"Then let us pray now."

Gideon was not surprised that the bishop chose Psalms 23:4.

The Lord is my shepherd; I shall not want. He makes me to lie down in green pastures; He leads me beside the still waters. He restores my soul; He leads me in the paths of righteousness for His name's sake.

Yea, though I walk through the valley of the shadow of death, I will fear not evil; For You are with me; Your rod and Your staff, they comfort me.

Head bowed, Gideon murmured, "Amen." These were words that did comfort him. In that moment, he knew he had been right to uproot his *kinder* and move. His Lord had led him here, to a bishop both wise and kind.

Amos did ask him for the names of the students who'd been so eager to tell scandalous tales to their friends. Betrayed as Gideon felt, at least none of the parents were ones he knew well, although he thought the boy, Yonnie, might be Rebecca King's younger brother.

The bishop looked pained, and said, "They need to be

reminded that Matthew told us, 'Therefore, whatever you want men to do to you, do also to them, for this is the Law and the Prophets.'" He smiled at Gideon and laid a hand on his arm. "For you, 'Then Jesus said, Father, forgive them; for they know not what they do.'"

The verse from Luke was also familiar to Gideon, who replied, "*Denke* for the reminder. Yesterday, I let myself feel too much anger. I thought to go talk to the parents myself, but that would have been a mistake."

"Taking time to reason with yourself before you act is smart when quick action isn't required to help another person."

Gideon rose to his feet. "Talking to you has eased me. I'll let you get back to work, while I do the same."

On the trip home, he urged his gelding to a brisker-than-usual pace. It would be good to accomplish something before stopping for lunch.

Even more, though, he sought the reassurance of seeing Hannah.

Instead, as he started up the driveway, he saw a young Amishwoman coming from his house to the road. She stepped hastily to one side to let the buggy pass. Not more than sixteen or seventeen years old, she was the schoolteacher's assistant.

Gideon reined in his horse. "Daniela?"

"I brought Rebekah home. She didn't feel good. Probably part of this sickness going around."

A new worry. He bent his head. "*Denke.* I'll go see how she is."

The girl hurried on, and he snapped the reins.

HANNAH WAS GLAD to hear the buggy, and peeked out to be sure it was Gideon.

She gently stroked a strand of hair back from Rebekah's forehead and tucked it under the *kapp*. "Your *daadi* is home. Do you want to wait to see him, or go straight to bed?"

Her eyes widened. "I want to lie down. If . . . if I can take a bowl with me."

"Of course you can." Hannah grabbed a sturdy ceramic bowl and ushered the six-year-old upstairs. She sat on the bed while Rebekah changed into her nightgown, giving passing thought to Julia and Miriam's promise to come to Gideon's house a couple of afternoons this week. She was grateful this was not one of those days.

When Rebekah was ready, Hannah tucked her in, hung up her dress and *kapp* on pegs on the wall, and closed the curtains. "I'll check on you often, I promise, but yell if you need me, *ja*?"

Rebekah's head bobbed.

Hannah bent to kiss her cool forehead, smiled again, and went downstairs just as the back door opened and closed with more force than sometimes.

Gideon was waiting for her at the foot of the staircase. "I saw Daniela Wagler."

"Oh! I was embarrassed because I didn't remember her name."

"She said Rebekah is sick."

"I just tucked her into bed, but . . ." She hesitated. "Can we talk in the living room?"

He nodded and let her go ahead of him. There, she sat in a wooden rocking chair and waited until he sank onto the sofa.

Then she said bluntly, "I don't think she's really sick. Daniela said she asked for permission to use the bathroom and came out saying she'd thrown up. I haven't taken her temperature yet, but she's cool to the touch, and she amended her story when I expressed surprise that she doesn't have a cold like the other sick *kinder*. Suddenly, she has a sore throat, too."

"You think it's an act."

"*Ja.* You saw how she was yesterday. She told me she didn't want to go to school today. I wish I'd said something to you."

His jaw tightened. "Lying isn't acceptable."

"No, but she's young. Maybe her stomach really *is* upset because she's so anxious. It's also possible one of those *kinder* taunted her before Teacher Tabitha called them in."

Gideon sighed and reached up to knead the back of his neck. "Back home, before we moved, Zeb did this once. The other students were talking then, too."

"But why? If their mother died in an accident . . ."

"*If?*" he snapped. "Do you think *I'm* lying?"

Stung by what was really an accusation, she exclaimed, "Of course not! But Zeb and Rebekah couldn't have been the first *kinder* in your former church district to have a parent who died. I know it can be awkward. Even as an adult, it's hard to know what to say to somebody who just lost a loved one. But if the talk was malicious . . ."

His shoulders were held tensely, almost braced. The stare from his dark eyes hadn't softened, either. "Malicious?"

Of course he didn't know what "malicious" meant. He was fluent, but that wasn't exactly an everyday word. "Nasty. Meant to be hurtful."

"Back then, it wasn't that, I don't think, but the *kinder* were curious, and too ready to share what they'd heard at home. I kept Zeb home from school for two weeks, but longer might have been better."

She'd sworn she wouldn't question him, but she needed to say this.

"I think you didn't tell them everything—"

"At their ages?" Once again, anger honed an edge to his voice.

She kept her back straight and her chin high even though

she trembled inside. "Yesterday, I wondered if Zeb was old enough to notice how little you did say."

He glared at her long enough for her to think maybe she'd overstepped, but for his *kinder*, she couldn't let herself back down.

"It's not my business," she said as calmly as she was able, even as she wished that weren't true. "I know that. But how can they counter the talk if they don't know the truth?"

He was not a man who liked to back down, either, and he held her gaze longer than was comfortable. Then, suddenly, he closed his eyes, pinched the bridge of his nose, and let his head drop forward.

It was all Hannah could do not to leap up to lay a hand on his shoulder. Odd, when she'd never been much for casual touching, but she often had to fight the impulse where Gideon was concerned.

Because she wanted to touch him. She wanted *him* to touch her. The admission was humbling and even embarrassing, especially since he was such a guarded man. Except with his *kinder*, touching wouldn't come easily for him, either.

But he lifted his head just then, his expression holding a world of pain. "I don't want them ever to think less of their mother," he said hoarsely. "How can that be good for them?"

Did she wish she'd never learned what her own mother had done? Hannah asked herself. Mom had never been reliable, but Hannah had always believed she did her best. That she loved her daughter. Now she'd lost that certainty, might never be able to piece together a relationship. Would she go back, if she could?

She had to speak for Rebekah and Zeb, not herself.

"I think it depends what happened that you want to keep from them," she said softly. "Here, you didn't have to worry about it, and maybe they were better off, but now, somebody thinks they know everything."

"They don't know," he said gruffly.

"It's almost as bad if they're only guessing. Or maybe it's worse."

He surged to his feet and left her in the living room. A minute later, she heard his footsteps on the stairs.

Chapter Seventeen

❖◆❖

REBEKAH LAY CURLED in bed with her back to the door. Pretending she was asleep, Gideon thought. A ceramic bowl sat beside the pillow.

His daughter looked so small like this, reminding him of when she was a *boppli*. Not so long ago, and yet it seemed forever. Back then, he'd spent more time than he could afford doing nothing but standing beside the cradle and then the crib looking down at her, marveling at this second gift from God, watching for the next breath, and the next.

Knowing that he would do anything for her, as he would for her brother, by then a sturdy, active toddler. As he would have for any child of his.

Now, Gideon sat on the edge of her bed, his weight compressing the mattress. If anything, Rebekah stiffened. Squeezing her shoulder, he said, "If you were afraid to go to school, you could have told me."

She rolled toward him. "I'm sick! I am!"

He smiled at her. "Hannah told me not to worry because you don't have a fever."

"She didn't take my temperature."

"Usually when they're sick, people feel hot to the touch."

"Oh." Then, subdued, she said, "I did throw up."

"I'm sorry." He slid his hand around her neck and began to gently knead.

Tears flooded her eyes. "*Daadi*, why are they so *mean*? Why would my friends say things like that about *Mammi*?"

"Was it your friends?"

She snuffled, and wiped her wet eyes with her sheet. "Not my . . . my special friends, like Adah and Beth. And Naomi. And today, Adah and her big sister Emma were waiting for me and Zeb to say they were sorry, that the people talking were nothing but *doppicks*. But . . . but . . ."

"But?"

"But that Bernice ran over and said, 'Why didn't your *mamm* take you when she went? Of course she left Zeb, who'd want him, but you'd think she'd take her daughter.'"

Why hadn't he kept his *kinder* home today, to give Amos time to speak to the parents? They were young; he'd been foolish to think they'd be able to confidently retort, *No, you're wrong,* Mamm *wasn't leaving us, she was with a friend, not a man, it was just an accident,* and then brush off any repeat of hateful rumors.

My fault.

Knowing his rage would be of no help right now, he tugged her toward him. Crying in earnest, Rebekah wrapped her arms around his waist and pressed her face into his torso.

"Did you say, 'My *mamm* wasn't leaving us, you don't know what you're talking about'?"

Her head shook. "Zeb threw himself at her and they fell down in the dirt. Tabitha separated them and talked to both of them alone. She made them *both* sit facing the wall. Except not near each other."

"She was right to do that. Do you know why?"

This head shake was more vigorous. She actually sat up

so she could see his face. "Bernice was being *hateful*, and Zeb was just mad because she was so mean to me."

"*Ja*, and I understand that he thought he was protecting you." And was maybe mad because Bernice had insulted him, too. "But you know we don't believe in hitting other people, no matter how mad we are. Our Lord tells us not to resist an evil person. 'But whoever slaps you on your right cheek, turn the other to him also.'"

She gazed at him with beseeching eyes. "Is Bernice our enemy, like in the Bible?"

"Do you think she is?" he asked, curious to hear how she'd respond.

After a long moment, his daughter shook her head. "She helps me with my schoolwork sometimes, and when Toby fell playing *eckball* and skinned his knee and was crying, she put her arm around him and led him to the schoolhouse so Teacher could clean up his knee and put a bandage on it."

"I'm glad you remember the kind things she's done. I think she just got excited because she heard her parents talking about what happened to your *mamm*, and she didn't stop to wonder if they'd been told wrong information. So she whispered to other *kinder*, and none of them thought, 'Will it hurt Rebekah and Zeb's feelings if we ask questions or tell them what we heard?'"

She stared at him, teardrops still clinging to her eyelashes. "I should have said, 'Why would you say things like that, when you don't know what really happened? Why are you being mean?'"

He smiled. "*Ja*, that would have been good. Much better than pretending you were sick so you could come home."

She heaved a sigh. "It's just . . . why did *Mammi* go with Brooke if she drove her car so fast? Why didn't she yell, 'Stop!' or make her go slow?"

His own eyes burning, Gideon pulled her convulsively into another embrace, and whispered against her head, "I don't know. Maybe she did, and Brooke didn't listen."

"That's what I think. I'm glad you wouldn't let us ever, ever, *ever* go in the car."

"*Ja*. Me, too."

They stayed quiet, holding on to each other, for several minutes. Finally, he used his forearm to swipe at his eyes to be sure any dampness was erased, then set Rebekah away from him.

"Usually, we'd talk about why you don't tell lies."

Her lower lip trembled, but she bobbed her head.

"Today, though, I only have a question for you. Do you want to spend the day in bed, or would you rather get dressed and help Hannah in the kitchen and the garden?"

Her face lit. "Can I?"

"*Ja*." He kissed her forehead. "Now I must go to work."

He left her scrambling out of bed to collect her clothes, and went downstairs. Hannah was wiping an already clean table, her head coming up the minute she heard him on the stairs.

"We had a talk," he said gruffly. "I told her she could spend the day with you."

First relief transformed her worried expression, then joy. "I can't think of anything I'd like more."

It was all he could do not to step forward and cup her cheek with his hand. Bend his head towards her—

Her eyes widened. He saw something in them that frightened him. Even so, stepping back was hard, wrenching. He wanted to run away from her, as he did too often, but first there was something he had to say.

"*Denke* for talking sense to me. For making me think before I said the wrong thing to my daughter."

She had pulled back into herself, appearing dignified and untouchable, but still said, "*Gern schehne*." You're welcome.

Gideon nodded, grabbed his hat from the table, and went out the door. He must first take care of his horse, no doubt patiently waiting where he'd been left even though Gideon hadn't tethered him before running into the house.

* * *

AFTER HEARING ABOUT the morning from Rebekah, Hannah was not surprised to see Zeb's mutinous expression that afternoon. Fortunately, this was one of the days Susan Miller had walked the *kinder* to school and picked them up, so Hannah only had to wait at the foot of the driveway and wave when he appeared. Rebekah had hung back.

He didn't even acknowledge them, keeping his head down. More worrisome, he didn't bother looking for traffic before crossing the road.

Susan looked sympathetic, but with a toddler on her hip, a little girl clutching her skirt, and Enoch already running toward his house, she couldn't stop to talk.

Hannah smiled ruefully and waved. When Zeb marched past her, she touched his shoulder, but he jerked away from her touch and kept going. He stomped past his sister without a word, too.

It would be interesting to see whether he tried going off by himself to sulk, or waited for a snack and then did his chores. After being in trouble all day at school, did he really want to anger his *daad*, too?

Well, both *kinder* had been not only obedient, but exceptionally cheerful, since Hannah started to work. That had to wear off eventually. She had no intention of *letting* him sulk, even if that made him mad.

He was nowhere to be seen when she and Rebekah reached the house. If he wasn't in his bedroom, would Rebekah know where he liked to hide?

In the quiet kitchen, Hannah said, "Well, it looks like Zeb doesn't want his milk and cookies."

"*I* do," Rebekah said hopefully.

Hannah laughed. "You've already had plenty of cookies." As a helper, of course Rebekah had to do taste tests. They'd tried a new kind today, a plump cross between a cookie and a muffin, using pumpkin puree. Rebekah had enjoyed squirting orange and green icing on them. Both of them had agreed that these were as good as oatmeal-raisin or sugar cookies.

Ready to start preparations for dinner, Hannah decided to give Zeb a few minutes before going looking for him.

"Rebekah, will you sweep the mudroom?" she asked. "And then the front porch?"

Rebekah nodded eagerly. It was good for her to do chores she could handle on her own, instead of always being the helper. Hannah hadn't thought of it that way, but taking over the cooking, grocery shopping, and much of the housework when she was young had allowed her to feel as if she had some control over her own life. She had hated feeling helpless, the big decisions always out of her hands. No surprise if Rebekah felt the same, if for different reasons.

To fill the time, Hannah took the vegetable drawers out of the refrigerator, emptied them, then washed and dried them. She had just put the cabbage, greens, peas, and carrots back in the drawers when she heard footsteps on the stairs. Not Zeb's usual fast clatter that sounded like a horse galloping down, but a pace so slow, she felt the reluctance.

She'd hidden her smile by the time he entered the kitchen. "Oh, good, there you are. You still have time to have a cookie or two before you start your chores."

"Why didn't *she* do them, since she got to stay home all day?"

"That's unkind," Hannah said quietly. "Rebekah has been a help to me, and is sweeping the mudroom right now. You're bigger and stronger, so you can do things she can't."

He rolled his eyes. "She could clean the chicken coop. She's just scared she'll get pecked."

"Weren't you, when you were younger?"

His mouth twisted, but he mumbled, "I guess so."

Hannah poured a glass of milk and set it in front of him along with a plate holding two cookies. Then she sat across from him, watching as he studied them dubiously before taking a bite and then gobbling.

After the first had disappeared, Hannah said, "Your *daad* talked to Rebekah when she first came home."

Something like despair flashed in the boy's eyes. "Of course, she told him everything. She's such a *blabbermaul.*"

"Wouldn't you have admitted to your father what happened this morning?"

Shoulders stiff, he stared at the remaining cookie without reaching for it. Then those thin shoulders slumped. "If I don't tell him, someone else always does."

"That's the way of the world," she agreed. "And your *daad* understands better than you think. I bet he got into trouble as a boy, too."

"*He* didn't have someone say she was glad because his mother left him!" he flared back, his dark eyes filled with anger.

"I wasn't there," she said. "When your *mamm* died, I mean. So I don't really know what happened."

"Bernice wasn't, either," he said spitefully.

"*Ja,* that's true. But what I'm trying to say is that, from what your *daad* said, it sounds like people did a lot of talking back then, too, including other *kinder.*"

"Some said it was *Daad*'s fault." Now he looked desperate. "That he'd let *Mamm* ride around in the car with an *Englischer,* that he should have *known* something bad would happen. It made me so mad!"

"You were only . . . five? Six? Just think what your father was hearing. But he worried most about you and Rebekah."

As if, by using her name, Hannah had summoned Zeb's sister, she appeared from the mudroom, clutching the broom that was really too tall for her. Her gaze went from Hannah's face to Zeb's.

"What are you talking about?"

Zeb whirled in his chair. "None of your business!"

"But . . ."

"Zeb, apologize to your sister," Hannah said firmly. "It's never necessary to be rude. You could have said, 'I need to talk to Hannah by myself,' and Rebekah would have understood."

His lips thinned in mutiny, but after stealing a look at Hannah, he muttered, "I'm sorry."

"Then can I stay?"

Hannah leveled a look at him, and he managed to keep his mouth shut. Looking at his sister, she said gently, "You and I had all day to talk. Now he needs some of my time. Please go sweep the porch, too."

Rebekah never liked to be shut out, but she went, albeit dragging her feet.

Once Hannah heard the front door open and close, she said, "Learning to control your anger is part of growing up. I imagine that sisters and brothers often get mad at each other—"

"Don't you have any?" he asked in amazement.

"No . . ." She blinked. "Well, now I do. Emma and Adah are two of them, but I didn't grow up with them. I didn't even know they existed."

She watched him absorb that. After a minute, he said, "She's always following me around. I want to be *alone* sometimes!"

"*Ja*, but you also want her to play with you. You and she have been through so much that nobody else understands, that ties you together. Weren't you mad at Bernice this morning partly because she hurt Rebekah?"

"*Ja*." He did look thoughtful, which gave her hope.

"Back when you moved, did your *daad* talk to you about his decision?"

"*Ja*, but that doesn't mean I know why we *really* moved."

She smiled at him as she pushed back her chair. "Well, think about it."

He snatched up a cookie.

"I'm going out to the garden to see what's ripe." She opened a cupboard. "You'll tell Rebekah?"

He screwed up his face. "She's coming in now."

"Oh, good. She can come with me." She found a lightweight bowl she could use to collect peas and cucumbers and rhubarb for a sweet bread, making a mental note to retrieve the heavier bowl from Rebckah's bed. Circling the table, she was able to bend and press her cheek to Zeb's dark head. "Find your hat before you go out."

WHEN HANNAH ARRIVED at her father's house that evening, he was waiting to unhitch Clover. She'd become accustomed to helping now, her hands going automatically to buckles.

Samuel looked at her over the mare's back. "I hear there was more excitement today for Zeb and Rebekah."

Glad of the concern in his voice, she nodded and told him the latest. "I was proud of Emma and Adah, though. Rebekah said they waited outside for her and Zeb to say they were sorry for the talk."

"They're good girls," he said with satisfaction. "Just like their older sister."

"Now, how do you know I was a good girl?" she teased, helping him pull the lightweight buggy into the barn, while Clover, freed in the pasture, lowered herself to the ground and began to roll, hooves kicking the air.

"Because I think you're a good woman now," he answered seriously. "And I wonder if your *mamm* wasn't a better mother than you think."

She stared at him in shock. "How can you say that, after what she did?"

"Would you be the woman you are now, good-hearted, happy taking care of other people, able to have faith in the Lord, if she hadn't raised you with love?"

Her mouth hung open, and for a full minute she couldn't have formed a word to save her life.

"Come. Sit down," he invited.

The hay—or straw?—bales were handy. She took one, her *daad* the other.

She blurted, "Taking care of other people?"

Why had *that* come out?

"You're so good with your sisters and brothers. You sat with Zachariah when he was sick and read to him, for his sake and for Lilian's. You are happy when the food you serve pleases people. Sunday, I saw you with Gideon's *kinder.* The way you touch them, smile at them, and the way they trust you."

"I didn't know until I came here how much I like *kinder.*"

"You try to live as God asks of you."

"The first time I remember going to church I was seven or eight, maybe. *Mamm* was dating a man who was a churchgoer, so . . ." She glanced nervously at Samuel.

He nodded his understanding, his expression holding a depth of acceptance, even serenity, Hannah couldn't conceive.

"I loved going to church. Whenever we moved, I found a church within walking distance. *Mamm* . . . never understood, but from the first time I went to a service, I felt as if I was being embraced. God's word taught me who I wanted to be."

"A fine woman," he said contentedly.

"Denke."

Not until now, she realized, did she see clearly what she'd found in those churches—and what she hadn't. Her attendance had always been taken for granted, but not remarked on. She hadn't been enfolded the way she craved. In some churches, pastors lectured their congregants in ringing tones about sin, while others focused more gently on hope and forgiveness. Especially as a child, she'd wanted a blueprint for how to live based on God's will, but no one ever gave her one. Probably, she'd come to believe, that was up to parents to provide for their children.

A silence settled over them. Samuel neither moved nor spoke, his patience seemingly unending.

There were questions she hadn't yet dared ask. This seemed like the right time. "How did you meet her?"

"In town. I was young." He shrugged. "I sometimes went to the Mill Café."

Englisch owned, Hannah understood, versus the Amish-owned Country Days Café. Samuel had been kicking over the traces, in his modest way.

"Your *mamm* was a waitress there. She flirted, and I took her for a ride in my buggy. Your *mamm* . . ." He hesitated. "Jodi was pretty, of course." His sidelong glance held humor. "To a man in his twenties, that matters. A boy, maybe, not a man."

Hannah laughed.

His gaze became unfocused. "She was always smiling. She made me laugh. I started to think about what it would be like to spend my life with a woman so joyful, a woman who seemed to shine from within. Always happy."

"Was she ever really like that?"

"I don't know," he said simply. "Once we spent time together, her certainty seemed as great as her joy. She learned the language, took the necessary classes so that she could be baptized." He glanced at Hannah. "She'd grown up in her parents' church, so she had a start. We got married."

Hannah reached for his work-worn hand. He started, as if he'd forgotten he was talking to someone else, but then his calloused fingers closed around her hand.

"There were things I hadn't noticed about her," he continued, voice heavier. "When you came, you began right away to help: in the kitchen, the garden, with the housework, as if you didn't know how to sit and be lazy. Jodi had visited, and I thought she was just shy with my *mamm* and sisters and the others. But once we were married, I found she didn't know how to cook and didn't want to learn. At first, she did a little housework, talked about what a big garden she'd start."

Oh, Hannah knew all of this. Her mother talked, but expected others to do the work. And, no, that wasn't altogether fair; Jodi had held job after job after job, in between being taken care of by the men who eventually grew impatient with her, if she didn't get tired of *them*—or have to flee from them. Most often, she worked as a waitress. At least she could whirl around a room from a family group to a couple to a single man or woman. She loved to chat, to flirt, to laugh with people. But she always lost those jobs because she was too slow, because other waitresses had to take some of her tables, because she didn't do her share of the cleaning and prep work. She thought nothing of arriving five minutes late, too, and was invariably surprised when her bosses lost patience with her unreliability.

"She became unhappy right away. Lonely, when I worked all day. She'd say, 'There's nothing to *do*!'" He shook his head in genuine puzzlement. "There was much that was important to do, but she ignored it. Once we expected you, she became happier, although then she claimed to be sick to her stomach or so tired she couldn't do housework or cook. She skipped our worship a few times, too, sick, she said. She dreaded hosting when our Sunday came around, then insisted she was only nervous that people would think she hadn't done what she should have."

Hannah understood his bemusement. She'd now heard enough women talking to know how excited they were to hold the worship in their own homes. Scrubbing and polishing in advance was part of the happiness at truly being part of the congregation.

"I hired a woman to be here," Samuel continued, "as

Gideon has with you, for the days when my female relatives were too busy with their own families to help. You were only a *boppli* when I found old friends of hers were picking her up, and both of you were gone all day sometimes."

This was far and away the most Hannah's father had ever said in one sitting. A quiet man, he enjoyed having his family chattering around him, but except for the occasional interjection, only listened. "He says that's what he's best at," Lilian had confided one day, laughing softly. "Listening."

Like Gideon, Hannah couldn't help thinking.

But her *daad* must understand Hannah's hunger to know how she'd come to be born—and why everything had gone so awry.

"We both must have known we'd made a mistake, but we had you. And for me, marriage was for a lifetime. But when I pressed her to be more of a partner, she became angry. All I wanted was a housekeeper, she said." He sighed. "But when I told her she could visit her friends, but she couldn't take you with her, she . . ."

Rather than waiting while he groped for words, Hannah said, "She threw a screaming fit."

"Ja." He was still perplexed, she saw. "But I stood firm, and she was furious with me after that. I don't know why she stayed as long as she did."

"Because she had to have money? An idea of someplace to go?" But especially money, Hannah realized. Her friends were likely as young and free and easy about finances and responsibilities as Jodi had been—and still was.

Or had Mom actually been happy to leave her small daughter in someone else's hands? Someone who would change stinky diapers, potty train her when the time came? Start teaching her to cook, to sweep floors, to pull weeds?

Then Mom could flit home at the end of the day and

delight her child with fanciful stories and overflowing love that probably made the other women in the young child's life seem dour and lacking in joy.

Oh, yes, Hannah thought. *I was probably thrilled the day my mommy said, "Today, you're coming with me. We'll have all kinds of adventures!"*

Samuel broke into her thoughts. "I do not like speaking harshly about her. You know your *mamm* better than I ever did—"

"She never changed. She could be happy and fun. I always knew she loved me." *Did I really?* Hannah asked herself. Should love be so careless? But as a child, she'd never dared let herself question the depth of her mother's love. How could she, when Mom was all she had? With a sigh, she went on, "But Mom was also wildly emotional, inconstant, longing to have a man to take care of her. I'd say she was unreliable, except she never abandoned me. We were a team. That's what she'd say. So . . . I suppose she did teach me to love, and I learned to be practical, because she wasn't, and I think that's a good thing."

"Ja." He squeezed her hand again. "I think the same."

Hannah bent forward, feeling as sick as Rebekah had pretended to be. "And so I love her, but I still can't forgive her."

"Forgiveness will ease your burden," her father said mildly, but then they sat quietly for a time, feeling no more need for speech.

Samuel Mast was infinitely reliable, kind, she thought; a rock that would never break, any more than he would betray the smallest of trusts. For a woman who flitted through life, he must quickly have gone from irresistible to intolerable. Probably dull, infuriating. Certainly not *fun*. The two had been ill suited from the beginning, and too young and foolish to see that.

Hannah laid her cheek against her father's solid shoulder,

and wondered how it could be that she was so much more like him than she was like the mother who'd raised her.

She didn't wonder at all why she was so powerfully attracted to Gideon, possibly even falling in love with him, another man she had not the slightest doubt was steadfast, trustworthy . . . and capable of tenderness.

Chapter Eighteen

❧ ◆ ❧

JULIA AND MIRIAM arrived Thursday afternoon, as promised, to help Hannah cut out and sew a new dress and aprons. Knowing their lives were as busy as hers, she felt blessed by their friendship, offered with no expectation of anything in return.

Her *aenti* Sarah had given her two older dresses that didn't fit Hannah well, but given her daily activities, that didn't really matter. When she apologized for not having Julia's dress and apron ready to return, she admitted that the last time she'd worn it, she'd stained the apron red as she baked strawberry pies, then splattered grease on it frying pork and sausage for a pork potpie.

"I soaked it, but I haven't had a chance to wash it and make sure I really got the stains out."

Julia only laughed. "Aprons are meant to get dirty," her new friend assured her. "There's no way you can cook and take care of your garden and house while staying spotlessly clean. Though I admit, I never look forward to *weschdagg*."

Hannah already knew that was "washday." She and the

other two women had evolved to speaking a hodgepodge of *Deitsh* and English, the *Deitsh* increasingly dominating as her fluency grew.

While they cut out lilac cotton for her first new dress, Julia told Hannah about the lessons Miriam had given her in speaking *Deitsh*, back before she'd even consciously considered converting. "She'd quiz me. She made me learn to say, *'Ich hab en aker grummbiere geblanst.'*"

Hannah put that together. "'I planted an acre of potatoes'?"

Miriam let out a peal of laughter. "You understand! Now you can say you speak *Deitsh*."

Hannah laughed, too. "I'm sure there are more useful things I could learn to say."

"*Ja*, like *'Sell kann ennichpepper duh.'*"

Her hands went still while she thought. "'Anyone can do that'?"

Both the other women crowed in triumph.

In a teasing way, they threw out sentences and phrases while they were there, including some that were undoubtedly meant to help her understand the next service.

Er hot net der glaawe. He doesn't keep up the faith.

Do I? she asked herself silently. *Or do I set it aside when it's inconvenient—or when I'm not willing to do God's bidding?*

Looking at the two kind, friendly women here to help her, Hannah wondered whether there was any way to compare her faith to theirs. Was hers even close to filling her to the brim, as she imagined theirs did? Would either of them cling to anger, like she was?

I mostly had *forgiven Mom*, she realized. Accepted that her mother's love wasn't quite what she'd wanted, but was the best she could do. The sharpness of Hannah's anger now was new, from when she learned how she'd been cheated out of family—and how much Jodi had hurt her own parents and Samuel.

But how much of that anger was ultimately selfish, Hannah asked herself, because it was on her own behalf?

She gave herself a small shake. Right now, she needed to immerse herself in these new friendships, and the sense of belonging Julia and Miriam gave her.

In the few hours the other women were there, they finished the dress and cut out the apron and a shirt for Zeb. Hannah paid Miriam for the fabric and supplies she'd already brought, and put in an order for enough fabric to make a new dress for Rebekah as well as a second one for herself. "And aprons, too."

They both nodded, leaving with cheerful waves and promises to be back tomorrow.

Did she need another dress? The request had just popped out of her mouth. If she was only to be here for a few more weeks, even a month or two, she could get by with three dresses if she was diligent with her laundry. It wasn't as if she'd ever have any use of them again, except maybe when she visited. She could leave them at her father's house.

The picture of herself cheerfully changing back into her *Englisch* clothes—blue jeans and a T-shirt, say—and driving away as her family stood in the front yard waving refused to form. This wasn't the first time she'd felt as if a crater had opened somewhere in her chest or stomach when she tried to envision her future.

Eventually, she'd really have to sit down and make some decisions . . . but right now, Hannah cleared off the table. She had to be able to serve supper—once she'd actually applied herself to cooking.

Thursday evening, Gideon had visitors. He recognized the two adults as they emerged from the buggy, but not the older girl.

"Stay in here unless I call for you," he told his *kinder*, and went out the back door to intercept the family. They had been crossing the lawn toward the rarely used front door, making the statement that they felt they didn't deserve to be welcomed as close acquaintances, far less friends.

He waited until they saw him approaching, and nodded. "Paul." He had to grope for the wife's name; he didn't think they'd ever spoken, even though their church district was of typical size. If he had a wife of his own, he would undoubtedly be more familiar with the women. Fortunately, the name came to him before the pause became awkward. "Claudia. And I think you must be Zillah."

Hers was one of the names he had passed on to Bishop Troyer.

The girl tried to squeeze her body into a smaller space, but she had the courage to look up and meet his eyes, hers desperate.

Older than Rebekah and Zeb, for sure, he decided, but likely no more than ten or eleven.

"We're here to tell you how sorry we are for the talk that went around at school," Paul said, direct. "Zillah wants to say the same to both your *kinder*."

Gideon looked at her with a friendlier eye, although he reminded himself that she might be here, planning to say the right words, only because her *mamm* and *daad* were mad at her. They would not have enjoyed being chastised by bishop.

"That's good of you," he said. "Did Zillah hear these rumors from you?"

Her father's lips tightened. "No. She has lately become friends with several girls who are older than she is. They're of an age to be thinking about boys and talking about their *rumspringa*—and gossiping."

Gideon relaxed slightly. He had liked Paul, always willing to join any work frolic, and the two of them had often discussed farming. Paul had advised Gideon, when he first moved here, on the best choice of crops, seeds, and fertilizers.

"I'm glad," he said. "Please, come in for a cup of coffee and some applesauce cake. The girl who works for me is a fine cook." He wished Hannah were here. He'd become so used to talking to her, hearing her advice.

Claudia's face brightened. "*Ja*, I had a slice of friendship bread she baked. I wonder if she'd share the recipe."

He smiled at her as he led them toward the back door. "I'm sure she would. Hannah Mast is a generous woman."

Rebekah and Zeb looked up when the group came through the mudroom to the kitchen, their eyes widening. Rebekah scrambled off her chair and backed up a few steps, while Zeb stared defiantly at Zillah. Gideon wished even more for Hannah's presence, this time for the sake of his *kinder*.

"Sit down," he told them gently, and waved the guests to other seats. Paul hung his hat on a peg, and his wife and daughter removed their bonnets.

Coffee was on, so he only had to pour. It took barely another minute to dish up squares of moist cake topped with a drizzle of icing, but none for him or his *kinder*. They'd had plenty already.

Paul looked at Zillah, who sat across from Rebekah and Zeb. She stole a peek at her *daad*, then raised her chin and said in a voice with a quaver, "I'm sorry for the things I said. I didn't know what I was talking about. I wanted Bernice and . . . and Yonnie to like me."

Especially Yonnie, Gideon suspected. Was a girl her age old enough to like a boy in a special way yet? From her blush, he thought yes, although the heat in her cheeks might just as well be shame.

Rebekah surprised him by speaking up with no prompting from him. "*Denke* for saying that," she said with great dignity. "None of that was true, but it hurt my feelings anyway. I still miss my *mamm*."

"It made me mad that people were saying such bad things about our mother," Zeb said sharply. "None of you *knew* her."

Zillah bit her lip and nodded.

"Zeb," Gideon felt compelled to say.

His son looked momentarily mulish, but finally bit off, "I forgive you."

Well. Gideon supposed that was the best he could hope for, unless he hauled Zeb outside by the scruff of his neck and lectured him on accepting an apology graciously.

Fortunately, amusement crinkled the skin beside Paul's eyes. He had at least three boys, if Gideon remembered right. If Zeb was any example, they were harder to raise than girls, even if Gideon had worried more about Rebekah since the move to Tompkin's Creek.

Zillah thought Bernice had gotten her information from listening to her parents, but she wasn't sure. "It could have been Emmie . . . ," she said doubtfully.

Gideon pictured another older girl but couldn't remember a last name.

"Not Yonnie?" her mother asked.

"He's a boy. I don't think he cared that much."

The adults turned the talk to the farming that was their livelihood, and boredom set in among the *kinder.*

Zeb asked if Zillah wanted to go outside. He'd pitch so the girls could both hit the ball. They agreed with alacrity, and all three raced out the back door.

Claudia said humorously, "*Kinder* never seem to hold grudges."

Gideon smiled. "Not when it gets in the way of having someone to play with."

She set down her fork. "I hope this doesn't make you regret settling here. We've been so happy to have you."

"*Denke.*" He hesitated. "I doubt that will be so. There was talk back home, before we moved." He told them the basic story: his wife had been killed in a car accident with her friend, who was driving. "They'd grown up best friends," he said. "Living next door, you know how it is."

"*Ja.* I don't see why there was talk, instead of the sympathy and caring you should have been able to expect."

He unclenched his jaw. "Our bishop believed I should never have allowed Leah to get in the car with her friend. He thought I'd let her set aside her faith."

"What?" Claudia stared at him. "After such a tragedy, he blamed *her* as well as you?"

"*Ja,*" he said tightly. It still rankled, when he should feel humbled instead. Of course, he blamed himself, too. The suggestion that Leah had brought on her own death had particularly angered him.

"You had good reason to move," she declared. "I had a close friend, an *Englischer,* from my girlhood, too. I don't see her much anymore, because I grew up in Iowa and met Paul when his brother married my cousin. It's so far, we mostly write letters."

Like the one Gideon was guessing Bernice's mother received from a friend or family member in New York. He chose not to say that.

Not much later, the Schwartz family left, exchanging smiles and even a hug for Rebekah, given by Zillah, who also whispered into her ear.

Watching the buggy recede down the lane, Rebekah said, "She was nice. Wasn't she, Zeb?"

He lifted one shoulder. "She's okay."

This smile, Gideon hid. When he said, "Time for chores," both his *kinder* groaned.

Gideon reflected that it was easy to forgive a young girl who had only been trying to impress older friends. He wondered what Willard and Ava Kemp would have to say, and Lois and Matthias King.

He reminded himself to ask his *kinder* more about who this Emmie was.

* * *

FRIDAY, JULIA CAME alone. The owner of the quilt shop had unexpectedly asked Miriam to work today.

"I don't know if Ruth has hired anyone to replace Miriam yet. There are plenty of quilters out there, but most of them have families and no time to spare. Although . . ." Her forehead crinkled. "That gives me an idea."

"You thought of someone?"

"*Ja*, a cousin of Miriam's husband, David Miller. Her parents belong to a different church district, but no farther from town. Ketarah is only seventeen, I think, and I can see her excited to have a job in a fabric store. She and her *mamm* both are very fine quilters." She gave a decisive nod. "I'll ask Luke to talk to Ruth tomorrow. She may not have thought of Ketarah."

Hannah smiled. "I see you brought more fabric."

"And no *boppli*. Deborah—Luke's *mamm*, you know—begged me to leave both Nathan and Abby with her for the afternoon. Think how much more we'll get done, especially since we don't have Miriam to take turns with him!"

Hannah laughed. "Just think, once Miriam's a mother, too, Nathan will be walking."

"Walking? He'll be running the minute he can figure out how not to tip over!"

"I think you won't get nearly as much quilting done as you used to."

Julia smiled softly. "I quilted so much, I had piles of my own quilts. I'd given ones to everyone I knew. I'd sold plenty of them. I quilted because I was alone so much. I still love to quilt, but I'm not sorry that my life has become busy with a husband and *kinder*."

"No." Hannah had a feeling her answering smile was more complicated. "I was hoping that, while we work, you might be willing to talk a little more about your decision to convert." She braced herself for the other woman to ask whether she was considering doing the same, but Julia only smoothed any wrinkles from the fabric. So Hannah asked, "Was Luke a big part of it?"

"Of course he was, but not all." Even as they laid out the fabric and pinned the pieces of one of Julia's discarded dresses, adjusted in small ways to better fit Hannah, Julia talked readily about why she'd been so drawn to the Amish. She'd switched to speaking English, probably aware that Hannah's *Deitsh* still wasn't up to such a serious discussion. "Two reasons, most of all," she said at last. "I never felt as if I had a personal relationship with God. As if He might hear me. I went to church and I said prayers before meals, but that's all. I didn't make daily decisions by asking what God would expect of me. I saw immediately that the Amish do. Most Americans see it as a ridiculous sacrifice. And there are sacrifices, but mostly small. When you add them all together, you find that God is more present in your life. You don't think of Him only on Sundays. And what was I really giving up?"

Of course, the question echoed Gideon's, resonating with Hannah. *What would I be giving up?* How many times had she asked herself that now? Yet she wondered whether that was the important question, or whether she should be asking herself what she would be reaching *for*?

Some instinct—or was it cowardice?—had her lightening the moment, though. "Buttons? Velcro?"

Julia giggled. "That's about right. I dress differently, I don't listen to loud music or watch television, I don't drive a car anymore—" She shrugged. "My parents and my brother love me. I always knew I could go to them for anything. But now, I have so much more. My life is rich with family, with love, with the *kinder* I always wanted, and with a sense of the Lord's presence that I never had before."

Hannah paused, scissors in hand, to watch the flow of expressions across the other woman's face. Julia radiated joy.

But her mood became darker as she talked about being attacked when she was nineteen, about the years of terror because her assailant was never identified or arrested. "My life revolved around him. There was fear, and anger, and even hate. What he did to me was bad. I'd still rejoice if he was arrested, so that he couldn't hurt any other woman. But when I opened my heart to God, I was able to forgive him, to accept that hc may have been abused himself, and had to express his own rage somehow. Because his DNA has never been collected at another crime scene, as far as we know—" She glanced at Hannah. "You have to understand, my brother will never stop searching for him."

Hannah nodded.

"So I hope and pray that the man horrified himself so much by the attack on me, he has never done anything like that again. I even hope he can forgive himself. Being able to forgive, living my faith, has brought me peace."

Too moved to say a word, Hannah didn't even dare start cutting for fear she'd make a mistake. Was she letting her bitterness and new fury at her mother stunt her own life? Close her off from God?

"Have you met Luke?" Julia asked her.

"I . . . no," she managed to say. "I might have seen him."

"You probably did. He's tall for an Amishman, over six feet. David's close to that, as is Gideon. Oh, and Luke's brother, Elam. Luke has dark hair and blue eyes." Color rose in her cheeks, more noticeable for her redhead's creamy skin. "He's handsome."

Hannah laughed. "I'm not surprised you think so."

"In a different way," her new friend mused, "Gideon is as striking."

Hannah lightly whacked Julia's arm. "Knock it off."

Their conversation turned to the church service, and some of the people Hannah had met. She commented on what an extraordinary voice the man who'd called out the first hymn had.

Julia nodded. "John Mast. I think he's your father's cousin. First or second, I don't know. He's what we call the *Volsinger*. He always chooses the hymns for that Sunday, and lifts his voice to lead us."

"*Auslanders*," Hannah said, "would say he's wasting his talent."

Julia's eyes met hers. "What do you say?"

"That he uses his voice to praise God, and to help others do the same. That's a lot more important than a recording contract."

Julia clasped her hand and squeezed.

They were quiet for a few minutes, only the snip, snip of the scissors to be heard, but then Julia exclaimed, "Oh, I almost forgot! Luke wanted me to pass on a message."

"A message?"

"He bought lunch yesterday at the bakery a few doors from the furniture store. He said while he was in line, he heard two women talking. Their *kinder* came home from school—oh, it must have been Tuesday—and they said gossip was going around. It was about Gideon, and his wife's death. Luke pinned one of them down—Dinah is married to a cousin of Luke's, Jerry Ropp." She grimaced. "Yes, the relationships hereabouts are awfully tangled. Anyway, Luke said he'd have stopped yesterday on his way home, but his buggy horse had developed a limp, and he remembered I was coming over here today anyway. Just in case Gideon's *kinder* don't say anything, Luke thought he should know."

"Oh, we know." Hannah reported on most of the past few days' happenings. She didn't say, *I don't think Gideon told his children everything about the accident.* She didn't say, *I think his grief is mixed with other, even more painful, emotions.* "Gideon said the parents of one of the girls who was passing the rumors around stopped by yesterday evening to apologize. I guess Bishop Troyer has talked to all the parents."

Julia gave an exaggerated wince. "I don't envy them."

Although Hannah didn't have much sense of humor where all this was concerned, she did laugh. When Amos Troyer had welcomed her last Sunday to the service, she'd seen how kind his gaze was, but also how unnervingly perceptive. She wouldn't want to try to keep a secret from him.

When she said as much, Julia smiled. "He's been so good to me. To get baptized, I had to take classes and, eventually, convince him that my conversion was genuine. I imagine that's always true, but in my case, he'd already guessed that Luke had fallen in love with an *Englischer*— and probably that *I'd* fallen in love with an Amishman."

"So saying, 'I want to marry Luke,' didn't cut it as a reason to be baptized, huh?"

"No, and I'm glad. The bishops and ministers have to guard against young men and women, madly in love, not having any idea what they're getting into." Her eyes rounded. "Oh, no! I'm so sorry! Me and my big mouth, just rattling away."

"No, it's all right. I'm . . . painfully aware that my mother's conversion wasn't genuine." She paused. If it had been, Hannah couldn't imagine Jodi being willing to make even those small sacrifices Julia had talked about. "What she didn't understand was what her life would be like within the Amish community." She tried to smile, but her lips didn't want to cooperate. "She insists that Amishwomen are slaves to the men, their only purpose to work nonstop and bear and raise children."

"We do work hard."

Hannah heard how wholeheartedly Julia included herself in that *we*.

Her own forehead wrinkled as she thought about it. "Part of the trouble is that Mom was never very domestic. She didn't cook, cleaned as little as possible, had no interest in gardening, never mind sewing, quilting, canning. *Daad* said he thought they both knew they'd made a mistake fairly quickly, but then she got pregnant." Hannah could only shrug.

"I don't think Amos was the bishop—what was it, twenty-five years ago? I'll have to ask Luke who was."

"Somehow, I don't see my mother slipping past Amos Troyer's net," Hannah said ruefully. She couldn't help thinking that her mother and Samuel both would have been better off if the then bishop had declined to baptize Jodi Hinsch.

Except, of course, they wouldn't have had a daughter together.

Chapter Nineteen

❖◆❖

GIDEON RARELY ALLOWED himself to cut his workday short. He lost enough time when he and the *kinder* were on their own, or when they needed him to attend school functions or to stay close when they were sick. Today, he had inspected the raspberries, his devastating experience with rust on his mind, determined that they were healthy, and detoured to look at the blueberry bushes. As he'd told Hannah, they were not large yet, but were fruiting prolifically.

He stood at the edge of the pond, enjoying the silence and the cooler air. A rabbit bounded through the long grass; a vivid red cardinal tipped its head and studied him from a branch of a redbud, past blooming season. Staying still, he noticed a long-necked cormorant on a twisting branch that must have blown into the pond. The cormorant watched the surface of the water with an intent eye, ready to fish for supper. The wildlife was abundant here, on the fringes of Gideon's land. He could almost always hear the rat-tat-tat of a woodpecker working in the woods. Today he saw a small flock of yellow warblers and a wild turkey strutting away from the water. He liked this band of native woods, slanting up toward a ridge too steep for farming or building. Occasionally, Gideon hunted here. If he'd had a gun, he might have brought down the wild turkey.

Except, Hannah had not yet asked him to kill a chicken, so she might still not know how to pluck the feathers. A smile twitched at Gideon's mouth. If she had her way, he'd end up with a flock of geriatric chickens.

Ja, if she weren't planning to leave soon.

Pushing the disturbing reminder away, he thought he'd bring Zeb up here to fish Sunday. They hadn't done that in a long while. Zeb could clean their catch, and even Gideon knew how to fry a bluegill or bullhead catfish. The thought made his mouth water.

That was when he decided not to start another job. Dinner couldn't be more than an hour away, and the worry about how the day had gone at school for the *kinder* had lurked at the edges of his thoughts all day.

He replaced tools in the barn and came out to see Hannah stretching to pluck wooden clothespins from the line and drop them into a cloth sack. So graceful did she look, it was as if she'd paused in the middle of a dance, the ballet he'd seen in pictures, her arms held high. A basket filled with folded sheets and clothes sat at her feet. He saw her pause and tip her chin up as she watched something in the maple tree above her. Then he heard a low laugh, followed by a flick of movement among the leaves.

She spotted him a moment later and smiled. "A squirrel had his eye on me. They're so cute."

"They are." That smile, so beautiful, so happy, made his heart swell until it didn't beat quite right. He had to clear his throat. "Have you been up to the pond? I was just there, checking on the blueberry bushes I planted, and I saw half a dozen different birds. A cormorant seemed to be planning on fish for supper."

She chuckled, but her eyes shied from his. "I'll walk up

there tomorrow. Rebekah would enjoy that, certain sure. Oh. You know Julia Bowman was here this afternoon?"

"*Ja*, her and Miriam, you said."

"Miriam had to work at the fabric store, so it was just Julia. She asked me to pass on a message from Luke."

Gideon listened in silence, something easing in him at hearing what Luke said. He was friend enough to want Gideon to know about the rumors as soon as possible.

He nodded acknowledgment. "Where are Zeb and Rebekah?"

"I'm teaching Rebekah how to sew a seam. She's practicing on some scraps of fabric. She's excited, because I'm making her a new dress, and she wants to help. I think she's plenty old enough."

"That's good of you."

"No, it's fun." Hannah wrinkled her nose. "I think. I haven't actually done that much sewing myself, and if I can make a pair of pants for Zeb, she can probably do as well."

A smile spread on his face. "Just don't look closely at the seams?"

"Something like that." Her laugh was a happy ripple. "A while back, I thought about insisting on harnessing Clover myself, but then I imagined what would happen if I didn't hook something up right, and halfway to *Daad*'s the buggy and horse parted ways." She pursed her lips. "Then I thought, what if the pieces of Zeb's pants part ways when he's running with his friends? And just . . . fall off?"

They shared a laugh.

He waited while she grabbed the last few clothespins, and lifted the full basket before she could.

"Clothes dry so fast at this time of year," she commented, "but what do you do in the winter?"

"They dry on the line if the sun is out, even if it's cold. Or we set up racks in the house, usually near the wood stove in the living room. They fold up for storage. You may have seen them in the cellar."

"Oh! I wondered what those were."

"You didn't say where Zeb is."

"I think in his room." She looked a little less happy. "He did his chores and then thought Rebekah would play with him. I think he's bored."

"I can find more work for him."

"I'm sure he'd be happy, if he's working with you." There was a tiny emphasis on the *if.*

Gideon wasn't so prideful that he resented a nudge like this. Hannah was right, and he liked that she cared enough about his *kinder* to see what he sometimes didn't. He should have taken Zeb along to check for rust on the raspberries and to see how well the new blueberry bushes were doing. Gideon had a library of books about farming techniques and the particular crops that he had grown or might try someday. He'd find pictures of the pests and diseases that could threaten his crops and even livelihood. Watching for rust on the raspberry leaves was something Zeb could take over.

"I thought I'd take him fishing Sunday," he said.

Hannah's smile warmed at his suggestion. "He'd love that. He seems . . . quieter than usual."

They had reached the back door. He stopped with a hand on the knob. "Did it go better at school today?"

"I think so." She sounded less certain than he liked. "Rebekah was cheerful. She said Zillah played with her at recess. Zeb . . . I'm not sure. He wasn't mad, but he didn't have much to say."

Gideon nodded. "I'll talk to him."

Once he opened the back door, Rebekah squealed and came running as if she hadn't seen him just this morning. He picked her up and swung her high, then said, "I've probably made you dirty."

"Hannah doesn't mind. Does she?"

"Hannah doesn't mind at all." She smiled at his daughter in that gentle way she had. "*Kinder* should play and get dirty."

Rebekah's face lit. "And I'm going to have a new dress! Did Hannah tell you, *Daadi*?"

"She did. The way you're growing, you may need more than one."

"*Ja*," Hannah agreed, "but having her dress an inch or two shorter than it should be isn't as obvious as Zeb when his ankles and wrists are bared. I think he must be having a growing spurt. If he's going to be tall like your *daad*, he has a lot of growing to do."

"I can be tall, too," Rebekah protested.

Hannah smiled at her. "I'm tall for a woman, but look how much shorter I am than your *daad*."

He grinned and pretended to rest his chin on the top of her head, but almost immediately regretted letting himself get so close to Hannah that their bodies brushed. Self-conscious and . . . uncomfortable, he stepped back. But Rebekah giggled, seeing nothing wrong with his foolishness.

"How tall was your *mamm*?" Hannah asked. Her cheeks were pinker than usual, but nothing a *kind* would notice. "We can get our height from either parent, just as we do the color of our eyes or hair."

Standing behind her, Gideon frowned, not sure he liked her talking about Leah. But he saw his daughter's eyebrows scrunch together, as if she was trying to remember.

"*I* think *Mammi* was tall," she said, but uncertainly.

Of course she wouldn't remember. How could she? She'd been only three when her mother died. Even Zeb might be forgetting his *mamm*'s face. Gideon held Leah in his heart more than he envisioned her face, yet that would be hard for the *kinder* as their scant memories faded. When he moved them from New York, there'd been little he could bring along to help them hold on to memories. The Amish didn't take photographs; they didn't collect pretty statues or paintings or anything fancy for the kitchen. If Leah had been a quilter, the *kinder* could have wrapped themselves at night in quilts lovingly stitched by their mother. She did sew, but they'd long since outgrown those clothes even before the family moved.

He was conscious that Hannah had turned and was watching him with what he thought was warm encouragement. She expected him to talk about his wife, make her live for his *kinder* by his words.

That was something he hadn't done well, he realized. Closemouthed by habit, he found it easy to avoid painful topics. He couldn't escape the realization that, for all his fears, Hannah was good for him. The ache he usually ignored flared like a coal finding new fuel.

Yet somehow he managed to tease his daughter. "You think your *mamm* was tall because you were so short. She wasn't as tall as Hannah." He held a hand sideways on his chest. "The top of her head came to about here. Do you remember how short your *grossmammi* was?" His hand lowered to waist level.

Rebekah giggled again. "Oh, *Daadi*! She wasn't *that* short."

He smiled. "No, but short. Zeb has always been tall for his age, but you have, too. You're taller than Beth and Adah, aren't you? Girls usually stop growing sooner than boys do, though, or so my *mamm* said."

"And you never know," Hannah agreed. "I'm about the same height as my *mamm*, even though my *daad* isn't tall for a man."

Rebekah frowned again. "Who is your *mammi*?" Her face cleared. "Lilian."

"No, my *daad* was married to my mother long before he knew Lilian. My mother is an *Englischer*, so you've never met her."

"That's why you wore pants."

"*Ja.*" She bent, and kissed his daughter's cheek. "Now, why don't you put your sewing away, and we'll start dinner. I think your *daad* must be hungry, ain't so?"

She nodded. "*Daadi* could have a cookie, couldn't he?"

"I could," he said, relaxed enough now to be amused, "but I think I can find them myself." And, truth be told, Hannah had fed him so well at noon, his belly was content to wait awhile longer for another meal.

While she and Rebekah took dishes and ingredients from cupboards and the refrigerator, he scrubbed his hands and then brought the ledger he used for tracking expenses and income to the table, along with a pile of receipts he hadn't yet entered. Usually he did this work in his office, but today he wanted to be at the center of activity. He opened the ledger, but watched Hannah and his daughter. Especially Hannah.

After Hannah had such a strange childhood raised by an irresponsible woman, how had she become so instinctively kind and giving? Samuel had said she was twenty-seven years old. Why hadn't she married? Did she care more about her career as a cook—no, a chef, that was what she'd called her job—than she did about having a family?

If that were so, why had she so willingly set it aside for the sake of the grandparents and father she hadn't even known? And how was it that she knew just what to say to Rebekah and Zeb, *and* to him, and how to touch them when that's what they needed?

No, he didn't understand this woman, but he wished he did. Most of all, he couldn't understand why she intended to leave the *kinder* and him.

SUNDAY, HANNAH AGAIN attended church with her grandmother, and planned to make a midafternoon meal for them afterward.

In the car, Helen said, "I told Jodi she's welcome to have dinner with us, but not when we expect you. I won't play any part in another ambush."

"It wasn't quite that."

"It was, and I should have known better." She compressed her lips, not saying anything else until they turned in to the parking lot behind the handsome old church. Huge sycamores grew around it, casting welcome shade. Helen said softly, "I wish so much we'd been able to have another child. I think I loved her too much."

Hannah braked to wait for another car to maneuver into a slot. "I don't believe it's possible to love too much."

Her grandmother shook her head. "It's not healthy when you pin all your hopes on one person. The weight of those hopes—"

She didn't finish. Hannah parked, set the emergency brake, and turned off the engine. She groped for the right thing to say. How was she supposed to know anything about how a family should function? *I do know what I experienced—and what I missed*, she thought. She was learning more about family from Gideon and his *kinder* than she could have imagined.

Into the silence, she said, "Parents can ruin a child. Physical abuse is passed down from generation to generation, people say. But I don't believe you ever let Mom down. You and Granddad are too loving and kind. She was fun and loving, in her way. She held jobs she hated so she could support us. She never hurt me physically, or looked the other way if anyone else hurt me. She never abandoned me."

Helen had gone still in the act of releasing her seat belt, the very hope she'd talked about in her eyes. "You're remembering what your mother did right. Have you forgiven her?"

Hannah gave her head a small shake. "I wish I could, but the lies she told were so huge, so unnecessary, and they hurt so many people. I can't get past that."

"Then?"

"I'd like you to remember that two children born to the same parents, raised very much the same, turn out quite different. I always thought Mom couldn't see consequences. I didn't know that word when I was a little girl, but even then, when I saw her turn off the alarm clock and go back to sleep, I'd think, 'If you're late to work again, Eddie will fire you, and then what will we do?' But Mom was always blithe—another word I didn't know—sure people would give her a break because she was pretty and charming and bubbly."

No wonder, Hannah thought, that she'd never wished she possessed those qualities. In fact, she'd spent her life trying *not* to be like her mother. Or was it that she'd wanted desperately to measure up to the members of her Amish family, who'd provided her with a solid foundation?

After a moment, she continued haltingly, "I think she always believes that whatever she does will be forgiven and forgotten. That the next job or the next man will be perfect. No matter how it ends, she puts it behind her and is just as certain the next time. It's as if anything she does wrong doesn't count. As if . . . so much of the past doesn't even exist." As a child who was scared something terrible would happen, Hannah had never understand Jodi's ability to do that. She finished, "No matter what, Mom doesn't learn from mistakes. I don't think you taught her any of that."

"I always wondered—" Helen didn't finish her speculation.

"Did you ever take her for counseling?"

Her smile was pained. "We tried, but not until she was a teenager, and I swear she charmed the counselors. That"—she rolled her eyes—"and she didn't show up for appointments if I didn't drag her there."

Hannah squeezed her grandmother's hand. "I often think of her as changeable, like one of those days that goes from sunny to breezy to rainy and back to sunny, but really she hasn't changed at all."

"No." Helen sighed and reached for Hannah, managing a hug. "Finding you has been such a blessing."

"I think the blessings have all been on my part," Hannah whispered.

They both had to dab at their eyes with tissues she had put in the glove compartment.

A minute later they made their way to the wide front steps of the brick church. Somehow, it was no surprise at all when Hannah saw a slim woman with shining blond hair mounting those steps ahead of them, her hand on the arm of a handsome man with salt-and-pepper hair.

Of course Jodi would decide to attend church, demonstrating how pious she was to her latest escort, and where else but here?

GIDEON HAD TO walk the *kinder* to school Monday morning, after Enoch ran out of his house and said, "*Mammi* doesn't feel good. She made breakfast, so *Daudi* doesn't know, but she's lying down. She said I should ask you—"

What could Gideon say but, "*Ja*, come along." The boy carried a lunch pail, so his mother had gotten that far. But should she be left alone, her sick and her other *kinder* so young?

No, he decided, and took the time to detour to Isaac Miller's house on the same property. When he knocked, it was Enoch's *grossmammi*, Judith, who came to the door. Enoch rushed to tell her the tale, too, and she shook her head in dismay.

"Ach, she should have sent you over to let me know! I'll just turn off the stove and go right away."

Of course, Gideon offered to pick the *kinder* up, as well, an offer Judith accepted. He worried about Susan all day, and was relieved when he brought Enoch home to have Judith come out to the porch to say, "Feeling better, Susan is. *Denke*, Gideon."

His *kinder* were quieter than usual, but not seeming distressed. When he asked about school, Rebekah told him about reading aloud and how she hadn't stumbled over a single word, but Zeb only mumbled, "It was okay."

Tomorrow would be better, Gideon couldn't help thinking, because Hannah would be here.

That turned out to be so, Zeb telling her enthusiastically over supper about the *big* fish he'd caught all by himself, and how he and his *daad* had caught several others, but Rebekah had only watched. "They tasted so good," he declared.

Rebekah pouted. Gideon caught Hannah's eye and grinned. As sometimes happened, she looked startled and then blushed, which gave him a *gross feelich*—*ja*, a big feeling—in his chest.

He made a point after that of being careful *not* to meet her eyes. And even though he knew he should ask when she intended to leave, he didn't. The week was good; he hoped the gossip about Leah's death was past.

Therefore, do not worry about tomorrow, he reminded himself. It seemed as if the Lord was nudging him to put aside his worries about the future. He could do that—at least until tomorrow.

Chapter Twenty

❖◆❖

DAVID AND MIRIAM Miller were to hold church this coming Sunday. Grumbling that she wished she'd known in advance so she could take a day to help, Hannah baked up a storm on Saturday so at least she could contribute in this way. Poor Miriam, pregnant, and having to scrub every inch of her house and probably the barn, too, Hannah told Gideon.

Amused at her fussing, Gideon reminded her that both David and Miriam had large families. "I doubt any of the women let Miriam lift a finger."

"Oh, because—" She stopped.

He gazed blandly at her. "Because?"

Hannah wrinkled her nose. "You know perfectly well."

"You will be there tomorrow?" he asked, the question careful, as if he really wanted to know.

"Certain sure." She narrowed her eyes. "Half the food might not make it out of this house if I weren't there to notice."

He laughed. "But then what will we eat Monday?"

She pretended to look grumpy. "I kept back some bread, and bacon muffins, and split pea soup you can warm, and a funnel cake. Oh, and those gingerbread cookies you like so much, too. You won't starve."

He suspected he would also find a full meal or two in the refrigerator, labels affixed to the lids that told him what was inside and how to warm it. Hannah took care of them even when she wasn't here.

Gideon hated imagining the day when she was truly gone. He only wished her cooking was what he'd miss most.

He would look for a good-natured, older widow this time, he decided, even if she were slower moving. Amish-women learned to cook from the time they were *kinder*, as Rebekah had begun to do. He would live without meals that had Hannah's special touch. He could only hope that Rebekah had learned about some of the spices and different ways of cooking from Hannah.

Although nothing would replace Hannah herself.

His mood was dark when he finished harnessing her mare and saw her horse and buggy receding down the lane. Reminding himself that she would be there tomorrow didn't help.

For at least the hundredth time, he told himself he shouldn't have hired an *Englischer* . . . although how could he have guessed that she would knock down all his de-fenses and leave him open to feelings that endangered ev-erything he was? He didn't understand himself. As shocked as he'd been at losing Leah in such a way, how could he have allowed himself to care so much about a woman who would always be anchored in the *Englisch* world, whatever decision she made in the coming weeks?

Yet it seemed every time he turned around he was re-minded of everything she'd done for his family. Sunday morning was one of those moments; he was pleased to see how well dressed his *kinder* were. One more improvement in all of their lives. Hannah had finished the new dress and apron for Rebekah, who had rushed down from getting dressed to twirl to show him. His own father would have chided her for vanity. Gideon only smiled.

"That looks very fine. I was starting to think you'd soon be wearing those short skirts, like the *Englischer* teenage girls do."

She giggled. "That's 'cause I'm growing, *Daadi!*"

"*Ja*, I have noticed. I hope Hannah has time to make you another new dress."

"She says she will. She's sewing another pair of pants for Zeb right now. 'Cause *he's* growing even more."

"That's true," he agreed. "Boys do that." He opened the refrigerator, hoping by some chance Hannah had made one of her breakfast casseroles, and there it was. He toasted slices of the lemon–poppy seed friendship bread, smiling when he remembered her teasing that he wouldn't want to bring anything she'd baked to share. In truth, he liked having such good food to offer; he'd rarely been able to make any contribution to the fellowship meal until Hannah started working for him.

Once he and the *kinder* had eaten, he shook his head when Rebekah jumped up to clear the table. "You don't need to get spots on your new dress before you even leave the house. While I clean up, will you gather everything Hannah made for the fellowship meal? Zeb, go to the cellar for a basket or two."

Zeb looked just as fine in his new shirt and pants. He and Gideon both put on their best straw hats. Gideon had a suspicion that Zeb's new clothes would not look the same by the time they came home. How could a boy play baseball without sliding into base, diving for a ball, or getting hit by a pitch? He only hoped Hannah would see the two before the service.

As it happened, they arrived shortly after Samuel, Lilian, and their younger *kinder* in the family sedan, and Mose and Hannah in the small buggy she drove to his house five days a week.

She saw them, beamed, and hurried to hug Rebekah.

Gideon smiled at her and asked if she'd like to inspect the baskets to be sure they hadn't forgotten anything.

She laughed at him and said, "No, I trust you." Her smile quickly died, and she continued to study him as if perplexed. At last, she said, "I do," so softly he thought he was the only one to hear her.

When he turned away, it was to find himself almost face-to-face with Bishop Troyer, who had raised his brows as his gaze moved from Gideon to Hannah and back.

Fortunately, Hannah was admiring the new clothes and praising Rebekah for stitching one long seam all by herself.

Zeb said, "Can I go ahead, *Daad*?"

The moment Gideon gave his okay, Zeb broke into a run.

Hannah shook her head, smiling at Amos. "He is so hard on his clothes."

Amos unbent enough to smile in return. "Maybe you should teach him to sew up rips. He might be more careful."

She just chuckled. "When he's playing or working, he shouldn't have to worry about his clothes."

"Nancy mended many tears while we raised our *kinder*."

"I'm sure—oh! I abandoned Lilian." She rushed away. "Adah, I can take that, it's too heavy for you."

Rebekah chased after her.

"As much energy as your Zeb," Amos commented, as the two men started walking. "Hannah and Rebekah."

"*Ja*, I've begun to wonder whether I have gray hairs and just haven't noticed them."

Amos smiled, but said nothing. Gideon braced himself.

"I think if Hannah was Amish, you might consider marrying her," the bishop remarked after a minute.

Gideon wanted to lie, but couldn't bring himself to do that, and to Amos of all people. "*Ja*," he said, "but I haven't forgotten that's not possible. There has been nothing between us you wouldn't want to see."

"It might still be best if she leaves soon," Amos said gently.

"She hasn't said how long she means to stay," Gideon admitted. "Not since I first hired her. I don't know what she's thinking."

"Does she still see her mother?"

"*Ja*, but not often. At church last Sunday, she said, but briefly. I think she's still too hurt to want to visit."

"Perhaps I'll talk about forgiveness today," Amos said thoughtfully. "Will she understand me?"

The two men had reached the open ground between the house and barn, where most people had gathered. "Sometimes she'll ask for a word," Gideon answered, "but she is close to speaking *Deitsh* like one of us."

"Well. I should join Josiah and Ephraim. But I must counsel you to be careful." Amos nodded once and walked away

Roiling inside, Gideon joined a group of men his age, including Luke and David.

MOVED BY THE service but also flushed with anger, Hannah looked for Gideon among the men carrying the benches out of the barn and setting them up for the meal. She didn't like to be the bearer of bad tidings, but he needed to be warned before he overheard the talk himself.

There he was, taller than most of the other men and with a beard darker than was common, too. She saw him turning his head in search of his *kinder*, spotting Zeb with a group of boys, and Rebekah, who was solemnly placing a platter with sliced bread on one of the makeshift tables.

But Gideon continued to scan the gathering until he saw Hannah. For an instant, he was all she saw, his face stern enough to seem harsh, except she'd learned that he was harder on himself than on the people he loved.

Hannah started toward him. Between the broad brim of his hat and his beard, she couldn't tell what he was thinking, but he waited until she reached him.

"Hannah."

Reasonably sure no one else was within earshot, she said urgently, "I overheard some women talking in the kitchen."

His mouth tightened. "What did these women say?"

"Nothing new, but one lowered her voice and said her sister wrote that everyone knew that 'his' wife liked the bottle too much, so it was no wonder she was in the car with a drunk when the accident happened. And that . . . that those two women killed a boy, too. *Englisch*, not Amish, but still, she said."

Gideon's dark eyes bored into hers. "Did the woman see you?"

"No. I quit listening and hurried out. Gideon, how can they talk like that? And even if it was all true, why *would* they? It's hateful!"

He tore his gaze from hers and looked away. "I don't know. But if they're still talking, their *kinder* will be, too."

"That's what I'm afraid of. No." She scowled. "It's unkind for your sake, too. I should have stepped in and told them."

"An *Englischer*, telling them what to think?"

She recoiled, both from his scathing tone and the dislike she swore she saw on the face he turned back to her. "You're right," she choked out and started to back away. "I probably shouldn't have told you. It's nothing to do with me."

"No!" he exclaimed. "Hannah, my anger is at them, not you. If Rebekah will be crying when she comes home from school Tuesday, it does have to do with you."

She stopped, a lump still stuck in her throat. Her gaze dropped to his big, powerful hands, curled into fists.

He looked down, too, seeing what she had, and deliberately relaxed his hands. "Don't be afraid of me."

"I'm not." That, she could say almost steadily. "I've never seen you violent, even when you're angry."

His eyes closed. For some absurd reason, Hannah noticed how thick his black lashes were. He rolled his shoulders, then opened his eyes. "Did you know who these women were?"

She hesitated. "Not all. And several of the women in the kitchen were listening but not saying anything. They may have disapproved."

"But they didn't say, 'Enough of this talk.'"

"They may have after I left."

His grunt told her what he thought about that.

Naming names made her feel like a tattletale, but she hadn't like the speaker's avid tone.

"I think her name is Ava."

If his expression could grow any grimmer, it did then. "Ava Kemp is Bernice's mother."

"Oh."

"I hardly know her husband, Willard. He's a butcher. Also the man you call if you need a dead animal hauled away."

She didn't quite shudder, but his mouth relaxed at her expression.

"You don't approve?"

Hannah made a face at him. "I'm squeamish, that's all. Um . . . I don't suppose you know the word."

"I think I can guess."

Was that a smile? No, it couldn't have been.

He bent his head toward the tables, where men had begun to take seats for the meal. "I'll ask Luke what he knows about the Kemps, and then talk to Amos again, but maybe not today."

"No, but . . ."

"But?"

"You might talk more to Zeb and Rebekah, so they aren't surprised."

"Telling me what to do again?"

Her eyes widened. "I'm sorry! I didn't mean that—"

"You're right." He nodded. "I'll do that."

And, in that infuriating way he had, Gideon left her without a backwards glance.

GIDEON WAITED UNTIL the women were eating, Rebekah beside Hannah, and the men gathered in groups to talk before he sought out Luke Bowman. He caught Luke's eye and didn't even have to ask if they could talk privately. Luke eased himself out of the cluster and came to Gideon.

"Something's wrong."

"*Ja*, you could say that." He paused. "You heard some of the talk about my wife's death."

Luke's face hardened. "I did. There's no excuse for it."

"I went to Amos, and he spoke to the parents of the *kinder* gossiping at school."

Luke waited, his blue eyes keen.

"Jacob and Claudia Schwartz brought their daughter to apologize to my *kinder*. They said they aren't the source of the rumors."

"I wouldn't expect them to be. Have the other parents apologized?"

"No, although it's been quiet at school. The Schwartz girl plays with the younger *kinder* instead of following what the older ones say to do."

"That's good."

Gideon sighed. "Hannah told me she just heard Ava Kemp in the kitchen throwing around the same report. Ava's sister wrote to her saying that 'everyone' knew my wife was at the bottle all the time, that it was no wonder she was killed in a drunk-driving accident."

Luke frowned. "She wouldn't have driven a car, would she?"

Gideon told him what had happened. "If 'everyone' saw Leah drunk, or ever *taking* a drink of alcohol, I must have been blind. Either Ava's sister didn't like Leah for some reason I can't understand, or she just enjoys stirring up trouble." He made a sound in his throat. "I don't even know who Ava's sister is."

Luke scratched his jaw. "This is just between you and me."

Gideon nodded.

"Ava is a couple of years older than me, if I remember right. She wasn't well liked, even as a girl. Learned from her mother, probably, because my mother told me once that Phoebe had a nasty tongue. From what I've heard, Ava got worse after marrying Willard. There are those who say—" He grimaced. "Here I am, passing on possibly unfounded rumor, but this is a common one. I've heard from several people that Willard has a temper."

"He hits his wife."

"So it's said. *Daad* told me that while I was away, Amos put Willard under the *meidung*. He had to confess to all the members to be forgiven and reinstated."

Shunning meant his wife couldn't sleep with him, or hand him dishes at the table. Stunned, Gideon thought how humiliating the confession would be, and not only for Willard. David Miller had fled to the *Englisch* world for six years after a tragedy, and had been required to confess before the brethren about punching a man and serving a term in jail, but that would be nothing compared to admitting that you hit your wife.

Trying to be charitable, Gideon said, "Perhaps Willard learned his lesson."

Luke shrugged. "I don't know, but Ava is always at worship now, no one having to make the excuse that she's sick or fell and bumped her head."

Gideon blew out his breath. "I don't want to ask Amos to speak to her again, but I think I must. Not for my sake, but for the sake of my *kinder*. It's most likely Ava and Willard's daughter Bernice who started the talk at school, because she heard it from her parents . . . or maybe only her *mamm*, I don't know."

"If you don't mind my asking, who were the other parents?"

"Mathias and Lois King. Although Zillah didn't believe their son, Yonnie, was very interested in any rumors he passed on. Just friends with Bernice, I guess, and some other girl named Emmie."

"I wonder, sometimes, how many of the *Leit* don't listen to the sermons or scriptures when we worship," Luke said wryly.

"And do they read the Bible at home? Or pray?"

Luke shook his head. "For Ava, passing on spicy gossip was probably exciting. As far as I know, she has no interests outside her home. She doesn't keep bees and sell honey, or quilt, or make and sell cider from their apples, or have a vegetable stand."

"Is Bernice their youngest?" asked Gideon, now curious.

"No, two older girls are married, my mother said, but I think there may be three or four younger."

Gideon felt a stab of familiar pain for both Leah and the unborn *boppli* he'd lost. No one else had known she was pregnant, and he'd never wanted to tell anyone afterward.

"Mathias and Lois, I don't know well," Luke said. "I can ask my mother or father about them."

After giving that a moment of thought, Gideon shook his head. "I think I must leave this in Amos's hands."

"*Ja*," Luke agreed, although he looked regretful.

Gideon wondered how much, after so many years out in the world, the other man had struggled to humble himself before the Lord and the bishop. Yet he seemed to have succeeded. Gideon hadn't had any such struggle . . . until the aftermath of Leah's death. He'd found some peace here in Tompkin's Mill, in part because he respected Amos Troyer and the two ministers, too.

He sighed and said, "*Denke* for your honesty. These are not troubles I expected to have after moving."

"These aren't troubles you *should* have had, here or in any other Amish settlement!"

"There is gossip anywhere."

"But not usually so mean-spirited."

That was blunt, indeed, and also true.

"I may leave early, once Rebekah has eaten and helped clear the tables. Zeb won't like it, but—"

"Your place isn't so far. We'd be glad to bring him home later, if he wouldn't mind."

"You plan to stay?"

Luke smiled. "Abby will be happy to play with her friends when she's done eating, and Julia put Nathan down for a nap just before she sat down. His schedule is never convenient."

Gideon grinned. "Except that Julia has a chance to eat in peace."

"Oh, she'd have had that, anyway. *I'd* be holding him."

Despite his wry tone, Luke's happiness was apparent. And why not? He had what Gideon had wanted and once had: a loving wife, a family, and satisfying work.

A minute later, he spoke to Zeb, who was next up to bat, and then Rebekah, who wanted to play with her friends, too. It was no surprise when Hannah said, "Mose and I have room for her. I'd be glad to watch over her after you go." Her smile for Rebekah was reassuring, her eyes anxious when her gaze met Gideon's.

"I'm fine. Just not wanting to stand around talking."

"Okay." She touched his arm, so lightly he barely felt her

fingertips rest on him for an instant, yet his skin might as well have been bare.

He thanked her, too, then walked down the lane to reclaim his gelding and buggy, glad to escape the bustle and endless talk, even as he wished for the impossible.

Chapter Twenty-One

❖◆❖

HANNAH TOOK HER keys from the ignition and unfastened her seat belt, but then just sat there in front of the Mill Café, where her mother had suggested they meet for lunch. The fact that this was where Jodi had met Samuel disturbed Hannah. Did her mother even remember?

Pushing back the dread, Hannah made herself get out of her car and walk into the café. Not a buggy was parked here; if any Amish were having lunch in town today, they would more likely have gone to the Country Days Café or the bakery, both Amish owned. Or possibly the Sonic Drive-In; the sight of horses and buggies in those outside spots had struck her as incongruous.

The cool air inside took her by surprise, so accustomed had she become to the heat. The hostess approached her, but Hannah saw Jodi in a booth at the far corner and said, "My mother is already here."

Walking toward the booth, she saw double for a disconcerting instant. She must have been a young adult, out on her own, pleased to see her mother. The illusion was maintained because, from this distance, Jodi could have been in her thirties or even younger, her smile as carefree as ever, her delight intoxicating. In the here and now, Hannah would have liked to be almost anywhere else.

Well, she'd been a coward long enough. She'd make herself listen, and then judge for herself . . . but she prayed her mother didn't tell more lies or embellish the ones she'd already told.

She nodded as she slid into the booth. A menu lay on the table in front of her. Hannah reached for a glass of ice water.

"Hello, Mom."

Her mother flashed her brightest smile. "I've missed you so much! I can hardly believe we have the chance to talk at last, just the two of us."

"Let's order first, shall we?" Hannah picked up the menu, scanning it with little interest. When she was a kid, this would have been a treat. Now, well, she'd attended culinary school, worked in a restaurant that prided itself on innovation, and had more recently immersed herself in learning and expanding on a cuisine that was subtly different from the solid American fare you'd find at most places like this, probably anywhere in the country. Truthfully, she wasn't very hungry, but the act of ordering and eating would provide a diversion, and maybe have a civilizing effect.

Mother and daughter, having lunch, catching each other up on their lives.

So, she imagined herself saying, *I'm getting to know Daad—you know, the father you always claimed was dead? He's super nice. We're having such a good time.*

An older waitress with bags under her eyes appeared. "What can I get for you girls?"

Jodi laughed happily at being called a girl.

Once they'd both ordered, they looked at each other across the table.

"Sweetie, I don't understand what's been happening *at all*. You've gotten so *cold*!"

Jodi's teenager mannerisms and voice, all high drama and urgent exclamations, really grated today. In her own teenage years, Hannah had hardly noticed. Mom was just Mom. In the past six weeks or so, Hannah had become a hundred times more critical. More so than she liked.

Her Lord expected her to forgive.

But first, just once, she'd like some real honesty.

"Two months ago, I learned that you'd been lying to me for as long as I could remember," she said quietly. "From little lies, like convincing me I'd never been in an Amish buggy, to the huge ones: claiming my father and grandparents were dead. It was just us."

"It was!"

"Yes, it was, because you made sure of it." When the waitress brought their drinks, Hannah bit down on everything else she wanted to say.

Then, resolved to stay calm, she continued. "You ran, and you keep running, whenever any authority might have had reason to look into my history. Or maybe it was *your* history you worried about—after all, you could have been arrested for kidnapping, couldn't you?"

Jodi's mouth rounded in horror. "That's ridiculous! You're my daughter. I was entitled—"

"No, you weren't. You can't possibly be that naive. You know that it's illegal to take a child without the permission of the other parent."

"He was hurting you!" Spite transformed Jodi's usually breathy voice. "Samuel, and all those awful women he made sure were there to watch me when he couldn't. If I did a single thing they didn't like—"

"*Daadi* never hurt me." If Hannah knew anything about the early years of her life, this was the most important. "I loved him. Those 'other' women were my aunts, my grandmother."

"I could never do anything right. They hardly trusted me to change your diaper."

Hannah couldn't imagine her mother *wanting* to change a diaper, but she didn't say anything.

Jodi's face flushed with anger Hannah hadn't seen in a long time.

"They'd cluck their tongues and snatch you out of my arms. Take the pins out of your diaper and put them back in *their* way." Her voice kept rising. "If I warmed a bottle, one of them would grab it to check the temperature before I was allowed to sit down with you. They were scandalized if I let you run around in shorts and a T-shirt. Nothing *I* cooked was ever good enough. *They* stuffed their faces, and insisted Samuel had to eat ridiculous amounts of food or he wouldn't be able to work hard. He was my husband, but I had zero say in how we lived. I was supposed to give up all my friends, and learn to harness and drive a horse. Cars are evil!" She clapped a hand to her chest. "Gasp! If any of those witches saw me get in one, she'd report to Samuel. You were my daughter, and I couldn't take you with me when I went to town."

Hannah realized she was finally hearing honesty. In a romantic haze, Jodi had married an Amishman without understanding that his faith, his life and culture, didn't allow her to flit from one interest to another the way she always had. She'd somehow believed that marriage wasn't any different than the jobs any teenager or young adult took, the college classes she could quit if they bored her. Fun for a while, but one day she'd seen that this might be forever.

Hannah could imagine her mother, first squirming, then panicking. Feeling trapped. Of course she wanted to run away, but she had a child now. Hannah knew Mom had loved her. She never doubted that. Jodi wouldn't have considered leaving her. Seeing that Samuel and his family could give her little girl what she couldn't would have demanded selflessness of which she was incapable.

If she'd even hinted to her parents that she wanted a divorce, she'd have seen their disapproval. The concept would have been unthinkable to the husband she hadn't understood at all.

Suddenly, Hannah felt pity for her mother, despite the many lies.

"They were stealing you," her mother said bitterly. "Teaching you to be just like *them*. If I'd waited any longer, you'd have fought me. Don't you see? You were *my* child. I *had* to get you away before your world shrank to the size of *theirs*." There it was again, the disgust. "I was saving you! And what thanks do I get? You act like *I* did something wrong."

Their lunches came. Hannah was able to thank the waitress despite the tension between her and her mother. She felt how tangled that space between them was, like wild blackberry bushes, thick old canes bristling with razorsharp thorns, the more supple, new canes as painfully cutting.

Once she and her mother were alone, Hannah tried to ignore the ache in her chest and the softening of her feelings. "You did do something wrong, Mom. How can you not see that? Grandma and Granddad loved me, too. So did my Amish *grossmammi*, *Aenti* Sarah. And *Daadi*, most of all."

"Don't use that language with me! Do you have any idea how much I despise it?"

"But they *are* Amish, and that's their language. It's *my* language, as much as English."

"That's ridiculous!" her mother exclaimed. "You're twenty-seven years old. Nobody even remembers the stuff that happens before they're five! You can't tell me you understand them talking to you."

"At first I didn't. But, you know, *Daad* especially speaks perfectly fine English. I suppose you wouldn't have married him if he hadn't."

"I wish he hadn't. If he'd jabbered at me in that stupid language, I'd never have thought it would be fun to take a ride in that . . . that *buggy*. His accent was different, exciting. He was older than the boys I'd dated."

Hannah liked Gideon's accent, too, except that now she hardly noticed when they were speaking English or *Deitsh* or a mishmash of both. She just liked Gideon.

"Well, here's news, Mom. I must have spoken *Deitsh* fluently when you took me away." *Kidnapped me.* "Because I've soaked it up like a sponge. I didn't have to learn it. I absorbed it. Whether you like it or not, I'm half-Amish."

A different kind of horror appeared on her mother's face. "You're not thinking of *joining* them. Please tell me you aren't."

Hannah opened her mouth to say, *Of course I'm not, but that isn't the point*. What came out was, "I feel at home here. We never had a home, did we? Maybe . . . maybe if you'd settled down, and I'd been able to stay in the same school district, make lifelong friends, feel like I belonged anywhere, I'd be a different person now. But I could never trust that tomorrow night, I'd sleep in the same bed. I quit unpacking. Did you know that? I had to be sure there'd be time to pack up the kitchen stuff, so my clothes stayed in that scroungy old suitcase." She knew she was hurting her mother. Guilt battled with her need to be honest, too, if only this once. She hesitated. "There's something else, too. I can't tell you how much I love the faith I see among the Amish. You remember I was always a churchgoer."

"Oh, church. I never understood."

"But you grew up attending with your parents."

"And I was bored every minute," Jodi said sharply. "Although that was nothing compared to those awful Amish services! Three hours, and I only understood one in three words! Just try it and you'll see."

"I have, and I felt closer to God than I ever have before."

Her mother stared at her in horror.

"The Amish who have chosen to be baptized believe so much more deeply. Their faith may shake, but it's unbreakable. It shapes them, defines them. I'm drawn to that, Mom. I would love to have some certainty in my life. Sometime, somewhere."

Sometime? In Gideon and his *kinder*, hadn't she found what she'd always sought? Gideon would never let down anyone he loved. Or anyone whom he had the power to help, for that matter. He tried to keep some distance from her, but often failed. And he was always, always, trustworthy. She'd seen how gentle he was with Zeb and Rebekah, how he listened to them. How he listened to *her*, and changed his intentions because of what she said. He'd even, on occasion, let her see the softness he hid because it made him too vulnerable.

Could she possibly have fallen in love with Gideon Lantz? Or was she making the same mistake her mother had, all those years ago?

Since he very likely didn't feel the same, her yearning would come to nothing.

Mom shook her head. "I can't believe this. Everything I did for your sake, and it was all for nothing."

Forgiveness came to her in that moment, a powerful wave of emotion. It was time, she knew, in part because her mother *had* been honest. Hannah was able to see clearly that what she'd told Helen was probably true. The young Jodi Hinsch might simply not have been capable of changing, maturing. Perhaps she *had* done the best she could.

Peace flooded through Hannah, washing away every negative emotion. The feeling was astonishing. Tears stung her eyes. How easy this was.

Peace I leave with you; My peace I give to you. Not as the world gives do I give to you. Let not your heart be troubled, neither let it be afraid.

God had seen that she was ready. Perhaps what she'd felt earlier wasn't pity at all; it was acceptance. Much of her childhood had been frightening, but without its challenges, she wouldn't be the woman she was now. The one who didn't want a life hampered by anger.

I can forgive her, she thought. *I do.*

On a deep breath of relief, she reached across the table and took her mother's hand in hers. "I love you, but I'm not like you, Mom."

Jodi snatched her hand back. "I suppose you think you're like *him*."

"He makes up half of me. In the five years we lived with him, he did influence who I am. How could it be otherwise?" she asked gently.

Grabbing her purse, Jodi slid out of the booth. "If you join the Amish, I'll never see you again."

Was that grief? Or a threat to cut her off?

"That's not true," Hannah said gently. "You'll always be my mother. You'll make a wonderful grandmother, you know."

Jodi's eyes filled with tears. "I don't know if I can."

Hannah hurriedly stood, too, and embraced her mother. Jodi stayed stiff in her arms, but didn't wrench herself away immediately, either. "I love you," Hannah whispered.

Jodi clutched her daughter for one convulsive hug, then tugged free and fled. Hannah had one last glimpse of her mother's face, wet with tears, before she hurried toward the exit and rushed out to her car.

Close to tears herself, Hannah looked down at her untouched sandwich, then felt a fragile moment of humor. Naturally, it hadn't even occurred to her mother to leave money for the check.

But her heart felt light when she dropped bills on the table, and when she, too, walked out.

"Thank you," she whispered to a God she believed heard her.

*   *   *

Monday, Zeb came home from school sullen, even angry. When Gideon tried to find out why, his son refused to talk about it. In stubborn silence, he ate two of Hannah's cookies, drank a glass of milk, and stalked out to do his chores.

Gideon blew out a breath and sat down across from Rebekah, who was nibbling daintily on her second cookie. "Do you know what's wrong?"

She looked worried. "I saw some of the older *kinder* talking to him. Teacher was busy with Timothy, 'cause he backed up trying to catch a ball and ran into the wall. He was bleeding and crying."

"Was he all right?"

"*Ja,* just a bump. Some of the boys were laughing at him."

"That was unkind."

She nodded firmly. "I told them *they* wouldn't like it if someone laughed at *them* because they got hurt."

"Good. I hope they understood." He held Rebekah's gaze. "Now tell me about Zeb."

"I don't know," she said hesitantly. "On the way home, I asked what the big kids said. He wouldn't tell me, and he won't tell you, either, because he thinks you'll lie."

Gideon hoped she didn't notice how rigidly he held himself. "Why would he believe I'd lie to him?"

She ducked her head and mumbled something.

"Rebekah?"

"I don't know."

He suspected that wasn't true, but recognized her stubborn expression. She didn't like tattling on her brother, and he didn't blame her.

Zeb stayed closemouthed over dinner, too, and Gideon decided to let him get away with it, this once. He would be angrier, except that it was true he hadn't told either of his *kinder* everything. Hannah had somehow heard what he *didn't* say, and it seemed she was right that Zeb could, too.

How was it that she saw him more deeply than anyone else ever had?

After Gideon had gone to talk to Bishop Troyer again this morning, it was likely Bernice's and Yonnie's parents would have to explain themselves a second time to their bishop. Gideon would not want to be in their shoes. Tomorrow, they'd see what happened at school.

Hannah was quieter than usual when she arrived in the morning, only nodding politely at him as he took charge of her mare. He saw her hug Rebekah as always, though, and lift Zeb's hat off his head so she could ruffle his hair. No eight-year-old boy would like to know he was blushing by the time she placed the hat back where it belonged.

"Now, let's go see what we have for lunch," she said.

He went straight to work, leaving Hannah to do her job. Taking advantage of the cooler temperatures before the sun got too hot, Gideon took down a good-size maple tree and began cutting it up. Maple was one of his favorite woods for heating the house, and if he cut it into rounds now and then split those rounds, it would have plenty of time to season before winter. This afternoon, Isaac and Jake Miller had promised to join him to make some repairs on the barn roof. It wasn't a job he'd want to do alone. When they needed help in turn, they'd call on him.

By the time he hacked the limbs off the tree, he'd acquired scratches on his face and hands. He took time to separate the branches that were large enough to be worth sawing for firewood from the ones he'd leave in the woods to compost.

When he went into the house for the midday meal, he didn't immediately see Hannah, although she couldn't have gone far, since good smells came from the oven and stove.

A small mirror hung in the downstairs bathroom so that anyone using it could be sure a *kapp* was on securely or to clean up more effectively. Gideon splashed water on his face and started to reach for a towel, but took a look at himself first and grimaced. Oh, *ja*, that was why any exposed skin stung. He washed more carefully before he risked using a towel. At least his beard had provided some protection, although he had to pick leaves and twigs out of it.

When he returned to the kitchen, he saw a crock held ham and beans, and Hannah had baked his favorite cornbread, as well.

With her back still to him, she said apologetically, "I should have set the bread to rising earlier, but I brought some cabbage rolls I made yesterday at *Daad*'s house, and I can run down to the cellar for applesauce. I did make a streusel cake—"

"I will not starve, Hannah. That's plenty. I saw the clean clothes on the line."

She poured coffee for him, and they took their places at the table. He bent his head in prayer and knew she was doing the same.

The moment he lifted his head, he reached for a muffin and the butter.

Hannah dished up a small helping of ham and beans for herself. "You look like a rabid barn cat leaped on your head this morning."

One side of his mouth lifted. "That's what it feels like. I'm cutting up a tree for firewood. Branches have a way of springing back unexpectedly."

Her gaze moved over him, taking note of the damage to his forearms and the backs of his hands, too. But when she spoke again, it wasn't about his scratches. Instead, she said, "Zeb was quiet this morning."

Hearing the note of inquiry in her voice, Gideon said, "Last night, too. Rebekah admitted that some of the older *kinder* talked to him when they knew Tabitha wouldn't notice."

"Oh, no," she said softly.

"*Ja*, so I think." He filled his plate and ate for several

minutes before saying tautly, "Rebekah says he won't talk to me because he thinks I won't be honest with him."

He hadn't intended to tell her that. Maybe he'd been fooling himself. His worries had been like muscle cramps, waking him frequently during the night. Sharp and painful, easing, then making themselves felt again.

Being able to talk with her about the *kinder* had become important to Gideon. He didn't always like knowing that, but it was true. No, the compulsion he felt to talk to her wasn't limited only to the *kinder*. He liked knowing she told him things he had no doubt she usually kept to herself, too.

She stirred food around on her plate, but didn't actually take a bite. Still, it was a minute before she lifted her gaze to meet his. "You know, I had the impression, when you talked to Zeb and Rebekah, that you were holding back some of what happened. Maybe you only did because I was there, and you didn't like saying too much in front of me."

That would have given him an excuse, but he didn't take it. "No," he said gruffly. "I hated some of what was said after Leah died, and I thought the *kinder* were still too young to hear it. Or never needed to."

"But they're hearing plenty, anyway," she pointed out, in her gentle way. "And Zeb, at least, is old enough to guess there's more you didn't say. He's probably been thinking ever since of what that 'more' could be, and some of his ideas might be worse than the reality."

"Does he need to know that Leah's drunk *Englisch* friend hit another car head-on?" Gideon demanded. "That she killed a boy, barely seventeen, along with herself and Leah? That their *mamm* had just told me we were to have another *kind*, but our *boppli* died along with her?"

He groaned and let his head fall forward. Even Leah's *mamm* didn't know. But here it had just burst out of him.

"Oh, Gideon." The ache in Hannah's voice echoed the hurt inside him.

After a minute, he lifted his head and looked at her. Of course, her face had softened with sympathy. Just seeing what she felt was a balm to him.

"You won't tell anyone?" he asked.

"No. Never."

He nodded. Why not finish this ugly story? "There was talk that Leah was drunk, too. I never saw her drink. A time or two, a smell of alcohol seemed to cling to her when she came home from visiting her friend, but I thought it was like cigarette smoke. Her friend smoked, too."

Hannah only waited.

After a moment, he continued. "That day, she had lunch with her friend. Brooke. The police chief talked to the owner of the restaurant where they ate. He knew what time Brooke and Leah left. The accident didn't happen until three hours later."

"Maybe they went to this Brooke's house."

"Maybe, but if so, nobody noticed her car." He shrugged. "Neighbors might have been at work. I don't know. Now, we'll never know."

"Surely if they'd gone to a bar, or, I don't know, a tavern, someone would have noticed them. An Amishwoman would have stood out."

"*Ja.* The police chief asked if I wanted him to test Leah's blood for alcohol, but I said no. How could I doubt her? She was a good wife, a good mother. I refused to believe she would ever drink alcohol, and especially when she was pregnant."

Hannah heard something in his voice he hadn't meant to betray, because she said, "But?"

He looked at her in torment. "But I did doubt her." The next words were torn from him. "I blamed her. How can I ever say that to my *kinder*?"

Chapter Twenty-Two

❖❖❖

HANNAH TWINED HER fingers together. To keep herself from reaching out to him?

"That's a normal, human reaction, I think," she said carefully. "Not something that you need to feel ashamed about."

His throat worked. "She would have trusted in me."

She groped for the right thing to say. So much of life, she'd watched from a distance. But she'd started this, and she couldn't have stopped herself from offering him solace.

"I think . . . we always want to believe a tragedy didn't have to happen. We insist on believing that, if only she'd done something different, everything would have come out fine. Worse yet, we think, 'If only *I'd* done something different.' Of course, you asked those questions. But do you still blame her in any way?"

Gideon stared at her with those burning dark eyes. "No."

"If she'd made a mistake, you would have forgiven her, surely." Oh, how much easier to say this was now that she'd forgiven her mother!

"Ja." He sounded hoarse.

"Whatever the answers are to your questions, you have to quit torturing yourself, Gideon. I've . . . seen what a good man you are." She nibbled on her lip, wondering who she was to offer counsel. But he'd been open with her, and the best she could do was summon the same Bible verse that had so perfectly described how she felt after forgiving her mother. "Do you remember this passage from John? 'Peace I leave with you; My peace I give to you. Not as the world gives do I give to you. Let not your heart be troubled, neither let it be afraid.'"

He didn't move or break that stare for the longest time, but at last he closed his eyes and made a muffled sound. "I thought I'd found peace, until all this started again."

Oh, this was none of her business, but . . . "Weren't your parents a help?"

"No." A familiar gruffness in his voice meant he was reluctant to make this admission. "My father is a stern man, a minister in our church district. He never allows himself to depart from what he believes is the right way."

"The narrow way," she murmured.

"Ja. My mother . . . she would never argue with him, never quietly speak a word he wouldn't have approved, never sneak a treat he wouldn't have liked to one of us."

Hannah pictured him as a boy with tousled dark hair, defiant eyes, and a questioning mind.

"Did you get in trouble?"

He grimaced. "Often. Sometimes when I hadn't done anything wrong. Nobody would listen to me. I resented that."

"And vowed you would be a different kind of father." And husband, it occurred to her. Of course, his parents hadn't supported him.

"We don't make vows."

"You know what I mean."

"Ja." He pressed his lips together, and then resumed eating.

Hannah hopped up to grab the coffeepot, and topped off his mug.

"I hope today goes better for Zeb."

"Ja."

His usual short answer made her feel as if he'd decided to shut her out. He was probably right to do so. She was an *auslander*, however she dressed and whether she spoke his language or not. He had talked to her only because she was taking care of his *kinder*, not because he felt close to her.

Her cheeks felt hot. She shouldn't have asked about his childhood.

He knows all about mine.

They hadn't agreed to share and share alike. She worked for him. He'd hired her only grudgingly, probably because Samuel had asked him to. If sometimes it felt as if Gideon, Zeb, and Rebekah were her family, this the home she'd craved all her life, she'd been deluding herself.

I should be applying for jobs, she thought, with a familiar surge of panic. *Not . . . not lingering here, as if—*

She swallowed, trying to dislodge a lump in her throat. *As if I intend to stay.*

Had she really made that decision? If so, maybe that had been a mistake.

Confused, sad, angry with herself, she rose to start clearing the table. She dished up a slice of the vinegar pie she hadn't been able to resist trying and set it in front of him while averting her gaze from his face. The filling did taste astonishingly like lemon, without any citrus in its ingredients. Still, she vowed to make some lemon meringue pies this week.

"You're not having any?" he asked, when she started running dishwater.

"No, I'm not very hungry."

She didn't look at him once until she heard the sound of his chair scraping back.

"I'll talk to Zeb tonight," he said. "You were right in suggesting I need to be more honest with him."

She turned. "I don't remember saying that. Well, not exactly."

He actually grinned, making her pulse skip.

Oh, she had it bad. How could she keep working here, now that she couldn't block out her awareness of him as a man? When she couldn't stop herself from blushing? And, yes, she was doing it again.

"You're good at prodding me to do what you think is right," he said, amusement lingering in the curve of his lips. "Any man with sense listens when a woman like you—" He broke off, his shock apparent.

She was stunned, but tried to counter it with a smile. "When a woman won't quit nagging, you mean?"

"*Ja,*" he said slowly. "Something like that."

"Speaking of, unless you're going back out to do battle with that tree, you should put some antibiotic ointment on those scratches. The deeper ones, anyway." Not letting herself see how he'd react to another order, Hannah took a tube of ointment from a drawer. She'd used it just the other day on Zeb's knee after he'd skinned it.

"The scratches will get dirty, anyway." His voice came from right behind her.

Hannah jumped before she summoned enough dignity to turn to face him. "Better put this on before dirt gets into them."

"*Ja.*" But he didn't reach for the tube. Instead, he looked down at her.

Her heart pounded hard, but not from fear. She wanted . . . she needed . . .

He bent his head slowly, as if to give her time to retreat. How could she, with her feet rooted to the floor? Creases between his brows formed something like a frown, but not quite. Hannah waited in breathless hope.

His lips touched hers, softly. She lifted her hand to his cheek, liking the texture of his beard and the hard line of his jaw beneath it. He kissed her again, and this time she rose on tiptoe to respond.

Cupping her face with his calloused hand, he adjusted the tilt of her head, and kept kissing her. Hannah heard herself make a sound—a small whimper?—and was sorry when Gideon straightened.

But then she heard what he had: a horse and buggy passing the house, stopping at the hitching rail. One of Gideon's horses in the pasture let out a nicker.

"I . . . maybe that's Julia?" she said shakily.

Gideon's hand dropped to his side and he took a step back. "No. Jacob and Isaac Miller are here to help me replace shingles on the barn roof."

"Oh."

He didn't allow himself to look away, but she hated the expression on his face. This was the well-guarded man she'd first met.

"I shouldn't have done that," he said. "I let myself forget you're an *Englischer*." His lips tightened. "And you work for me."

Mind whirling, Hannah couldn't think of a single thing to say.

"We'll talk about it later," he said. Ignoring the tube of ointment in her hand, he clapped his hat on his head and went out the back door.

Hannah stood where she was, fingertips pressed to her lips. Tears stung her eyes.

THE ENTIRE AFTERNOON, Gideon berated himself. Several times, he caught himself about to make a mistake because his attention wasn't on what he was doing. That was especially foolish when he sat on the steep slant of the barn roof, high above the ground. Yet he couldn't seem to prevent himself from thinking about that kiss.

He hadn't smooched with a woman in three years, not since Leah died. He hadn't wanted to. He'd been driven to make a good living from the land, to protect his *kinder*, to raise them to be confident, caring, and solid in their faith.

Despite the attentions of single women back home and then here in Tompkin's Mill, too, he hadn't even been tempted. He was honest enough with himself now to recognize that changed the minute the strange *Englischer* had rolled down her car window to ask him a polite question. Hannah, and only Hannah, had tempted him from the beginning, although he hadn't let himself acknowledge the truth at first.

If he had, he couldn't have hired her. When he spoke to Amos about her, it didn't occur to him to say, *I like her too much*, although even then . . .

He heard a scraping sound and turned his head to be sure Jacob hadn't slipped, but his neighbor was only pulling a bag of shingles closer.

The sun baked them, and Gideon's sweat stung where he was scratched. He might have felt better if he'd applied the ointment.

If he'd spread the ointment on his scratches, he might not have surrendered to impulse and kissed Hannah. Perhaps the burning on his hands, face, and neck was God's way of rapping His knuckles on Gideon's head as a reminder that a believer should keep a distance from unbelievers.

For what fellowship has righteousness with lawlessness? And what communion has light with darkness?

He felt a stirring of rebellion. He couldn't equate Hannah with darkness. Her faith in the Lord was a deeply felt part of her. Nor was she lawless.

Still, if he let this go on, he would do damage to himself.

Letting himself love a woman from outside his faith would tear him apart. And trusting that, even if she did convert, she would never have regrets about giving up the life she once had? No.

He liked even less knowing how much Hannah would be hurt, too. Her strength, her belief in God, her instinctive generosity and ability to love covered the sadness she couldn't entirely hide, her damaged ability to trust. She might not be able to endure yet more wounds.

I should ask her to find a different job, he realized, even as his rib cage tightened until he couldn't draw a breath. If he did that, he'd be protecting himself, but stealing something precious from Rebekah and Zeb.

He came in for dinner not knowing what to expect. What he found was much as usual: Hannah and Rebekah bustling to prepare dinner, while Zeb sat at the table scowling over a book and notebook covered in his messy writing.

When Hannah exclaimed, "Here's your *daadi*," the *kinder* didn't act as if they heard the same false note he did. Rebekah ran to him for a hug, but stopped short, looking horrified.

"*Daadi*, what happened to you?"

Before he could answer, Hannah shook her head in dismay. "I always thought bobcats were shy, but today one jumped out of a tree onto him. Your father wrestled with it." She sighed. "And now I have to figure out how to cook bobcat meat. Maybe a stew?"

Both *kinder* stared from her to him in shock.

She burst out laughing. "I think it was a tree that attacked your *daadi*."

"Not a bobcat?" Zeb sounded disappointed.

"No bobcat," Gideon confirmed. "The scratches do sting."

Hannah gave him a pointed look. "I put the ointment on the sink."

He grimaced, gave Rebekah her hug, and then went to

clean up. And, *ja*, the ointment was messy but also soothing. As he stared at himself in the small mirror, it occurred to him that Hannah hadn't really looked at him. Not when he first appeared, not when she was teasing the *kinder*.

Wasn't that what he wanted?

He shook his head impatiently and returned to the kitchen to sit down with Hannah and his *kinder* to eat dinner.

If he hadn't been apprehensive about seeing her and finding out whether Zeb's mood had improved, he'd have noticed the smell of chicken frying sooner. As it was, he raised his eyebrows at the sight of a large platter of chicken in the middle of the table.

"Did you—?"

Her gaze almost, but not quite, met his. "I brought the chicken from *Daad*'s. Lilian showed me how to pluck it and cut it up. Next time, I'll let you know."

He nodded and reached for a piece that looked like white meat. Flavor exploded in his mouth. The spices she'd used in the breading were different, and delicious. The meat itself was moist.

Rebekah was eager to talk about her day, Zeb less so, although he seemed often to be sulky lately. If he were a few years older, Gideon might have blamed Zeb's up-and-down moods on the approach of the teenage years, but couldn't seize on that easy answer. Zeb was certainly more hotheaded than his sister, but Gideon recognized that from his own boyhood. Boys worried about their standing among other boys, a form of pride the Amish didn't admire. Yet it seemed to come naturally. Learning to recognize *hochmut*, to overcome that kind of foolish pride, was part of growing up.

Gideon didn't push. It might be better if he didn't talk to Zeb in front of Rebekah. While Hannah and Rebekah were cleaning the kitchen after dinner, he did encourage Zeb to come out with him to harness Clover and back her between the shafts of the buggy for Hannah's short drive home. He let Zeb do as much as he could, and praised him. If Zeb could take over this task, Gideon wouldn't have those strangely intimate minutes when he said good night to Hannah. He would miss that time, just the two of them, but that was one of the changes he needed to make if she was to stay working for him.

Just as Hannah emerged from the house, Zeb let his father down by running to the chicken coop to start a chore that he was supposed to have done earlier. Perhaps tonight it was just as well. He and Hannah did have to talk.

She stopped in front of him, holding herself with dignity, and said, "I should quit staying for dinner every night. I've gotten in the habit for no good reason. Tomorrow—"

He interrupted. "We'd miss you. I'm more concerned about *middaagesse*. Perhaps I should take food with me like the *kinder* do, so I don't need to come in."

"No. I'll prepare lunch and either eat before you come in, or after. I'll go back to my work while you eat."

The midday meal would never be the same again, but Gideon nodded. "That might be best."

Without saying anything else, Hannah got into the buggy, picked up the reins, and clicked her tongue at her mare. She didn't even glance at Gideon.

He stood watching her go, a great heaviness inside of him.

AFTER READING BIBLE verses aloud that evening, as he always did, Gideon sent Rebekah to bed, but asked Zeb to stay behind.

Her expression grew mutinous. "Why does *he* get to stay up?"

"He's older, and we have things to talk about." Gideon let her see that he wouldn't hear any argument, but she still made a huffing sound and stomped upstairs, making a great deal more noise than usual.

His *daad* would have followed and punished Gideon or

any of his sisters and brothers for even an unspoken rebellion like that. Other families among this church district might be harsher than Gideon was, but he thought his *kinder* should know he listened to their protests. He never wanted them to be afraid of him.

He returned to the living room to find Zeb looking wary.

"Did I do something wrong?" he asked.

Gideon shook his head. "Will you tell me whether the other students are still gossiping about your *mamm*?"

Zeb shrugged, or maybe only hunched his thin shoulders. "Not so much today," he mumbled. "Yesterday, Bernice and some of the other *kinder* said you must be lying to me, because Bernice's *aenti* knew what happened."

"Did she say her *aenti*'s name?"

Zeb frowned. "Don't you know?"

Gideon shook his head. "How could I?" And then he said, "I hope you set them straight. How can some woman in our church district claim to know more about the accident than I do? If something bad happened to Miriam Miller, I wouldn't tell everyone I knew better than her husband or parents unless that accident happened right in front of my driveway and I had been there to help. If I wrote to Bishop Raber, he would speak sternly to this woman for spreading falsehoods. She could have no good reason to brag that she knew more than anyone else."

Zeb looked startled. "Maybe you should send a letter to Bishop Raber."

"I can't do that when I don't know which member of his congregation to name."

"Oh. That's why you want to know?"

Gideon held his gaze. "No. My hope is that you'll use your head when you hear irresponsible talk. That you'll take time to think about what's said, and recognize falsehood from possible truth."

Zeb seemed to shrink. "I just got so mad."

"Part of becoming a man is learning to control your

temper, but it isn't always easy when you're provoked." He paused. "I also decided you're old enough to hear more about the accident. When it happened, I wanted to protect you and Rebekah. You were too young to hear everything. The talk being flung around has taught me that I can't always protect you. You need to be able to hold up your head and say, 'You can't tell me anything I don't know.'"

He thought that was trust in his son's eyes.

"Your *mamm* was with her friend, Brooke, like I said. It's true that Brooke was drunk. She was speeding when she crossed the yellow line on the road and hit another car head-on. The other driver died, too. He was only a boy, seventeen. He hadn't been driving long."

"An *Englischer*," Zeb whispered.

"That doesn't matter. He was still a boy. Brooke could just as easily have hit a buggy. As fast as she was driving, she could have killed an entire family."

"So that part was true."

"*Ja.*"

Zeb looked stricken now. "I wish *Mammi* hadn't gone with her."

"I understand, but we both have to accept that God called her home to be with Him. We can't understand His purpose, but how can we? What I don't like is knowing how scared your mother would have been. Thinking about us, praying that she would make it home safely."

"Had she been drinking the alcohol, too?"

"I can't say for certain sure," Gideon admitted, almost steadily. "The police chief offered to check her blood to find out, even though she wasn't to blame for the accident since she wasn't driving."

Zeb waited, unblinking, but his eyes were wet.

"I said no. How could I not have faith that she wouldn't have done something like that? I had never seen her with a bottle, never seen her act strange, stagger when she walked as drunks do. I believe exactly what I told you: that her friend sometimes drank when they were together, but your *mamm* didn't understand what could happen. One extra drink could have made the difference, but not been something your *mamm* would have noticed. Maybe that day she worried, but wasn't sure how to get home and told herself Brooke had never had an accident before." Gideon moved his shoulders. "It would have happened fast. They told me she died right away. God was merciful."

Tears ran down his son's cheeks now. Gideon stood, and joined Zeb on the couch, resting a hand on his shoulder.

"That's the truth." Gideon took a deep breath. "The talk afterward was about me. Bishop Raber hadn't liked me letting your mother ride in the car with her friend. He didn't like her spending time with an *Englischer*. Sometimes, I think he might have been right, that I was to blame for her being in the car when the accident happened."

"But . . . you said we're not forbidden from riding in cars."

"No. I never saw Brooke drunk. I liked her."

"She was nice to us," Zeb said in a small voice.

"She was." Heeding thoughts of Hannah, Gideon told Zeb about his own childhood and, finally, why he'd decided to move. "I'm glad we did. Bishop Troyer is a good man, not as restrictive as Bishop Raber was. I accept his word with an open heart, because I can tell he respects the ability of all the sisters and brothers to make the right choices. He thinks and listens to God before he tells us we made a bad choice."

"Do you miss *Grossmammi* and *Grossdaadi*?"

"Not as much as I miss your other *grossdaadi*." Leah's mother had died unexpectedly almost ten years ago now.

"I liked him best, too. I mostly miss fishing with him."

"*Ja*, I'm thinking soon we'll go for a visit. Maybe this winter, when there's less work to be done on the farm. Now," he said, "do you have other questions?"

Zeb swiped at his tears with his forearms. "Should I tell Rebekah what you said?"

"No, if she has questions, she should come to me."

Zeb turned and threw his arms around Gideon, who hugged him convulsively.

"I love you," he murmured.

Zeb rubbed wet cheeks on Gideon's shirt. "I think you're the best *daadi* in the whole world."

Gideon laughed. "Probably not that, but I try."

"And . . . and I wish Hannah could be our new *mamm*." He pulled himself free, jumped to his feet, and ran toward the kitchen and the staircase.

Left reeling at a wish he couldn't fulfill, a wish that devastated him, Gideon didn't move for a long time.

Chapter Twenty-Three

❖◆❖

FRIDAY MORNING, HANNAH barely had a chance to nod at Gideon before he hurried out the back door. Usually, he paused long enough to tell her where he could be found, but apparently he didn't want to bother today. She was just as glad; it hurt to see him. Increasingly, she was thinking she had to resign, only . . .

She couldn't bear knowing she'd never see any of them again. Well, except at church, but that would be from a distance, and only if she chose to be baptized and stay.

Rebekah chattered, a welcome distraction, as Hannah put together school lunches. It was her turn to walk them as well as Enoch all the way to school. Once they reached the foot of the Millers' driveway, Enoch came running, cheerful as always. He liked silly jokes, and told several that had Rebekah in stitches and even Zeb and Hannah laughing.

Hannah greeted mothers dropping off their *kinder* and chatted for a few minutes before starting home. She didn't always bring her phone with her, but had this morning because she'd talked to her grandmother Wednesday, and learned her grandfather was struggling.

"I almost called for an ambulance, but he doesn't want to go into the hospital again," Helen had said, voice betraying the tears that she had to be shedding. "I've been afraid before, but he's bounced back. This time—"

She didn't have to say anything else. Hannah had driven to town Wednesday evening to sit with Robert, holding his hand, talking gently when his eyes focused on her. Listening to his desperate struggle to breathe had been agonizing. She finally left when an aide came to help Helen get him to the bathroom and bed.

Last night, when Hannah called to find out how he was doing, her grandmother only said dully, "The same."

She was just passing the phone shanty when her phone rang. For once, she prayed the caller would be her mother, but the number that showed belonged to her grandparents.

All she could think was, *Oh, no. Oh, no, no, no, no.*

"Grandma?"

"He's gone, Hannah. I'm waiting for the doctor, and the . . . the . . ."

Hearse.

"I'm so sorry." Tears had begun to blur her vision and run down her face. "So sorry."

"It's not as if I didn't know it was coming, but . . ." Helen's pain-filled calm evaporated. "I woke up this morning beside him, and realized he'd died during the night. You know what his breathing sounded like! How could I not have noticed when it stopped?" she cried. "Or . . . when his struggles increased? He died alone."

A car passed on the road. Hannah turned her back so the driver couldn't see her tears.

"Not alone," she choked out. "You were right there. You know he couldn't have talked."

"But *I* could have! I could have kissed him. I could have *seen* the moment he slipped away."

"He was probably asleep."

"It doesn't matter! I should have sat up with him! Oh, Hannah, I wish . . ."

"He knew you loved him until the very end. He'd have never had a single doubt. You gave him that. What more can any of us can do?"

All Hannah heard was weeping.

Crying herself, she said, "I'll be there as soon as I can. I need to stop at *Daad*'s house to get the car. You just hold on."

"You don't have to—"

"I do."

Once she ended the call, she lifted her skirt and ran. Near the top of the driveway, she saw Gideon coming out of the barn, pushing a wheelbarrow. His head came up when he saw her. He let go of the handles, not seeming even to notice that the wheelbarrow tipped over and the contents spilled out. By the time he reached Hannah, he was running, too.

His hands closed around her upper arms. *"Was is letz?"*

For a confused instant, she couldn't translate his words. But then her brain switched gears. He'd asked what was wrong. He must fear something bad had happened to one of the *kinder*.

She looked up at him from eyes that felt as if they were trying to swell shut. "My grandfather." Her voice emerged rusty and tremulous. "He died. I just . . . my grandmother just called."

"Ah. It's sorry I am," he said in English. "What can I do?"

"I need to go. I told her I'd be there as soon as I can. If you'd hitch up Clover . . ."

"*Ja*, and I'll drive you."

"But . . . you'd have to walk back. Or . . . I guess you could bring the buggy back here, and I could have *Daad* drop me off tomorrow, or . . ."

"Those aren't important worries."

She gave an undignified sniff. "*Denke*. I have to get my bag from the house."

He was already slipping the reins through rings in the buggy when she returned, having washed her face in cold water. There wasn't much improvement.

Gideon studied her, but didn't comment until he had set Clover to trotting down the farm lane. "Should you drive the car? Taking you to town would be no trouble."

"I'm sure I can. There's so little traffic. It would be more convenient to have the car."

He bent his head in apparent acquiescence. Clover turned onto the road, her steel-shod hooves ringing out against the pavement as she gained speed.

"I hate to desert you," Hannah said, trying to gather her thoughts. "There's sliced ham for sandwiches, and sauerbraten left from last night."

"I can feed myself, Hannah." He sounded remarkably gentle, even tender.

She wished she could wrap his deep voice around her, as if it were a wondrously soft shawl she could tug close to hold in warmth.

"There is pecan pie, too," she said, "and some oatmeal-raisin cookies, too, that I froze."

"No need to worry about us. We'll be fine tomorrow, too, if you want to stay with your *grossmammi*."

"But . . . it's Saturday."

"We survived before you came to us."

She hated knowing that they had, that if she never came back, Gideon would only hire another woman. Hannah thought Rebekah and Zeb would miss her, but Gideon might be glad if she *didn't* come back to work. If she chose the life she'd put on hold, in time she'd recede in all their memories, but she'd never forget them.

The buggy swung around the sharp bend in the road and she saw her *daad*'s mailbox and phone shanty up ahead.

They slowed down on the hard-packed dirt driveway, but it seemed no time at all before the buggy swept up to the house.

"I'll unharness your horse," Gideon said. "You go ahead and do what you must."

She would have given almost anything for him to take her in his arms, to be able to rest against him, if only for a moment. Borrow some of his strength. But of course that wasn't possible.

She mumbled more thanks and clambered out of the buggy. She should hurry, but her feet felt leaden.

Gideon's voice stopped her. "Hannah?"

She turned.

"This is a good time to pray. Remember that the Lord is near when you most need Him."

She smiled shakily. "I'll remember."

He was right. As Hannah trudged up to the house, she thought of a passage from Isaiah.

Fear not, for I am with you; Be not dismayed, for I am your God. I will strengthen you, Yes, I will help you, I will uphold you with My righteous right hand.

Her heart still ached, but her step felt lighter.

THE DAY WAS hard, but seeing the relief on her grandmother's face when Hannah walked into the apartment made every wrenching moment worthwhile.

Since Helen couldn't quit crying, it was Hannah who talked to the doctor when he came.

"At least we know the cause of death," he said. "It's a miracle Robert lived this long."

Hannah said only, "Yes," not knowing whether he was aware she'd known her grandfather such a short time. She'd have liked longer, except she knew that was selfish. He'd been suffering.

And was now at peace, she reminded herself.

She held Helen, turning her so that she didn't see when the mortuary workers wheeled Robert's body out. She changed the bed, so her grandmother didn't have to do it, and washed and dried the bedding. When a hospice supervisor called, she confirmed that he'd died and was assured that they would pick up the oxygen tank and wheelchair.

Hannah finally asked whether Helen had called Jodi.

"I'm ashamed of myself, but no. I will later. I think . . . I just wanted you today."

Hannah hugged her. "And here I am."

Midafternoon, she persuaded Helen to eat a few bites, and suggested a nap, which Helen refused. Hannah doubted she was ready to lie down on the bed she'd shared with her husband.

Mostly, they talked quietly, with long lapses in between. Knowing her grandmother had some favorite daytime television shows, Hannah suggested she watch as a diversion, but Helen refused that, too. The screen on the wall remained dark. Helen was inspired to ask about photos, and Helen brought out albums. It was immediately clear this was just what she'd needed.

Some of these, Hannah was seeing for a second time. Robert Hinsch was so tall and handsome in wedding photos, the expression on his face when he looked down at his new wife luminous with love. As the pages turned, Hannah watched the years pass. Helen smiled now and again. She'd shown Hannah some photos of Jodi as a child, but now she saw more.

"I have a few of you," Helen said suddenly. "Not as many as I would have liked. You know how the Amish feel about having their pictures taken, but I did sneak a few when Jodi brought you here."

She disappeared into the bedroom, returning with a small wooden box, the inlaid top beautiful. "I keep some precious things in here."

She took out what couldn't be more than a dozen photos

and handed them to Hannah, who was instantly riveted by the picture on top.

The baby, bundled in white, gazed vaguely over her mommy's shoulder. Jodi looked so young, and her smile was as luminous as Robert's at his wedding. Hannah's heart squeezed, and then she thought, *That's me*. And: *Mom did love me*.

How astonishing. When she was seven or eight, she'd wanted to see pictures of herself when she was younger. Jodi explained that a pipe had burst in a house where they'd lived—"Don't you remember?" she asked—and the photo albums were ruined.

Once Jodi got a smartphone, she'd started taking digital pictures, but those weren't great quality. Still, she'd forwarded what she had to Hannah so she was able to see herself as a teenager, anyway.

Now she set aside the first photo, and there she was at maybe a year old, beaming at the camera. Even then, she hadn't had the chubby cheeks so many babies had. Instead, she looked more like an elf someone had just plucked from a flower-strewn meadow. Her hair had been the white-blond rarely seen in its natural state on adults.

In another picture, she grinned triumphantly as she toddled unsteadily across the room. Oh, and there she was, staring in fascination at a birthday cake that held just two candles.

Only in the last photo was she dressed Amish. Jodi must have bought *Englischer* clothes for her young daughter so she could change her for visits to friends and her parents.

Hannah touched the picture with a fingertip. Her hair was still so pale then, tucked into a white *kapp*. Somebody had made the apron and light green dress just for her. Her feet were bare, curled into the mowed grass. Hannah hardly recognized the radiant smile on that little girl's face.

Words whispered in her ears. *This was the life I might have had.*

Helen couldn't seem to look away from this photo any more than Hannah could. "That couldn't have been more than a week or two before she took you away. You were so cute, and so happy."

"I can't believe I forgot everything and everyone," Hannah whispered.

"But you didn't really, did you?" The grief on her grandmother's face had softened. "By that age, your aunts and grandmother had you helping them cook and serve meals. When you visited us, you were so eager to help." She was quiet for a moment. "And then there's the language."

And the faith in God she had somehow held on to, despite the gap of years before she found another way to worship. Eyes stinging, Hannah nodded. *No more tears*, she told herself.

"You were such a happy, confident child," Helen said softly. "And you grew into a lovely woman. One who never behaved as if we were strangers to her."

The shock was faint, but real. "You never *felt* like strangers."

Her grandmother smiled at her. "Because we weren't."

A few tears did escape.

SHE DID WORK Saturday, sorry to be the reason the *kinder* were so subdued. Her mother was to spend the day with Helen. Gideon looked at her with kindness, not remote at all. He encouraged her to sit down when she served lunch. Rebekah gaped at him. "But, *Daadi*, Hannah always sits with us."

Gideon's eyes met Hannah's briefly. "*Ja*, but I think she isn't eating enough because she's sad."

How did he know? Then she realized he didn't; he'd just thought up an excuse for his *kinder*, who didn't know he and she no longer sat down to meals alone together.

She did nibble, taking a few more bites after he nagged,

but was eager to leap up and wash dishes. It was more difficult to mourn or to brood when her hands were busy. Perhaps fortunately, she had only brief snatches of time alone since the *kinder* were home, and Rebekah was at her side helping most of the time.

The grief was real, but as the afternoon went on, Hannah was brought to confront one cause of her uneasiness.

She had committed herself to staying in Tompkin's Mill until her grandfather died—and now he had. That theoretically freed her to start serious job hunting. Her certainty about the decision she needed to make had steadily become more solid. How could she possibly pack up and go? Next thing she knew, she'd be in a restaurant kitchen again . . . and living alone in another apartment that would be home no more than her previous ones had been.

But she couldn't stay because *this* house felt like home, or because she had fallen in love with a man *and* his children.

She knew what she wanted, but she had to come to terms with what she'd be giving up, and what her commitment to the faith and this life meant. She would have to accept baptism with her whole heart. Hannah had her mother's example to chide her. Becoming Amish would turn her life on end. She had to resolve any doubts at all before she considering stepping onto that road.

The one that might lead her ultimately to the narrow gate.

The hardest part of all? She couldn't convert to being Amish in the certainty that she could have a life with Gideon, become a mother in truth to his *kinder*. He'd kissed her, and sometimes she'd thought . . .

Hannah shook her head impatiently. That could have been no more than a moment of temptation. He'd certainly regretted the kiss. He might have no interest in asking her to become his wife. If she couldn't have him, Zeb, and Rebekah, would she learn to be content living so close to them? Worshipping with them? Potentially having to join the celebration when he married another woman?

That was no excuse, she told herself sternly. After baptism, she could join one of the other church districts surrounding Tompkin's Mill.

Her mind reverted to the wealth of issues she had to consider.

What if she began to chafe at restrictions, as her mother had? Geographically, her world would shrink. She would never drive a car again, never fly in an airplane. Make any decision that was counter to the *Ordnung*, the rules that defined the Amish. The whole concept of *Gelassenheit* was alien to her, too. The giving up of self-will to God's will, as interpreted by the bishop and ministers—and potentially her own husband.

A society that was patriarchal, in many ways.

I need to talk to Julia, she realized. Not tomorrow; it was the off Sunday, when the Amish did go visiting, but chances were that Julia, Luke, and *their* kinder would go to his *mamm* and *daad*'s, or his sister's, or . . .

But Monday, they were more likely to be home. It was worth a try, Hannah decided.

At that point in her ruminations, Rebekah poked her.

"You said the blankets aren't dry."

Hannah blinked and realized she was removing the clothespins securing a wool blanket to the line.

She smiled down at the little girl. "*Denke* for reminding me. My mind was wandering."

"Where did it go?" Rebekah asked very seriously.

"Oh . . . thoughts of the funeral, worry for my *grossmammi*." She didn't add, *Thoughts about* my *future*.

"Oh."

Hannah had a very bad feeling that she wasn't the only one brooding about the near future. Rebekah knew that Hannah hadn't intended to stay long term. She'd already been here two months . . . and Rebekah hadn't hidden her hope that Hannah would never go away.

And that gave her another painful thought: What if Gideon decided to marry her for the sake of his *kinder*, not because he loved *her*? Would that be better than the alternatives? Or unbearable?

She shook her head as if she could rid herself of the stack of worries, and said, "I think we should start on supper."

"Me, too." As they started for the house, Rebekah gave her a sidelong glance. "I'm already hungry."

"Which means Zeb will show up any minute, begging for a snack," Hannah said with a laugh. "What do you say, carrot sticks?"

Rebekah made an awful face.

Dinner was pleasant enough. As Hannah and Rebekah cleaned the kitchen, Gideon and Zeb went out to hitch up her horse. When she came out, Rebekah trailing behind, Zeb called to his sister, "Let's do something." She brightened, and they ran to the wooden bin that held balls and bats and even some nets that Hannah had yet to see untangled and hung.

Gideon watched them for a moment with an unreadable expression before his dark gaze turned to her.

"You'll be going to church tomorrow with your *gross-mammi*?"

"*Ja*, I promised."

He nodded.

"She left me a message," she continued. "The funeral service is already set for one o'clock on Thursday afternoon. I know that's inconvenient—"

His expression prevented her from finishing. "Of course that must come first. Will your *daad* attend?"

"He said he would, but he didn't yet know when it would be."

"We'll survive another day without you." Lines formed on his forehead. He opened his mouth again, but closed it.

Had he intended to ask when she would be leaving, but decided this wasn't the moment? Probably, Hannah decided, her mood plunging anew.

"I'll see you Tuesday morning, then," she said with what she hoped was an adequate pretense of serenity.

He only nodded and stepped back, although when she turned onto the road at the foot of the driveway, Gideon still stood where he'd been, watching her go.

Chapter Twenty-Four

❖❖❖

RIGHT AFTER LUNCH on Monday, Hannah arranged with Lilian to take Clover and the buggy, her stepmother giving her directions to Luke and Julia Bowman's home.

"We had church there not long before you came," she said, smiling. "Just remember to be home in time for me to pick up the *kinder* after school."

This was the farthest Hannah had driven in the buggy, but she'd become more confident. Only a handful of cars passed, and the mare ignored all of them, never appearing even the slightest bit alarmed.

The Bowmans' farmhouse was set well back from the road that led into town. Hannah knew from what Julia had said that their house and barn weren't on anywhere near the acreage Gideon owned, since Luke was a furniture maker with no interest in farming. Still, they had plenty of land for a large garden, an orchard, and woods screening the house from neighbors. The long driveway led alongside a pasture that held only two horses and a dairy cow. That both harness horses were here meant Julia and Luke were, too, right?

Indeed, when she reined Clover to a stop at a hitching post near the house, Luke came around the corner.

"Hannah," he said with a smile. "Your timing is good. Nathan just went down for a nap, and we're hoping Abby fell asleep, too."

He was speaking in unaccented English, which momentarily disconcerted her until she remembered he'd spent over a decade out in the world.

"Oh, good." She climbed out. "Since I couldn't call, I decided just to drop in."

"We never mind visitors." He tethered Clover for her. "Go on in the back door."

"*Denke*. Thank you," she amended, and he chuckled.

It appeared Julia had been baking, but was washing her mixing bowl, measuring cups, and spoons when Hannah walked in.

"I'm hoping to match your applesauce cake," she declared. "Luke had some at the fellowship meal and keeps mentioning how much he liked it."

"Feeling a little pressure?" Hannah teased, before smiling. "I'm sure it'll be delicious." She agreed that she'd love a cup of tea, and sat at the long table in the kitchen. "Did Abby conk out?"

Julia laughed. "I'm still tiptoeing around, but I think so. She's at that in-between age. She doesn't want to nap, but she gets cranky if she doesn't." Once she'd poured the tea, she spooned sugar into her own cup. "I'm so glad you came. I meant to visit you on Friday."

"It's lucky you didn't."

"So I hear." Expression warm with sympathy, she said, "You know how everyone talks. You must be sad."

"Yes." Hannah sighed. "Except that, in some ways, it was a blessing. Struggling for breath must be one of the most awful feelings in the world."

"But you will miss him."

"At least I had a chance to get to know him. I worry most about my grandmother. They were married for fifty-three years. She told me she's never lived alone."

"That would be hard."

"What I hope is that she'll stay busy and not just huddle in the apartment. You know? The facility has plenty of recreational opportunities. I'm not sure about the aerobics, but they also have classes, trips, movie nights, and ice cream socials. I don't think she's tried anything, because she felt she couldn't leave Robert alone. Or maybe I should have said she didn't *want* to leave him. She had to have been painfully aware of how little time they had left together."

"I'm guessing, once she's past this first week or two, she'll find she feels some relief, too. Both their lives have been dominated by his illness for a long time."

Hannah thought about that. "I hope so."

The timer went off, and Julia took the cake out of the oven. It smelled amazing, and Hannah didn't protest when Julia served them each generous squares.

After the first bite, she declared, "It's every bit as good as mine."

Julia laughed. "What else could you say?"

They talked about other things for a few minutes, but Hannah kept expecting one of the kids to wake up, or Luke to come in and join them.

So finally she nerved herself and said, "I promised to stay until my grandfather died. Now . . . now I'm trying to figure out what I want out of life."

"You're considering converting."

"I am, but I have a lot of qualms."

Julia reached across the table to squeeze Hannah's hand. Only briefly, but that human contact was reassuring. "I did, too. I took weeks to work through what was most important to me, and what I'd sacrifice to have it. I told you that my parents and brother were opposed, didn't I? I do think they're all reconciled. Ask anything you want. I suppose giving up your career is one of those qualms. I'm not sure I can help you with that, because I'd had jobs, but never a career."

"I dreamed for years about becoming a chef in the kind of restaurant filled with diners who'd had to reserve their seats days or even weeks in advance." She made a face. "But cooking for Gideon and his children has given me more joy than I've ever had working in a restaurant. I've learned that what I really wanted was to make people happy with the food I made. That's something I never had. I took over cooking from my mother when I was only ten or eleven, but she's never been all that interested in eating. She'd have been fine with warming a frozen meal, or grabbing fast food, or having a salad out of a bag."

"You didn't have an appreciative audience."

"That's one way to put it. Now I know that having a family who loves my cooking makes me happy. I suppose . . . back then, I was trying to make her happy. Thinking everything would be different if she was."

Her cooking *had* made Gideon and his *kinder* happier.

She expressed her feeling that, as welcome as her *daad*'s family had made her, she was also in the way. Lilian was a good cook, too, and her daughters were learning at her side. "I can't stay there forever."

"You could just as well marry and start a family in the *Englisch* world."

"In theory, but I'm almost twenty-eight, and I don't even date that often. For one thing, the hours a chef works are pretty limiting. And then there's the fact that most men I meet either aren't churchgoers at all, or it's just a Sunday thing they do."

"They don't live their faith."

"No. And I'm finding I want the depth of faith I see around me. I . . . believe I am finding it."

Julia was frank that she'd never found the *Ordnung* restrictive in a way that affected her life. "I married Luke, though, and because he'd lived and worked out in the world for so long, he's more . . . flexible, I guess is the right word, than most Amishmen would be. So that makes a difference. I will say that my mother-in-law and Miriam both have strong voices in their households, too."

"This is probably none of my business, but did you know when you converted that you'd be marrying Luke?"

"No. I'd sometimes hoped, but he was doing his best to keep his distance by then. I understood that I could make such a big decision only because I wanted to worship the way the Amish I'd gotten to know did. Most of the things I had to give up weren't important to me. I went to Bishop Troyer without any idea whether there would be a future with Luke and Abby. I was in a panic about where I'd live, how I'd get around when I knew next to nothing about horses."

She reminded Hannah about the instructional classes she'd need to take before she could be baptized.

"That gives you time to work through any hesitations, or change your mind if you come to believe it's the right thing to do. Amos will want to be certain sure"—Julia gave an impish smile at the typical Amish phrasing—"that you are seeking conversion for the right reasons."

"Unlike the bishop who oversaw Mom's baptism and married her and my father."

"I can't imagine. I take it you don't think her conversion was genuine."

Hannah smiled sadly. "I truly don't know. She has a way of latching passionately onto new enthusiasms, sure they'll last even though they never do. She didn't bother going to church after we left. Still, from what she's said, I think it was mostly the life that she grew to hate."

"But with the Amish, you can't separate the two."

Hannah sighed. "She certainly didn't understand how intertwined the Amish faith is with their lives. Plus, she missed the concept that the *Ordnung* spells out behavior that's not allowed. Mom . . . doesn't hear what she doesn't want to know. She was outraged to find out she was supposed to quit spending hours hanging out with her *Englisch* friends. And the idea that, as a wife to a hardworking man, she'd be expected to work hard, too? No. The whole thing probably seemed really romantic. I can see the movie running in her head. I suspect she'd have left *Daad* a lot sooner if I hadn't been born."

"But she cared enough to take you with her," Julia said gently.

For better or worse. But Hannah didn't say that, only nodded and managed a smile.

She spent another hour with Julia, who talked frankly about restrictions, and expectations, too, none of which surprised Hannah after living with her Amish family and working for Gideon for two months.

"I'm sure there are domineering men among the faith, even in our church district—but that's not limited to the Amish," Julia remarked.

"Unfortunately." Jodi had found quite a few abusive men along the way.

Finally, as Julia walked Hannah out to her buggy, this new friend said, "Your mother would be horrified, wouldn't she?"

"Yes. We . . . already touched on the subject. But I can't see having much of a relationship with her going forward, no matter what. I think she's broken in some way. I feel sorry for her, and I have forgiven her."

"Did you feel better once you had?"

"It was like I could breathe for the first time in a long while." She smiled. "I hadn't realized what a heavy burden my anger was."

Julia clasped her hand and squeezed. "I remember the moment when I let mine go."

Warmed anew by the friendship, Hannah said, "Forgiving her doesn't wipe from my mind and heart what she did to her own parents and to *Daad*. Everything that's happened since I found out I had family has shone a harsh light on Mom, forcing me to see her in a way I never let myself acknowledge. What I've learned is that I have to accept Mom for what she is. She'd be a fun grandmother if I ever have children, as long as she knows not to undercut the values I teach."

"Your grandmother?"

"Oh, I know she'd be happy, since that would mean me staying here in Tompkin's Mill. Samuel stayed close to her and Robert, you know." She was quiet for a moment. "Reimagining your life isn't easy."

"No." Julia hugged her, their cheeks pressed together. "If you choose to join us, you will be warmly welcomed, I know that." A hint of mischief showed in her smile as she drew back. "I wouldn't be the only member tripping over words in the Ausbund, or sticking my foot in my mouth in ordinary conversations."

Hannah was laughing as she got into the buggy and picked up the reins.

Even as she watched nervously for traffic, she felt the comfort of knowing that, if she took this step, she wouldn't be alone.

TO THE BEST of his recollection, Gideon had only been in a church three times in his life. Once for an *Englisch* neighbor's wedding. Once for Brooke Stephenson's funeral, and the last time for the funeral service held for the teenage boy killed in that same accident. It felt important that he express his sorrow for Brooke as well as Jerrod Smith. Gideon had stared a long time at a blown-up photograph of the boy.

Ach, and here he was for yet another funeral service, this one for Hannah's grandfather. He saw three other horses and buggies when he arrived. He recognized all three horses: one Samuel's, one belonging to Bishop Troyer, and the last, the black gelding, Luke Bowman's. He was a little relieved to know the stares wouldn't all be directed at him.

Hannah had come to work Tuesday and Wednesday mornings, just as always, but had been more subdued than usual. A few times he met her eyes and worried at what he saw there. He could tell Rebekah and Zeb felt apprehensive, too. Was she already pulling away from them, preparing to give her notice? He couldn't decide. Wednesday afternoon, she reminded him that she wouldn't be working tomorrow because of the funeral. When he said, "*Ja,* I have not forgotten," she only nodded.

Now, when he entered the church, he found Luke, Julia, Amos, and Samuel sitting in the back pew, with room to spare. Gideon slid in beside Samuel, and they exchanged a few quiet words. Amos leaned forward to greet Gideon.

He assumed Hannah and her grandmother would already be here, right in front. Hannah's *mamm,* too. Gideon was curious to set eyes on her, after all he'd heard.

Although he would never feel comfortable worshipping God in such fancy surroundings, he'd concede this was a handsome church, with a soaring ceiling and richly colored stained glass windows depicting Jesus, the disciples, and Mary and Joseph on a donkey. A shiny casket surrounded by flowers rested atop a stand in front, near a podium. Around them murmured conversations continued, and once he heard a phone ring.

At least it was silenced quickly.

The service wasn't long. One elderly man who apparently had been a longtime friend of Robert Hinsch went up front to speak about him, praising him for his kindness, his generosity, for a life well lived.

None of the women spoke. Gideon guessed that Hannah's grandmother was too overcome to be able to put words together.

Barely forty-five minutes later, everyone stood and waited while the minister and the three women started up the aisle. The one that had to be Hannah's mother was sobbing uncontrollably, leaning heavily on a man Gideon didn't recognize who had stepped out of a pew to offer her an arm. Instead of leaning on someone else, Hannah had a supportive arm around her grandmother, while the minister hovered behind them. As they came abreast of the last row, Hannah's gaze flashed to Gideon first, then to Samuel, Luke, and Julia. She tried to smile and failed, yet something about her seemed different. Gideon tried to decide what that was. Perhaps it was only her strength showing, the strength her grandmother needed right now.

Then they were past, and others in the congregation crowded the aisle. Gideon glanced at Samuel, who hadn't noticeably reacted to his former wife's presence or big display of grief.

So worked up she was, Gideon couldn't say how much she looked like her daughter.

At the foot of the stone steps outside, Hannah stood with her grandmother, who spoke quietly to people. Her eyes were red and swollen, but she kept her composure. Hannah stepped forward to hug her *daad*, then Julia. She and Amos talked longer than Gideon would have expected, even stepping aside from the others. She seemed grateful when they parted. At last, she came to Gideon, her lips trembling. He remained stiff when he would have liked to put his arms around her. He might have done it if the bishop weren't been watching.

"I didn't know you planned to come," she said. "Any of you. *Denke*. It's so good of you." She blinked back tears. "Most of these people are strangers to me. I'm so grateful you came for my sake."

"Of course I came." He felt almost angry because she hadn't thought anyone except maybe her father would care enough about her. She was easy to love; look at how his *kinder* had fallen for her. Gideon still didn't entirely understand why she wasn't married and raising a family.

Except that wasn't altogether true. She had become used to standing alone because of her *mamm*, the woman who was still sobbing over by a car, collecting sympathy.

Not a kind thought, Gideon corrected himself . . . but, unfortunately, also true. Jodi Hinsch had chosen not to see her mother and father for twenty-three years, led them to believe she and their granddaughter were dead. Yet now she was crumpling instead of supporting her own *mamm*, who had just lost her husband.

Had guilt made her grief so extreme? Gideon would have liked to believe that, given the alternative, which was that she just liked attention.

"Will your *mamm* stay in Tompkin's Mill?" he asked.

Hannah's gaze followed his. "Probably as long as she's involved with Todd Wright, the man with her. He's a bank manager. Apparently they dated in high school. He's recently divorced. And, of course, she may wait for the divorce to become final."

The divorce from Hannah's *daad*. He glanced at Samuel, who was watching his daughter with concern, showing no interest in the woman he had once married but not seen for over twenty years. Gideon wasn't surprised; Samuel was well known for his unshakable faith and good nature. Although even his air of contentment and calm must have been strained by the disappearance of his wife and small daughter.

"My *grossmammi* is taking this very hard," Hannah continued. "I know it's a lot to ask, but could I take tomorrow off, too?"

"*Ja*, of course you can," he returned readily, even as he hurriedly ran through his plans. In the early afternoon he had an appointment at the produce auction house. While he was in town, he'd go to the bank and stop at the hardware store for a replacement handle for his ax, too, but he should be home, no problem, before his *kinder* left school. Just to be certain, he'd hurry, best anyway because there was talk of a storm tomorrow. He didn't mind getting splattered, but it was his experience that some *Englischers* didn't drive sensibly when the road was wet and slick. "We'll miss you," he continued, "but it's good your *grossmammi* has you. And that you had time with your *grossdaadi*."

"Ja." Hannah gave him another tremulous smile that made him want again to do more than stand here, as stiff as the statue of some Civil War general that stood in the park. That statue cared about nobody. *"Denke,"* she whispered, and turned to hurry toward her *grossmammi*, who had walked as though exhausted to one of the cars, accompanied by the pastor.

THE FOLLOWING MORNING started with a bang. Her eyes almost swollen shut from weeping, Jodi was already at the small apartment when Hannah arrived.

Hannah toasted the friendship bread she'd brought and made coffee for all of them. Helen gave her a grateful smile when she accepted the delicate cup with coffee.

"I've hardly eaten a thing, but that bread smells really good. What is it?"

"It's lemon poppy—"

"What if Daddy never forgave me?" Jodi wailed.

Setting her cup down on the coffee table with a small click, Helen looked at her oddly. "I don't remember you ever *asking* for his forgiveness. Or mine, either. How could you, without first admitting that you did anything wrong?"

"I had to leave," she whispered. "I had to. You wouldn't have understood. But . . . but the death certificates . . . When I asked Kevin to make them, it was Samuel I was thinking about. He'd be able to remarry and have a new family. I knew it wasn't fair."

Was it remotely possible that was true? The very softness of her mother's voice was more persuasive than her usual histrionics.

If anything, Helen's back stiffened. "So, you didn't think about your father and me, at all? It was fine for us to grieve for you and Hannah?"

Fresh tears welled in Jodi's eyes. "I couldn't let myself think about that! I knew eventually I'd be able to call you. And, well, you hadn't seen us in years anyway."

"So that made everything fine." Helen shook her head and gazed down at her hands.

Hannah didn't say a word.

Jodi jumped up, but the pain on her face looked real. "I never meant to hurt anyone. Can't you believe that?"

Helen lifted her head at that. "Then tell me." She sounded hard. Not like herself. "Why didn't you take the time to get a divorce?"

"It would have taken forever! And . . . and I was losing Hannah. What if they'd hidden her? Even if they didn't, I was terrified of letting Samuel have her even for weekends."

Not weekends, Hannah thought. Unless the judge had been biased against the Amish, he or she should have given primary custody to Samuel, who owned a home and had a solid income and family members willing to care for his small daughter during the workday. Jodi hadn't had even the prospect of a job or apartment, never mind the means to pay for day care. Perhaps she'd assumed her mother wouldn't offer to help given her disapproval of her daughter's behavior.

Mom might really have lost me, Hannah realized with sudden clarity. Jodi had made her choices out of what she called love, however misguided they'd been, however damaging to her daughter, however hurtful to her husband and parents. She would never understand the appalling selfishness of everything she'd done.

Hannah's strongest feeling for her mother was deep pity. Did Mom understand that even if Hannah continued to include her in her life, in most meaningful ways she had now lost her daughter for good?

Jodi was looking desperately from her mother to Hannah and back. "Neither of you believe me. Oh! I never should have come back."

"But you needed money," Helen said.

"I could have found something. I just wanted—" Her face twisted, she spun away, and an instant later the apartment door slammed shut.

Hannah set down her own coffee to hold her grandmother, who had broken down in tears again.

"Didn't you hear?" A large man whose belly strained against the striped fabric of his overalls had paused just outside the open double doors to the auction house to talk to an Amish farmer who looked only vaguely familiar to Gideon. "There's been a tornado watch issued. A small one touched down in Oklahoma, and there's a warning out for Arkansas."

Gideon slowed to eavesdrop, and felt some alarm he quickly dismissed. Tornadoes hadn't been a problem in upstate New York. Even in the time he'd been here in Missouri, however, he learned that at this time of year, tornado watches came frequently. Last summer, there were several warnings specifically aimed at this corner of the state, but none had formed in this county.

Nonetheless, this was why he'd made certain that Rebekah, Zeb, and now Hannah knew the location of the shelter.

He overheard more talk about the tornado threat inside, and then at the hardware store. Nobody sounded especially concerned. Dark clouds had formed, and he expected rain and even hail, but these clouds didn't form the specific "wall" others had told him to watch for. Nor was there any hint of rotation.

His business at the bank completed, he guided his gelding down an alley behind the bank and its drive-through, and out onto a cross street with parked cars and pickup trucks on each side. He saw a man just ahead jump into one of those massive pickup trucks and heard the engine rev, but Fergus continued placidly on. The light ahead turned green. They could turn and follow the same road all the way home.

The horse and buggy were abreast of the black truck when it pulled away from the curb right at Gideon. The front fender struck his buggy, the fiberglass side crunched inward, the right wheel buckled, and the gelding staggered and fell to his knees.

Shocked by how quickly the collision had happened, Gideon took an instant to be sure he was uninjured. Then he leaped out to go to his horse's head.

Chapter Twenty-Five

❖

WHEN A NEWS ticker appeared along the bottom of the television during one of Helen's favorite daytime shows that afternoon, Hannah sat straight up, devoured the message, waited until it repeated, and then jumped to her feet.

"I need to go."

"But . . . I don't like thinking of you out in your car if bad weather hits," Helen protested. "Wouldn't you be safer here?"

"Is there a shelter for this building?"

"Yes, in the basement. If the siren goes off, staff will be knocking on doors and helping anyone who can't make their own way down."

"*Daad* has a tornado shelter, too, and I'll bet he and Lilian could use help with the younger children."

"Oh, dear." Her grandmother looked at her worriedly. "If you're sure that's the right thing to do?"

Hannah had been wavering, but at that moment she had the strange sense that she had to go, that she was needed. "I'm sure," she said. "Do you understand?"

Helen smiled shakily. "I understand that you've found more than you expected to since coming home."

"I have." A sting of tears in her own eyes, Hannah grabbed her handbag, kissed her grandmother's cheek, and rushed out the door.

The sky was ominously dark for midafternoon. Wind snatched at Hannah's hair as she sprinted across the parking lot to her car. Her hand shook as she started the engine, and she didn't even know why. Tornado warnings were common at this time of year. Sometimes, if a tornado actually did form, it would be two states away.

Anyway, if one had been sighted anywhere in the vicinity, she'd hear the town siren. Summer storms happened. It wasn't hailing, or even raining right at the moment.

Still, that inexplicable sense of urgency stayed with her as she drove the familiar route toward her father's house. This was the rare moment when she wished he had a mobile phone—and that Gideon had one, too. Neither of them was likely to bother going down to the road to check for messages at the phone shanty. And what would she tell them, anyway? She just wasn't used to the idea of being unconnected.

There were other cars on the road, and she passed a couple of buggies. When she saw a third, she recognized Luke Bowman's horse, so she braked and rolled down her window. On this straight stretch, she'd see any oncoming traffic.

"Do you know anything?" she asked.

"No, but I don't like the looks of this weather. *Daad* and I decided to close and get home."

Since Eli wasn't with Luke, one of those other two buggies had likely been his.

"You have a shelter?"

"Anyone with any sense in this part of the country does. You're going to your *daad*'s?"

"Yes. It was that or get stuck in town with my grandmother."

"Then drive safely," he said.

"You, too." She rolled up her window and accelerated away from him, passing his house only a few minutes later. Julia would be relieved to have him home.

Perhaps it was her earlier thoughts about phones that had her braking when she reached the phone shanty the Mast household shared with several neighbors. It wouldn't hurt to check for messages. Someone might need help.

She parked on the shoulder of the road, and got out. Her nerve endings prickled as if something wasn't right. Hannah stopped and looked around.

What she could see of the sky *was* a strange color now, tinted greenish. A dark wall of clouds reared to the south. But it wasn't the clouds that had caught her attention. It took her a minute to realize that the whole world had gone quiet. Not only the wind had stopped. It felt as if no one existed but her. The birds were silent, even the cicadas. She wasn't even sure she heard the faint crunch of gravel underfoot when she jogged to the crude hut with one open side.

A red light blinked on the answering machine in a way that meant there was only one message. Probably it was completely routine. Someone had left it earlier wanting to book her *daad* to shoe a horse, or a neighbor to make a delivery. Still, she pressed the Play button with some apprehension.

The voice she heard electrified her. It was Gideon, and he sounded frantic.

"Hannah, if there is any chance you get this message, can you go to my house? I'm in town, and a car damaged my buggy. I'm going to try to ride Fergus home, but I don't know if I can make it before this storm hits."

Hannah cried out and covered her mouth with her hand.

"Susan always assumes I'm there and lets the *kinder* run

up to the house on their own. I pray they will know to go into the shelter, but we can't hear the siren that far out of town. Please, if there is any chance—"

He was still talking when she ran back to the driver's side of her car. Even if no tornado formed, or there was one but it didn't come close to Gideon's farm, Rebekah and Zeb would be terrified at the strange weather and their father's inexplicable absence.

Hannah made a reckless U-turn, uncaring that her front right tire left the road and the car tipped sideways for an instant. She couldn't take time to let *Daad* or Lilian know where she was going. They wouldn't worry, she told herself; they would assume she'd stayed with her grandmother.

She drove faster than she ever had before on this relatively narrow, two-lane road. This time, she didn't see any other traffic, and especially not a man riding on a horse wearing a harness rather than a saddle.

She almost skidded into the driveway, and accelerated up toward the house, where she sprang out and ran for the back door.

What would she do if the *kinder* weren't here? Assume they had gone to the Millers'?

She prayed as she'd never prayed before. *Please, God, keep them safe. Keep Gideon safe.*

She was halfway across the yard when something struck her. Another smack on her shoulder, then her head.

Hail, the size of a golf ball.

Hannah threw her arms over her head as she kept running.

NOBODY HAD EVER ridden Fergus, and he wasn't happy to have Gideon on his back now.

The *Englischer* who had pulled out of a parking slot without checking his rearview mirrors or turning his head had been horrified. His relief had been almost as great as

Gideon's when Fergus heaved himself to his feet. Gideon unhitched him and walked him for a few minutes, but he didn't even have a limp, although he might have sore knees by tomorrow.

The *Englischer* had more carefully moved his pickup truck and helped Gideon drag the damaged buggy into the empty parking spot. He'd given Gideon insurance information, but said he would pay himself for any repairs, or even a new buggy if that appeared necessary. Veterinary bills, too. He'd been decent, and Gideon didn't hold a grudge.

He did desperately want to get home. He'd have accepted a ride from the man, except he couldn't abandon his horse in the middle of town. If only he had the number for Hannah's cell phone with him! He knew Samuel's number, though, so he borrowed the *Englischer*'s phone and called to leave a message for her. Probably, she was still with her grandmother and this would do no good, but he had to try.

After hearing him, the man said, "If you have a name for the grandmother, I can try to track her down and get a message to this Hannah."

"*Denke*. Thank you. If you'd do that, I'd appreciate it. I'd meant to be home by now, before my children get out of school. I wouldn't like them to be alone, but usually I wouldn't worry so much."

The *Englischer* nodded in concern. "This weather isn't looking good. I understand."

He jotted down the names Robert and Helen Hinsch, and was calling information when Gideon swung himself up on the gelding's back, gathered the too-long reins in a bundle on his lap, and squeezed his legs while clicking his tongue.

Fergus danced sideways and hunched his back, but was too well behaved to actually buck. After a few bumpy strides, he reluctantly broke into a trot.

Ten minutes into the ride, Gideon was wincing as his thighs rubbed painfully on the thick leather of various parts of the harness—and as he bounced up and down on the gelding's back.

Eventually, he caught the rhythm, and the ride became smoother as his horse's stride lengthened. In his urgency, Gideon wanted to gallop, but the long, ground-eating trot was all Fergus would give him.

The sky darkened. The wind returned with new strength, breaking branches from trees bordering the road, sending leaves and twigs whipping around them and dancing across the road beneath the gelding's hooves. Gideon thanked God for Fergus's acceptance.

Over the wind, he heard an unfamiliar sound, a high-pitched, distant shriek. That had to be the tornado alarm, and he was at least two miles from home.

If only Hannah had been there today. He could have put his trust in her. As it was, Gideon's only comfort was the word of God, the promises He made to His faithful.

And those who know Your name will put their trust in You; for You, Lord, have not forsaken those who seek You.

Silently, Gideon prayed. *I beg of you, if You need someone, Lord, take me, not my* kinder.

Not Hannah.

HANNAH STUMBLED UP the two steps to the back door, fighting for control of it against the renewed wind, and all but fell inside.

"Hannah! You're here!" Face wet, Rebekah flew at her, oblivious to the fact that Hannah wore a knee-length skirt and sweater rather than her Amish garb. "We're so scared! Where is *Daadi*? Why isn't he home?"

Zeb appeared behind her, not crying but his fear apparent, too.

"We'll be fine," Hannah said, gathering in the little girl and holding out an arm for Zeb. "You'll see. Your *daad* left me a phone message. He was in an accident—not hurt," she added hurriedly, "but the buggy was damaged. He said he was going to ride Fergus home, but asked if I could get here faster."

"Is there going to be a tornado?" Rebekah asked. "Bernice told everyone she'd seen one lift a horse up into the sky."

"Bernice thinks she knows everything," Zeb burst out. "But she doesn't!"

Hannah squeezed him. "No, she doesn't, but a big tornado can tear the roof off a house, and it can toss a horse or cow or even a car as if they weighed nothing. That's why we have a storm shelter buried in the ground, so we'll be safe as can be. I don't know if a tornado is coming or not, but the weather is very strange. Listen."

They all cocked their heads. Even here on the ground floor, they all heard the hard pounding on the roof.

She held up her hand, using her thumb and forefinger to show them how big those balls of ice were.

"Zeb, you run upstairs and get some blankets. Where's your coat? Rebekah, find your cloak. I'll get some food, then we have to go into the shelter."

They separated to do as she'd asked. Hannah found a plastic lidded container heaped with two different kinds of her cookies, and took a pitcher of milk from the refrigerator, too. Rebekah knew where they kept the disposable cups used for fellowship meals.

Then the three of them went out the back door. There was no longer anything like silence. Hail slammed down on the barn and house roof, and bounced on the ground. She saw a chicken running and squawking. A giant wall of dark clouds reared from the direction of town. Protecting the *kinder* as best she could with her own body, she urged them toward the refuge she had never dreamed they would need.

She managed to get the door open. The dark hole within sent a shiver through her, but anything was better than staying out in this wild storm. Two kerosene lanterns and a book of matches sat on a shelf right inside, but she wouldn't be able to light either until they closed the door.

"Inside, inside," she urged.

Zeb put his arm around his sister and did as Hannah asked, but at the last minute he turned, shouting over the sound of the wind, "What about *Daadi*?"

Hannah's heart hurt at the question. "I know he's coming as fast as he can. We'll keep the door open until we see the tornado coming at us."

On their faces, she saw grief, fear . . . and trust.

Hannah turned, praying to see Gideon galloping up to the barn, but even if he were there, she wasn't sure she would see him, not with the branches of the trees dancing wildly, the hail thundering down, and a torrent of debris whirling in the wind.

She whispered a prayer for him that was snatched from her mouth.

God would hear her no matter what, she thought. Of course He would.

WHAT SOUNDED LIKE a freight train bearing down on them finally frightened Fergus into a gallop. All Gideon could do was hang on. Fortunately, Fergus knew to run home.

Gideon almost parted from his back when his horse swerved onto the lane, but his grip on a piece of harness held. They were nearly at the house when the hail abruptly stopped.

He turned his head and, to his horror, saw a massive wind funnel. The sight was partly blocked by trees, but it couldn't be more than a couple of miles away.

Groaning, he looked toward the house instead, and saw Hannah's car. She'd come when he called for her, or even without her ever having heard his message. She loved his *kinder*.

He hadn't absorbed the relief and joy when Fergus

reached the barn doors and skidded to a stop so abrupt, Gideon pitched off his back. He picked himself up from the muddy ground, his ears ringing from the monstrous sound that seemed to come from everywhere, as if even the ground cried out in pain. One glance told him the tornado was coming this direction. He fumbled with the hasp and got the doors open, leading his horse inside and to his stall, then unclipped the reins and dropped them in the aisle. The other animals were out at pasture, but there was nothing he could do for them now but pray—and the barn might not be the refuge it seemed.

One of the broad doors had slammed shut. He had to use all his strength to swing the other against the wind and close it. He took one more look at the advancing tornado, then ran for the shelter. Surely Hannah would already have the *kinder* inside it.

The heavy door stood open against the bank of earth. He was nearly there when Hannah poked her head and shoulders out. The increasing strength of the wind whipped her hair across her face. She lifted a hand to contain it.

She saw him first, her face transforming from anguish to gratitude so profound, he knew she felt everything he did. He thought she called out his name, but then she looked past him and saw the funnel. Her mouth rounded in horror, but her instinctive response was to hold out her hands to him rather than duck for safety.

For one moment, they clasped hands, his muddy, hers cold, yet the connection meant everything. Then she retreated down the narrow, steep steps as he crouched to pull the door closed over the top of them. He fought the most powerful wind he'd ever experienced, but finally the door dropped into place and he shoved the latch to secure it. The sudden cessation of noise was almost shocking, the complete darkness disorienting.

From the darkness, his daughter asked, *"Daadi?* Are you really here?"

"*Ja*, thank the good Lord, we are all together."

"We were scared."

"I was scared, too," he admitted, sliding his foot carefully to be certain he'd reached the bottom. He didn't dare take a real step until there was some light.

"We have two lamps." Hannah's voice shook. "Zeb, can you get a match lit?"

The scratch of the match was followed by a tiny flicker of flame that glinted off glass. To his mild surprise, she and Zeb succeeded in lighting the lantern, and she carefully fit the chimney back in place. She adjusted the wick, and golden light flared, letting Gideon see the tiny room with benches and nothing else.

He hugged Zeb, then Rebekah, and lifted the chimney from the second lamp so Hannah could light it, too. Holding it high, he looked at his family, and choked up. Everyone he loved was here, safe.

He should never have let himself love this *Englischer* woman, but it was now too late. Losing her, when she went back to her previous life, would hurt more than he thought he could bear. But right now, he wouldn't let himself think about that.

No matter what they found when they emerged from this bunker, the Lord had given Gideon what he needed most.

WITH REBEKAH NESTLED on her lap, Hannah tugged a blanket more closely about them. On the opposite bench, Zeb leaned against his *daad*. The lanterns cast light from the end of each built-in bench. If she were alone, she might feel claustrophobic, so tiny was the space, but with Gideon here as well as his *kinder*, Hannah felt an inner glow of happiness completely new to her.

"We should pray," Gideon suggested in his deep, calm voice.

A smile curled her lips. "Let's start with the Lord's Prayer."

He lifted an eyebrow, but said, "*Ja*, why not?"
As one, they recited a prayer they all knew by heart.

Our Father who art in heaven,
hallowed be Thy name.
Thy kingdom come.
Thy will be done
on earth as it is in heaven.
Give us this day our daily bread,
and forgive us our trespasses,
as we forgive those who trespass against us,
and lead us not into temptation,
but deliver us from evil.

They had barely finished when Rebekah shouted, "The Lord did give us our daily bread, and I'm hungry!"

Hannah chuckled, bent, and from behind her feet, lifted the container full of cookies.

"And we have milk, too," Rebekah told her *daad*, who laughed.

Gideon's gaze stayed on Hannah's face. "With a tornado bearing down on us, only Hannah would have thought to provide us with cookies and milk while we wait out the storm. Suppose we eat, and then sing."

None of her baked goods had ever tasted as good as these cookies did now, shared with these three people, washed down with milk.

Then Gideon, with some help from the *kinder*, sang "Das Loblied," the best known of all hymns from the Ausbund.

She had left her phone and handbag in her car, Hannah realized, never giving them a thought. The roaring sound was muted by the earth that surrounded them, but the tornado could have snatched up her car and flung it half a mile into a cornfield. She wasn't even sure she'd shut the car door behind herself.

Once more, and so powerfully, she felt the peace of certainty, of faith. Of course the decision she'd made over the course of the last week was right for her. Of course it was.

She wouldn't need the car, or her phone, or most of the contents of her purse again, Hannah thought. It might be fitting if all those possessions treasured by an *Englischer* were spun out of reach by God.

Happiness swelled in Hannah's chest as she watched Gideon lift his voice to their Lord. The hymn ended, and she looked down to see that Rebekah had fallen soundly asleep. Gideon noticed, and smiled. He murmured something to Zeb, who leaned more securely into his father's arms and closed his eyes.

Neither adult said anything for several minutes, although Hannah couldn't make herself look away from Gideon.

He spoke quietly. "I was glad Amos came to your *grossdaadi*'s funeral."

"That was so kind of him." She hesitated, but when better to tell him than now? "I've been wanting to talk to him," she said simply. "We arranged a time."

Chapter Twenty-Six

❖◆❖

GIDEON STARED AT her. He hadn't dared let himself hope.
Was it possible . . . ?

Remembering to breathe, he asked, "When will you
meet with him?"

"It was supposed to be tomorrow morning."

In the shadows, he couldn't tell if Hannah was blushing,
but for some reason he felt sure she was.

"I want to convert," she said in a rush. "I don't want to
leave. I've felt as if I'm home ever since I came to stay. As
if I'm *meant* to be here."

He felt . . . so much. But disappointment and worry were
in the mix. "Your commitment must be to our faith. You
could stay in Tompkin's Mill as an *Englischer*."

She shook her head, her tangled, loose hair swaying. He
could just see a dangling pin. "Julia said that, too, but it's
not the *place* that's home. It's how faith weaves through
your lives. No one is ever truly left alone to bear a burden.
That's a big part of what feels right to me. As if everything

I do will have a purpose, be part of a whole. Do you know what I mean?"

"*Ja*," he said huskily. "Of course, I do."

"I've been talking to Julia, since she was so recently baptized and has made the adjustment from a life not that different from mine. She claims not to have had a single regret."

He glanced down at his son, to see that Zeb, too, was sound asleep. To keep from awakening him, Gideon kept his voice low. "What about your work? You trained for a long time so that you could come up with new meals in a restaurant."

Hannah bent her head enough to brush a soft kiss on top of his daughter's head. Then, voice equally soft, she said, "I love to cook meals that make people happy. I think I started cooking in the first place because I wanted to please Mom. I've discovered that seeing your family and my father's eat what I cook, being at the table with you, gives me so much more joy than having a server mention that a diner complimented my potato-lentil croquette, or seeing a review online remarking on a dish that I'm responsible for at the restaurant."

Some of what she was saying, he didn't entirely understand, but the important part he did. The taste of her molasses cookie lingered on his tongue, a reminder of how delighted he and the *kinder* had been by her skill, and by the forethought that allowed her to feed them even in a storm shelter that might be in the path of a raging tornado.

Little creases formed between her eyebrows. "I also suspect that I loved to cook because of my *grossmammi* and all the other women in *Daad*'s family who encouraged me to help when they prepared meals and baked, even though I was too young to really contribute anything." She sounded slightly tremulous now.

Her heart had been touched by those long-ago memories,

Gideon guessed. The memories, and sense of belonging, that had led her to give the same to a motherless little girl.

"Somehow, I thought, if I could do what they did, I'd make everything right. Only, it didn't work." She bent her head again, as if she didn't want him to see her face. "I was so lonely." It was barely more than a whisper. "Until I came home. Until . . ."

She raised her head slowly, almost reluctantly, her gaze touching on Zeb first, until her eyes met Gideon's.

Until I met you.

He heard what she hadn't dared say. Unless she was encompassing his entire family, and that wasn't so bad. He needed her to love him first, and always, but he had no question in his mind that she loved his *kinder*—and how could he love her if she didn't?

Perhaps feeling embarrassed, she changed the subject. "So. How will we know when we can look outside?"

Jolted by the reminder of where they were and why, he said, "Let's wait a little longer, to be sure the tornado has moved on."

"We could find the house gone. Or the barn, or the crops you've worked so hard to plant and tend."

She grieved at the very idea, he could tell, perhaps because she'd lost so many homes over her lifetime.

"*Ja*, and if any of that is true, we'll rebuild, plow again, plant again." He heard the tenderness in his often-gruff voice. "We would do that even if lives had been lost, trusting in God's purpose, although it would be much harder. But, thanks to you, and to our Lord, we are all safe."

"You made it home in time. I was so afraid for you."

Gideon smiled at her. "I might not have been if I'd had to go to the house looking for Zeb and Rebekah. They would have had more time to be frightened, or decide to run to a neighbor's. And even if we'd made it to the shelter, you would not have been with us."

Her lips trembled, but she said lightly, "You'd have had no milk and cookies."

"And no Hannah."

"You're a good *daad*. They could both have slept in your arms, knowing they were safe and loved."

"Now they feel loved by two adults. They trust you, Hannah."

"I know. And I'm so glad."

"I shouldn't ask you so soon, but—"

"I do want to keep working for you," she said in a rush. "If . . . if—"

"That's not the question I was going to ask you." What if her answer was not what he wanted it to be? Their remaining time in the shelter would be difficult, and her continuing to work for him awkward.

And yet, he felt the kind of certainty that should be part of love. As he had felt certainty and trust in Leah. At that moment, he was stunned by a realization. *Of course she wasn't drinking alcohol.* Why had he ever felt the first hint of doubt?

I can and do trust Hannah as much, he realized. She had lived most of her life in the *Englisch* world, but that no longer frightened him. She was not a woman who would ever break a promise. Ever be unkind to anyone, for any reason. Ever fail his *kinder*, or him.

She would certainly never abandon them.

"Will you marry me, Hannah?"

SHE WAS TERRIBLY afraid she gaped at him even as her eyes burned. "You mean that?"

The corners of his mouth quirked up. "*Ja*, Hannah. I love you. I have been fighting my feelings since your first day of work. I told myself I shouldn't have hired you. I should be glad if you left as soon as you first thought you would. But that would have been a lie. I didn't want you to leave. Not ever."

Tears spilled from her eyes. "I fell in love so quickly. When you said you couldn't be alone with me anymore . . ." She shivered.

"I missed our meals," he said huskily, "just you and me, able to talk about anything."

"So did I." Oh, she sounded so watery! "That's not anything I've ever had before."

He hesitated. "I did with Leah, but . . . it wasn't the same. We grew up knowing each other, saw most things the same, never had any reason to argue. You help me see through new eyes. Because of you, I'm closer to both of my *kinder*, instead of only a stern *daad*. I'm a better father than I was." He paused. "Also, better fed."

Hannah stifled a giggle with her fingertips.

He looked both rueful and frustrated. "I want to hold you."

She wanted that, too. And more, but they would have to wait.

Zeb stirred and lifted his head. "Is the tornado over?"

"Perhaps it's time we take a look," his *daad* said.

Zeb straightened. "Can I?" he asked eagerly.

"The door is too heavy for you. Even for Hannah, I think."

"Did the tornado come right over the top of us?" his son asked in worry.

"I've never seen one before," Gideon reminded him, "or had to hide in the shelter, but I think we'd have heard more noise if it was that close."

His eyes met Hannah's, and she knew Gideon was less certain than he'd sounded, but Zeb had noticeably relaxed.

"I want to see!" he exclaimed.

"*Ja, ja.*" Gideon ruffled his hair. "You are not so patient." But he stood and went to the steps.

After gently awakening Rebekah, Hannah rose, too, so she could lift one of the lanterns to enable Gideon to see what he was doing.

A few steps higher, he reached above his head. With a metallic clang, he heaved the door upward. The hinges squealed as gray light spilled into the shelter. Gideon went up a couple more steps, and then called down, "It's still windy, but not even raining. The buildings are all standing. It should be safe for us to go to the house."

Hannah blew out a breath. Relief lasted mere seconds, however, because any of their neighbors and friends could have suffered the horrific damage from which Gideon's farm had been spared. What if it had hit *Daad*'s place? Or the Bowmans—any of the Bowmans? Or poor Esther Schwartz next door, or the Millers, or— She thought of all the students at the school and their families, of Teacher Tabitha, of Bishop Troyer and his wife.

The tornado had surely not turned around and gone an entirely different direction. Anyway, whatever its path, homes would have been in the way. People endangered.

Gideon climbed out, waiting to take first Zeb by the hand to help him, then to swing Rebekah out and hold on as she wobbled down the steep slope. Last, he extended both hands to Hannah, and for one moment, they gazed deeply into each other's eyes.

As if she were made of glass, he said in a low, deep voice, "Anyone whose house or outbuildings or even fields were damaged will have the help they need to rebuild, just as we will receive help when we need it."

"*Ja*, I know that," she said. "And I like it when you say 'we.'"

"It might be the best word in any language." His head turned. "The *kinder* have run to the house, so I think we can have that kiss."

She lifted her face to his, uncaring of the wind or deep gray skies, feeling as if she were bathed in sunshine.

Gideon loved her, and now his lips met hers with tenderness, gratitude, and enough urgency for her to wish for more than this stolen moment.

INDEED, THE COMING weeks were to be spent helping with the cleanup. No lives had been lost, but news spread quickly so that everyone knew there'd been significant damage. Among their church district, Martha and Enoch Beiler, an older couple, had suffered the worst loss when their old farmhouse was leveled while they huddled, safe, in their shelter. The minister, Josiah Gingerich, and his wife would need a new barn, as did their next-door neighbors, the Waglers. Otherwise, fences had been ripped from the ground, fruit trees blown over, shingles scattered everywhere, sheds destroyed, and animals killed. A dozen or more farmers would need to replant some of their fields.

And, of course, *Englisch* neighbors had their own losses. The Amish would pitch in to help them, too, as they were able.

By morning, work parties were already being formed to clean up debris and repair roofs while plans were made for barn and house raisings.

Hannah had accompanied Gideon and his *kinder* to Sol and Lydia Graber's home for this first day. Like many families, they would have rain leaking through into both their barn and house if patches were not made to the roofs. Hannah had been told that Sol and Lydia lost their oldest son a year ago when a car had hit their buggy, severely injuring Sol as well. How dreadful yesterday would have been, the two of them hugging their other *kinder* tight while the storm raged. They'd have been aware on the deepest level how quickly a *kind* could be snatched away. Like Gideon, they had known that their property meant nothing compared to those precious lives.

Their yard was a mess, littered with tree branches, fence

posts, toys, and tools. Hannah and Rebekah had gone to work with a will, joined by Adah and Emma once Samuel and his family had arrived. Hannah kept an eye on several other *kinder*, too, whose parents were working on the barn or in the house.

She and Gideon had agreed that they wouldn't tell Zeb and Rebekah about their plan to marry until she'd spoken to Amos. She assumed the Saturday appointment she'd made with him would be postponed. There were many needs greater than her own.

Yet, when another buggy arrived, Hannah recognized the bishop when he got out and tethered his horse. His glance swept over all the workers, stopping when he saw her. To her surprise, he walked over the grass to her.

"It's good of you and Rebekah to help."

Hannah smiled, as much at the sight of the little girl earnestly dragging a small branch to a pile where they would be burned as at what Amos Troyer had said.

"Of course we want to help! Gideon and Zeb are with the men rebuilding the corner of the barn and reroofing. Mose and *Daad* are here, too, up there." She pointed at the pitched roof of the house, crawling with men hard at work.

"Is Lydia inside?"

"*Ja*, she and several other women are putting together a meal and watching the younger *kinder*."

"I'll go say hello, then. I'm trying to find out how everyone in my district fared, and where and when we'll need to hold work frolics. Bishop Ropp and I will be able to plan them so that we can have the most helpers possible at each. Will you be able to take a few minutes to talk once I stick my head in the kitchen to greet people? I may not have a chance tomorrow, and why wait?"

"*Denke*," she said gratefully. "I'd like that."

Amos dipped his head. "Then I'll be back in a few minutes."

Hannah asked a woman she'd met when dropping off the *kinder* at school to keep an eye on the girls, and told Rebekah what she'd be doing. Ready when she saw Amos returning from the house, she left her work gloves on the grass next to the trunk of a plum tree that had lost several branches.

He fell into step with her, saying nothing as they strolled along the side of the house. She'd asked for this meeting, so apparently it was up to her to start it.

"I want to convert to the Amish faith," she said simply. "I think it's been my faith all along, and I just didn't know it. I've always been drawn to the teachings about forgiveness, nonviolence, and trusting in the Lord without knowing I'd heard them as a young child."

Under his gentle questioning, she told him some of what she'd already confessed to Gideon. Her loneliness, a faint frustration because, even as she took to heart the teachings from services held in countless churches as she and her mother moved around, she had never known how to integrate them into her life.

Amos stopped walking at that moment, and smiled at her, the skin beside his eyes crinkled. "From what I've seen and heard about you, I think you've done that better than you believe. Everyone who has spoken to me about you mentions your warmth, your instinctive kindness, how readily any of the *kinder* trust you. Your father is proud of the woman you became. Sad that he didn't have the chance to see it happen, but he forgives your *mamm* because she raised you to be generous, helping others without a second thought. It seems to me Rebekah has blossomed under your guidance."

"I love her."

"*Ja*, so I've noticed. I think it's not only Rebekah that you love." His sidelong glance held shrewdness as well as kindness.

"That's true," she admitted, voice stifled.

Of course, that was the moment her gaze turned toward the barn just as Gideon stepped into sight. He'd probably been checking up on Rebekah, but now he looked at Amos and then her. Although their eyes had barely met, Hannah felt both heartened and strengthened, knowing she had Gideon's support, and always would.

He nodded at them both before going back around the corner of the barn and out of sight.

Amos's eyebrows had climbed. "You are not alone in your feelings, I think."

Hannah couldn't lie to this man. "No. Just yesterday, we admitted what we feel for each other. Gideon stayed silent," she added hastily, "until I told him I intended to talk to you about getting baptized."

They walked and talked for another twenty minutes, Amos wanting assurance that her decision was one of faith, not romance.

"That's not a mistake I would ever make," she told him. "Not after seeing how many people were hurt by my mother breaking trust because her commitment wasn't sincere."

Amos gave her another of those shrewd looks, and stroked his beard. "You seem to be a steady woman who sees herself clearly."

"More clearly than I did before I came home."

"Good." He outlined his expectations for her: several more meetings with him and perhaps one or more ministers, and then her participation in the series of classes that would take place in October and early November, taken both by converts like her and the Amish young preparing for baptism. "Most Amish weddings take place in November, too," he said. "Should you be ready to plan for such a thing."

Her cheeks heated, and he was chuckling as he left her.

Hannah could hardly wait to tell Gideon about the conversation.

* * *

GIDEON HAD NO idea how Hannah managed to put such a fine meal on the table barely forty-five minutes after they returned to his house. Rebekah bustled beside her with increasing confidence. Even after the day of hard work, Zeb willingly helped his weary *daad* feed the animals and finish chores. Not all the chickens had returned to the coop yesterday evening, but all had tonight, a particular relief for Zeb, who took care of them and knew each individually.

Once they sat down at the table, Gideon's prayer before the meal was heartfelt. How had God found him worthy of so many blessings? Once he cleared his throat, the others raised their heads as well.

He and Hannah had had less than a minute to talk privately this afternoon, but that was long enough. "Before we eat," he said, "I have something important to share with you."

Zeb had been reaching for a sourdough biscuit, but he stopped with his hand short of the basket. He and his sister both stared at Gideon, who looked at Hannah. The sadness seemed to have left her; her green-gold eyes brimmed with emotion.

"Important?" Zeb asked.

"*Ja.*" Gideon had to clear his throat. "Hannah is to be baptized, and she has agreed to be my wife."

The stunned silence did not last long. As always, after swiveling in her seat to look at Hannah, Rebekah spoke up first.

"You'll be our *mammi*?"

Joy and gentle love made Hannah's smile beautiful. "*Ja.* I don't want you to forget your own mother, but since she can't be here, I hope I can be what you need." She turned that smile on Zeb, too. "Both of you."

Zeb whooped, and Rebekah flung herself at Hannah and burst into happy tears. Gideon gave his son a quick, hard embrace, and decided that this evening, he wouldn't take Zeb out with him to harness Hannah's mare. He had nodded stiffly while keeping his distance too many times. He was eager to hold Hannah close, to kiss her, and to start counting down the days until November.

Acknowledgments

❧ ◆ ❧

I owe huge thanks to everyone I've worked with at Penguin, starting with my editor, Anne Sowards. Her insight and encouragement helped make writing this trilogy a real pleasure. The rest of the team, particularly Miranda Hill, Natalie Sellars, and Stephanie Felty, have been wonderfully positive as well, keeping me informed and staying patient with my more-than-occasional absentmindedness. Thanks are also due to my agent, Jill Marsal, for suggesting this project in the first place. And, finally, I don't know what I'd do without my equally patient daughters, who have always believed in me.

About the Author

The author of more than a hundred books for children and adults, **Janice Kay Johnson** writes about love and family—about the way generations connect and the power our earliest experiences have on us throughout life. An eight-time finalist for the Romance Writers of America RITA award, she won a RITA in 2008 for her Superromance novel *Snowbound*. A former librarian, Janice raised two daughters in a small town north of Seattle, Washington.

Ready to find
your next great read?

Let us help.

Visit prh.com/nextread